AFFAIRS OF A
DOG MAN

AFFAIRS OF A DOG MAN

Albert Gordon

AFFAIRS OF A DOG MAN

iUniverse books may be ordered through booksellers or by contacting:

iUniverse
1663 Liberty Drive
Bloomington, IN 47403
www.iuniverse.com
1-800-Authors (1-800-288-4677)

ISBN: 978-1-4917-9036-6 (sc)
ISBN: 978-1-4917-9037-3 (e)

Library of Congress Control Number: 2016903328

Print information available on the last page.

iUniverse rev. date: 02/29/2016

PREFACE

The old man was seeing the signs of age, he wasn't walking as far as in the past, he no longer cared about sex, now his memory was slipping. He knew there were things he could not remember but certain words if he repeated them whenever he thought of it, kept them close enough to recall. Words that started with "M" such as Marquette, or Mark Messier, Melatonin, seemed to be in a forget channel but repeating them really helped him to remember. Frequently he mentally went over them but kept forgetting to include words. Words that he had written about long before in the history of dogs he always remembered. Why was that? Maybe it was because he kept thinking of them. Each day he practiced crossword and jumble puzzles that came in the local paper; it also helped.

A few years earlier while in the car he had been having a disagreement with his common law wife over which was the right road to take to get home from a long trip. Suddenly he found he was unable to speak. He had been trying to tell her to go to a nearby restaurant to discuss the route but nothing would come out of his mouth; he couldn't speak, his head was aching-- so uncharacteristic. He had forced himself to relax, he thought he might be having a stroke or dying but if he was he was determined to go out peacefully. He employed a relaxing technique, making all his muscles go limp. After awhile his headache subsided and by the time he was able to speak they were past the restaurant and on their way home in the wrong direction--the route his wife had chosen.

When he was able to speak he quietly suggested a different way to proceed and after another quiet discussion they made their way home--his way. For some time she had been doing the driving because he had given up his license when he realized his vision was failing. Yet he understood maps; invariably he did the navigating,

When they reached home his wife had taken him to the hospital where a number of tests were done but they were unable to determine whether or not he had had a stroke. The doctor at the hospital recommended that he take a small aspirin daily and let them know if the problem recurred. Three years later there had been no recurrences. His daily walks were not as long as they had been in the past but he tried to get out every day and when it was snowing he would spend time climbing stairs in the apartment building. He depended a lot on his computer, his companion. It was the source of so much that he needed to know. On this one occasion he was deleting no longer relevant material; it seemed to be jammed up with junk but where was his folder on Poems? He must have deleted it by mistake? He looked at a story drafted long before. It was about dog people. He had spent a lifetime working with dogs. Was this story about him? So many things he couldn't remember, looked like an accumulation of stories about dog people. The names he did not recognize. He thought he must have written it as things happened. Was the story true? He no longer even had a dog. He stopped the computer reorganization--and read on.

CHAPTER 1

Goodwood

There is a place in Southern Ontario called Goodwood or at least there was half way through the twentieth century. Grew Tuckett and his wife had a place about two miles past the town where they raised dogs. The area is real. It formed the beginning of what turned out to be an ongoing saga of people connected to dogs. Grew Tuckett recalled how for some time he had collected information that had gone into stories of the people that had passed through his life. So much of the source of the stories began around the time when they had a kennel not far from Goodwood. It was a place in his life where stories of women he had known or become involved with started. Many of the short bits that he had placed in his draft took him back to that time when they had lived in that area and to the adventures and happenings that shaped their lives in those days that in turn affected what became of them afterward.

As he thought back he wondered if his life had been programmed, directed by an unknown director who was to take him into danger and out, into love and out and to guide him through the periods of remorse that he felt for those who had gone on into a life away from him or had died, leaving him to live on without them. Grew Tuckett had lived his whole life in a different way because he was born blind in one eye. Although he was tall, lean and relatively strong he could not play the usual sports. His parents were always afraid something would happen to the other eye. Still he had practiced throwing a baseball at the wood shed and for a brief period he pitched for a local baseball team until his parents got wind of what he was doing. Running and hiking became his sports which led to him getting a dog that became his constant companion. Perhaps it had something to do with him adopting a life working with dogs.

The first time they followed the road to Goodwood it was pretty well broken up with potholes and areas where the road had been repeatedly repaired with patches of tar. It was in an older green Ford and they had followed Highway 47 bouncing over the rough road through a town called Stouffville, then on through Goodwood. Marilyn and Grew were not married at the time. They were on their way to meet his friend, Fred Burr who lived off the 4th concession. Fred had just moved to the area from the Eglinton and Dufferin area of Toronto where Grew had been working for a veterinarian. The two friends, both in their twenties, had met and talked often in the local convenient store that also had a coffee counter and a TV that Grew had often sat and watched. They had a common interest in dogs. Fred had no children but a wife that at first seemed to be almost always miserable which was in stark contrast to the demeanor of Fred.

As Marilyn and Grew drove through the town of Goodwood Marilyn noted the Esso station with one car filling up at the pump. "Look, gas is only thirty seven cents a gallon, we should fill up on the way back."

Next to the gas station was a general store and post office. It was small with steps leading up to a small platform before the door. A little further along the road was a BP station with an old stake truck parked to the side. It was red but the paint had deteriorated some time before and it looked like the mud had never been washed from it. This truck was later to play a part in their lives. Across the road from it was another general store and there were a few houses scattered around, down side streets, then they were past Goodwood. The road went up hill and wound a bit, on the right was an expanse of gravel pits almost as far as one could see. By the twenty first century this whole area was covered with estate type homes, each one with a few acres.

While visiting the Burr's in their new home, at least new to them, a modest house with two bedrooms, they had talked of the area and the openness, the Burrs mentioned that there was a property for sale down the road but that it was only a shack with no water, yet it had five acres. They decided to look at it. Grew had brought along his female German Shepherd that they left in the car as they visited.

When leaving the house Marilyn noticed it first as they moved towards the car. She quickly turned around and faced Grew who was still talking to Fred. "I don't think you are going to like what you are going to see, turn around slowly." she said.

Grew turned and through the window of the car saw the material hanging. Bisket had torn the lining out of the car while she had waited impatiently for the two to visit. Grew should have known better. When they had arrived he had not let her out to relieve herself and in her frustration had decided to make her own way out.

Grew let Bisket out of the car and she promptly squatted beside the driveway on some unkempt grass. Grew stood at the door of the car, gazed at the cloth hanging from the ceiling inside and quietly murmured that it was his fault. His anger was hardly evident; through his years working with dogs it was not unexpected-- it was only a car. He reached in and tore the hanging cloth loose, which left a ragged display of bare metal on the ceiling with bits of cloth hanging around it. He never displayed any anger to either Marilyn or the dog but as he looked around and caught Marilyn's half smile, suddenly they were laughing.

Marilyn and Grew were both taken with the rural open fields around the Burr's house so they drove down the highway to look at the five acres. They were both on the athletic side, Marilyn was a bit heavier build, she had grown up working physically for most things that she had achieved, had worked her way as a youth cleaning horse stalls so she could get to ride. Grew had also worked his way in life, first by learning to cook in the west and worked at that for a few years but then he had turned to dogs as a choice of his way to make a living, cleaning dog kennels at the veterinary hospital in Toronto and earlier at a large kennel in Michigan and one in Vancouver.

For Grew, what made it worthwhile to look at the property was the five acres. The appeal for Marilyn was that at that time Grew was living in one room at the animal hospital and she was living in one room at a rooming house. The only way he was going to marry her was if they found a place to live. Such a place was also going to have to accommodate their few dogs; he had two and she had a small black poodle. Marilyn who also had a small eye problem, one eye wandered, would probably not notice anything different about Grew. In the breast area she was well endowed but the main thing about her was her warm personality, she was a friend of everyone.

They walked up the hill from the road towards the empty shack. The grass had grown long around the one building. There was a rusty padlock on the paint chipped door that had seen better days. The outer walls were of a sort of plaster that had been painted over long before and patches of paint had peeled off leaving a pinto effect. A black peeling trim surrounded each window, two on the front and one on the side with no conformity as if each had been scrounged from some dump. The house if it could be called that was perched near the crest of the rise.

They walked together with Bisket, the dog running free, ranging out over the property then looking back to see if her people were coming as they moved over the crest. There before them appeared a large field, a couple of hundred feet wide, flat and deep with a forest of hardwood trees at the back standing naked and alone in the fall, quietly watching the intruders. On one side of the property there were planted evergreens and on the other side the property fell away to the highway that wrapped around the lower side, where they had come in. It was a property all on its own, invisible from neighbours on either side or from across the road.

A rabbit popped up from somewhere and Bisket took off after it, apparently she had caught its scent and had been looking for it. Soon after she appeared trotting towards them without the rabbit but with tongue hanging, there was an expression of satisfaction as she wagged her tail.

They returned to the shack on the property and walked around it wondering if they could make it livable. It was built on a cement slab placed on gravel, in fact the whole hill was gravel. The cement slab idea found favour in the area and worked on gravel or rock base. The roof seemed square as did the walls and in good condition. It looked like it would hold up and had stood the Snow Belt winters for many years before.

Grew's father sent $1000.00 as a down payment for the five acres. Five miles further along the road from the property was another town on what was at that time Highway 47 but later bypassed. As reported, this property had no water but the two young people regarded it as an excellent place to raise dogs. They were going to rough it. They lived there for five years, each day returning from the city with plastic gallon containers of water, piled in the back of cars that suffered from the wear.

The true potential for this property was not realized until years later when someone else owned it, someone who could afford the necessary improvements--like water. Those people that came later also dug under that same house, putting in a full basement.

On top of the hill, people later built a small barn for horses. When Grew was to look at the property years later he was envious and sorrowful that he had really missed the opportunity he had been handed. He could have borrowed money from the bank to do the same thing.

At the time though, the property was an ideal piece of land for their purpose. There was no trouble getting the kennel license. Grew referred to it as their "Seclusio". There was sort of a rough driveway on the first part that sloped down to the highway and on the bottom of the hill they built a very basic shelter for the car, as they knew through the snowy winter they wouldn't be able to drive up the hill.

It was in the fall when they took possession of the property. Priority time was taken up in putting in a wooden floor over the cement slab. With the help of Marilyn's brother and brothers in law, they also fixed up the wooden shed that was on the back of the building making it a combination outhouse and dog kennel. To use the toilet one had to be in the company of the German Shepherds who were in pens, that had been built for them, complete with swinging dog sized doors that let them come in and go out as they chose into the separated dog runs attached to the shed. The runs were built with cedar posts sunk into the gravel and then connected with six foot 12 gauge chain link fencing. People that knew the area had warned Grew that flooding happened every year in this structure when the snow melted so Grew had conceived the idea to dig a ditch around the upper perimeter of the dog runs. He found the digging quite easy in the gravel and the substantial ditch was soon put in place. In five years flooding was never a problem.

When they first took over they put a space heater inside the house in what was designated the living room. Marilyn's father, who she had for a long time never spoken to and she regarded as a creep, designated the property as "a fire trap". The interior doorways were without doors, it was left open into the kitchen; a bamboo screen was put across the bedroom door. They built on another side room, which extended the living room a bit into the porch. In doing this they had to take down a couple of walls.

As the walls came down they found that the builder of the place had used as insulation in those walls, pages of a book on skiing, written by Mr. Maison. The book looked to be informative. Marilyn and Grew looked at the pages with a combination of respect and humour for the author who had apparently written a creditable book on skiing. Supposedly the book had not sold well so had become insulation.

They had had a quiet wedding with the Henry's from Hamilton being the only others there. Previously they had been conscripted by Grew to find a position at their kennel for Marilyn for eight months while she endured a pregnancy that had been kept quiet from her seven sisters and all but one of her four brothers or half brothers. There was an unexpected psychological affect on Marilyn when the baby was adopted out. She had agreed to it as being the sensible thing to do but years later Grew had wondered if it wouldn't have been possible to keep it. The pregnancy was the result of an unfortunate encounter Marilyn had become involved in before meeting Grew and shortly after the death of her mother that she had been looking after.

After they were married, living in the country "estate" Marilyn had a job in downtown Toronto while Grew still had a job with the same animal hospital that he had started with but was about to move on to another. It was 25 miles from home--hers was much further.

Mr. Maison originally built the Tuckett house as he had others, all built on cement slabs put on the ground. Scattered around the area were a number of these houses that Maison rented out. Mr. Maison and family were a story in their own right, as was the whole area the Tucketts had decided to settle in. Maison lived next door, down the hill in a valley and behind the young evergreens, planted trees that separated the two properties. Tuckett's land, Maison had sold to someone else with five acres but there was no well on the property.

The Maisons had moved in shortly after the Second World War in order to get out of the way of the Mounties who had him pegged as a communist, he did look wild, with long hair and a beard but he also looked and acted healthy. His wife was heavy and very backwoods looking, the children were good looking and fit. They owned and rented out most of the other houses in the area.

Mr. Maison was a charming fellow as were many of his children and certainly they were outspoken. Probably he got the communist label for being overzealous in the labour movement. Strangely, in later life he would likely become considered a capitalist. He had bought the sixty acres and later more land when it was practically valueless. Later he leased it out to gravel companies. They raised kids, cows, chickens and corn from their little enclave.

His young and pretty girls would stand beside the road and sell the corn when it was ripe, with their wild blond hair and country complexion they were a charming set. Grew didn't miss the beauty but confined his association with them to buying corn. The boys were named after the Gods of Greek mythology and were a varied but healthy lot. Thor and Lott were prominent but there was also one named Frei. One son had shot himself, another had been partially paralyzed through an industrial accident as he worked as an electrician, others had other stories of interest. The corner near the property, Rock Road and Highway 47, had rightfully taken on the name of Shotgun Corners. That story apparently had been given because of another domestic shooting, domestic strife almost a contagious disease of the area.

The Maisons eventually worked a deal with a gravel company for the gravel on their land and became quite well off even though they never changed their life style. To enter their house, which was done seldom by Grew and Marilyn, was like going into something one might expect from a hillbilly domain, with clothes scattered everywhere, hung on interior clothes lines, and even the odd window boarded up. It was dark in the house on the main floor that was at ground level, the smell of wood smoke filled the air and as one looked around for a place to sit, it was noticed that every old chair was covered with clothing of some sort. Piled boxes of things lay around on the floor. There were narrow alleys between the junk where it was possible to walk.

Grew and Marilyn were getting along quite well with the Maisons. Mr. Maison had written at least the one book and in discussions he presented an interesting political point of view as he related his own disagreements with the Canadian Government. The winter provided an abundant covering of snow that first year. Mr. Maison could often be seen doing spins on his own design of ski that he called figure skis. This was long before the development of snowboards, and the hotdog skis of the nineties. At the time of Mr. Maison's exhibitions he would have been well into his sixties.

Most of their association was with the son Tie who for some time traveled with them to the city so he could go to trade school. The hour ride often got pretty hot and heavy in discussion but Grew was one who enjoyed a different point of view. Tie also used to come up to the house to talk, sometimes with the two of them, sometimes with Marilyn alone. He got to know the dogs and to a certain extent learned what the two of them were all about, presenting informed and interesting points of view and obviously he had been taught to think things out for himself.

Across the road from the "Seclusio" was a tenant of the Maisons who also raised chickens. The husband Charley, worked at the G.M plant in Oshawa, about twenty miles south on Rock Rd. They too were an out of the ordinary couple that had grown up in rural Ontario, developing ways to do things that to the city folk seemed strange. Grew learned partly about the way they were when their chicken house roof caught on fire. As Marilyn and Grew observed the flames rising from the roof of the chicken house from across the road, before rushing over to help Grew shouted at Marilyn to phone the fire department. The chicken house was about twenty feet long and about ten feet deep and only about six feet high. As Charley and Grew worked frantically, bending as they kept returning into the shelter, picking chickens from the roost-- chickens that appeared to be enjoying the warmth coming from above--throwing them out the door, the fire department arrived.

The fire had started because Charley had decided a fire on the roof would melt the snow that was getting abundant enough that it threatened the stability of the roof. It did melt the snow. Charley was really put out because the fire department had been called. Considering the mindset of Charley, that is what would have been expected.

There are other little stories about the Goodwood area that appeared amidst some of the overall picture of lives on the balance, mixed up relationships and people searching for some kind of contentment and sexual satisfaction.

The kennel name was decided as "Chloe". It was a name Grew had chosen years before while passing through Chicago. He had picked up the sheet music to the song, *"Chloe"*. The words were those of a wanderer, searching the world, through swampland, fire and hell, the difficult areas of the world, looking for Chloe. Chloe was the personification of perfection; the song has her as a woman, Grew wanted the same with his dogs, Chloe was the symbol of his inspiration.

They went on to breed a number of excellent German Shepherds that made their mark in the background of breed pillars in North America. Later they also bred a number of Champion Pembroke Welsh Corgi's. These little dogs became the bread and butter dogs of the kennel. They were sold as pets and they were just great at it. Buyers never returned these little buddies who, if not great show dogs, became part of the families they were sold into. One of their own poodles was shown and got points but was eventually eased off from breeding because it developed epilepsy.

The two of them gave all indications they were satisfied in their little home. They got through the first winter in relative ease. The dogs were content in their pens out in the toilet shed and in the second year a litter of puppies was born there and appeared quite happy in the frigid environment. The people used the chemical toilet quickly in the cold weather and the dogs got used to seeing people eliminating in the other part of their home. Often the dogs were brought into the house to be enjoyed and to share the comfort or to be studied by guests that often arrived. In the spring and summer these same guests walked with either Grew or Marilyn as they walked with the dogs running free out to the end of the property and beyond into the surrounding empty fields. They bathed by heating water and then standing up in a two and a half foot diameter tub and washing. They had a small television across from a pull out couch in the living room. There was also a table with two chairs in the kitchen, a counter to prepare food on and an electric stove. They had a small fridge that had been picked up from somewhere. In the bedroom there was a double bed. Everything had been picked up second hand and very little was owed anywhere except that they had traded in their Ford and had purchased a second hand Volkswagen on time. The wooden floor that they had put in the house had been covered with tiles so they considered their abode as quite comfortable.

Grew was always searching for water on the property. At one time he had hired a well digging company to come in and dig a well but their equipment was limited to sixty feet, so they left the hole on the side of the hill and pulled out. Grew covered it with plywood and gradually filled the hole with garbage. Further down the hill at the lowest point on the property he dug another hole but only got about eight feet deep then stopped, leaving it for another time. Another spot would gather water in a storm so he would try there, with the same results--nothing.

One day in the spring Grew watched from outside the door of the house as a Volkswagen raced around the curve of the highway that skirted the property. (The highway actually made almost a U turn and dipped as it went around the property.) The car went out of control as Grew watched and suddenly it had gone into an end over end somersault. It rolled about three times and then landed, right side up on the lower level of the property. Grew called into the house for Marilyn to call the police and ambulance as he started down the hill to check it out. At first he didn't see anyone. As he approached the car Grew called out.

At first there was no answer. Grew couldn't see a driver inside the car either. Then he heard the voice coming from the bottom of the hole, beside the car, "Hello up there, watch where you step. I'm down here."

The driver had landed right side up, stepped out of the car right into one of Grew's dry well holes. Good thing there was no water. He was drunk and the police took him away muttering. The car was hardly damaged and it's not known how the driver made out. The next day the car was gone.

While they were driving to the city one Friday, Marilyn told him that she was bringing a girl who worked with her, home for the weekend. The pull out couch certainly could accommodate a guest, one that was prepared to rough-it. Grew had no problem with the idea but when he met the girl he was astounded at the beauty and personality as they set out for home. He knew at the time that he would have to be careful with this one, he had previously seen the jealous nature of his wife pop to the surface. Years later Grew would wonder, knowing the way Marilyn was, why she would have brought such a girl home. Was it a test? He wondered about the sleeping and toilet arrangements, thinking of their confined space. He knew though that he would have enjoyed seeing more of this girl.

It was snowing as they started off from the city. As they proceeded towards the outer limits of the city they ran into heavier traffic, the snow was becoming exceptionally heavy. No one was getting up the hills. They did spend a lot of time together in the car, laughing and joking. Grew thought everything was okay but as they went further the weather got even worse, so bad it became a task to get the young lady Joanne even close to where she lived.

They decided it was better to drop off Joanne. After she left Marilyn made it quite clear that she was disturbed over the attention Grew had paid to the girl, who was single and unattached. She knew Grew well enough that she should have expected it. She was always making comments about him turning to look at women as he drove. They found a bed themselves at the home of one of their Toronto friends. Marilyn was still upset but they were also worried about the dogs but couldn't get any closer to home.

The next day, as soon as they could, the two of them set off again with the Volkswagen, were able to get within five miles of home but from there could see snow drifting right up to the tops of the telephone poles. The road was completely blocked. Grew had rubber boots on and she had snow boots. They decided to park the car by the side of the road and walk the last five miles. With any other woman he wouldn't have attempted it but knew she was tough. As they walked along there were places that were almost clear right down to the road, then the snow had drifted to the top of the telephone poles again and they would have no choice but to climb the drifts. Hand in hand they climbed over the drifts. Each time one of them would sink through the snow crust they would drop and lay flat, crawling on hands and knees or wiggling on their bellies until they felt it safe to try again. Several hours later they made their way to the snow covered door, packed with snow up to the roof. With gloved hands they dug in the snow until they had uncovered the door. Inside they found it to be quite warm. Right away they both headed for the back door where they found all the dogs happy to see them. The dogs had kept their swinging doors clear by periodically going out side. The water they had been left with was not even frozen and there was still some left in the pails. The heater had worked well on low and although the house was pretty well covered by snow, they felt satisfied that it had withstood the storm exceptionally well. With all the dogs they fought through the snow dunes on the back of the property and took them all together for a romp in the white and fluffy. The dogs were happy and loved plowing their way, the small corgis working their way under while the German Shepherds made their own trails over the top.

The following week Grew had visited Marilyn's place of work and for some reason she was not there. Joanne, who was about to go out to lunch, was quite willing to go with him as he too went to get something to eat. He talked to her about getting a gift for Marilyn but in reality probably was coming on to her. It was something that Marilyn had always picked up on. However since Grew had lived to 27 years before getting involved with a woman and then married was used to being free to communicate freely. It was something that took him a long time to understand.

Just then Marilyn responded by taking it out on Joanne but in fact she herself was probably out eating with a male co-worker. She had painted herself as being deceived. She withdrew within herself at work, not co-operating with the other staff. Grew felt that he was never quite able to deal with or smooth the damage done from her previous experience with the father of the baby. Marilyn lost the job over her attitude with the rest of the staff.

She had befriended a man from work and after giving him glowing reports on the quality of Welsh Corgi's as pets, she had helped him import one from England. The information she got on Corgi's she had learned from Grew who had never considered there was a problem with her associating with this man. Grew had also arranged for the breeding of the female the man had purchased and for all the help given they had received a female puppy that was the start of their corgi breeding stock.

Joanne had struck Grew in his emotional need, maybe even awakening thoughts of Judy. Marilyn knew there was something not right about their relationship. Marriage did not provide the answer she had expected. Perhaps Grew felt he had been pushed into marriage although he had adjusted well and was contented with the life it had become. He was confused himself as to his feelings for Judy. The impression on him of this new beauty, Joanne with a personality to match brought it all back to him but he never saw her again.

It didn't make him happy. How was he to deal with what he saw as Marilyn's over control of him? He was not used to being controlled. It was not life he was satisfied with, something was missing, but at the time he could not admit it, certainly not to Marilyn. His devotion to a life style with dogs was compatible to life with Marilyn. His experience with women before Marilyn had been minimal. He had spent a lot of time in the wilderness and didn't suppose his family upbringing with one sister helped his understanding. He could remember sitting by while his mother counseled his sister on the evils of men wanting to steal her virginity. Marilyn was not from the same ilk, she was sexual, yet her over sensitive possessiveness only worked to push him the wrong way, giving his very independent nature a feeling or excuse of being over restricted and not trusted. He discovered in time, that those who trust no one are usually not to be trusted themselves.

CHAPTER 2

Roughing it

As he recalled his life lessons he realized lessons learned had not kept him from stepping into the same situations of love that would end in the same way, yet with each happening there was a new lesson about life. His thoughts went back to the dog he had purchased for fifteen dollars as a fifteen year old. This dog had followed him everywhere but with a word of command would stay home, waiting without restriction, on the front boulevard of the property until Grew would eventually return; it was not the same with women. The same dog, if he allowed it to come with him would follow him as he delivered his newspapers or would wait outside the school for him, would play football with other students chasing like one of the boys. The dog had been his best and often only friend as they walked back into the hills from his coastal home. He looked back thinking, Leo was as good a dog as he had ever run into, a thinking animal. Leo purchased as an Alsatian, without papers and later to be followed by a registered German Shepherd brought him into a life with dogs.

Little had he known at that time that it was to set the course for what his life was to become. Grew had rejected a life of being a cook because of resistance to him bringing his dog to logging and mining camps. The boat jobs he understood that he could not take a dog to. He had decided to learn how to groom dogs instead of cooking and do whatever else went with it. From that life decision he had landed in Goodwood married to Marilyn.

Why had he become so involved with dogs in the first place? Why had he not known where the plan called for him to step next? He decided it was the way it was meant to be, being moved like a pawn from one square to the next, and for which he would have to live with what it brought with it. He reflected as he read of those days long ago in the place--because of the promiscuity-- he had dubbed "Good would". The memories did not return in order they moved through his mind as they would. The memories of some things triggered other thoughts of the past; sometimes recalling them hurt.

Grew had met Marilyn at the dog training. She had a miniature poodle that was a picture of enthusiasm doing all the training exercises with precision. Sammy was such a happy working dog that everyone was noticing him. In one obedience trial she had defeated the woman whose dog had a lock on high scoring obedience trials. Grew was noting the enthusiastic working qualities of the owner handler combination. They were an incredible team. Sammy could not be missed but Marilyn was not quite so obvious, still she did not go unnoticed.

Marilyn was not a classic beauty but in some ways she tried to be. When Grew had first become aware of her she had bleached her hair almost a white blond. It was something that to him would have been a distraction rather than attraction but even the distraction could not take away from the warm friendly way she treated people. She was at that time and normally so, a bit on the heavy side, of medium height, a pleasant face with a pale smooth complexion, very light skin, that actually went with the blond hair. Her legs were a bit on the thick side and slightly bowed below the knees, her demeanor was one of health and good condition.

But it was in the face that Marilyn displayed what she was. In spite of one eye that tended to wander slightly from time to time, the expression was almost unique. Character and courage were written in her face but in addition to that was a sexuality that almost shouted out saying,

"I am woman, I'm sexual, make your pass, let's see what'll happen, I'm not afraid. Are you?"

Grew would admit at the time that he missed a lot of the message about her. To him she was just a very friendly person that this lonely man enjoyed talking to. After the lessons they would go as part of a group to a restaurant called the Dufferin Gates. They had coffee and treats then all went their own separate ways. The extreme capabilities that went far beyond sexuality of this woman he missed. She was one of a kind. One of the first memories of that time was when, Art a married man, had struck her hard on the ass with his hand and although the tears were evident in her eyes, she brushed it off as nothing.

During the time when they all were going to the armouries the German Shepherd Club put on a dance. At that time Grew had an old Plymouth car that barely held together so he went to the dance alone in his only suit, the perpetual designated bachelor. He had learned to dance years before, attending dances at the Y in Vancouver.

At the dance, he danced with Marilyn but was more impressed with her sister in law that was married to her brother, who she had talked into coming with her. As Grew remembered this one was tall and a better dancer than Marilyn, at least at that time. Grew believed that to dance with him one had to be pretty good. It was at a time that to him, the woman he might be with had to give the right impression, but also had to be able to side step him when dancing. At that dance he got up and sang one of his Frankie Laine impressions that had always given him a high. No, he didn't take Marilyn home either. He was shy and missed the signals, certainly slow with the girls.

The dog training classes stopped for Christmas, his day spent with Margaret and her family, the waitress from the snack bar. It was a pleasant time at Margaret's and he appreciated her efforts to put some pleasure into his social life. Long before he had decided that life to him was more of a looking in rather than being inside living it, it was not always to be that way, still after supper he had been happy to get back to the animals and semi isolation at the animal hospital.

New Year's Eve in the afternoon he had received a call from Marilyn at his home at the animal hospital, surprised to hear from her and even more surprised to hear what she was proposing. She told him of a New Years Eve party that was North of Toronto that she had been invited to take a guest to. It was at the home of a dog handler-breeder that he had briefly considered working for, someone with Alaskan Malamutes. For some reason Grew had decided not to work for her but they were still good friends.

Since as might be expected he had no other plans and he wouldn't turn down a person who had raised the nerve to phone, he accepted. It should have been him that was asking her but he was still dealing with this fear of rejection.

It was a nice party but the two of them left early. He didn't find it awkward to be there with her. They had driven for an hour to find the place and in that time had had pleasant conversation, mostly about dogs. New Year's Eve can be an awkward time for a first date. However it did give him an excuse to kiss her that he might not have done if it had been at another time. There was so much for him to learn about women. Marilyn was never made aware of how much she was appreciated and just how naive this young fellow was that she had found. Years later Grew regretted that he had not been more open with her about his fears and misunderstanding of women. He was slow but she went along with him, pausing as they went, always talking about their mutual interest in dogs.

When they got back to Toronto they had sat for a long time outside of a restaurant. Then they had gone in and had a piece of pie each and a coffee. There was something holding them together, neither wanting to end the evening. It was the same outside the house where she had a room, and they had kissed some more. Her kisses were warm; it was something that he had been doing without for a long time, arms around her barely moved as they traveled on the sides of her breasts that were nice and soft. He didn't want to be too forward but she didn't stop him so he continued to gently stroke. The sides of her face and jaw line warmed as he moved his fingers. Grew had played with her ear lobes and the tickling had made her wiggle and giggle. Since he had no expectations of getting sexually involved at that time he had to stop as he felt himself getting turned on. They had said goodnight but he promised to call her.

The next day he had called her and asked if she wanted to go out in the snow with the dogs. She was going to stay at her brothers place to look after his two daughters that evening so Grew agreed to pick her up there. Suddenly Grew had come to life. It was a short walk to a golf course that was covered with snow. Together they had trudged through the white stuff while the dogs tore around after each other, the young German Shepherd and the somewhat older little poodle. The dogs were like they had always lived together, a couple of buddies. It was a friendship that went on as long as they were together.

Their own friendship was becoming more comfortable too. Obviously there was a connection between them but he was still sensing a reserve. He felt there was something Marilyn was not telling him--almost like she was resigned to the relationship not progressing further. She seemed to like him though and certainly he found her a real joy to be with but he thought it must be him that was the problem. Still he never wanted to leave her. She did ask him to come to her brother's house to baby-sit with her. It was an overnight thing for her. Her brother and sister in law greeted him in a friendly way as he met them again. The two nieces were gorgeous young things with a close relationship with Marilyn. After the parents left they took the two girls Pricilla and Cathy with them out into the snowfields where the four of them built a snowman. Grew had always felt close to those girls after that.

Grew had stayed and had supper with them and then later in the evening the two girls quietly went off to bed. Marilyn and he were alone. For a while they sat on the couch and watched the newest version of television. But they had other ideas, soon Marilyn led him off to a bedroom where she was to sleep. Together they lay on the bed and necked and stroked each other, her not objecting as he uncovered full well formed breasts.

She was sounding like it was something enjoyable so he just kept squeezing, sucking nipples and moving his hands over the translucent smooth skin. She was so white and as he uncovered her lower body he discovered that the bleached blond was not quite the real colour but her hair was rather a light soft blond that it was a shame to hide. She had spread her legs as he moved his hands in her pubic hair and as he fingered her reluctant passage it slowly became wet. Tight muscles had closed on his fingers.

After a while she took out his penis that was by then hard and stroked it gently. She looked at it, pushed the skin back and forth, slow action, so gentle and unforced, like she knew that she could ask him to stop at any time, a guy so naïve just going with the flow. In those days there was always the fear of pregnancy and he knew that he didn't have a condom. So as they played with each other, her seaming to enjoy the sexual stimulation while he stroked the beauty of her he expected it and was not surprised at all when she started to back off.

He asked her, "What's the matter?"

She responded, "We can't keep doing this. We are only a step away from having sex. I don't see you going for any protection and I don't have anything. We have to stop."

So they did but during their conversation while they were cooling down he picked up the signals that there was something else. Again, he thought that he was the problem and wondered what he had done to turn her off. *If it was to be the end of this friendship, maybe I could learn what I had done wrong.* This was one insecure young man. He kept pressing her for answers until, as they sat in the living room with all their clothes back on she told him that he would be better not to get too involved with her.

And again he was asking what it was about but he was also becoming suspicious about where this story might be leading. As they sat side by side she told him of how she had been living with her mother who had been dying. She was the last of eight girls. All the others had married and moved away. She was barely twenty-one years old at that time but for the three years previous she had been looking after her mother who had been separated from her father.

Marilyn had had no use for her father at that time, she believed he had only one thing in his head. It was sex, her mother had been the recipient of his wishes. Over the years she had born ten children by him.

Grew listened quietly as she went back to the beginning of her father and mother relationship. Her mother had been supposed to come to Canada from England to marry. Her fiancé at the time was denied access to the country because he had TB but in some way her mother ended up in Canada with one son and no money to return so found a housekeeping job with a gentleman that also had a son. Whether she was pregnant when she arrived or became pregnant by the new man, wasn't known but she married the new man anyway. After that son was born the lady had eight more girls. There was a set of twins but other than that they just kept coming. Marilyn was the last. Living with her mother she was subjected to the bitterness of being told of perpetual demands for sex. Her mother drumming into her youngest daughter the evils of men and how they only were motivated by one thing, the demands of the penis and getting it into a soft warm vagina.

She had suddenly stopped talking about the real problem, deciding it was better not to say anything. There was something "I have to find out about first". Was it to check her other options? Grew had left her then, wondering about her problem, but he was used to being disappointed with women.

Grew got the story a bit at a time. The next time they had gone out with the dogs he took her back to the animal hospital. In his small room, the room with only a bed and a dresser, it was not long before she was stretched out on his single bed with her clothes lying on the floor, her bra and panties topping the pile with both their jeans and t-shirts below. The dogs had been placed back in the kennels. His sexual impulses were stimulated with the white smoothness of her skin, her breasts stood full above her chest, the nipples hard. There was no question about contraception this time and he had wondered why not? She was urging him on. As he had pushed into her, he found her tight--foreplay, at that time it was as if he had never heard of it.

She had winced at the first push but he had kept easing it in and it wasn't long before they were having tight fitting slippery sex with both of them sweating profusely. To him it was great but he was pretty sure that he had come too soon. He worried about pregnancy but she told him not to. It should have told him something.

It was then that the rest of the story came out. Grew knew and wondered before she had finished telling that there was another person involved, was that her other option that she had decided against? It is possible but maybe she had just decided to tell him the story. Her stories were explicitly graphical-- it was the beginning. Grew became her priest, her person to confess to, the one to absolve her of blame. At the same time she would confess to him she would expect that he too could not look like he was any better than her; he could not talk down or sound superior.

Marilyn had the same desires as her mother, and perhaps her father and had fought against them. Although she had obeyed her mother's wishes as she worked at the city hall she had made friends of male co-workers. She became interested in bird watching that she shared with a married co-worker who was not a forceful friend but was nonetheless interested in her. She knew that he wouldn't have turned her down if the opportunity had been presented but it wasn't their time. Grew believed she had sensed his own excitement as she revealed the details of her predicament, even in the beginning; it was obvious,

It had been her resolve to keep the relationship with the co-worker on a friendly basis and she had done it quite well. Although curious about the man, fantasizing how it would have been to have sex with him as they sat with their binoculars in isolated swamps or bush areas, quietly watching birds, she had teased but not enough to get him to the stage where he would make serious moves on her. The bird watcher had expressed an interest in her dog when she had first brought Sammy around but it had also created a problem when the little dog scared up a few birds. Adjustments were made and Sammy had to curtail his urge to chase the birds.

This man had been very sympathetic, had tried to fill the void that was eventually going to come when the mother could no longer hold on, encouraging the way Marilyn was looking after her mother. He was a good friend and perhaps softened Marilyn's man hating training. The two of them often went out for lunch and on out of town journeys would stop for supper. It gave her a break from constantly looking after her mother, one who had become more and more demanding and of course, critical of her new found friend.

That night as Grew drove Marilyn back to her home, she told him she was pregnant, also told him that it was why she wasn't worried about him getting her pregnant; she was already there. She chuckled a bit as she had let him know in somewhat of a flippant manner. (Had she not known the week before?) Once again Grew listened intently as she told him of the affair she had had with a contractor who she had met at the city hall. Grew was learning that from her he usually did not get the whole story of her adventures all at once. It was a good thing; the whole story might have really scared him away.

This construction man she talked of, who was obviously well off had kept passing her desk, chatting with her a few minutes at a time, had always been getting permits for construction projects. One had to know Marilyn to realize how friendly she would appear. At first it was offers to go to lunch that she persistently refused. She laughed at his dirty jokes, was attracted to this man but she remembered her mother's teachings of the evils of men. Her bird-watcher friend had advised her against seeing this man out of work, it was moving into another league of men. Was it an unintentional challenge? Her mother had kept her last child, the daughter who looked after her--pure.

Then her mother was dead. Marilyn missed her terribly, was not quite ready to look after her own destiny. The way she told it to Grew put him there with her. As she talked, Grew would periodically ask questions of confirmation, getting excited, living it with her. Years later Grew was to learn that it was a method of therapy identified as humanistic, where the therapist just listened, occasionally asking questions. His problem with becoming the listener/therapist was in keeping detached from the person relating the experience. There was a condition called transference where the patient transferred the feelings over to the therapist. Of course Grew wasn't aware of this then. He was just being a friendly listener and in the beginning had no idea of any way that he would be able to help improve the situation. So on another occasion she continued with her story of the contractor.

Grew pictured the scene as she related it. The contractor had kept coming back as his business took him by her desk. Each time he would tell her raw jokes and as always she laughed with her enjoyable outgoing laughter. Perhaps he had not been aware of the death of Marilyn's mother. She handled the jokes like one of the guys, giving the impression that she was really with it, eyes would sparkle and she would laugh freely.

It was not too long after her mother's death that she did agree to go to lunch with this man. There was nothing wrong with that; the man behaved himself. "Why wouldn't he?" She felt no threat in any way but knew that he was married. She had been out to lunch with other married men. Her bird watching friend had never been a problem. In a naive way she seemed to dismiss the married thing as something beyond her responsibility, only going to lunch with them. It was a beginning thing but no special reason not to go again. The occasion had been pleasant, simply a nice time with him at lunch. The little touching things he did, brushing her ass or breasts, crude jokes, she accepted as simple teasing.

She had also accepted his offer of a trip on his boat. The warnings from her bird watching friend were rejected, thinking he was being jealous. After all he too was married. Even so, there was a lot of hesitation before she finally went along and accepted going for the boat trip. She knew this guy was a womanizer but that made it even more exciting. This guy had told her that he was separated and spent his weekends, not knowing what to do with his time. Finally she agreed to go, not worrying-- feeling she could handle him.

"You went out on his boat with him?" Grew asked.

"I was trusting, I like men, and he was fun and I too was bored."

She continued to relate her story to Grew about how she had enjoyed the day out there on the water. This man still didn't come on to her in any way that she couldn't handle. She would tease a bit, then move away, then he would have her in his arms again as the boat cruised through the water on cruise control, again as if on cue, she would slip away but she was beginning to like the man and the attention. When they came back to shore it was only natural for them to go to supper. They had drinks that made her a bit woozy but still she felt in control.

As they had parked in front of her rooming house he had turned off the motor and reached out his arm to encircle her shoulder and pulled her towards him. His mouth was on hers almost before she was aware that his lips were there. Their mouths crushed together, she felt his tongue passionately pushing her resisting lips apart. She didn't pull back, allowing her lips to be separated. Bodies moved together, warming as she felt his tongue, delving deep into her mouth. He was making up for lost time and it was not long before she felt his hand on her knee, gently rubbing, pushing up her inner leg to her shorts. He was moving fast. Fingers gently stroked up her warm smooth thigh to the crotch of her shorts before she could close her legs. Her hand took his wrist stopping the advance as he tried to move his hand under her shorts but she did not remove it; she liked the stroking on her bare inner thigh, it made her skin tingle, a new feeling.

Bob had almost jumped out of the driver side, over to the passenger side and pulled her hand out of the front then opened the back door. "Come with me". As he had pulled on her hand she had wondered what he was up to.

She had resisted as he had tried to push her into the back seat. "Bob, I don't want to get back there with you. We have had a great day, it was a lot of fun, and I'm tired."

"Just for a few minutes, I want to hold you but it is too restrictive in the front seat. Do you want me necking with you out in the street?"

She had still resisted so he took her in his arms by the side of the car, she had felt his hand on her soft buttocks, kneading the flesh, and then dragging the material on her leg upward. She was aware of her buttocks becoming exposed as she was being pushed backward through the still open door, falling on the seat in a semi prone position, him following her in. She had accepted where she was with a laugh. There had been some concern as to being put in the back seat but after a few minutes complaining that she really had to go had accepted his renewed lovemaking, "Okay just kiss me good night then," she had said. But he was doing more.

He had taken her in his arms and as he had pushed her sidewise his knees were on the floor moving her towards a prone position on the seat. Kissing her again, he had pushed his tongue at her closed mouth. For a while she had teased, keeping her lips firm, then slowly had opened them, admitting his tongue. She too was excited, enjoying what was happening, had felt his hardness as he had moved over her, not sure whether he had got it out of his pants but it felt hard against her belly as he had tried to lie on her. The feel of this thing had been exciting her even more. He brought her hand to the bare flesh of his penis. Her face was flushed as her hand closed on the stiffness.

As they had lain together, him trying to get over her as she kept trying to slip to the side, the kissing had become intense. She had held his hand back but in her own excitement had lost the hold on it. Her fingers had moved nonchalantly back and forth on the hard thing. Then his hand had gone between her legs, pushing, and spreading them further apart. She knew her control had been slipping as fingers had dug into the cloth of her white panties but the feeling had been ecstatic, the sensations had been taking over. Her panties were wet, as his fingers had pushed at the hot opening lips beneath the crotch band. Fingers had worked around the leg band, pushed it aside and into the soft wet center of her. She had wiggled with pleasure at the strange thing, the warm finger in the slippery entrance, on her clit, slowly circling, and stroking.

Trying to get over her, he had struggled more to bring her lower leg further onto the seat so he could get between her legs, to get her legs spread more, to get himself in position. Her hand had touched the flesh of him again, hard and hot. She had wiggled and struggled to stay on her side, muscles contracting to hold her legs together, squeezing his hand as it had stroked her.

In a panic, she had suddenly started thrashing, strength evident as she had dragged his hand from her shorts, shook her head, screamed at him, "Bob I said no. I know what you want but not now".

The loudness of her yelling and screams had stopped him as she had wiggled away from his hands. He had gone too far too fast. She had flipped the door handle above her head, pushed the door and crawled between them and he had let her go.

As she fought loose she had turned to him, red faced flushed, a not funny laugh, "Sorry Bob, I gotta get up in the morning, thanks for the nice time, I'll see you at work next time your in."

She had stumbled almost to the ground, then to her feet, wheeling away as he had reached for her, but she was gone up the stairs before he could protest further or catch her. She had straightened her clothing before going into the front door not wanting her landlady to see her disheveled state.

Grew was excited himself, listening to this story of near seduction and asked how she had felt about this man after that. She had held nothing back and what she had not supplied, Grew imagined in vivid colour. She was excited herself as she related it to him.

It was at a later time when her and Grew had become closer more used to each other, that she had told him about her feelings and what she had done when going into her apartment. As she had let herself into her apartment she still felt warm, hot and sweaty. She had talked to herself quietly. *Whew, that was close. I was just about to give in. That penis felt so strange, it really got me going. Boy it was close. Another five minutes and I think he would have had it in me. I could feel it, he had it out, it was hard, God that was exciting though, boy do I feel hot, but oh so nice.*

She had rubbed her crotch as she started to undress, feeling confident in the way she had handled herself but wondering if she had not cut it off quite soon enough, - *or maybe she could have let it go a bit longer.* She knew if she had not stopped then, he was going to get her panties off, she couldn't have taken that. She would have been fucked with that thing inside her.

She had gotten undressed and had had a shower, fondling her own breasts, rubbing below as the shower water sprinkled, tickling on her aroused skin. She had wanted something and as she showered she had felt unfulfilled. It was another week before she had heard from the contractor again and had been wondering why he had not called.

As he had passed by her desk he had barely stopped, said he was in a hurry. She had wondered, *had she cut him off too abruptly?* Thinking, *that if I hadn't stopped it then I would have said goodbye to my virginity right there in the back seat and as I have been told, the guy wouldn't want me after that and would move on to some other innocent girl.* She had wanted to save it for marriage. She recalled the thrill of the session. *How had I allowed him to get me in the back seat? Stupid.*

She had been getting sexy, just thinking about it and then as she related the episode to Grew it was not long before the two of them had found a place to neck, and shortly after get nude, soon they were thrashing together themselves with his prick driving in and out of her. He was learning fast, at least the rudimentary process of having sex if not the art of love but as he pulled back further for a harder push he fell out and together they had to reposition. With that first revelation Grew had felt as if he had been there with her, imagining every detailed feeling while it was happening. And when the excitement got too intense, right there in his own car on a back road, they had had sex. It was better than the first time they had gotten together. When they had come up for air it had been late. He had asked if she could tell him the rest of the story next time, as if he couldn't have imagined anyway. After they had kissed goodnight, he had driven home thinking about where this situation was likely to go, he knew that if he was smart he would keep going and she had suggested that if he had done so she would understand. A few days later Grew was back for more as they had started again with her continuing the story after Grew had encouraged her to tell him the rest.

CHAPTER 3
Marilyn's Awakening

She had continued her story. Another two weeks had passed and she was beginning to wonder if the contractor had moved on. Then out of the blue he had appeared again. She had been happy to see him. He had apologized for not calling her and had said he had been tied up with a contract, had asked her if she could go with him for supper that evening. She had wanted to go with him, delighted he had asked.

Too quickly, she had accepted without hesitation, and agreed to meet him but had had to go home to change first. She had been excited and happy as she showered thinking a bit about her landlady, who had not liked this man, but Marilyn had rationalized, *what did she know? Maybe she just did not want to lose her star roomer.*

They had had supper in a nice restaurant. ate lobsters and had a bottle of expensive wine to go with it. She had drank too much of the nice stuff as he had gone on about his penthouse apartment and the spectacular view of the lake, the lights and the Toronto skyline. The drink had been affecting her reasoning, she had known that it was the last place she should go with him, but wanted to go anyway, guessing what he was up to but the drink had given her courage. She'd enjoyed the previous date with him and felt that he'd respect her wishes when she wanted him to stop. As she had reflected on the last time together, in the back seat she was getting excited, she had been ready for a bit more necking with the exciting man. She had listened to him talk on, he was not at a loss for words, wondering whether to trust him. Then they had had another drink.

After some time she had been feeling tipsy from the drink, had even been getting giggly. She had told him that probably he had better take her home and that she would come to his place at another time.

Then mischievously she had added, "Are you sure you are not just trying to get me up to your apartment, you know, so we can go further with the lovemaking, I get the impression from our other times together that you weren't about to stop just because I wanted you to?" She was feeling teasey with the wine but she was also flushed and it had not gone unnoticed.

"Yes, I am trying to get you up there. You know I want you. I am proud of the place though. It really is as nice as I have told you. I want to show it off like I did the boat--soft music, dancing with you, sharing that very special place with a view. You seem to be able to look after yourself?" His sentences were filled with "I".

"Okay then take me home now, couldn't appreciate it like this anyway but will come up soon and when I do you have to promise to be good? I don't want to be wrestling with you and losing, don't want you to seduce me. You were too close the other night; I'm not ready. My mother just died, no sex with us, at least not yet, okay? It also bothers me that you're married, don't want to be the reason for your breakup--the other woman".

"Okay, don't worry though, you wouldn't affect my marriage. Would like to show the place to you, if you don't trust me I understand but promise to behave if you do come up." He was aware of her softer look--the eyes wet.

She was surprised when the car pulled up in front of his apartment. He spoke, "I have to get something before I take you home. I can park the car in the lot with the motor running or you can come up with me."

She had looked at him suspiciously, "Okay, we're here now, let's have a look." She slightly staggered as she had moved out of the car.

Grew had interrupted. "In the state you were in, you went up to his apartment; what did you expect?" He tried not to sound judgmental.

"I know it was wrong, but there was Something, --a feeling of anticipation in me."

They had entered the apartment together. He took her coat, leaving her standing, swaying slightly, in her black dress that dropped below the knees, slit in front. She had walked over to the full window and looked over a panorama of lights with the lake in the background. After hanging up her coat he had approached her from behind, he draped his arms over her shoulders and ran his hands gently over the front of her dress following the shape of her breasts, one in each hand and beneath them, down to her waist as he had kissed her neck and had then brought both hands up, cupping both breasts again, as he lifted them in his hands.

She spoke to Grew directly

"No I didn't resist, I felt secure and safe as I watched the scene before me. I didn't protest either as one hand moved to the front buttons or when he started undoing. My excitement was rising, my heart beating faster. His hand had moved beneath the cloth of my dress, beneath the cloth of my bra, fingers encircling a breast. He had been there before. I loved it, my whole body was vibrating." She was breathing noticeably in full breaths as she was telling Grew. And she had continued to tell her saga.

She had gasped slightly, feeling the hardness of the thing in his pants as he pressed himself closely against her soft warm buttocks, pressed into the crack of her ass. "It was comfortable there, I admit I knew where it was going. I wanted to have this thing in my hands again, even as fingers closed on first one nipple and then the other, gently rolling them between his fingers as they hardened, my breathing became ragged, and gasping as I felt the pinching. I reached back and felt the hard thing in his pants." Grew was breathing hard himself as she was telling him. It was as if he was there, as he listened to her telling the story.

His pulling on the nipples had intensified and she had felt herself flushing, getting hot. She had turned to face him with a reddish face. She knew she was flushed--had stared softly into his eyes and had said to him, "I thought you promised that we were not going to get into anything that would be a problem for me getting out of here in one piece". Her voice had been soft, ragged and slow.

And he had answered. "You can leave whenever you want, the door doesn't lock from the inside".

"Oh yeah, do I have to walk home now, if I leave or do I get a taxi? If so will you call one for me"?

But still for a few moments that seemed longer, they had faced each other while they had quietly said nothing, staring, studying each other. She had to admit to Grew that she had rubbed on the hardness of him as she had stood there. She hadn't moved. He had said nothing either, but slowly he had brought his mouth down on hers and she hadn't pulled back as he had kissed her lips softly, holding for awhile, gently, softly his tongue had pressed on her closed mouth, pushed between her lips and she had let him, let his tongue move deeper into her, and she had responded, the kiss had become more passionate, and tongues had swirled together.

Their bodies had rubbed and moved together as the passion continued, one hand squeezing her buttocks; her hand was on the front of his pants. Was it a tacit message? Was he allowed to go further? Grew had been fidgeting as she had talked.

She had detailed to Grew just how it had all happened; she had fought back as he pushed her towards the bedroom, her hands were slapping on his back wanting him to stop as he had walked her backwards towards the room that she had not even seen to that point; she had found herself landing on a full king-size soft bed, on her back.

She was breathing heavily as she was telling Grew and she hesitated as she quietly sat in the front seat of his car; they both waited. Grew put his hand on her knee and said,

"I think I get the message are you sure you want to tell me more? I can guess, you had sex and got pregnant."

She had started up again without an answer--really into it-- she wasn't about to stop.

"The hem of my dress had flown up as I had landed then I heard the tear at the slit as the material parted."

Grew fidgeted even more, twisting in his seat as she continued with the details as he listened intently to every word as if he had been there.

As she described the scene that then became a struggle she was getting louder, telling of the wrestling of bodies, her trying to free herself. Her legs had been spread as he had pushed his hand between them. He had continued to push until he managed to get his own legs between her legs. As they rolled on the bed together, the cool air fanned her flailing legs, his hands had moved to her upward tilted thighs. Her skirt had been bunched around her waist. She had felt his hands as they had worked at her underpants.

Grew imagined as she told of her screaming at him.

"No, No, don't do that Bob, please! You said that you wouldn't, you promised". Her legs had been everywhere as she had kicked. Rolling her body, her head clearing, bringing her arms forward, hitting him with one hand, she had been trying to hold her panties on and with her other hand. It was clear as she talked about it, reliving it that he had not stopped, wasn't going to stop. He was after what he wanted and had been determined to get it. Saying nothing, expressionless he had worked towards his goal, her kicking furiously as hair on his heavy muscled legs had tickled the soft skin of her inner bare thighs. She realized his pants were down and his weight had descended on her body, pushed her legs further apart, his arms draped on her thighs. His head had moved up between her breasts, his hands were holding her hips from moving as she had tried to pull herself up the bed, she had tried to wiggle away from him. Frantically, she had pushed uselessly at his shoulders, had pushed at his head, yanked on his hair. She had been pinned, he had pushed her at his erection; his hands had dug into her bare ass cheeks and hips.

She told Grew as he had sat silently but moving restlessly in his seat how she had kept wiggling from side to side as the bare flesh of the hard thing had kept hitting on her inner thighs, at the crotch of her panties as she had been tiring. The crotch was pushed aside the invader had reached her soft pubic hair, he had kept coming, forever pushing forward trying for the moving target. She had been unable to back up enough. With his hands on her hips holding her to him the downward thrust of his lower body had pushed into her upturned legs.

She was leaving nothing out as she related how the soft knob had separated her full lips, pushing them apart, she had been unable to get away from it. It had kept coming back to and into the entrance. Holding his prick in one hand, more and more firmly fixed in her center as she wiggled to get away, he had patiently, gently, pressed forward.

By this point she was really wound up in her story and hesitated again. Grew said nothing, listening to her soft full breathing, she looked over towards him again.

"I have to tell you the whole thing, you ready" He nodded.

"I pleaded as my ass was held with just one hand but still I couldn't back away. I begged, screamed at him, "please, don't do this to me"

She was crying a bit as she told him but insisted on going on.

"Even as I was crying out I could feel the thing right there. The knob felt soft with hard hot meat behind, my own flesh kept surrounding more of it."

The head had felt slippery and smooth to her, a round ball, moving around in her wet pocket of flesh. Her own wetness had lubricated the hard thing, (She had been so frank with her own feelings about it. She had admitted that it felt good, even as she had fought to dislodge it.)

This new sensation with a finger stroking her clitoris had seemed to go on endlessly, exciting her, even as she battled. She knew she had been getting wetter from her own warm moisture inviting the thing in. The feeling had been pleasing no matter how much she had fought it--totally new to anything ever felt before. But she had felt she couldn't just give in.

His strong hands, both of them were back on her hips, had held firmer, digging his fingers into her backside. It was her best chance to get away but she wasn't quick enough, or maybe she really didn't want to end the pleasure. A final effort could not get her free--it had gone deeper. The hard bone had pushed the soft knob into her-- deeper and deeper.

She had really got into the describing of the pain, the tearing sensation, the bone hard thing, forcing itself into her, too tight, spreading her, forcing even more within her, pushing her vagina apart. She had been unable to do anything more, it had entered her.

She had relived how she had screamed in vane at him as it was going in, had screamed at him but knew her vagina was being plugged and filled but good.

He had pushed into her virginal center with a guttural grunt, had pushed more, worked into her as far as it would go. Her muscles loosened, juices lubricating the thing, it had felt slippery smooth to her, moving around in her wet pocket of flesh.

She was candid in her description, admitting that it had felt good, even as she had fought to dislodge it. New activity with a finger stroking her clitoris added to the sensations. It seemed to go on endlessly, exciting her even as she fought but then she wasn't fighting, she was going with the flow, enjoying the action. Her vagina had become wetter, looser. It had been a glorious sensation for her. The prick would slip a bit back, then drive again. It had become easier as it moved inside her then back and in again. The original pain had turned to pleasure. Involuntarily her body had started to move with him.

He started kissing her again with passion and she had returned the kisses as they drove together, becoming a mutual thing, the heat of their friction both blending, it had gone on, a sliding of wet bodies against and within wet body until finally she had felt an intense rush. She had gasped as his driving had increased, as did her own response. Suddenly there had been a most exciting release, she talked of the new liquid that had squirted within her. She had felt drained, wet, inside and out.

Grew had sat there, transfixed. "Wow, what happened then?" He couldn't think of anything else to say, the story had turned him on.

"We laid there quietly until his penis softened, I could feel myself pushing it out, my muscles were sore, my insides were sore. I rolled away and went to the bathroom. A few minutes later I returned, throwing a bit of skin at him. It was what was left of my hymen.

"Here is something to put in your scrap book" I said.

This sex thing became her pleasure. She had been awakened, about to feed her starvation for love. It was a part of what she was. At the same time, it was the birth of her belief that all men and women were driven by the same sexuality. Her hormones were special and about to take over.

Marilyn had sex with this man a couple of more times and then she went to a dog show in Bermuda, where she showed her poodle Sammy in obedience. While there she nearly had sex again with the husband of her hostess. She enjoyed the banter but remembered the previous experience with Bob. She had such a superlative time as this new man walked her around the island. They kidded around out on the beach in the evening while the wife looked after the kids.

As she had been about to leave Bermuda, again the magic of the moment almost caught her as this new man held her, they kissed and he slipped his hands under the edges of her bathing suit. She was beginning to like these man things, she had remembered the joy of the last sexual experience as her and this new gentler man tested the bounds of how far to go. He had been responsible and strong enough to stop, had not been aware of how hot she could be.

When she had come back to Toronto she found that the contractor was not coming around as much. She did have sex with him a few more times, but soon got the idea that sex was all he wanted, without commitment. She admitted that she had been insatiable, loved it. Grew thought that she had contacted Bob to find out whether they were truly finished before getting fully involved with him.

Marilyn missed her period around the time she first started to see Grew. He had listened intently as she'd related her story-- knowing he had the choice to walk away--as she had suggested and he thought about it, but that was not him and probably she knew it. He did have a lot questions for her but had the feeling that what had happened was not totally her fault, a thing that she was vulnerable to, yet he had no idea just what he was in for.

After wrestling with the situation a short time as he worked, he had approached his friends, the Henrys in Hamilton about the possibility of her staying there and helping them with their house and kennel. They were responsive enough to the idea but it was Noreen not Walker that was enthusiastic, she could now see herself being free to go to dog shows.

Grew had then come back to Marilyn with the idea and after a few weeks talking, everything was settled, agreed that Marilyn would go to the kennel. They did need someone to look after the dogs and their kids as they both went out to work. Walker seemed to be a little reluctant, judgmental and considered Marilyn to be promiscuous, a situation that she had got into by her own hot pants and stupidity.

Before she went to Hamilton, Grew had been driving his car down hill when the brakes failed. He lacked the experience to gear down so chose to put it into a hydro pole rather than take a chance on the cross traffic at the bottom of the hill. He was not hurt and there were no charges but the car was a right off. So from then on his visits to Marilyn in Hamilton were made by bus. Either Walker or Noreen would pick him up and take him to the kennel and time with Marilyn.

Noreen and Marilyn had hit it off right away. The little adopted girl, Gwen, had had some deep problems but the little boy was easy enough for Marilyn to work with. Marilyn was as good with kids as she was with dogs. Even Gwen came around after awhile.

Religiously Grew had kept coming every weekend even though another interest had developed. Sometimes the Henrys would go away for the weekend to dog shows and leave the two of them to look after the dogs. It was nice and as her pregnancy progressed, their sex became more innovative, working around the increasing belly size. It was quite clear that this girl had no hang-ups about sex. He was unable to satisfy her, she had found her life's love--it was sex. Later she was to excite him often by relating sexual adventures, at that point in time they had just started.

It was also brought out some time later that Grew's friend Walker had found Marilyn, later to be Grew's wife, to be not unresponsive and took quite an interest in her, even though he considered her to be some kind of loose woman. Nothing happened between Walker and Marilyn in the time that she was staying there that Grew knew of. The baby girl that Marilyn had, as they all had agreed, was adopted out, there had not seemed to be an alternative. Bob, the father, paid the hospital expenses and Marilyn moved back to live with her former landlady. Grew and Marilyn went through a difficult time for a while. He wasn't sure that he wanted to marry her but he also wasn't prepared to live without her.

While she had been in Hamilton Grew had become involved with one of the clients at the animal hospital, he remembered her only as Judy. She had brought an old German Shepherd in to be put to sleep. Its time had come as all its illnesses had added up. It had become a soul-searching decision.

Grew's lifestyle was more in line with Marilyn yet he had become close to Judy and had strong feelings for her. His spare time that had been taken up by sitting in the convenience/coffee shop across the road from the animal hospital had taken on a new meaning. He had thought of Judy often as something that might have been if things had been different. It just might have been. However when he took a moment to think back about Judy he thought of his own guilt, should have been honest with her in the beginning even though he realized that she too was just using him as a diversion from her baby sitting time at home conversing with her mother-in-law.

CHAPTER 4

More Moves and Judy

It was in the second year of their marriage that Marilyn lost the job in downtown Toronto. After that, she stayed home most of the time looking after the dogs. At times she had gone to the city and trimmed dogs in people's homes or worked part time in poodle parlours. She had always developed a good rapport with the owners of the dogs or shops-- often arranging to show dogs at dog shows for the people she worked for.

Grew was on the move, too busy changing jobs to worry about what was going on at home. No doubt his decision to quit at the time was accentuated by his own home problems, and insecurities with his wife. He had quit at the animal hospital and went to work at a nearby dog grooming salon. Before Marilyn Jill, the owner had worked with him at the animal hospital when he had first come back from the States. She had imported a number of cheap poodles from England as Toronto went through a mad craze for poodles. Grew had taught her a bit about trimming and took quite an interest in her dogs that she had kept in her down town apartment. She had constantly been into some kind of difficulty with her importing business and both Doctor Green and Grew had helped her wherever possible.

As her importing activities had become increasingly time consuming, Jill had left the animal hospital and opened her own place. The doctor was not happy because her place of business was almost across the road. Grew had had a difference of opinion with

Dr. Green over the way he had been treating staff. The doctor had tried to make Jill's place out of bounds with anyone that worked for him. The doctor was annoyed because people were not obeying his rule--more so when he had found Grew too had gone. Grew had left as a matter of principle something that from time to time had caused him trouble, as a believer in principles. As an afterthought he could see the point of Dr. Green.

As he drove back and forth from work where he was realizing it had probably been a mistake to move from the animal hospital, he deliberated on how it might have been if he had married Judy. Was it a mistake to move? His thoughts went back to wondering if he had made another mistake earlier by getting married. Would it have been different if he had not told Judy that he had been engaged to Marilyn or have told her when they first started training her dog? Would he have been able to make a life with her? She had left so quickly when he had told her there had not been a chance to explain how things had changed, and he had not expected to get so involved with her. For sure, he had not been honest with this nice person, in not telling her before he had. This young man was not very woman smart and with Judy he had not been fair.

This is how he came to be involved with Judy. He had had a litter of puppies in his room at the hospital, born on his bed. He had taken it in stride and eventually moved them back to the kennels in the hospital. It was not the best situation for raising puppies but there had been at least one left when the doctor suggested that Judy look at them. Judy was a widow with a four-year old daughter. She looked at Grew's puppies and did buy a nice female that fit in very well with their family life. Grew's connection with Judy started with Grew helping her train the dog so it would fit in with their lifestyle. Judy's young daughter and mother in law lived with her.

Grew had sat in the modest Forest Hill home, an affluent part of Toronto, drinking tea and talking to her about dog training; he offered to help her. The dog he had sold her was an enhancing four months old German Shepherd that she had agreed to let him show in the dog shows. The dog was too good to be spayed so wasn't. Grew was nervous as he sat talking, watching the misbehaving daughter and wondering what had happened to the husband. Gradually she informed him about her husband. Grew remembered the story; she had met her husband as a patient in the hospital where she had worked.

He recalled his first impression of this woman as too thin and too finicky. She did not appear as a strong person but tall, very pretty in the face, with high cheekbones. Black almost straight hair reached nearly to her shoulders, the eyes were dark and enhanced with makeup. Her legs were classically long, she spoke with an enhancing East European accent. The body appeared to be on the thin side but elegantly carried, hard to miss was the nicely shaped trim backside. It was full within her build tapering down to nice legs and it was exciting, bringing out the imagination. This was a glamorous woman, not tall enough to be a model but a woman that as she walked by would be hard not to turn and take a second look at.

She was secretive about what had happened to her husband. Apparently he had spent a long time in the hospital before dying. They lived in a nice house and she drove a fairly new Studebaker. Her clothing was always in style but it appeared that she did not work. Grew never considered her to be a devoted dog lover and the way she let her daughter control her bothered him. There was an appearance about her of looking for something to pass the time, dissatisfaction with her life as it was. Grew was very cautious about taking their friendship seriously--maybe he had been too cautious--was it one that had slipped by? At first he approached what they were as an affair beyond a permanent thing, a pleasure to be enjoyed at the moment.

Many evenings, they had walked the park behind her house as they trained the dog which responded well and it wasn't long before Judy too, was able to walk quietly and peacefully with the young German Shepherd free at her side. At first it was strictly a matter of going through the exercises of training her dog to obey. On occasion she invited Grew back to the house for tea. They sat in the little side room with windows all around as they drank the tea and the little girl showed off. She was not badly behaved but Grew knew enough not to encourage her to show off and usually she settled down. He confined his conversation to Judy and her mother in law.

Through the summer months the dog was growing up and looking far better than he had ever hoped it would. Cindy, the dog, was the result of breeding the male that he had kept from his first litter, the one he had shared with the Henry's with a female he had brought from the States.

Judy too was becoming very proud of her dog but he still had the feeling that she wasn't particularly attached to it. It was like another piece of furniture to show off, something for her daughter to play with. He got Judy to enter the dog in the German Shepherd Specialty show. That resulted in more training. Grew showed the dog, at that show as she didn't feel able to and it won its class. The show had been in September. Marilyn was getting closer to having her baby and things were closing in.

Judy had started to let him drive her car, which presented the opportunity to drive into rather secluded areas so the dog could run free. She never questioned where they were going. One evening while working with the dog, they had gone out for coffee at a small shop. When they had driven by a drive in movie he said he would like to see that show.

Judy answered, "Why don't we go and see it then"?

He certainly had the time available; there they were with her car, the mother in law was looking after the young girl. He looked sideways at her. "Well if you have the time I guess I have too", On his part it was an out of line suggestion, considering his circumstances but Grew too had found something to take up his spare time.

That first night at the movies he did not even hold her hand as they sat alone in her car. Things changed though. He had never spoken of his relationship with Marilyn. Judy never asked anything about him of a personal nature in all the time that they were together. After the dog had its run they'd sit and talk. Together they talked about things of the world, he delved into her past secretive history, enjoying each other's company. She had kept coming back for more training so the meetings kept happening.

As they had parked behind the animal hospital one evening, where Grew had driven for her to drop him off, before getting out of the drivers seat, he moved towards Judy and suddenly he was kissing tender soft lips. There is no doubt he made the first move. The lips were so soft, he knew that she was a willing participant. There was no resistance as after a short time he moved his tongue between those lips. She was not pulling away. Before long the necking was becoming quite warm and passionate, he didn't move to even touch a breast or rub a leg. One of his first observations when they had first started necking was the running of her mascara. The face was still picturesque but it became adorned with black streaks, as they both became hot--it bothered him at first. This was no natural but one that had used abundant makeup to enhance the beauty that he felt was certainly there. To him it was like a hiding of the naturalness. She declined his offer to come into his room or even the hospital. She was hesitant about his progress, a little slow to accept his moving hand, she would put her hand gently on his, stopping it from caressing her. Grew wondered if the reluctance that she exhibited towards his advances. It had given him a fixed impression that she would never be available to him and she was only allowing him token liberties in order to keep him as a companion? When he later considered this he thought that perhaps she had given him the wrong impression, and combined with his own feelings of inadequacy, he had never thought there was a chance with her,

Later when she did come in with him, it was always with the stipulation that she would not go into his room, like she was perpetually on guard, being very nervous. Why was she so on guard? There was one time though that he had carried her into his room. She became so nervous, alarmed and panicky as he had put her on the bed that he stood back-- letting her make her way back out of the room as fast as she had been taken in.

The first indication that she was accepting him was when she moved from that first position where she had stopped his moving hands from traveling up her soft thighs under her skirt. When she allowed such freedom he was quickly changing his conception about her being too thin. The thighs were shapely and full as he exposed them, he was delighted at the smooth soft warm feel of them. As their friendship continued, he devised plans to get her out of the front seat of the car that was so restrictive. In those early days it was onto the grass so they would have more room and perhaps--as his thinking went--he could get closer to actual sex with her. His attitude had not been one of looking after her interests but to conquer and enjoy her body.

Progressively he had become bolder, finding the opposition diminishing as he bared those exquisite teacup breasts. They stood right out all on their own with standout nipples, she didn't need a bra. They were super to suck on. Was his obvious appreciation and adoration changing her reluctance and bringing out her pride? This foreplay was allowed with apparently mutual passion. Not long afterward she began to spread those fantastic legs, letting him softly rub the warm skin between them. To him it was such a delight to stroke that resilient smooth perfection. Years later he remembered the warm smoothness. She was capable of handling the competition if she had wanted to but as he recalled, she too, had lacked self-confidence.

Judy was somewhat on the shy side about his penis being brought out. Once more, her hand moved to stop him as he had started to undo his fly but as they had continued to neck and as he had continued with his hand gently stroking her inner thigh, it was her that had then undid the zipper and fished out his hard prick. She had sat back and looked at it with it in her hand, hard and in full bloom.

Her hand had moved up and down the shaft on the skin and then she pulled back the foreskin, obviously studying the coloured knob. There was no hesitation as she handled this thing, delicately fondling, loving it. After awhile she bent over and took it in her mouth with apparent joy. Warm saliva surrounded his tube; it had been so fantastic.

The space in the car had been so cramped, there was a stick shift between them. He wanted her out in the grass where they could move. He tried and tried but she so vehemently expressed a fear of snakes that he gave that idea up. Then he tried to get her in the back seat, but that too never happened.

On the weekend he was back on the bus to Hamilton to meet Marilyn. Something about her attitude was mostly up but there was an obvious restlessness with the whole ordeal she was going through. At those times Marilyn would express her thoughts to him. She was putting up with what was happening because she had to but she was not happy with the way things were at the kennel. They had kept the secret away from her sisters who never did find out. To him those times were such a pleasure with only minimal thoughts of his mid week escapades with Judy, as the two of them would walk with the dogs through the back area of the kennel, hand in hand, talking about her problems with the little girl or the bad character of some of the dogs she was working with.

When the Henrys were away at dog shows they spent time on the bed trying to get around the growing belly and into eventual sex, even making it pleasurable, she was not willing to wait. They would laugh as she practically stood on her head in order to get lined up. She was quite a contrast to his during the week woman. Later he would realize Marilyn's psychic sense, she probably realized something was not quite as it should be with them but would not be able to place what it was that was bothering her. Grew too was starting to be flustered over what was to come.

While riding back and forth on the bus or at work he kept trying to figure how he was going to get his penis into Judy. It had become his goal. He wasn't thinking of the consequences, or what was the best for her. Grew had not learned about the value of pleasing the woman at that point in his life. His love for Marilyn at that time was not absolute either but he was expending himself each weekend, therefore sexually not as aggressive as he could have been towards Judy.

His Judy sessions had developed into him getting between her legs with his pants down, both of them crammed together in the front seat, while she worked on his hard prick, trying to bring it off. He thought it was her goal, trying to get it off before he could get it into her. In a way they were playing Russian roulette. While this was going on, even while she was jerking it, he would be trying to get her pants down or working the crotch band to the side so he could get his prick into her vagina even as they were invariably bent in the wrong direction. As he would pull down on her panties she would be pulling up with her free hand, the one not jerking him off. She would let him get his fingers inside of her and he worked her off until both of them were drenched in sweat but she always managed to keep the crotch band in a position that prevented the prick getting in.

If he could not get the panties down, he came up with the idea that he would have to do something about the crotch band. One day he took a pair of scissors with him and was considering cutting it. He had stopped for a moment as they had reached that point again where his three fingers were stretching the walls of her vagina as they plunged back and forth into her. Then he showed her the scissors as he confessed what he had been planning. It happened at that last moment with them both going at each other. He had been trying to get his prick in there, he had her spread and slippery, pushing panties aside, while kneeling on the floor in front of her, pulling her delightful butt towards him, advancing hot, hard prick, while she furiously jerked at the thing, jerking wildly up and down on the shaft with her hand. He showed her the scissors and confessed his plan.

It seemed to make an intense impression on her. Suddenly, she stopped jerking the prick, she removed her panties. Now the coast was clear, she was going to let him fuck her. She kept jerking on the prick though as it moved towards her wide open hot cunt that he had been hand fucking with three fingers for the last while.

As he had gotten closer to the soft wet valley, with her mascara running down her face, the two of them kissing, open mouth to open mouth, he could feel the knob of his prick, bouncing around at the entrance-- fitting in. He was going to get her this time. She kept furiously jerking back and forth on his prick though, she wasn't waiting for it to get inside her, something was happening within her too; she was hot and gasping, excitement affecting her as well as him.

They were about to do it, both willing. He just had to get it in her. The way her body was jerking back and forth she was coming with an orgasm almost out of control, he could feel it. Then she was pulling his prick back trying to hold it away from the entrance but still he was winning; it was lined up separating her cunt lips, enclosing the knob. Her body was pushing onto it. He was ready to drive it in, at the entrance but then he felt his own pulsing he pushed it into her anyway but it didn't go far enough. She started to struggle frantically to get it out as if she also felt his pulsing. She managed to dislodge it just as it shot all over her belly and leg.

She had looked disappointed as they lay together wiping the stuff from her soft bare skin with cleanex. They talked briefly as he felt her closing up. He too was disappointed but in a sense relieved. It would have been disastrous if he had got her pregnant but it would have brought his situation into focus. Life was getting hectic; Judy's actions were indicative that she was about ready to start having sex with him---an understatement. He knew what condoms did to his erection so did not want to get into using them. This was all happening at a time before the pill.

When he had thought of it later he had wondered at his dilemma. Would Judy have had sex with him, then want to get married? One of the vet's assistants knew Judy and also what Grew's other world was, he talked to him, telling that he should grab Judy and hold on. Grew could understand that point of view, how he looked at it, how he felt about the situation. His advice was well meaning and probably good advice. Could he have made a life with Judy? The assistant kept telling Grew not to mess up with Judy. It was no doubt, his choice for the young animal worker. Grew's choice was to tell Judy about Marilyn.

One evening he did tell her and the scene was not nice. She didn't give him a chance to explain his situation with Marilyn, she just left on the spot. Within the next few days the dog was returned, his phone calls to her were not. She had virtually disappeared and he never saw her again until ten years later outside of another animal hospital.

At that time they had had a few words, cordial words. Then she had cut off the conversation and rushed off. The veterinary hospital where he had met her was that of Dr. Relaishe who had also worked for Dr. Green at another time.

Dr Relaishe was married but Grew had known him well, having also worked for him too, and an experience also full of stories of personal involvements. He wondered if Judy had become involved with him. She had still looked perfect. Grew never saw her again after that but often wondered about her. She might have been the right woman for him. Certainly her troubles appeared tame compared to what he went through and was about to go through more of the same. Could he have made a life with Judy?

He didn't get along with Jill's husband, who was into a lot of supposedly illegal things, so Grew left there too, then got a job on the other side of Toronto with another veterinarian. It was soon evident that it was a job too far from home; it was very difficult to get to in the middle of winter. He had liked the doctor and staff but could not agree with the quality of work done there. By the end of the year he was ready to move again.

Marilyn spent more and more time at home, only going to town when she was either trimming dogs or was helping at one of the poodle trimming establishments. Grew didn't find anything unusual about it. She would tell him when various people came to visit. He was quite contented that she seemed to be accepting the community and some of its people as well as mutual friends in the dog business that might have a day off from work so would stop by to see her, to talk dogs. The two of them were totally involved in the breeding, showing and the kennel clubs involved with dogs. Still it was him that attracted the attention. It was their life but perhaps more his than hers. Some of his friends used to tell him of the enjoyable time they had had when visiting her, following along as she would take the whole contingent of dogs walking together, back in the field and beyond. They reveled in their stories, all finding it so enjoyable.

Marilyn had met a woman called Karen who lived on a urine farm a few miles away from the kennel. A urine farm is where they keep pregnant mares so they can collect the urine for some specific medication dealing with diabetes. Apparently it is the best source of this component.

This is where Karen lived with her boyfriend Stan. Stan was a horse rider at Ontario style amateur rodeos. He thought he was pretty good. Marilyn wanted to get a horse and suggested it to Grew. Together they walked through the barns at the farm, looking at a number of standing horses with bags to collect their urine. For a while they looked around at horses elsewhere, that might have been available and in due course she found what she wanted, They bought the young horse and Marilyn started using it to take the dogs with her as she rode in the fields behind their place. It took her quite a while at first to adapt. They kept running around the feet of the horse and the Corgi's almost got stepped on a few times.

CHAPTER 5
Casual Affairs

Grew had gone to work digging a hole in the side of the hill, his own idea of making a cheap shelter for the horse. It was almost like a cave where the roof was actually at a level with the slope of the hill. He then put holes in the floor of this dugout and fitted them with posts, then plywood behind the posts like a mine entrance. The posts provided the uprights for the roof that was constructed on the top of the posts. He put double half doors like a regular barn on the front. It was predicted that the whole thing would only last a year, tumble in a heap with the first winter snowstorm but it was still there ten years later. He had learned of the special drainage qualities when building on gravel hills.

These horse people were a partying group that Grew wondered about some of the things he had seen going on. The Tuckett's went to a party at the urine farm, where Grew's first impression was that Stan was hitting on a new girl, Susan, trying to get her off on her own--cut her out of the herd--so to speak. She was probably about seventeen, nice looking. Karen was onto what he was up to and was trying to be nonchalant each time Stan and Susan disappeared from the party.

Marilyn was concerned about Grew being too sympathetic to Karen because she knew that Karen was a swinger. Grew thought Marilyn had been talking too much about her husband and got Karen interested. Karen also knew things that he did not, at the time about Marilyn. Yes, Grew would have liked to have had a go at Karen himself. She was somewhat on the buxom side, built like made for fun but she seemed too upset that night about the disappearing boyfriend. People at the party had been getting quite drunk.

Marilyn had also been disappearing and returning as Grew had pretended to be drunk himself. In thinking back Grew believed Marilyn had been going out to see someone herself, she should also have known that Grew did not get drunk. Even though he had been becoming suspicious of his wife he decided to go home, not making any progress with anyone himself and realizing he was out of his depth as a swinger. The next time Marilyn showed back at the party he told her he was going to go home. He felt she was screwing around with someone.

She didn't respond, just stood listening to him talk but with her mind somewhere else, so he had left. He no sooner got home than she called for him to come back and get her. Why? Was she really calling to see if he had really gone home? He went back for her not knowing what was going on, and never did find out. He spent the way home defending the position that he was not coming onto Karen, which perhaps was only because he wasn't getting anywhere.

He found out from Marilyn that Karen had been promoting her promiscuous lifestyle. Perhaps Stan had wanted to try Marilyn out and maybe did but if it was a switching situation maybe Marilyn wasn't about to give Karen her turn. He had never been told what they were working on and guessed it all flopped. Later he had wondered if the Susan thing was just a screen and that Stan was coming on to Marilyn.

He didn't know it then but Marilyn had been developing a reputation in this very small community. What also might have been going on could have been why she got sidetracked away from Stan and called to come home. Maybe Grew had thrown the balance of partners out.

Two days later they went to one of those fun rodeos where Stan and Karen were doing their thing. Horses and riders charged around barrels in races, winding in and out as they charged to a finish.

There were no bucking horses or calf and steer roping or riding bulls. Soon after that Marilyn stopped seeing Karen and the horse they had bought became somewhat neglected until eventually he was sold to someone else. Had she lost interest in Stan? Was he not the great stud he was supposed to be or had Karen made her back off? To Grew, Karen looked okay. The possibility that Karen had expressed an interest in switching seemed likely.

Marilyn eventually decided what she was carrying inside was too much and decided to confide in Grew once again. Had she expected him to leave her when she revealed the truth about the life she was living? Maybe she did expect him to go when she told the truth but she might have also known that it was uncharacteristic.

As they drove from his work after she had been trimming dogs in the city, she started to talk hesitantly. He knew from past experience with her that to get the full story it was best to say little. So he kept quiet--occasionally asking a question--supporting her as he had done a few years before as she had then revealed her story of seduction.

She told him that one day she had left him at work and went back home to have the Volkswagen serviced at the local garage in Goodwould. The Corbetts owned the garage and also owned the general store next to it. Clarence owned or operated the garage and service station. Frei Maison worked for him. The idea had been that if they got the car serviced there, Frei could deliver it on his way home. Marilyn could stay at home, doing whatever she had to do and then pick Grew up later. It is not clear but this probably happened before the party.

Clarence, who was around the same age as Marilyn, decided to bring the car back himself. Was it because she had told him she wanted it back early so she could go to the city to pick her husband up? Or was it that he had spotted the very friendly wife living next door to Frei and wanted to check her out? Clarence was of medium build with medium blond hair and a charming smile. But it was his blue eyes that Marilyn had faced a few times before that fascinated her.

She had invited him in for coffee and he was quick to accept. While drinking coffee he stared into her laughing face as she made fun of life and the back-wood way they lived their lives. Here was two very outgoing people coming together. Clarence had a story to tell of his own. He talked of his children but made it clear that he and his wife were only living together for convenience, told her of the local dance by the lake and suggested that she and her husband come to it.

"You will see for yourself the interaction going on with my wife and another man." He also told her of his own involvement in the past with another local woman.

The lifestyle of Goodwood was intriguing Marilyn. It was quite common and almost the way life was in Goodwood, this switching thing. Clarence's status with his wife (and other women that he did not elaborate on too much) was apparently well known. They had switched partners with a couple for a while. He had told Marilyn that his affair with the other wife was over. No wonder people called it Good would.

Marilyn had listened intently. As the time passed, she put more liquor in the coffee she poured for both of them. After some time she had again come to put more coffee in his cup. He had taken hold of her wrist as she did and stood up, the coffeepot he then took out of her hand and placed back on the stove, still holding her wrist. She had stared into the blue eyes, the eyes that she had swooned about when telling her husband of this man. He had switched his left hand to her right wrist and suddenly was bringing her into his firm body, his right arm had gone over her shoulder. He tilted her head up with his left hand, he was only slightly taller than her so it was not so far. While this was going on she was not resisting or giving any indication that he should stop. Her eyes would have sparkled as she returned the look. They would have told him that she wasn't going to fight him off. Her mouth did not say a thing. She had still looked into those blue eyes as his mouth descended on hers, said nothing nor did she resist, even as he danced her backwards onto the living room couch. She laughed as their mouths parted on the way down.

Then his lips were there again as the two of them had landed on the couch cushions, lips back together, softly moving, slightly, until after an eternity when his tongue had worked between yielding lips.

His right hand had moved to her breast, messaging gently as it felt for the clothed nipple. She had felt warm and fluid. Not a thought in her had considered where this thing was going. She had just melted into the body next to her, one step at a time. She had painted the picture with words to her husband as he listened intently, almost afraid to interrupt for fear that she would stop telling him about it.

Then she had felt the buttons on her blouse being unbuttoned, hands behind her back, warm hands on her skin, quick release of bra, warm gentle hands moving on her bare tits, slowly moving over the skin of her. Her mouth had opened wide as she took his tongue into her, sucked on it, felt it travel around her own tongue, diving deep into her throat, thrilling her. Still no resistance as the button on the top of her jeans popped and she had felt the hand move on her smooth belly, under her panties. It had messaged gently for too long a time. She had wanted it to proceed, she had wanted to be fucked, didn't care anymore, but he had kept stroking, stroking her belly, her tits, her nipples. All the time while this was going on they were wildly kissing.

Her legs had moved apart as she felt the hand move up the enchanted passage, had moved into her soft pubic hair, then into the wet, warm slit, slowly playing with the clit.

He had known what to do, where to play her and she had loved it. She had moved her own jeans down her legs as he continued to play with her hot spot-- oh so softly. Her jeans were off her legs and his own pants were suddenly not there and he was moving with this little penis between her legs. She had wanted it in her but he had only teased her, moving his penis around her clitoris, for an endless time. She had had orgasm after orgasm before he had finally sunk the thing in her, furiously driving. She told Grew it had been enjoyable though small. He had had great sustaining power; she had been on her second orgasm before he came. They rolled apart, soaking wet inside. The sweat covered them.

He had been there for two hours, had to get back to work and she had to go and pick her husband up. She had bathed, standing in the washtub, moving the wet washcloth over her smooth skin, had quickly toweled herself dry, put on clean panties and jeans and had then gone to get Grew. On the way home that day, she had talked to him about the things that Clarence had told her but not a word about her adventure. He never guessed that she had had sex with him and she hadn't told him until much later, as they again drove from the city. Every time she told him about her affairs it would turn him on, as she talked of the things she had done he made a mental note to try the same thing with her and later he did. Sometimes he had wondered if she had made it all up but eventually he saw enough to realize it was the truth she was talking about.

They did go to the dance. At the time Grew still did not know what was going on but Marilyn had told him of the swinging. He was careful not to be too forward with Clarence's wife Helen, as he knew what had happened before. Whether Helen was still into something with the other husband he had not been aware but he had been aware of a tension at the dance. He might have been more forward with her when they danced, a nice looking woman but found her rather cool. He might have acted differently if he had been aware of what had been going on previously. It was all part of the Goodwood scene.

And it was all too much for Marilyn to hold back from him. They were once again clearing the slate as she had detailed her sex with Clarence. It wasn't just the one time either. She had used him as a model to broaden their own sex play, she taught Grew things that satisfied her. Did it make Grew believe that all women were that way? It could have had something to do with it. He was learning.

The Tuckett's had taken on the responsibility of running the German Shepherd dog newsletter that came out monthly. When first receiving the project Grew had no idea what to write so examined parts of books on the breed and would rewrite parts in his own way, often changing the focus. Marilyn was very good at re wording his material and they often spent hours discussing and arguing to get the meaning intended. It was done with no hard feelings or rancor between them. In that respect they had a mutual respect. She would edit articles written by him as she had tried to make them clearer but she also had talked him out of putting in some of his more controversial ideas.

Various people belonging to the club had worked with them for periods of time. These people usually looked after the printing, done on antiquated equipment that the club bought from others that had upgraded, then they too went from stencil to printers, to computers up grading as they went. Marilyn and he looked after the editorial content.

Grew continued to write about dogs and on the breed including things that he had learned about the most desirable and efficient structure. The Club reluctantly accepted his right to express opinions as his own but few openly argued about his concepts.

The newsletter committee would meet at one or the other of the member's houses to go over the ideas of what would be included in the next issue. The Brinks were a couple that volunteered to help with the production of the paper. George and Maureen had been struggling with their efforts to produce good dogs. They had made some gallant tries to breed winners but bred their own bitches to dogs without the solid background, dogs that went back to Canadian dogs that really were secondary. They were sort of involved in obedience classes but not enough to make a mark. There was a suspicion that George was rough with the dogs, abusive to his two boys, only the youngest being his. History also revealed an abusive relationship with Maureen. They fit in well with Marilyn and Grew. As things happened it has to be said that they fitted, "Too well".

Maureen was a rather tall, somewhat sophisticated, trim person who one would suspect was always in control of everything she did. As one might expect, accounting was her field. She looked the part, talked like an authority, had ideas but never wrote anything for the paper. George was a medium tall, husky fellow, dark hair that anyone would consider good looking, athletic build. Sometimes he worked at mechanical jobs, sometimes not at all, giving the image of being clean cut but not that bright. The four of them had some enjoyable times as they met and discussed mostly dogs and sometimes life. Grew believed that they were all compatible. No one would suspect anything unusual.

A job offer came in from a vet close to the center of Toronto on the north side and Grew decided to take it. He didn't know it at first but this vet was a rather paranoid jumping up and down individual, difficult to work for but was an excellent person with the dogs. He was a real character and when he wasn't around the employees survived by making fun of the strange Dr. Gleeson--a short fellow but a going concern.

From time to time and he did it more than once, Grew "lost it", with this man, slamming down the white apron provided and walking out but each time he came back. It was something Dr. Gleeson was used to. His partner and other workers had frequently done the same. The doctor would try to signal in front of the clients with expressions and head motions what he wanted his assistants to do while they held dogs on the examining table. He never had gone over what his charades meant, what he wanted and all his staff rebelled from time to time in frustration. It became apparent that the way he was wasn't personal. Grew managed to survive for two years at that hospital.

When he had been there a short time. Dr. Gleeson introduced the staff to the new summer student--Lisa, she was eighteen years old. She instantly got along with Tony and Grew who had shared the work, holding dogs for Dr. Gleeson, cleaning kennels and doing the trimming to that time. Tony, who had worked for the doctor for some time, had helped Grew to understand the strange doctor. However the pressure could have been telling on him. Tony had just broken up his marriage and treated his position with disdain. Grew often wondered if his job had contributed to his marriage breakup.

Tony was not an artist, at least with dogs, he didn't really care. His view of trimming dogs was to get the hair out of the way-- just a job. Dr. Gleeson had wanted to raise the level of quality with the trims. He had just bought out his complacent partner. The purpose of bringing Grew in was to raise the level of trims coming from the hospital.

Grew taught both Tony and Lisa a lot but Tony was resistant, not particularly responsive or interested but it was not the same with Lisa, she was a prime student. Tony though, was able to tolerate Dr. Gleeson better than Grew was and many times would sit and talk, smiling a bit through his stocky English face, with his teeth almost clamped together as he would point out the better side of the doctor that Grew also came to respect as he saw him bring animals back to life that elsewhere would have been dead.

Lisa and Grew became friends. At first he was more impressed with her mother who had that look of a woman needing loving. Lisa was just considered too young but she was very nice looking, medium height and weight, a little thick in the ankles, upper teeth that slightly overlapped the bottom contributed to a cute smile. She walked with a bit of a wiggle. Even after the summer ended she kept dropping in, wanting to learn dog trimming. Grew talked seriously about making each trim a work of art, each dog a model of its breed, trimming the hair short or leaving it to hide a fault.

On her own time she would sit down in the basement as Grew meticulously labored, he really enjoyed making the dogs look better and he had taught his wife the same basic structure points he had learned himself when he had first come to Toronto where he had studied the dogs at the shows and modified show trims into practical images of the same. He would show Lisa many of the same features, as he would stand a dog on the grooming table and move his hands gently over the structure. Lisa listened intently while he talked about his German Shepherds, telling her what it was that made them so special and what he had been trying to achieve as he sought better animals through breeding. She listened like a disciple getting the word from God. The fall passed to winter again with Lisa still dropping in. She was a natural to get the animal hospital job the next summer.

That fall Grew and Marilyn took a trip with Bisket to Pennsylvania to breed her to a dog that had come from Germany.

Grew, by then an expert on pedigree studies, had figured out that it was one of the best chances to get better breeding stock. Although it was pressing to them financially, they made the trip in their Volkswagen.

Together they had this connection with the dogs that they totally agreed on as to direction taken. Grew had seen the dog they bred to in the Shepherd magazine, had studied the pedigree with all the working degrees following the names of the parents and grandparents and as he was familiar with the German lines, determined that this dog should be the one to use. It was a testament to his knowledge of the breed, much of which had been gathered in order to write his articles. By November the puppies were born in the shed on the back of the shack. It was unheated but like little wolves the puppies were happy and contented as they snuggled into their mother's breast. It was part of the philosophy of natural survival. The bitch had a litter in which there were two that made their mark on the breed, so that too was rewarding.

Many weekends Grew had to work so could not get to the dog shows. Marilyn had to go on her own. As she won her share at the shows her confidence grew and on some occasions took to entering shows further away. She would catch a ride with handlers, as Grew required the Volkswagen to get to work. She even seemed to be able to handle staying in a motel alone and he never thought anything of it, as he felt the two of them had found mutual understanding in the management and working of their kennel. They did sell a few dogs, which helped to finance the showing but they were just hanging on.

Sometime later Grew found out from Marilyn herself about some of the activities at the dog shows, at the motels. There was a lot of drinking going on but it was not something that she had ever found much interest in, she would retire to her room. There were more stories about what went on there and she related them to Grew at a later date. There was one old friend of the two of them that came on to her so persistently that she gave in. Although Grew would come to believe she was more involved than she admitted. She said he didn't force her but simply kept coming onto her, feeling her wherever he could, on the breasts, the ass, in her crotch until she finally pulled him to her and kissed him. From there they undressed and he screwed her, which she said was anything but satisfying.

Her and Grew never made an issue about it because of the friends wife that they were both very close to. It was ironic; Grew had always had an attraction to his wife, would have loved to make love to her and felt the feeling was mutual. Then there was the other friend "Alex", who kicked in her door one night at a motel and was in her bed before she could do a thing about it. She also rated him as a poor fuck, being long and thin but without a complete erection. Was it from alcohol? That is what eventually killed him a few years later.

The word seemed to somehow be out in Goodwood about Marilyn being one hot sex thing. Grew had not been aware of it though, as usual the last to know. He only found out about it when Marilyn told him. It was well after the fact when they had their conscience clearing. Grew found that the revelations made her even more attractive to him. He delighted in hearing her stories--she should have been a writer.

One salesperson had come to the door while she was there alone and before she was aware of anything strange, he had reached out and fondled her breast. As she told Grew about it she laughed. She had calmly allowed the affront, not stopping him, even as he had undone the buttons and worked on the bare skin. It had been him that had backed off, she did not have sex with him. She didn't know who he was and as she had told Grew, she herself was wondering what was being said about her.

George Brinks was not so shy though and it was not long before he had realized that this woman could be available. He had arrived one afternoon in early summer. It had nothing to do with the German Shepherd Club. He said he was passing by so dropped in. She had let him in, why not? He was a friend. She made him coffee as she usually did. She found him to be an attractive hunk but she had never entertained the idea of getting involved with someone so close to his or her social group. She also had known that it was close to the time that she should have been getting back on her birth control pills, so would not willingly have gotten into something with anyone, even her husband without protection.

Nothing had crossed her mind about an affair with this man anyway, he had never tried anything beyond a pat or sneak kiss and she had always felt that she could control things with anyone now that she was more experienced. If something happened with any man it was because she wanted it to happen. Sex was something that she openly enjoyed.

He did catch her by surprise, almost as soon as he was in the door, as he had suddenly had her in his arms and was kissing her. At first she tried to pull back but soon realized the unusual strength of this man. That strength itself was exciting. Deciding she would wait for an opportunity to get away later--after a little necking--which she wouldn't mind with him anyway, she had enjoyed the attention.

Marilyn knew that his wife had the reputation of being cold, he had often joked about it and she had never made statements to the contrary, something often associated with men that are inadequate. Later evidence would suggest that perhaps making no comment would have been the safest route for her to take. Marilyn would be the first to admit that he was a desirable looking man. All past association with him had led her to believe he was a reasonable sort, she'd get him to stop when ready.

She lost track of time though, it was nice, she had felt warm. George was breathing heavy, getting more daring with his hands, more passionate every minute--and less controllable. She had started trying to get him to stop as she kept trying to move his hands out of her clothing.

"George, George cut it out, enough is enough. It is time to stop, no more. What are you doing? Hey stop that. I can't have sex now" she had exclaimed. Had somehow the word got out to him too--about her?

Still she had laughed but kept telling him to stop as he had been dragging the slacks down her legs, or really up her legs, as she had been dumped on the couch and as she had lain there with him holding her legs in the air, kicking at him, yelling and wiggling, almost in a fun way, he had kept pulling on her slacks until they were off.

Her underpants were gone with a yanking motion. His aggressiveness had now been scaring her a bit but also exciting her. Her blouse and bra fared no better, as they also were soon gone. Vehemently, he spread her twisting legs as she had tried to keep them crossed, - no use. She fought without a sense of winning. He was getting everything off. She had continued to complain and struggle but he had stripped her naked.

Between her legs he had quickly dropped. Before she could move out of the way, even once, he had her nailed with his prick--into her. Suddenly he was wildly driving himself into her, not what she would have preferred. Incessantly, he kept pumping his strong body onto her, punishing her, his hard muscled belly slapping on hers.

Her own body had reluctantly begun to respond. *What was the matter with me?* He had just kept going, an athlete, pushing it into her. She was involuntarily meeting every thrust with her own until she felt the gush--she had had an orgasm.

As he had softened and came out of her she had lain there and worried. She had talked to him, asking about what had brought that on. He told her of his frustration with Maureen who was always turning him down for sex. He also informed her at that time, that the two of them were not married, told Marilyn how she had always turned him on until he could just not resist any further. He knew from the way she looked all the time that she was a sexual thing, never satisfied, he'd had an idea that she was hot, he was right. There was no mention of the gossip.

Marilyn had to deal with her own feelings of guilt. She knew how she was but did not like it, what she had become was distasteful to her, was to eat at her through the months of secrecy, was not something that she would confess to Grew for fear of what he might do to this supposed friend, or what else, so she lived with it.

She was beginning to know what George had been talking about and the affect she was having on men. Was she sending out vibes to them all that she was available? There was no doubt that something was happening. She admitted she loved it but still felt guilty. Grew was never told whether she ever had sex with George again.

That night she had sex with Grew that she was more than willing to do although it is not known who initiated it. Had she planned it, just in case? He had been very satisfied with her but sort of realized that he would never be able to satisfy her, was lasting longer before coming than he had before, learning, but still had not been spending enough time on foreplay. It had felt that time that she could have had an orgasm as suddenly the flesh of her behind had taken on a feeling of mush and all her muscles had relaxed. Her talk was usually of unsatisfied sexual need but not that night. He had no idea just what was going on but that day was probably when she had become pregnant.

There were a number of women that interested Grew but he believed that if he had become involved that it would not help their marriage and Marilyn with her almost psychic abilities, would have probably known. As it was, she had given him the impression that she suspected him of having an eye on every woman out there. Perhaps she had wanted him to get involved with someone else to justify her own involvement and feelings of guilt. He didn't know; he too had feelings of confusion about their marriage. Even Maureen Brinks, he found to be an attractive woman that given the right circumstances, he could have enjoyed sex with and it almost happened a few months later, when things started to come out and unravel.

Marilyn and Grew had been driving home from the city one day and as they were driving she had suddenly announced that she was pregnant. Grew couldn't understand it but knew that sometimes she would start the using of her pills again very close to the cut off time for sex without them. Not even considering that she might have been having sex with someone else he wasn't upset, simply took her word for it. This man was so wrapped up in the dog activities that he was almost unaware of what was going on around him. The confessions usually came some time after the facts but he somehow felt there had been nothing going on while she was confessing what had gone on before. The fact was that she also had had sex with him on that fateful day so no one was really to know for certain and never would.

CHAPTER 6
Lissette

He would have liked to become involved with someone more predictable, someone he could better understand, but his wife being pregnant inspired a sense of loyalty. He had not been happy, was confused with the way she was, felt that she had been feeling that he didn't want to have sex with her, as she became more evidently pregnant. It was hard to understand, considering the last time that she had been pregnant when they had been having sex right up to the time of delivery. Later he was to realize that her sense of guilt had been part of the weave into their mixed up state of existence.

One day Lissette came to him while he was painting kennels, a job that they did periodically as a means of disinfecting in a more effective way. "Grew, can I talk to you about something?"

"Okay my dear" he returned rather flippantly.

She started in right away and talked seriously. "Well it's about this guy I always wanted to go out with. I always thought he was nice. Last night I met him at the variety store and he asked me to go for a drive with him. I went and he parked and kissed me and Grew, I couldn't control him or me. He was too much". She paused.

Grew had looked at her with a shocked look. He was excited himself, he put down the brush and faced her, thinking to himself, *"Oh no, not another one, she is going to tell me she got laid"*. Cautiously, calmly he asked her, although wondering if he should,

"What do you mean too much? What happened?" picking up the brush, Grew faced away.

"Grew, he got his hand, both hands in my dress. First he was holding my breast and I held his wrist, first with one hand, then the other. Then I hung on with both hands, but he kept kissing me. His other hand went up my skirt and when I had to go after that one, he got his first hand under my brassier. I thought I could look after myself but my body was not doing the right things. I couldn't or wouldn't even cross my legs".

Grew was smiling, "Lisa, are you sure you should be telling me about this, this is pretty personal stuff. You shouldn't be telling me this. Are you all right?'

Just so matter of fact she stated, "Well he didn't get me but boy, I really didn't put up a good fight. I'm embarrassed to say he got his hand in my pants. He made me feel funny, Grew he could have had me. I kept saying No, over and over again. But I didn't mean it. It felt so good. I guess you're right, I shouldn't be telling you this".

Grew tried to regain his calm, slowly brushing on the cage door with the paintbrush. Inside he was in frenzy, trying not to say too much, trying to calmly play the role of confident. "It's okay I suppose you have to tell someone, I guess it might as well be me. The thing I don't understand though is how you did not get got or laid as you might say? You sound like you were out of control to say the least. Are you telling me the whole thing? Should I even be asking?"

"Yeh----he didn't get me. I went into a kind of hysteria. He got my brassier off but he was being too forceful. I just couldn't handle it. He was pushing too hard--fingering me, trying to get my clothes off. I guess I just went wild, didn't know what to do, kept telling him no but he kept pushing, trying to force me. I started screaming, I couldn't handle it. He let me go, don't know what happened to me". She was talking confidently, smiling, almost laughing. She was sounding pretty excited and maybe disappointed. Grew wasn't sure what to say at that point.

"Hey, take it easy. All that happened is that your own built in protection system went to work. There's nothing wrong with you.

He went too fast. You are eighteen though. your body is developing, becoming receptive to man, your starting to be aware".

Grew just couldn't believe that he had said all those things, thought he sounded like an expert, knowing he wasn't, the words uttered had sounded good, even to him. She softened, calmed down, they continued to work together as if the matter had never been brought up. Inwardly though Grew was more than a little concerned about her ability to handle herself in a tough situation.

He blatantly continued with his "expert" thoughts and advice. "The only thing is, now you know your limitations on your control, I would advise you to stay out of cars when you do not entirely trust the guy your riding with. Also when you have a problem you should probably be telling your mother instead of me but you have already told me that you can't talk to her about these things. So I guess if you don't have anyone else to tell you can tell me and I'll do my best. I'll tell you what I think anyway for what that is worth".

Grew had thought she was sure a gutsy thing, even admitting to him that she felt good. Her story excited him but he felt that he had handled it well, without overreacting, like what happened to her wasn't too much out of the usual. What he did do though was go home, throw the conversation at Marilyn, to get her reaction. He got it. She threw in other ideas that he felt would make him a little more capable the next time he had to council. As Marilyn advised, Grew was unaware that anything was going on in her life that might have influenced the input she was throwing into the situation Grew faced at work. Was she setting him up?

That next time came up real soon, the next day. Lisa had gone out and found another boy. Grew wondered if she was practicing or what but felt she was sure giving him practice. This guy hadn't been that hard to handle for her so was thinking of going out with him again. Grew asked what she was hoping for and what she was prepared to give up.

She told him--straight at him as usual--she was a virgin and intended to stay that way, at least for then. She told him how on one occasion she had jumped from a car when she had accepted a ride.

She had smashed her pelvis a bit that time and it hadn't quite healed properly. Grew looked at her as she walked away and thought her backside looked all right, looked well shaped, and seemed to do the right things. She did roll a bit, but then a lot of women do have a nice roll. It is an attraction.

Grew felt excitement, as from day to day she told him of her adventures. Was he sending her out to test his theories on how to dissuade a man, making no promises and always expecting to be greeted the next day by a tale of seduction, in full detail? He thought she was enjoying telling him as much as he was getting his kicks from hearing all about it.

Their lunch periods were becoming heavy discussion periods on morality, the fringes of sexual stimulation, and abstinence as they sat in the parking lot on the cement blocks, sharing her grapes or fruit. There was much laughter but much deep thought in those profound daily luncheons. It was an area of unseen danger. He could not even take a walk up the road without her tagging along, he was unaware what was happening, only conscious of this pleasant, deep perceptive girl making him, a thirty year old man feel real important. She pulled thoughts from him that were only part of his deepest self. As he thought back, the flow of sameness of thought in those sessions amazed him,

How could the thoughts of a thirty-year-old man mesh with the thoughts of an eighteen-year-old girl? An idea would pop forward from the depths, profound and unusual, only to find agreement or familiarity with the idea, then tossed around, perhaps a slightly different twist from the other participant would come forward. The sessions continued, sometimes almost quietly, hardly anything being said, intermingling thoughts, words unnecessary, little chuckles or loud laughter invariably arose from the scene.

The summer moved fast. All the workers at the animal hospital had a certain camaraderie. Each one had to find his or her own way of putting up with the dictatorial Dr. Gleason. They joked and mimicked Gleason throwing his left foot to the side as he strutted down the hallways, arms flung sideways. They practiced his antics when he wasn't there. The doctor called each male "Laddie Laddie", he screamed at his wife, confusing her even more as to what he wanted, he talked in charades, especially before the clients. His assistants were supposed to understand what he wanted. One of his eyes looked one way, the other the other way. All these things were turned into sources of amusement to those working for him, the staff who put up with his constant nattering. Yet even as they mimicked him and made fun of him they respected the genius of this man.

He was in a class of his own in the treatment of animals. His devotion to making them well prevailed. Grew recalled him blowing a mixture of diarrhea medicine up a dogs rear and the dog got better. Beneath his paranoiac behavior he was kind, loyal, devoted to his wife and the people who worked for him. No one questioned his ability as a veterinarian but he was almost impossible to work for. He knew that and the staff knew it. The mimickery, the joking had been their way to survive, they united as a group because of it. Together in spite of everything they developed this close feeling for each other, particularly Grew and Lisa.

Grew was acting depressed, sure that his wife knew. She would be very aware of his silence. It was not like him. For someone that he was not getting along with too well, he appreciated the way Marilyn supported him, acted like she understood, was willing to discuss any part of the matter he wanted to bring up. What he didn't realize was that she too had secrets she was bearing and not revealing--not knowing who the father of the expected baby was, a worse secret. There were some discussions but he never had really spoken of how he felt about this young girl but Marilyn knew. His wife had spoken like she was encouraging his involvement with Lisa. Was it to get her self off the hook? He wondered just where she was coming from.

Was she serious about him getting more involved with Lisa? Young girl and he really had developed a thing for each other and Marilyn knew it. In retrospect he realized why Marilyn related to the feelings shared by the two of them. Lisa had been obvious; words were not necessary between them.

Marilyn even suggested that Lisa would be more compatible with him than she was, but he couldn't see how there was any possibility for a relationship with Lisa, could only see himself in jail if her parents found out that it had gone as far as it had. What he did not know at the time was that Marilyn was also working on an agenda of her own, the revelation came later but oblivious to him it was happening but he was too wrapped up in his own affair. Their own differences had led Marilyn and him to discuss whether it might be better if they went in separate directions, yet she seemed to understand the deep feelings that this girl and her husband had for each other.

Lisa was always asking him if she could go home with him to see the animals. He was not sure that Marilyn would be prepared to welcome Lisa into their home. Wifey thought that he had too much to say about Lisa as it was even though he purposely toned down his reports on his friend. Grew said as little about Lisa as possible even though Marilyn kept pressing for information; kept asking, about how his extra work project was going. Grew was having a tough time at home--trying to downplay the situation--he had not forgotten Joanne, nor had his wife. Grew blamed himself with self-guilt for the home controversy but perhaps he was just being setup. He tried to keep his home problems away from Lisa, but was not aware himself, as to the extent of those problems, and tried to keep the conversation light. He talked to Lisa of his plans as to where he was going to show his dogs and she expressed a desire to go to a dog show with him; it was going to be tough to manage with his wife knowing how he felt about her. He told her he'd try to arrange it sometime.

It was painful to live during that time. Marilyn had been so supportive, yet in a way envious that their love could not reach that intensity. Her own affairs had been without the emotional caring, perhaps because she had not let go of her feelings for Grew. Wherever they wandered, they still had chains holding them together. In a way her support and understanding kept those chains padlocked with a mutual respect.

Marilyn and he did have some long talks as they drove for water or went swimming at Island Lake. Island Lake was about five miles from Chloe and through the summer Marilyn and he would often swim there. Late at night she would swim out into the lake, out of sight. He wouldn't have been able to rescue her. While he shivered in the cold water near shore, he would plead with her, loudly shouting, not to go so far, she would go anyway. It was part of what she was, a disdain for danger. Was it a death wish?

In a way that he hoped wouldn't happen, he was trying to tone down his relationship with Lisa. This girl was becoming just too close to him. Tony looked at it as a joke. Perhaps Grew was becoming too concerned about his own feelings. Tony asked him one day, "Are you really starting to fall for this kid"?

That question scared Grew because it was true. It was August and he had announced to Lisa that he was going to start spending lunch hours walking in the park-- had decided to go on his own. She asked if she could come with him, her sad eyes melted his resolve.

He smiled, "Doggone you shouldn't be going everywhere with me. This summer is going to end you know, your too old to be my daughter, too young for me to have an affair with. You know they put thirty year old men in jail for looking sideways at eighteen-year-old girls; don't want to deal with your parents asking me what my intentions are--don't have any intentions. I'm unhappily married and my wife is pregnant or I would leave her and I can't say that to your parents. You know, I think you are one super kid. You're warm, gentle, thoughtful, real good looking and you don't look like an eighteen year old. You're developed and guess I could say more but I wont. You can come if you want".

He could not quite remember how things happened on that day but they almost marked a turning point in their friendship; he remembered lying in the natural park with flowers all around. Lisa without being invited to do so was lying with her head in his lap. Could it be the other way with his head in her lap? She was disturbed at first at an open display of affection towards her.

Her apprehension at the position they were in bothered him; she spoke of her misgivings. Grew told her that he did not have any real feelings of loyalty to his wife, even though in some way she had got pregnant--telling of his wife's sexuality. At the same time, he knew he had grown very fond of Lisa and did not hesitate in letting her know. He had no intention of getting her involved in his mixed up marital affair, sad expression prevailed, laughter absent. There was no doubt, he had fallen for this girl.

She became very quiet after what he had said. Together they quietly, contentedly admired the flowers. They were amused by the antics of a squirrel as it dared to adventure close, in pursuit of the remnants of their lunch. His eye caught the beauty of Lisa's exposed leg. Nonchalantly he ran the fingernail of his middle finger along her shinbone, up to her knee. Casually testing, perhaps, to give her the idea that she was getting into dangerous territory. She did not protest at the move, He came back down with the open palm of his hand, stroking softly, "You have the most delicate skin, so soft", as he wrapped his palm around her calf.

"Don't, we're so close that we can't get into a touching thing. I can't take that", she quietly, slowly purred at him.

He knew what she meant, her presence set up electricity between them that he had not run into before. This was not the sex thing he had experienced with Judy. It was not a matter of an experiment with her body to see if he could seduce her. He didn't want to seduce this young thing. He knew what she was thinking; he felt the feelings traveling between them. Touching did not relieve the pressure, it was like two wires suddenly connecting to let the power flow.

He said as he raised himself up, reached out for her hand, "Common it's time for us to go".

As she placed her hand in his, the soft heat from it flowed to his hand and he pulled her to her feet. Her eyes, softly, intently, lovingly, looked him in the face, "Grew I'm sorry. I don't know what is happening to me, I'm all confused and don't know what I want or even expect".

Their smiles met and he said, "Remember when you were having the problem sorting out your feeling with the boys? I told you to give it time, be patient. Don't expect everything to sort itself out right now, things will work out. Maybe you shouldn't see so much of me. After all we both know that we have this real deep feeling for each other, but rightly or wrongly I am married and with my wife pregnant, don't know what I can do about it. Besides when you are thirty years old I am going to be forty-two and so on down the line, going to be seventy-two when you are sixty. Don't you think it would be better if we were just friends? Find yourself a boyfriend. I'll line them up for you".

"I don't want a boyfriend and I only care about what is right now, not what happens when someone is old? Either or both of us could be dead tomorrow or in ten years, besides, why is your wife pregnant if the two of you are not doing it?"

They walked back to the car in quiet solitude, each a little sad and although not speaking it, both of them were put out that they should be thrown so close together, feel so deeply for each other and yet not be able to do anything. It had gone too deep.

They worked for the rest of that day without speaking to each other. They did their work in different areas so that they would not be confronted with each other. There was no animosity between them but a frustration, that they allowed themselves to be drawn into this impossibly deep relationship that could go nowhere. Grew wondered as he wrote, so long after, whether Tony and Dr. Gleason were aware of the connection between the two?

Things cooled off between them for a while. They both consciously tried to avoid running into each other. Their free moments were directed in ways where they would not meet. Summer was running out and Grew's own feelings were caught in the realization that Lisa would soon be going back to school and he would not see her again. He looked back, realizing he was really in love with this girl. Was she the true love that he had always looked for?

Labour day, Grew had to work. The staff had taken turns working the holidays and it was his turn. His wife had gone to a dog show. At that time the exhibition dog shows were benched, the exhibitors had to stay all day. Grew had to drive the twenty five miles home to look after the dogs that were left at the kennel, then go back to pick Marilyn up at the show. Normally only one attendant would work the animal hospital for the holidays but since there were so many dogs in for boarding, the doctor had decided to bring Lisa in to help. It was to be the two workers last day together--they thought.

After work, everything was all locked up and they stood in the parking lot, the same lot where they had traded lunch food and poetry. They talked softly to each other, expressing sorrow at breaking it all up. She had her own little Nash Metropolitan with her. After awhile he said to her in a questioning way, "Follow me?"

"Okay", that is all she said. He walked to his car; she walked to hers. He looked in the mirror as he drove off. She was following.

He hadn't the slightest idea where he was going. He drove down by a ravine to the edge of a golf course. They found a trail that bordered the course, threaded through the woods. She took his hand and they quietly followed the trail, neither one saying other than casual words; they were both walking with some kind of expectation. They stepped off the trail to a secluded mound that overlooked the valley. He pulled her soft warm hand to one side and faced her, gazed seriously, endlessly into her eyes, warm attraction between them, unexplainable, undeniable, and inevitable-- they both knew.

They just moved together. His lips softly pressed against hers. It was the first time they had kissed, meant to be a goodbye kiss but wasn't. Her mouth slowly slipped open, his tongue just drifted slowly around in her mouth, teased with her teeth, up behind her upper teeth, just floating around, wet in the warmth of her, exploring inner mouth. Their passion was slowly growing. His thoughts were that he must stop but she was making no effort to stop, not saying a thing, mewing, like a contented cat. He was terribly aware of the softness, the warmth of the body pressed against him, his hardness pushing into it.

While they stood there, he thought of the time she had told him of the boy who had driven her to hysterics. Was that what prompted

Grew? Probably not, he was into the love thing himself, not in control. He moved his hand to the front of her dress, undoing buttons, one at a time. Waiting, thinking it would start her defense mechanism, she would stop him. She didn't. His hand slipped between the folds of her dress... beneath the brassier.

He had her bare breast in his hand, pliant, smooth, and warm. The nipple was hardening in his palm, something about virgin breast taunted him. The situation was driving him totally out of control as he laid her down on the leaves. Slowly she had sunk down--went without a murmur of resistance; the passion between them was so gentle, in a way one sided but her response and total compliance was encouraging him on. Her gingham dress had slipped up her thighs.

He looked at the part of her legs he had not seen before, the valley between them, oh so stunning to him. As he gently moved his other hand on and around her legs, hand stroking them, Grew was terribly aware of the softness of those thighs...up them, between them, but still she was not pulling back. She spread her legs, spread wide, as his hand moved to the white crotch of her panties, rubbed there for a while...then up the silk covered belly to the waistband and under the waistband. His hand was stroking in soft pubic hair and she was showing absolutely no signs of resistance, her body was slowly moving with his hands. Nor did she object when he sunk a finger into the warm moist entrance. She was getting wet there as he slid his now wet fingers around in her.

She had no intention of making me stop; I know it now. He was starting to get real scared. Now he knew she was not interested in just a kiss goodbye either, but much more. It had gone too far, she was doing nothing to stop him or control herself. Grew was being seduced by his own desires into an abyss of unquestionable grief. It was going to be up to him and she was driving him on with an unmitigated passion, wild and abandoned. Grew had to stop. He did not even have a contraceptive with him, he knew she was a virgin, so she was not going to have anything. But maybe he was sterile, but if so he didn't know it then. He had to stop! He mustered every ounce of resistance and pushed away.

"Lisa we have to stop, if we don't in a minute I'll be doing it to you, I have no protection...come on we have to STOP!

"I don't care, just screw me. Please, do it to me. I want you. I don't care what happens".

"Oh yes you do, You'll care tomorrow and you'll worry until you know you are alright, and if you aren't you'll worry some more. And so will I. I can't go on. I just can't go on. Even though I wish we could, you know I want to".

His hands were out of her clothing by then. she came into his arms again and again they kissed as he pulled her up to her feet. He broke away, started leading her back to the cars. At the cars he had more trouble trying to get her into her own car.

Grew said to her, "If you get into my car you get into the back seat. If you do that you get screwed, now get into your own car, we have to go". He had two forces pulling in opposite directions.

"Okay, let's get into the back seat of your car, come on you promised". She had her hand on the door handle and was trying to open the door.

It was like she was drunk on the ecstasy of it and obsessed with getting herself devirginated before she left him. By this time he had to push her away but was at least in control of himself; had found that extra something to back off before it was too late, really very scared at the time, especially considering the way she had become. Never had he seen such determined passion. Later he would always wonder what would have happened if he hadn't stopped. As he thought back he wished that he hadn't. After more attempts back and forth, either in the car or out, he had gotten her to get into her own car, sighing in relief as he watched her drive off and as he walked towards his own car.

He had thought that it was the end for the two of them; he could readjust to living without her. Perhaps he could put his life back together with his wife, even though he was not aware at the time of the full state of that relationship. Could he save his marriage? He felt that after awhile Lissette's passion would subside, to him she would become a lasting memory in the back of his mind, something always to wonder about.

The day after Labour Day the school kids go back. It is a short day. Things were just like when Grew had been in school. At 11.45 a.m. there was a phone call. "What time are you going for lunch?"

It was Lissette phoning from school, "I will be going from 12.00 to 1.00. Why?" Grew responded, surprised to hear from her.

"I'm finished for the day; can I meet you in the restaurant?"

He was happy to hear from her even though he realized that he should have said "No". He had been sad all morning, stoically telling himself that he would get over her.

"Okay, I'll see you there," and he brightened for the last ten minutes of the morning.

They had lunch while she ran over everything she did and what her new classes were going to be. Then she spoke of "us" and how she just could not bare it without him. She made his heart flutter when she told him of the leaves that had stuck to her clothing, fallen almost at her parents feet. Whatever story she used as to why she was late, they bought. (What else could they do? They were just going to have to wait to see what happened).

It did not go unnoticed by Grew that she seemed to be enjoying the adventure on the edge. It was like she almost wanted to be caught in this thing. It was shaping up into a battle of wits, her and Grew against her parents and society (was it revenge on her part?). He had his doubts about where it would go--had been getting ready to settle back into his dull life, but she was extending the adventure. It was a game they could not win.

She had decided that she was going to meet him after five when he was off work. Her parents came home at six but Grew also was expected home about six thirty, so whatever they did was going to involve close timing. They met at their wooded rendezvous, they necked for just a short time then they planned communication. The plan called for him to start eating his lunch in the Laundromat next door to the animal hospital, supposedly doing his laundry. That day they never took the intimacy close to getting into total sex, there was too little time. So a short loving session was all for then.

The next day at lunch they put their plan into effect; it worked without a hitch. As they talked on the phone they planned another get together. The procedure continued day after day, each of them keeping the other up to date as to each other's availability. She talked of Dr. Gleeson, Tony, her classmates, or anything else happening on her school day.

He had driven home that evening contented that at least he could still get a bit of Lisa without danger of further involvement. Still he couldn't rationalize sensibly anywhere the affair could go. Maybe she'd soon tire of the phone calls. As Grew recalled, he could not remember ever doing any laundry at the Laundromat. She would phone at 12.05, if he got held up she would try again at 12.10. Sometimes they would then meet, in a plaza for a few minutes, for an hour after work, if it could be squeezed in, or after work when he did the Sunday turn at work. Time was precious but sometimes it would be stretched a bit too much and questions would be asked.

In some back wooded area he could be driving this young debutant to the brink of submission while she was literally begging to be "Fucked", usually in the back of his Volkswagen. When he thought about it years later, he was never sure how he had resisted. The obsession seemed almost to be rather in beating those that would break them up rather than in actually getting sexually involved themselves. Grew was emotionally in love with Lisa. The adventure had captured them both together, into a capsule, insulated against the world. Every day at noon she would phone the Laundromat. They talked while they ate. What could they possibly find to talk about, who knows? But it went on and on, into the following March-- From September to March--. Was it indicative of something, a March-- September relationship?

Grew by this time had moved his employment again, over to another vet. This was a doctor who he had worked with when he had been with the first vet he worked for. Dr. Relaishe, from Europe, of French ancestry. The doctor had purchased an ongoing practice that included living quarters on the third floor. It was an old house where kennels had been built in the basement. The treatment and admission areas were on the main floor.

When Grew had worked with this vet before they had lost a couple of animals while giving anesthetic. One was a cat in for castration. Grew would administer the ether for the operations. When feeling the animal relax he would remove the ether muzzle that fitted over the nose. That time when he wanted to remove it, Dr. Relaishe told him to keep it on. Grew thought he was just expressing his authority; after all he was the vet. He did as he was told and the cat went to sleep--permanently. The doctor then blamed Grew for not removing the ether in time. So it was with some hesitation that Grew took the job. In spite of this Grew knew he was a good vet. Under their agreement Grew seldom had to work in surgery with Dr. Relaishe; he liked to work with the girls, leaving the grooming to Grew. Grew's grooming prowess was once again basically the reason he was hired.

It was an interesting place. Past differences and association were put aside as they agreed on the terms of employment. Grew was given the time off to be with his wife when his son was born--a thrilling experience--exceeding the wonder of newborn puppies. They called the boy Charles after Grew's father. Fortunately he was a healthy child that adjusted to the roughing life. Charles and Grew instantly became friends as dad shared baby chores and play.

Grew was able to keep Lisa contained on the brink by having a sexually demanding wife at home, requiring his services to the extent of his capacity. It might have been part of the reason that he was able to resist copulation with Lisa. He did not want to stop. The alternative was at least the end of his marriage.

After persistent requests he arranged for Lisa to come to the kennel to see the dogs. It was the first time his wife had met Lisa; after a short time to say hello to Lisa, realizing something was up, Marilyn left for the day. Later she had said, "She looks at you all the time, be flattered. You obviously eat it up".

It was not what he wanted. When Marilyn was gone, he could see he was going to have problems keeping Lisa out of bed while they were there alone. He also did not trust his wife not to return at any time, he would expect it of her. While Lisa was in the house alone he went outside behind one of the sheds and masturbated. When he returned to Lisa in the house, although they rolled, played, fondled and necked on the bed she was unable to seduce him. She must have wondered why.

Lisa did go with him to a few dog shows in the country; the dog people loved her. This one time his wife had decided to stay home. It was like she was encouraging him to get into something that would allow her to get out of the marriage, or was she just content to have affairs? She too did not seem happy with the things she had gotten herself into. It was like a perpetual quest for satisfaction. Probably at that very time she was having an affair with another man that Grew was not aware of.

The men at the show wondered, just how this guy could get away with such a bold transgression of the rules. And he was soon labeled forever--a womanizer. He wondered himself, how it happened, but then he was enjoying his luck, not even thinking about what might be going on at home. This man was getting all the rope necessary to hang himself. On the way home they would stop to neck, aware that Lisa was now becoming more aggressive, handling his erection like she had a right, with courage and increasing boldness. It was getting even more difficult to stop.

It was difficult to find a satisfactory place to park. There were not great expanses of parkland at that time with parking lots. Those that were around were not private in the daytime. A spot with an isolated trail off the road was what he was looking for. As it was, he kept parking on the side of concession roads but kept getting interrupted before they could have sex. Grew thought back about his state of mind. He had been ready to go all the way and hang the consequences, which could very well have been his head in the noose.

Somebody had the bright idea for Lisa to keep one of their poodles at her home. This too could have come from Marilyn, as she steered the situation to her own advantage. It led to Lisa and Grew spending Sunday evenings together at the dog training class. This was the same dog training class that was run by The German Shepherd Club where he had first met his wife. Again though, it was like Marilyn was opening the door for him to find something else in life; she knew what was happening. Down the road she eventually told him of her own adventures.

While his wife stayed home, supposedly looking after their new born son but maybe more, one evening a cop stopped them as they sat in the window fogged Volkswagen. Lisa and him were in a park exercising the dogs after training, instead of at the after training coffee session. As they were about to leave the park the cop wanted to know what they were doing there. The guilt that they both shared made them scared but there was really nothing the policeman could do about them. They both calmly spoke to the officer about the dogs and the training, then looking at them strangely he left, continuing his patrol.

Five minutes earlier he might have caught a thirty year old in the back seat of that car, nearly screwing a panty less eighteen-year-old young lady. The cop probably did not believe them but what could he say at the time. Lisa spoke to him, not acting like she was being kidnapped. She had a cool air about her. Fortunately he did not ask who she was, it might have mattered if somehow the incident had found its way to her policeman boyfriend.

Sometime earlier than that experience, when Lisa had been coming to meet him after work at the animal hospital on a Sunday, she had an accident. Someone had opened a parked car door on the street side as she was approaching. Lisa's car hit the door. The cop that investigated, a nice young fellow named Harry, started pursuing Lisa in a most aggressive way. Her and Grew thought that it would provide a good cover for their own meetings. Harry was acceptable to her parents where Grew certainly would not have been. From the beginning she made it clear to Harry that Sunday evening was one time that she was not available as that was the evening when she trained her dog, - no spectators.

From time to time Harry objected strenuously to this arrangement but accepted her wishes. This was why Lisa and Grew were apprehensive about the police. They were never quite sure whether he would arrange for other police to watch out or follow them.

The intrigue of putting it over on her parents and then the policeman became part of the attraction that kept it going. Their love affair continued even in spite of the complications that arose because of her new romance, even though the cop was starting to reap the benefits of Grew's warm up exercises. This depraved virgin told Grew that she had not been to bed with the policeman at that time but the other romance had been seriously cutting into the time that she could now spend with Grew and he was feeling it; yet still he was not prepared to let go.

Grew then started rationalizing that if the cop was to have her it would not be before he had her first. He was psyching himself up to justify the seduction that he had so long been fighting against. One evening on the back roads behind her house, a high-class residential district, he was pursuing the usual course of foreplay. he had her pants right off, anything less would totally hinder his chance of entering her.

Alternating between his hands and mouth he had worked her vagina into an open, throbbing, hot, wet, receptacle, nestled between flailing legs. His erection that had learned to take all sorts of attention and abuse, was being nibbled, jerked and sucked into a formidable weapon. This was it. Grew swung around, his hands were on her young buttocks, pressing her hole towards his penis, approaching steadily, and it touched, entered gently into the slippery entrance.

She wiggled, her head rolled as she moaned softly. Her wiggling was making it difficult to find the spot. "Do it. Do it, please. Put it in, don't stop now, not this time, please! please!"

He wanted to make it easy on her, he nursed it, just the knob moving gently in the entrance, then. "God Damn it. God Damn it, I'm going to come".

He felt the pulsing, the warning, The unstoppable ejaculation on the way. He couldn't put it in her now. His eyes closed as he tensed, he went into a convulsive like tightening process and it came. It moved down and out--squirting as it came-- over her belly, in her pubic hair, on her thighs, but not in her. Then working at her he tried to bring her to an orgasm but she was disappointed, she had her mindset that this was going to be it.

After that the pressure of the situation became unbearable. The cop had legitimacy on his side, now biting into Grew's only available time. Grew finally conceded defeat when Lisa appeared to be bending to the path of least resistance. Avoiding her, he had talked to her parents but they told him that whatever she did was none of his business.

Her father said, "It is none of your business to worry about her. Its nothing to do with you". Grew was put in that most unenviable position and he knew it. It was over.

"You're right, it is none of my business, and I thought you might be able to use the information to help her, Goodbye".

Grew never saw the father again, but had spoken briefly to the mother when he met her on the street one day sometime later.

One day Lisa called him. He told her he thought that she probably was getting over involved the other way. They had a brief meeting that brought back the old fire, but he knew that they couldn't continue seeing each other even though he felt she was not right for the cop. Even then the cop was mocking her feelings, her sensitivity, preaching at her, materialism, hard cold prosperity and security as aims in life. It was a philosophy always contrary to Grew's beliefs and of course he was adamant about it.

At that meeting he had been cool to her, told her to go and marry the guy but if she was only doing it so she would get out from her parents control, it was a weak excuse. Grew didn't want her to bother with him, in a way he blamed her for his own marital stress but that was probably unfair; he had had enough. She described her parent's home as tantamount to a prison He wondered about her future home but had stopped telling her what to do. She seemed quite depressed when they said goodbye. There certainly had been no feeling of pleasure in him either as he quietly drove home, in a sense relieved but also feeling that he had missed out on something special. The dog man was bitter about losing her to such a jerk and before getting in his car, he'd told her not to come crying the blues to him and in all fairness to this guy, she should tell him what had been going on between them for the six months previous.

She let Grew know when she jumped from her parents prison and married the cop. It was sometime after March seventeen which was her nineteenth birthday. Through some source that Grew could not remember he heard that she had lost a child before it was born. Grew knew that it was not his. Maybe it had something to do with her getting married. Recalling their love often, he knew he would never forget her and as it turned out she too had not forgotten when years later she had suddenly knocked on his door and had once again implanted herself into his life. There is a lot that had gone on in those years between and as Grew sat in front of his computer and briefly contemplated, he wondered, just a bit, about the plan he was unknowingly following, the corollary consequences of each step taken, often without regard for the bodies falling by the wayside.

His son had now become his raison d'etre, bringing up the heir. There was a glitch in the story while they readjusted. Perhaps as his affair with Lisa subsided and he spent more time at home with his wife and son it created a closer association with Marilyn and Grew. Unknown to him at the time, this aspect had a negative side. It was no longer so easy for Marilyn to come and go as she pleased, meet her lovers and pursue her own sexual yet unsatisfying hobby. The Sunday evening, times which she had had to herself, other relationships to explore were no longer available. Marilyn was being asked to bring the baby along, go with him to dog training, she often did; there was no way to get out of it.

People loved the baby that in some ways made Marilyn the center of attention. It was nice for her, the dog people had always regarded her as a backup person to Grew. He had always been considered the expert, but without even her realizing it, her and the baby were now the center of attention.

CHAPTER 7

More Dog People and Affairs

It was around the time that Paul Adams showed up. Grew liked him so Marilyn agreed to put one of their brood bitches with him and his wife Mona. Paul was quite heavy and jovial he carried his weight well, he played the guitar and sang but did not know all the words of the songs he sang, "Ruby" was a favorite. Paul and Grew found a togetherness of thought on dogs. He was very interested in working dogs. He bought a puppy but it turned out to be a monorchid so he got a male from the same mother's next litter. This one was called Arno. These people kept weaving their lives together.

Marilyn's other friends had been asking about her too. Many other friends who had previously dropped in on Sunday night when Grew was at training were now finding there time squeezed. When spring started to look like it was there for real, Marilyn started going out alone after Grew got home from work. He hadn't objected, he had believed she had been there alone with the baby through the day. Feeling for her, he had thought she needed some time out. It was still light in the evening so Grew would take the dogs out for a walk out in the fields on his own, taking the baby with him, riding on his shoulders.

Other times the three of them would go out for a drive, sometimes to visit two gay friends, one of which, Alex, Grew had worked with for two years at the first animal hospital. These two gays now were living about two miles from the Tuckett home. So when Marilyn and Grew visited them they would take the water jugs to fill up. Sometimes Marilyn and Grew would get into their discussion about loyalty and relationships. It was on one of these occasions of conscience that Marilyn, couldn't hold it back, while they were quietly discussing his past with Lisa, it must have been too much. All of a sudden she told the story of her extramarital affairs.

Grew was totally shocked--devastated--it now became apparent, the significance of what had happened. This is what he had given up Lisa for. As they had sat in the car, him quietly listening, Marilyn agreed with him that he should have left her regardless of her pregnancy, taken whatever flack was to come by going the full way with Lisa. Grew often wondered why he hadn't. It was a period of honesty where partly for revenge Grew told her of just how far he had gone with Lisa. She in turn opened the book on Clarence, George and the fact that George could very well be Charles's father.

She told him of having sex with his friend Alex at a dog show where she stayed; he'd kicked in her door and took her without consent. She didn't even complain but knew she could have charged him with rape and of course there was Hans, more on him later.

Marilyn described the sexuality of each one of them, the too quick to come ones, with a low rating, especially the low rating of Alex, the great lovemaking of Clarence and the love without feeling, only for his own gratification of Brinks. Through it all though she expressed envy at the relationship that Grew had had with Lisa, she understood. That had been what she wanted, what she had been searching for. Grew also understood, but knew that there was nothing he could do. If he had known earlier he might have, probably would have, made the jump.

As Grew thought of the revelations, with a mixture of anger at her, his own "friends" involvements, guilt on himself for allowing their own relationship to drift in such a direction, he wondered if there was any hope for the marriage. He had a love for her but at that time could not quite figure out how and in what way. There was this holier than thow feeling within him, making him sorry for himself; he'd been wronged, cuckolded; this woman was unworthy of him.

At the same time, he knew that it wasn't true; she was a very special person. Was he worthy of her? What of his own infidelity? Knowing of his own blame, he couldn't scream at being done--been cheated on.

Together they rode in silence for a while. The picture in his mind was of the wife besides him being screwed by all these various lovers, vainly wondering how he fit in with the bunch--how he rated--but afraid to ask. The thoughts of it all made him horny and when they got home they went to bed. However sex was before, it had become great as he employed the maneuvers of her best lovers, making it last, sucking and licking at the special places on and in her body.

It was special--sharing a mutual love fest that was long and spectacular, ending with a wild and tumultuous flailing of bodies charging for the climax, like a combined testament of forgiveness unleashed. For a while after that he never bothered as Marilyn would go out in the evenings. They had agreed not that she would be faithful but that from that point on she would tell him right after, if she did get involved with someone.

Since they had survived to that point Grew felt that their marriage would survive with a mutual need but testing it he did not need. He agreed to do the same but had no intention to go this route again. Often she would say that she had just gone over to see the "boys" and he believed that she had. Certainly conversations with the fellows later indicated that she was there on occasion.

One evening he was out walking with the dogs after Marilyn had gone out. He decided to go through the fence and out to a road that was seldom used that cut across the vacant property behind theirs. It was there that he suddenly came on two cars. One of the parked cars was his. He could tell there were people in the other car. After returning the dogs to the kennel he came back without them. It was getting dark. Cautiously he approached the larger of the two vehicles. He could hear the impassioned sounds of love within. The grunts and moans sounded like they were having sex.

What could he do? Break in the car right there? Hit the car? Put a rock through the window? He decided to rush back home and confront her as she arrived. Shortly after he got home he watched his own car drive up the hill to the house.

When she came in the house he asked where she had been. As expected she lied. Loudly he confronted her with what he had just seen and heard. She cringed fearfully as he dragged her down on the kitchen floor, her screaming, "No, Grew, don't do this, not like this please stop it"

Her jeans and pants were torn from her as he lifted up her legs, dragged her shoes off and pulled everything off almost in one motion. Then he started smacking her on the ass, all the time she continued to scream and cry for him to stop.

He continued to yell at her, "Liar, Liar," but was getting turned on and could see that she was too. *For God sake she liked it,* she was getting turned on and so was he. The message got through; it was sexual.

Her legs were forcefully spread apart as he dropped between them. Pulling out his prick, which was now like a rock, suddenly he was in her kissing her and she was responding with kisses of her own. There on the kitchen floor they had wild passionate sex. She was sweating as was he and felt the rush as they both came. When they had finished they lay there in each other's arms slowly kissing, him forgiving her and her forgiving and loving him.

What a scene--Charles lay in bed--oblivious of the wild display by his parents. Even with the situation as it was, neither of them ever considered Charles to be less a son nor did either of them disagree on his upbringing. He was brought up like they did with the dogs, both of them of a total like mind how that was to be done.

It was not long after this incident that the news came out that the Brinks had separated. Maureen moved into an apartment in Ajax. George seemed to disappear somewhere but Maureen continued to befriend both Marilyn and Grew. Marilyn might have had some feelings of her own involvement causing the breakup. Although it was never talked about, it was not hard to figure out that Maureen knew of the thing with George and Marilyn. Maureen was also aware that her ex-husband or whatever he was could have been the father of Charles. The baby had a lot of the same characteristics as Maureen and George's younger son.

Maureen was now filling Marilyn and Grew in on George's past record of abuse. She was now faced with the task of trying to put her life back together, supported by one job. The kids stayed with George.

One Saturday night, the Tuckett's invited Maureen to go out to the Muscleman Lake dance with them since she was now virtually single. Grew danced with Maureen a few times but did not want to give the impression that he was interested in her. Marilyn danced with a few people herself, including Clarence Corbett and Grew also danced with his wife, Helen. Helen was a good-looking woman who danced well but he found it difficult to get into a conversation with her. It was almost that they both were aware of the thing going on between their respective mates. She didn't appear to want any kind of inter family fun.

Maureen became more than a bit drunk and through the evening attracted a suitor who from then on monopolized her dances. Marilyn and Grew decided to head for home after checking with Maureen who informed them that she was going to get home by way of the man that she was with. She had originally planned to stay the night with them. Grew thought she had drunk too much but it was not up to him.

Early the next morning, he was out with the dogs and noticed a car parked in the gravel pit across the road. He wondered, and drove the Volkswagen over to investigate. There in the front seat was Maureen, asleep. In the back seat was the guy that she had picked up at the dance. Grew woke them both up and told the guy to take off; he did.

He got Maureen in the Volkswagen, then drove her back to her new apartment in Ajax. She was very down and depressed. It would appear that she had picked this guy up at the dance, brought him back to the kennel where she was to stay but then had sex with him while parked in the gravel pit. Both had then fallen asleep where Grew had found them.

When getting to her apartment she wanted to have a bath which Grew ran the water for. She got in the tub with him right there trying to talk her out of her depression. While he talked to her he picked up the soap and gently moved it over her wet body. The soap was smooth on her skin, the water warm; he could not help but to be aroused. The small breasts with rather prominent nipples took him back to others of a like structure as he soaped around the smooth skin of them.

He had been getting turned on himself kneeling beside the tub and he kissed her. She spread her legs as she sat there letting him move the soap down her flat belly into her pubic hair. There was a long scar over her belly that they talked about for awhile as he then moved his hand between her legs, on the smooth lean inner thighs and then into her vaginal area. Her breathing increased noticeably as her mouth came open. She almost purred as he soaped her most private pussy.

The next kiss was longer and on an open and responsive mouth. He was ready to start divesting his own clothes, get in the tub and her when the phone rang. Grew had invariably been interrupted by telephones and doorbells. When he asked her about the phone, she nodded and he answered it. It was Marilyn, he then moved to the other room to talk to for a while, telling her what had happened at the house.

"Maureen is having a bath", he said and "is quite depressed", but did not tell her that he was ready to get in the tub with her.

In her supportive way, Marilyn told him to stay there with her for a while until he felt that she was going to be all right. He said that he would be home as soon as he could. It was never known how Maureen reacted to the phone call. Maybe she thought she was now causing more trouble in her friend's marriage. She did not know the full extent of Marilyn's infidelity.

When he returned to Maureen, she showed him an empty dispensing bottle. He asked her about the bottle, "What is it about; what was in the bottle Maureen and what have you done with whatever it was?"

She sadly informed him that it had been nearly full of sleeping pills that she had been dispensed with when she first got into the separation with George. She then informed him that she had just taken every pill left. "Maureen, how many were in there?" He didn't know whether to take her seriously at first but soon felt that he had better because of the way she was starting to look sleepy.

He went to the apartment next door and talked to the woman who lived there, had never met her before but told her what had happened; he asked if she could help getting Maureen dressed. She did very well but by the time she did Maureen was pretty well asleep. While she was getting her dressed Grew phoned the local hospital, telling them that he was on the way with a woman who had overdosed on pills. By then she was dressed and he picked her up in his arms, the pill bottle in his pocket, and while people were exiting there apartments on their way to church on a Sunday morning, he was seen stuffing this woman into the side seat of the Volkswagen.

The hospital had not been far; he was there in a few minutes. They pumped her out. When George arrived he instantly blamed Grew for causing the problem but when he got the facts he apologized for getting the wrong idea. Grew visited her at the hospital a couple of times, then they sent her to the psychiatric hospital. Grew also visited Maureen there once, in a common ward with a number of people in all sorts of various obvious mental disorders. Maureen sat quietly in the middle of this further depressing room. People sat in a state of what looked like semi sleep. Others walked in an ape like sort of movement with heads bent forward, mouths open. Some blubbered undetectable words as they looked at him, the newcomer, probably wondering why he was there.

The hospital gave her electric shock treatment that made her forget everything. Then they released her in George's care. Six months later the two of them were separated again, this time for good. Years later Grew found her married to a fireman and breeding Shetland Sheepdogs. She seemed very happy and content with her new environment.

There was a young divorced woman with a son that worked at the animal hospital. Sandra was about five foot two, very attractive, medium weight, a noticeable breast development, her smile enhanced a pleasant face. Her mother looked after the baby. She had bred collies, which caused a lot of discussion between her and Grew as to the relative merits of what she was breeding and dogs in general. He felt that her ideas were rather basic-- the same as he would have thought, about the ideas of most collie breeders. It was a pleasant atmosphere as the two of them casually discussed the merits of dogs in the animal hospital. It was his impression that the over concentration on heads rather than the structure of the whole dog was leading the Collie breed in the wrong direction. Sandra had a lot of respect for Grew but she had gotten involved with a charming handyman at the hospital who had been hired to do some work around the clinic. The work went on and on. Everyone seemed to know that there was something going on between Sandra and Sven, often in a secluded corner of the basement.

Sandra gave the impression that she was in the process of trying to figure out just where and what she was going to do in her life. Yet with her life in some turbulence she was still able to get some dogs entered in dog shows. Grew was impressed with this young lady; he gave her a lot of credit for her initiative, sorry she had connected with wrong men. It was in a time when the Sportsmen Show was in full swing, a benched show requiring dogs to stay all day. Marilyn and Grew had some dogs entered, as did Sandra.

He was standing by ringside talking to Sandra as they both watched some dogs being judged. After awhile he said to her, "I have to go home and look after the dogs, do you want to come with me? I'll be gone for about an hour and a half. I'll be going alone, if you do come I'm not telling Marilyn, she wouldn't trust me alone with you."

For awhile she didn't answer as if preoccupied with the dogs in the ring, then said, "I have to let my dog out in the exercise pen which will take about fifteen minutes, then I can go. Can I trust you?" She smiled sideways at him as her eyes lit up.

He thought for a minute before replying, "Trust me for what? My wife is probably afraid that I will get you out there and have sex with you. I don't know, guess it depends on you and me, but you can trust me, think you know I wont rape you."

In the next fifteen minutes they met out by the car. He had told Marilyn he was going home to look after the dogs but did not tell her he was taking Sandra. When they got out of the city he realized just how bad the blowing snow had become. It was driving across the highway, he was beginning to wonder about the wisdom of even going home; might have been better just to let the dogs wait until they all came home but that would ruin his plan with Sandra.

They did manage to get to the house without much trouble. She took a quick look around the small interior while he was feeding the dogs. She put the coffee on for them. When he finished with the dogs she poured them both coffee. They sat on the couch side by side and talked briefly about the German Shepherds that he had there, he brought a few dogs in the house for a while to show her and then locked them all up in their separate pens. They were all ready to go back.

Her coat was there beside her on the couch. She was about to reach for it when Grew picked it up. She stood up thinking he was going to hold it for her, but he placed the coat on a chair in the kitchen, returned to her while she was still standing, came right up behind her and put his arms around her, then turned her around to face him.

Lips came down on hers as he held her firmly, their lips moving against each other's, they continued to kiss, neither backing off. He pushed gently on her shoulders, bringing her down to a sitting position on the couch, while he kneeled on the floor facing in front of her. She had to lean forward to maintain contact. They continued to kiss passionately as he then eased her into a prone position on the couch, still kneeling beside her. She allowed herself to be positioned. He slid up onto the couch laying beside her, against her, feeling every curve of her body against him, his erection pushing at her. A hand moved to her sweater, up inside the front of it, onto her nice medium full breasts. It was only minutes until the bra was off. He was massaging the well-shaped and bouncy glorious things.

Getting no resistance at all he continued, she was undulating with him as he worked hands and mouth over her, their bodies moving at each other in a mock gentle sex thing with clothes on, right hand worked up the nylon covered legs of her, shapely things; he reached the bare flesh above the stockings, she wore a garter belt with bare flesh beyond the top of the nylons, a real turn on. He felt the straps of the garter belt as his hand caressed the smooth flesh.

They were both enjoying the lovemaking. It was not a life commitment but they were both obviously on the same track. She wiggled to allow him to pull her skirt up to her underpants, right up beyond where he had been feeling the bare expanse of flesh. Now it was all in view, panties peeking out from her garter belt. Hesitating, as she looked up into his face proud of what she was he moved quickly to pull the panties down, her legs moving and bum rising to accommodate the removal.

His own pants were down in a second aware of his stiff protrusion, aware that she was now looking at what was going to be inside her. Her legs willingly spread, rising around him as he came down, softly. His hands were only in her for a short time, she was wet, willing, pulling to get the thing in her, making it quite clear what she wanted.

When it impaled her she rolled and bucked from side to side as she pushed back at the thing pushing in her, filling her vagina with flesh; her slightly rounded belly slapped up at him. Hands grabbed her ass, squeezed, pushed her onto him, then he relaxed pulling back, then driving in her again. Far too soon he came but such wild activity made it happen. She too had been enjoying it; she had enjoyed hard sex, getting what she wanted, as was he. She had been a treasure appreciated.

He had felt guilty as they dressed hoping that Marilyn had not noticed that Sandra had gone too. When they got out on the highway again the weather had turned worse. The snow was drifting even as they reached the main highway. He'd kept imagining how he was going to explain things if they went off the road. Then it happened, they hit an icy spot, Sandra gave a slight expression just less than a scream as they did a complete three sixty whirl off the road. He got out, took a look and got back in the car.

Slowly he tried to back it out. The amazing Volkswagen responded. Again they were on their way. When they returned to the show Marilyn said she knew that he had taken Sandra with him, "I hope you had fun." He never gave an answer but admitted she had gone with him.

At the animal hospital Dr. Relaishe had hired another nice young lady that reminded Grew a bit of Lisa-- a bit older, twenty-one at the time, on guard against men as her mother had kicked the husband and father out years before. Beverly was an effervescent sort, friendly with everyone, and a natural victim for either Dr. Relaishe or him. The impression was athletic. The general shape of her looked good with ample hips, and well shaped buttocks, about five foot seven, a little heavier than average, a bit wider in the chest area separating full breasts, legs straight. Grew soon found out that she was the doctors girl, he used her for reception and helping with treatments. She did relate to Grew though, expressing quite an interest in his dogs.

She wanted to see the dogs so he invited her to come out to the kennel he'd talked to Marilyn about it and of course she was suspicious about him getting involved with another young girl. (Who could blame her)? Marilyn agreed but said that she would not be there. She had met Beverly and could see the other side of what could happen. Grew and Beverly, drove to his home in her car as his wife had theirs; he got her to bring her bathing suit so they could go for a swim at Island Lake. He was looking forward to seeing more of this girl.

They arrived at the kennel and he let the dogs out. She loved them all, running with the pack as they ran back into the fields, through the woods to the fields beyond. Grew felt warm having her with him. When they came back to the house he suggested that she could get changed in the bedroom. There was a rattan blind that dropped down from the bedroom door that he had checked before. The way the light came in the bedroom window one could see through the blind from the living room but could not see through the other way. Beverly went to go in to change as he sat on the couch in the living room waiting for the show, not knowing what he would do when he saw her naked on the other side of the blind, wasn't sure he could handle just watching, could picture himself going in there, throwing her on the bed and doing his thing but he could not lower himself, the moral degradation--even to watch.

Just as she was about to start innocently taking her things off he called to her, "Beverly, wait a minute, something I want to show you. You can't get changed there I can see right through this blind. It would be very nice for me to watch you change but really, just can't do this to you." Why didn't he just plain and simply go to the other room, the kitchen or outside?

Her reaction surprised him, had she known that he would have been able to see? As he thought about it some time later he realized that if she had looked through from the living room she would have known that he could have been watching. Perhaps she knew that he would have been able to see her. Maybe she was expecting him to at least go through with the show. Anger he had not seen from her before welled up in her. She got annoyed at the whole scene, acted like she had been taken advantage of when in fact she had been saved from whatever might have happened. She wanted to go home right then. They did ride out to a place to get something to eat but if there was a spell it was broken. He wondered later what might have happened but he was unable to take advantage just as he was unable to take advantage of Judy with the scissors finding there was a point in taking advantage he could not go beyond.

Down stairs at the animal hospital he had his own assistant who did not like the doctor at all. Sandra had left. One day she had worn a pair of blue jeans with a slight hole in the thigh. While working with the doctor he had put a finger in the hole touching her leg letting her know that it was unprofessional. She reacted with anger, in no uncertain terms telling him to get his finger out of there or else maybe it would be broken.

On another day, before the doctor came down from the third floor to work, her and Grew had had the dogs in and out for their morning exercise. They had stood by the door to the runs that they had just cleaned on top of the stairs down to the basement, her a step above him, he was explaining something to her. Somehow the conversation had become personal, she told Grew how her husband had raped her when they had first met. Grew perked up at the very descriptive details in her story and yes it did turn him on. Still standing face to face she then got into how her husband wanted to fondle her breasts but she claimed that there was no feeling in what appeared as smallish bumps in her shirt.

Grew had started down the steps again, with her disclosure he had stopped to face her again and they were standing almost next to each other--face to face-- Grew had looked in her face then up and down her body and commented "Is that right?"

As he had spoken he had reached out his hand and took hold of her breast. "What do you mean that you have no feeling? Everyone has feeling. Do you not feel this?"

His fingers worked around her covered nipples as they had continued to speak, she had not told him to back off. He had known it was a bold thing to do, expecting to get at least a slap. She made no suggestion for him to remove his hand. Instead the conversation casually went on for some time as if he had not touched her--his hand still there. She talked some more about her relationship, Grew was getting hot. As they quietly talked he could feel a hardening in the nipple, he knew his pants must have also been sticking out.

All of a sudden the girl was in his arms wildly kissing him, his hands manipulated her breasts, now both of them, undid the buttons one by one, uncovered her chest shoving the bra up, He worked his hands gently on the smallish bare tits. His mouth was on hers-- both wide open as they furiously worked at each other's tongues. Her hand was on his crotch, rubbing up and down on the hardness of him.

As she stood in a standing position, he picked her up and carried her, still kissing her, her feet six inches off the floor--their difference in height--into the first kennel room, down to the end where there was a large open kennel. He placed her down, prone in the kennel, still kissing her wildly, mouths open, undid the button on top of her front flied jeans, undid the zipper and was pulling them off her legs, as she spoke." No, No, we can't do it here, not in a dog kennel Grew." but he wasn't stopping.

His hand was inside her panties, working fingers into her warm pussy. She continued to complain. Her hole was wide open and wet. In her hand was his penis, she had fished it out, she was gently moving the skin back and forth but still saying," No, No, not here."

The front door bell rang. At first they ignored it but it rang again and then again. Grew knew that the doctor would wonder what was going on if someone did not go to the door. Then he would come down himself.

Breathlessly Grew spoke, "Some ones gotta get the door."

He pulled himself away as she lay sprawled in the painted cement kennel, her legs spread, her jeans and panties off, ready to be fucked. Sorrowfully he noted the spread trim legs, erotic expression on her face, willingness to have sex, apologetically looking at him, as he left.

Pulling his pants up, he made his way to the front reception area-- smiled at the lady there, standing in Bermuda shorts, holding the grossly overweight domestic cat. What a silly picture they presented. He smiled to himself again as she told him the name of the cat, "Flub"-- appropriate for the occasion.

The lady down stairs had dressed herself, was doing up her pants as he returned to the basement. She also chuckled at the name of the cat but they never got back to where they were right then, it was too close to opening time, the doctor would be down soon.

The two of them met one afternoon. They drove down to the area where he had first been with Lisa. Before they got too deep in the lovemaking she asked if he had ever been there with another woman. She wanted to leave when he told her that he had. They went back to her apartment but when they started to make out there, she had feelings of guilt. Grew understood how she felt and left. The doctor also kept after her, she kept turning him down. She was willing to have an affair with Grew but soon after quit work.

There were more Marilyn confessions. Hans was a big stocky sort, balding, jovial, aggressive, often rubbing people the wrong way by defending the Nazi policies of WW11. He had a job working with the city where he was able to get days off from time to time in the week. Years later he got into a very successful kennel operation of his own. For a while he even had his own dog club. He was closely linked with Grew through the dogs--but as it turned out, even more so with Marilyn. After seeing Paul's dog, a monorchid but a good obedience animal Hans bought the dog. Hans liked the type of dogs coming from the kennel and came to see the kennel. He then bought another male from the Chloe.

He had sacrificed getting married so he could raise his brothers but was not above getting sexually involved wherever he could. His befriending of Grew had side benefits as he openly jousted with Marilyn. Grew did not think that he was the type that she would be attracted to, his mouth would tend to put most women off. Yet Marilyn did respect him for what he had achieved and his commitment to his family so he was a welcome guest at the kennel. Marilyn would tell Grew when he had come by from time to time. Some time later, committed to sharing, she included Hans on her list of confessions. She laughingly detailed the incident to Grew.

Hans had come by one afternoon while she was alone and they had gone out for a walk with the dogs. As usual they had their joking around, their discussion had gotten into a sexual thing. As she related it to Grew it sounded like she had sort of kidded him a bit too much about the sexual story he was telling her--people tended not to believe him--always giving the impression of boasting when telling of something he had done. This story seemed to be something about how long he could keep going without coming while having sex. It also included a version of how he had wrapped his partners legs on the back of the bed board, not the type of story he should have been telling in that venue but regardless she had listened intently, obviously amused. This was Marilyn, the way she was.

She looked at him laughingly, saying, "Hans, who are you trying to convince? Your a great guy but you don't have to convince me your a super stud, I believe you. What is this thing about the headboard?" Her eyes would have been sparkling as she smiled at him.

He responded, "Okay smart ass, you don't want to believe me, let me show you the thing with the headboard, if I'm right we have sex, okay?" It was a bold right up front move, typical of him. He said what he wanted. She was too with it to be offended.

Taken aback, she had looked a bit shocked, but also excited at the suggestion. She had been wearing a blue gingham dress at the time and reflected how exposed she would be, if she did what he was suggesting. "Hans, what a con game, I'm not going to go along with that." Still she had been laughing as she answered.

They were in the house at the time having coffee, moving around to where she stood he took her wrist and started pulling her towards the bedroom. "Come on Marilyn, let me show you. We don't have to have the sex." He dragged her to the bedroom, as she laughingly pulled back, but still moved unwillingly along with him.

As he got her to the bed, she allowed herself half heartedly to be pushed onto it with him coming down beside her, she took hold of his side hair, pulling his head towards her own. She said, "Just in case we might have sex, let's have a little warm-up first. We can do that". Was it a challenge? He slid next to her as they kissed; the idea of it all raised her anticipation.

Almost right away he was fondling her breasts, had them out of their containers and was sucking one after the other--she loved her breasts being worked on-- in between he was gently kissing her neck, tonguing her ears and French kissing her mouth. She was finding him to be a gentle lover, didn't rebuff him as his hand went up her skirt. That hand was soon in her pants, gently rotating her clit. He moved the pants down her legs. His thick fingers were inside a wet, receptive cunt, stroking gently in the right places, she was ready.

He stopped kissing and fondling her, started moving her legs around. As he did he placed her ankles under the bar at the top of the headboard. She was spread fixed in a doubled position. When she saw his thick but short penis working its way towards her exposed and open vagina, she realized that as the back of her ankles pushed up on the bed bar the only thing she could do was to double more to get them out. She was trapped. His penis was so thick he had to force it as he pushed in her. She wished it was longer but certainly it was hard. He pushed it in her hard, it hurt as it entered. It didn't pop out either as he continued to bash in and out. His big hard belly kept slapping at hers. She had orgasm after orgasm, he just kept going until finally she felt it blast inside her. She was soaked, felt very wet as he finally subsided. He was right he had kept going as he had said. She knew her legs would be sore and they were after that experience. She laughed as she told her story to Grew. He laughed with her. What kind of wife was this? There was more.

CHAPTER 8

Dr Secks and More Affairs

There was an acquaintance of Grew's, son of a man who brought dogs in from Germany that had been used as studs for Grew's dogs. This person had grown up in the dog game from a young boy. He handled German Shepherds aggressively, intimidating judges wherever he could. Grew was more associated with Sid's father, also a judge. Grew and Sid often had lengthy discussions as to what their opinions were, but Sid really only seemed to care about winning.

Sid was known as a ladies man but Grew knew that he seldom talked of his affairs, also knew that he usually became involved with women not because of his own advances but more because of prestige. When he almost seemed to ignore them as he talked about dogs and his expertise, they ended up making advances on him.

Grew had met him at work one day, invited him home for supper. It was on a Sunday. Grew had planned to go to the obedience classes that Sid didn't want to go to. When they got to the kennel and had supper Sid had been in deep conversation or disagreement with Marilyn about something. On dogs she was an authority in her own right. Grew wondered if the two of them would get it on if he left them alone but also knew Lisa would be at the training, it was at a time when she still had the poodle. Around the time that Grew was about to leave he kept asking Sid if he was coming but said that he was welcome to stay talking with Marilyn if he wanted to. Sid had been there with his own car.

Sid finally said, "Naw, I better be heading for home soon anyway, I'll just stay here for awhile and convince your wife that she doesn't know what she is talking about,"

So Grew left without him. Down the road a bit he had wondered if he would be able to hear or see anything from the bedroom window. Turning around, he drove back and parked the car at the gravel pit. Behind the horse barn he had snuck up the back over to the bedroom window. It was not long before he could hear them talking.

He couldn't see anything though and even what he could hear wasn't worth it, couldn't make out anything but the two voices did seem to be coming from the bedroom. He realized it was his own fault if there was something going on. Returning to the car he went on to the training class still wondering just what went on at home.

When he got home Marilyn was alone, her first comment was, "You set me up you bastard. What was I supposed to do with him?"

"I don't know, I was leaving, you two were into your heavy discussion, I told him I was going, he didn't need me to tell him how to get home, so I left, what happened?"

She laughed then as she told him of the sexual experience, "Well we did have sex if you can call it that and he is so small I could hardly tell he had it in, no wonder he doesn't come onto women. He actually did make the moves though, I figured you probably knew he would, you might have broken in. We rolled around on the bed for quite a while which was fun until he finally got down to business. He wasn't what I would call eager"

Grew smiled as he listened to her story. It wasn't about to make much difference in their life. Sid never came around again, at least, that Grew ever knew about.

From time to time in deep conversations it became apparent that she was still smarting over Lisa. Her efforts to screw her way to equality were not working out too well. She would get into a depression over it. They decided to see a marriage councilor. No one including doctors seemed to know where to find one so they looked in the yellow pages. There was one advertised as just that, with quite a large ad. They phoned in and made an appointment.

When they came into the "doctor's" office together he listened intently to their concerns about the marriage for a while then after a brief time alone that he had requested with Marilyn they came out and he spoke. "First of all Grew the problem is not with you, your wife has taken on some ideas that are causing her no end of pain. She is the last child in the family she came from; she has always been the last in line. She had to look after her mother in her last days. The mother indoctrinated her on the evils of men yet she had kept having more babies herself. How was she having them? Not by immaculate conception. What I want to do is have a number of sessions with Marilyn alone. I will work on changing many of her ideas or hang-ups. I stress to you though, DO NOT, I repeat, do not ask her about the sessions that her and I are having."

Grew listened intently as the man was talking, a little apprehensive that he wasn't included. "Why do you want to do it that way?

"Your involvement can destroy all the benefits I can give to her. Are you willing to live by those rules? If not the two of you might as well leave now. If you agree I will ask you to leave her and I alone for half an hour right now. Go have coffee or lunch then come back."

Grew sort of shrugged, perhaps pleased that at least someone didn't believe that he was at fault. He did go to have lunch down the street and half an hour later he came back to pickup Marilyn. She looked a little strange. She wanted to talk to him about the session even though he had agreed not to discuss it; she was not sure, uneasy about continuing with this guy. Naturally Grew asked why? She thought that possibly the guy might be too forward but after a bit of discussion agreed to see him at least a few times.

She said, "I'll take it one session at a time".

It was probably after the third time Marilyn had seen this man that Grew knew there was something really bothering her. She had been giving Grew indications as one sitting followed another that she was not quite sure about continuing with Dr. Sechs. One day she broke down crying. Grew finally decided, that whatever he had agreed to, she should let him know just what had been going on. He had always listened to her concerns, had been her friend. As they sat in the car after getting coffee the whole story came out.

From the first day that Marilyn had been left alone with Doctor Secks it had begun. She had young Charles with her and Secks had asked her if she had to feed him. She had responded, "He is about due and if you would like to wait for a bit I will take him in the ladies room or it wouldn't be too bad if he waited awhile."

He had replied, "That wont be necessary, I have seen tits before, do it right here while we talk, it will help you relax. Here let me help you." he had reached over and took the buttons of her blouse in his hand, while he looked her in the eye, he popped the buttons loose, then with knowing hands flipped a tit out. "There how is that?" as he was continuing to hold the breast, gently fondling it.

She had brought Charles up to her breast--let his mouth find the nipple. She defied the doctor with her eyes. The doctor did not let go but also met her eyes. Right there was when she had to get up and leave if she was going to but didn't. This was the same woman who had let another stranger come to her door and fondle her bare breast. There is no doubt it turned her on. As the doctor manipulated the breast she received the sucking sensations from her son. It had been a very sensual experience.

The doctor had talked gently to her as they sat almost next to each other. She did relax as she talked of her experience of the first time she became pregnant, admitting her enjoyment with the sex that she had with that man. They went on to talk of orgasms, how often she had had them during sex, how much foreplay she had been used to, how it fit into her sex life.

She had become soft, receptive as he talked, answering his questions. She also admitted enjoying his fondling, even allowing him to take the other nipple, gently play with it as they talked. She had smiled, eyes sparkling, at him as he squeezed her nipple. The session had been over too quickly for her--just a half hour. She admitted she would have jumped in bed with him right there. When she had met Grew after that she had still been aroused.

The second time that she came in he greeted her by taking both her hands as she had walked into his office. He led her over to his couch and sat down with her, had asked her how things had been. She told him that things had been all right. She had been a bit bolder when having sex with her husband. There had been no one else. She did not have her son with her this time. The doctor asked about him and she went into some detail about how Charles had been.

Then he took one hand away from hers, reached across to her breast and gently squeezed, continued to massage as he talked to her and undid the front of her dress as she watched. She felt the excitement as he did but she made no move to stop him. He had pulled the dress down from her shoulders leaving her sitting bare to the waist except for her bra. For a while they continued to talk. He told her how special her breasts were, how nice they felt as he tweaked the nipples through the cloth. She sat there, sometimes giggling a bit at his funny jokes, enjoying the nice things he was saying about her body. To Grew, she didn't deny enjoying the attention, the nice things he was saying and the touching, as it continued.

The doctor asked, "Can I take your bra off? Are you going to let me look at your magnificent tits again? My you are gorgeous, your face is starting to redden a bit. Are you getting a bit excited?" He had continued to question but had not waited for answers.

She quietly nodded at him as she felt the back catches on her bra release with his arms around her. She sat back on the couch as his arms had then moved to her front, taking a breast in each hand. Slowly, a bit breathlessly, he had continued to talk to her, feeling every bit of her breasts, massaging, commenting on the beauty of them, asking her questions about her past sex experiences, throwing in the odd sexual word like fuck or cunt, asking if she had ever sucked prick, asking her to describe how she felt when being fucked, asking if she felt wet and slippery in her cunt? She had been getting hot while he talked and was getting hot while telling Grew.

He had continued. "Marilyn, do you want to feel my cock? Will you play with it if I pull it out? Oh my God your tits feel ravishing;

look at the nipples harden." She had looked as he moved the nipple of her own tit into her view.

She noticed his open fly. "Marilyn, put your hand in my pants, feel what you've done; pull my prick out."

As she had obeyed his command she had been ecstatic when she felt the hardness of the prick in her hand, had looked at it as she moved it from his pants. She had clasped the hot thing in her hand and slid the skin back and forth, slowly as she exposed the knob then back again, gently playing with the thing. He had told her what to do with it next, what to do so he would get the best sensations from it.

There had been no more talk of her past. On that day they were both too wrapped up in the present. They sat side by side on the couch, her leaning over him moving her soft hand on his erection as ordered.

"Marilyn, now slowly, over that ridge, gently underneath, that's it, softly. Oh! That is the way, your hands are so soft, don't stop."

After awhile as they sat, both of them quietly breathing, his right hand came over to her legs, on her knee, it gently rolled around the bend, smoothing the fine skin, gently his hand moved up her thigh, pushing the hem of her skirt, exposing skin as it went.

Then he was rubbing on the cloth of her panties, picking at the pubic hair underneath from time to time. Slowly he had separated her legs as he slid his hand between, rubbing in the warm wet crotch of her. He told her it was time the session was over. She hadn't believed it. She had been ready to fuck him right there. She told Grew that she wanted to.

Boldly she had said to the doctor, "We can't quit yet, I want that thing inside me. Doctor, I want you, please fuck me, don't stop now. How can I go out of her like this, I have to have something. Put this thing in me...please."

The doctor was worked up too. Marylyn got the impression it was not easy for him to stop. The session had been into overtime. He said he had never run into a woman like her before. "Okay, tell you what, you can suck this thing off, I'll get my hand in your pants, I'll make you love it."

"No. Get your pants off." She was hoping he would fuck her, wanted it and admitted it to her husband.

But she did as ordered. Gently he moved his hands around her vagina, hitting all the right places. At the same time she took his penis in her mouth without hesitation. She had never done this before but had learned from the doctor about the sensitive parts, where to lick, where to move her tongue. She sucked as commanded as her spread legs undulated in time to the doctor moving his hands around the lips, the clit, and deep within her until she let go.

As she did she had wildly sucked and jerked on his cock until he ejaculated into her mouth; she felt the juice of him, squirting, she sucked more, drinking it down her throat. A few minutes later the doctor told her that was it for then. People were waiting in the office.

As she walked out of the back door to the office she had felt exhausted but satisfied. It had been an earth shattering complete feeling, a feeling of having been completely satisfied sexually. Had it ever happened before? It reminded her a bit of her times with Clarence, but Clarence had never exhausted her so completely.

She had some feelings of guilt as she made her way home. Was this what Grew had experienced with Lisa? How was this going to solve her marital problems? She had another appointment the following week, she wondered about it. She was getting frightened about the legitimacy of this guy and what it might lead to.

Still the following week she had been there again. At first he had asked her more about her past love life. Then he had wanted to know how her week had been with her husband or anyone else. He wanted the details of some of her love sessions, wanted to know how many times she would normally have orgasms; had asked before but was it any different? Again he talked to her about some of the sexual things that she had found satisfying and had called her over to the couch again. Always it had been her that had to go to him--willingly.

Before she even realized it, he had been kissing her. It was a different approach. She only then realized that it had been the first time he had kissed her. It was smooth, soft, and nice, she smelled the clean smell of his mouth. Eventually their mouths had opened and they had sucked at each other, playing tongues.

Freeing her breasts he had felt again at her nipples, soon his hand had been moving up and down the skin of her legs. It had tickled and her legs would not stay still. Her shoes had come off by his hands, he had her toes in his mouth, had divested himself of his pants and soon she had been playing in the way she had been taught with his hard penis. His tongue licked along the length of her thigh then licking and nibbling every bit of her legs, her body, her tits and her nipples. She was wet with sweat as his tongue had found its way within and around her vagina, driving it to wild involuntary motion. He sucked on her clit, he drove his tongue in her, and she had an orgasm and he didn't stop, she didn't want him to, she was building in excitement again, then another climax. And she had another climax as he had then worked on her with his hands.

She had worked with her hands on his hard penis until it too squirted its product out into the room. She had looked at it, thinking that the last time she had swallowed that stuff. It had excited her even further. Then they had begun to subside and as they did he had talked to her of the unbelievable sexual person she was, had wanted her to meet him out of the office but she refused. He had even talked of what he could do for her if she would leave her husband, had even talked of leaving his own wife. In twenty-seven years he had never run into anyone so sexually responsive--so totally into the enjoyment of it. He wanted her for himself. She did make an appointment for the following week. As Grew thought of this as he was writing it years later he realized what had happened. By awakening the amazing sexual potential of this woman, he had become a slave to it himself, something once brought to life, he was unwilling to give up. Of course she would not realize the extent of what she had done to him.

Before attending the next session she had confessed it all to Grew. As she was confessing she felt that the doctor was not helping her at all but Grew had not been so sure. On her part she compared it to what Grew had been doing with Lisa. Grew had to agree that what she was saying was probably true; it had also been a great education for Lisa. As Grew had been teaching, totally, subconsciously, into the sexual thing with her so had Marilyn been into the same sort of things with Dr. Secks. Ironically the lessons with Lisa were not concluded until years later.

Marilyn had made Grew feel good by saying he was capable of doing this "work". They later found that there was no certification that allowed Dr.Secks to "practice". She talked to Grew about her following weeks appointment and he didn't know whether to advise her to go or not. The danger in where it was going he too could see. Had the doctor got too wrapped up in his treatment himself? Again Grew felt violated, but more by the doctor than by Marilyn.

She had decided she was going to call the doctor, tell him that she had spoken to her husband, to tell him that she would come for the appointment but wouldn't pay so that he could get his jollies. It was an approach that Grew did not particularly agree with, felt it was fraught with danger, she would be matching wits with the doctor. What was her point, did she want revenge because he had misled her, had she wanted one more go at the sexual satisfaction and would that be enough; would she be able to resist the psychological tie to the doctor?

With all the worries Grew was ready to let her go, at least once more but only because that is what she wanted to do. Her sexual experiences with the doctor were getting him turned on partly because the routines she was now employing in their own lovemaking. It had moved into a much more satisfying thing, more caring for each other, he would be the first to admit that. making love had seemed to be becoming a more satisfying thing. Had it been because of the doctor?

When she had called the doctor, he wanted her to come in for her usual appointment. When she then talked about not paying, he suggested that it was something they could talk about. Looking back Grew knew that if he could have gotten her secluded the chances were that he would have had her--totally as his. Maybe she would not have come home at all. Grew accepted the possibility that is what might happen and suggested it to her after the phone call.

She had told the doctor that her husband was objecting to having to pay for her sex. While talking to him on the phone, he offered to meet her sometime before the appointment, it was the wrong thing to say, he had played his hand wrong, alerted her to the dangerous game they were playing. He wanted to take her out for supper where they could talk. Marilyn knew herself well enough to know she would be trapped if she met him, she'd been there before. Was she learning her own limitations?

She agreed that she would keep the appointment but at that time she would not meet him for supper. At the last minute she told Grew that she too felt that it was too dangerous. "The doctor has gotten too emotionally into the case himself". She felt that when he had been kissing her he had gone beyond helping her with someone else, wanting her himself and quite open about it. She never cancelled the appointment but never kept it either. She had learned her lessons well.

It was during the spring or summer of the doctor that Brad Hoare started coming around. He was supposed to be a friend of Grew's or for some reason they had started talking somewhere. Grew was probably interested in the breeding that he did with the pigs Perhaps Brad had come out to see the dogs with some thoughts about buying one to work with the pigs. At first they watched dogs, as Grew would explain differences. Brad was not the sort of person one would think that Grew would have to worry about--it snuck up on them. Brad looked like an ordinary farmer, not even clean.

It was after the doctor thing that Grew later realized that Brad Hoare was coming around more often. By invitation both Marilyn and Grew had gone over to his place to see his pigs. The pigs were crammed in a barn hardly able to move. The air was thick with flies; if one opened their mouth they would be spitting out flies. The place was a mess.

Brad's wife was unable to speak, something she had never done, and he spoke to her with signs as Grew wondered what their communication was about. It was understandable that Brad was a quiet fellow. When the Tuckett's first met them they had three children, mostly looked after by the wife. She was a pleasant looking but sad lady. The pigs were well fed though with slop. Marilyn and Grew went with him once as he did rounds to pick it up. Probably he had agreed to take Grew in order to get Marilyn to go with him at that time. The impression Grew got was that this was an unhappy man. While they were driving, Marilyn sat between them.

When Grew thought back about it he wondered if something was going on then that he was not aware of; but there were no obvious indications, it would not have been unusual for her to sit between them.

After awhile Marilyn started going out at night again. Grew was not too concerned for a while but in time noticed that she was getting home later and later. Often he would detect the smell of cigarette smoke on her-- thought that she had started smoking. When she was wound up, sometimes she would smoke but had never kept it up. She knew that he was against it but felt that sometimes if others smoked she would too, just to be sociable.

At the vet hospital Dr. Relaishe had found himself a blond assistant who put up with his pawing advances. Helen was a nice quiet Dutch girl in her thirties, divorced, of medium build, on the slim side. She spoke to Grew when the doctor was not there about her predicament. She really did not like the constant attention of the doctor. This included frequent visits to her apartment for sex. Grew had listened as she went on about the doctor wanting to come to her place in off hours, he wasn't paying for that time, nor contributing to her apartment rent. She had sex with him while the arrangement lasted but eventually he over used his welcome and she quit.

CHAPTER 9
Coming to A Head

Grew was beginning to realize that Marilyn was meeting Brad Hoare at night and was torn between letting her get this one out of her system or whether he should interfere. He could understand just how it would get started. Knowing Marilyn, she was so warm with people she was always subject to being taken advantage of. This affair with the quiet man--the pig farmer--had started with daytime visits listening to her sorrows making them more serious than real. She had agreed with Grew to live the way they did. It was more her way of letting Brad know that she was not exactly happy with things at home. or was it just a way of getting him to make love to her. There were a lot of things that she could complain about, no water, no shower, not much of a house that was overrun with dogs but it was the lifestyle they had chosen, as Brad had with the pigs.

Brad, wanting to get on with this woman himself, would encourage her dissatisfaction, building on it, making her feel hard done by--even though he kept a woman at home in far worse conditions, perpetually pregnant and in isolation. That woman was deaf and in her own world. Really all Marilyn wanted was more sex. She wanted to be held, this man wanted someone who would talk and was happy to hold whomever it might be. It did upset the path of their lives though.

They probably got into the sex thing first, right there at the house in the afternoon. She never spoke of it but Grew could imagine that it was long sustained and gentle. She would be not only co operative but would be employing her new sexual knowledge to give this man sex how he had never had it before. They hit it off very well, which had increased their insatiable desire--needing to be together.

They started meeting at night which was not difficult. Grew never stopped her going out. Brad's idea of evening entertainment, from years of living in silence at home, was to sit in bars with his friends, smoking, watching bar television and talking to the girls wherever possible. He would have affairs without conscience but always go back to his wife who couldn't complain, satisfied because he was looking after the needs of his family. Maybe he had been trapped by his wife's pregnancy.

Now he was taking Marilyn into this out of the home environment, proud of his new companion. At first she enjoyed being out, rationalizing her infidelity as deserving more than a mere existence. The change from watching television especially with a husband she didn't trust, who seemed more interested in doing his dog activities than making love to her was welcome.

The listening support of Brad with him verbally making her believe she had been hard done by lent support to the idea she should have more with him. Did she ever stop to think about his negligence of his own family? It was hard to imagine what her expectations were. The Brad and Marilyn night meetings became more frequent, went on night after night, finishing off with them having sex, sometimes in a motel where she could have a shower afterward, before going home.

These meetings were not enough; he wanted more. He kept wanting her to stay longer and longer. One night Marilyn had not arrived home by midnight. Grew was starting to get more than suspicious. He was getting exasperated. With his son in bed, no electric appliances on and no heat in the house, he decided to walk the two miles into Goodwould to see if the car was there. It was there at the BP station. He settled down to wait for them to return, getting more and more worked up as he waited. Why didn't he just take the car? Even with a usual calm to this man there was a part of him that would sometimes look within, feel he was being taken advantage of, see himself as a sucker that he didn't want to be perceive as and he would get angry.

After half an hour he was even more annoyed. He ran home, sweating as he arrived, got out some paint and a brush. He painted right across the front of the house so everyone driving along the highway would see, "BRAD HOARE IS FUCKING MY WIFE". The way the house was located, the front was like a signboard facing the highway. Then he waited.

Another hour and she still had not arrived so he ran back to town again. The car was gone but Brad Hoare was there just getting into his truck, the same truck that they had seen parked beside the PB when they first drove through town.

Grew confronted him as he backed out of his truck facing him. Grew stood there and shouted at him, "Where the hell do you think you are getting off? How long do you expect to keep keeping my wife out all night? You son of a bitch, you whoring bastard, you have a wife of your own. Why do you have to be out fucking my wife?"

As Brad approached him, Grew came forward swinging as he came, he might have got a couple of good swings in but got too close and Brad grabbed, wrapping his arms around Grew's body. Then Marilyn drove up. She had been home and saw the message on the front of the house. She was distressed herself but said very little. She did manage to get between the two combatants as Brad let him go.

Then she was yelling, "Grew get in the car, in the car, common we're going home", then louder "GET IN THE CAR OR I AM LEAVING WITHOUT YOU!."

This had all taken place in the middle of Goodwood at two o'clock in the morning. Considering the volatility of the confrontation it was amazing that it ended in such a complacent apparently passive manner

Grew did get in the car and they drove towards home but she drove past the place first, she wanted him to cool down a bit before getting out of the car also wanted to see the sign. As she parked on the way back looking up at their house, she just shook her head.

She looked at him and said, "You must have really been distressed; does it bother you that much? I thought you really didn't care what I did. In the same situation I might have done something similar."

As Grew read what he had written he realized that she was such a tremendous person to take it in the way she did. She had been going out because she didn't think he cared. Unfortunately he felt that he never did get her over that idea.

They drove up the driveway, after two in the morning, got out of the car and looked closer. Together they felt that they could cover the whole thing with newspaper and paint over it the next day. They covered it and then went to bed.

Neither one went to work the next day so they came out rather late in the morning. The paper had blown off. She screamed when she saw the sign again. It had been there in plain view in the morning for everyone to see as they drove to work. They got out the paint and painted over it. From time to time, the lettering bled through the covering paint so had to be painted again. It was the nature of the wall covering that did funny things with paint.

Things almost seemed to settle down after that. If she was seeing Brad Hoare it was in the daytime and Grew did not know about it. Besides, she started working almost full time for The Elegant Dog so most days she was not at the kennel. They had some long talks and it almost appeared that they were both back in a mode that would go on forever through hell and high water.

One day he came home to find her quieter than usual. She told him that she was going to move into a room in the city close to where she was working, take Charles with her to the room and into the poodle place with her when she went to work. Grew was upset, he didn't know what to say; he knew she was going to do it. He accepted it, she refused to tell him where she was going to be staying.

It was a terrible time for him. Even as he read what he had written years later. The days had passed with him totally depressed, his work was done mechanically. Was their life together finished? He missed her and had missed his son perhaps even more. Life had become empty, each day he drove home, let the dogs out, walked them through the fields, perhaps to him therapy, and watched television, then to bed. It went on day after day. Friends didn't mean anything anymore; his job didn't mean anything.

The doctor had hired a replacement for Helen. Her name was Doris, a very unlikely candidate. The staff was surprised. They mused that the doctor's wife might have had something to do with the hiring. Doris was not pretty nor did she dress to look good. Her priority was her horse. She would be about one hundred and twenty pounds, not thin or heavy, well muscled limbs, straight with body parts insignificant. Her face was simple, serious, complexion almost freckled and with nothing done to enhance her facial image. Her hair was a mousy red, medium length, not enhanced by style.

She was one of those types of people that do whatever they do capably. She had a nursing assistant background. She kept her horse in a barn in Mississauga. This was a natural veterinary assistant, except she was not the type that Dr. Relaishe would hire. In spite of her simplistic appearance she was a congenial person who Grew quite enjoyed the company of. For a while she had resisted the advances of the doctor but after a while decided that it might not be too bad. She was already in a relationship with a guy who never seemed to take that extra step to either move in or marry her.

One evening during the separation Grew was having with Marilyn, Doris asked him if he wanted to come out and see her horse. They were all aware of what he was going through and possibly there was a feeling of sorrow for him. It was a most welcome invitation since he only had to look forward to whatever was at home. He decided to let the dogs wait and go with her

They drove together after dropping his car near highway twenty-seven so he could pick it up on the way back. The horse was spectacular, Grew was getting another perspective of this very nice woman and what she really was, as she opened up. The horse barn was her element, rubbing the nose of the animal, with the horse responding with a pushing of his face into hers; Grew saw a beauty he had not seen before. She vigorously curried the horse all over then went for a ride around the inside exercise area while Grew watched, impressed with her horsemanship as she put him through his paces.

On the way back to his car he was seeing a different type of person than he had been used to. She was warm, confident, almost outgoing in her conversation. When they stopped to pick his car up, he thanked her for taking him out. Almost in a spirit of friendliness he reached out to kiss her as they stood outside the two cars beside a grassy area next to the highway. She came into his arms, surprising him with the warmth of the kiss. It was a soft kiss with lips gently moving, neither of them were pulling back. The kiss continued, and mouths were opening, still neither backing off. The kissing had become more passionate as his hand found her breast-- nice feel.

She didn't stop him, not even as he pulled her down in the long grass. The buttons easily came loose as his hand worked inside her blouse--her bra. The breast was warm, supple, firm, a lovely thing that had been amazingly hidden behind uncomplimentary clothing. She was kissing him--as he was her--with warm passion, she softly moaned.

Even as he undid the zipper of her riding breaches she didn't stop him, neither did she as he pulled on the belt, the underpants beneath, pulling it all down her legs. It was not easy to get them off; he couldn't get them off her legs so he didn't. He dove his hand into the soft center of her curly pubic hair, and found the wet slit waiting there, surrounding his fingers as they gently caressed and pushed into her and the surrounding flesh.

She had undone his pants, had his hard penis out and in her hand, pulling the skin back as she did. He felt the gentle manipulation getting him even more excited. Then he had fingers right in her, pushing in, slowly pulling out and in again. Ridges within her were holding onto his fingers as he finger fucked her, but just couldn't get the damn breaches off. Trying to get his prick into her from behind, they were both laughing, as they were hand working each other off.

Grew turned her around into a bent position, was about to work it into her when they heard footsteps. FOOTSTEPS! Out there, on the side of the highway. They had both stopped.

"Shhsh!" one of them said.

There was someone walking, they could hear him or her close by. "Sh... "he whispered again, "someone is coming." They lay still, almost joined in the middle, while footsteps came closer then moved beyond. His penis subsided, it was over, foiled again. They started to dress.

It was too late then, the moment had come and gone. She was doing her clothing up as the footsteps receded into the distance. They laughed again as he held her close.

He kissed her again and exclaimed, "Wow you are something, I never expected that. Can we try again sometime."

"Your still married. Is there any point taking it any further?"

A positive answer could have been in order, but he wasn't ready for a new commitment at that time, yet he often wondered as he recalled the incident and thought this woman could very well have been what he needed. She was probably available. Grew in his honesty answered that at the moment he was not sure where his marriage was going. To his credit he wouldn't lead her on. He needed to sort one thing out before getting into another. He wondered if it might have been better if he had taken his chances with Doris, an exciting person with similar priorities. They got in their separate cars and went in different directions those directions went beyond that evening. They never did get together but he always remembered her as being so nice, one splendid sexual surprise.

Grew had still been trying to figure out where Marilyn had gone but he wasn't about to nor did he follow her. She had made her decision to do whatever she had done. Had she somehow realized though that she had let something go too soon?

One day she phoned him at work, asking if he wanted to see Charles. He should have said no. Instead he asked where she was staying but she wouldn't tell him. Since she wasn't going to tell him he said he'd just as soon not see Charles or her. It had probably been at least six weeks since he had heard from her but more like a couple of months. He was getting over her, ready to put her and Charles out of his life. She had never asked for money. He hung up.

Soon after she called again. Grew agreed to see her after she had told him that she had a room with Jill in a big house with extra rooms. Then he asked if she was seeing anyone? She said that she was but that it wasn't serious. She expressed a concern about the way Charles was relating to her boyfriend, that he had not been well and had picked up some pockmarks. She felt that he had missed his dad and would like to see him.

Grew asked, "Why don't you see if he can visit George?"

She seemed terribly hurt by that remark for which he apologized. They agreed to meet at a mutual place. She didn't want him to come around Jill's house. He wondered why not, but didn't make an issue of it.

They met in a restaurant by the animal hospital. For a long time they talked. Charles was very happy to see him--play time for a while with dad. He consented somewhat reluctantly to meet with her again soon. That night by agreement he did follow her to Jill's. She invited him in. Jill and he talked, saw Marilyn's room and then he left. She had seemed to be living alone. Grew patiently waited after that, not calling her, knowing she had problems that were no longer his concern. Grew was still ready to let go, he still thought of Doris but that was not his nature.

The next time they met she told him that she had been seeing Brad Hoare. She told him she went in to pick up the mail and the girl at the wicket asked her if she wanted the mail for Tuckett or Hoare? It was clear the whole town knew. The girl, who she had known well and considered a friend, had been very sarcastic and unfriendly. Marilyn had felt hurt. She had also found that she could not keep relating to the bar scene, didn't like Brad flirting with the woman. She had also found out that his wife was pregnant which must have happened since Marilyn had been sexually involved with him. Grew often wondered just why but said he wanted her back, even admitted he missed her and Charles.

She said, "Brad won't let me go. He's possessive. To him, I'm his now, he expects me to be loyal, even though he isn't loyal to me, it won't be easy".

"Well why are you bothering me by calling, what do you want?"

Why would anyone expect loyalty from either one after what had happened? He put it straight to her. Grew stated it was going to be up to her whether she came with him or not. If she didn't come with him then he would not be asking her again. She would be free to do whatever she wanted with her life but he would have nothing to do with her. He told her that he would not even want visitation rights.

He continued, "If your coming pick a day, I'll come to Jill's, have the police there so that that Brad doesn't interfere. I'm asking you to come with me."

Soon after that they did meet outside her rooming house ready to go. Grew had arranged for the police to be there who at first were not willing to come. He told them that if they were not there, he would be there with an axe handle, if this guy tried to stop his wife from leaving with him, he would be doing whatever necessary to get her away, as long as she was willing to go. After much discussion the police did agree to show up. Brad Hoare was also there. Brad talked to Marilyn for a long time. She then came over to Grew, telling him that Brad didn't want her to go.

Sarcastically Grew said, "We knew that. Why am I not surprised? I have no doubt that he cares for you, even that you care for him".

Grew was distressed and nervous himself, not feeling too sure of his position and that she would make the decision to come with him--did know though and probably she did too that this was her last chance and if she didn't come with him, he would not be asking again. He had withstood nearly two months without her or even hearing from her and was confident he could readjust his life and eventually settle with someone else.

"Marilyn, I want you, I love you, our life is different but it is something that you and I do well together. It has to be up to you though, I have said before, you're going to have to make up your mind, right here." At that point he was undecided himself whether to walk away or not; impatience at the situation was also affecting him, knowing it had to be done right then. Was it his own ego that he had to please?

She said, "Okay, I'm coming but let me go over to talk to him again for a minute." She went over to Brad and started talking again.

He took hold of her arm, trying to lead her away. Grew walked over to where they were, telling him to let her go. He told Brad that he was not going to allow him to drag her away. She was going to have to make up her mind on her own.

The police officer stepped up to Brad and said, "Let go of her arm, if she wants to go with him you are going to have to let it happen."

He let go. She hesitated for a few minutes, still looking at Brad then back to Grew. They all knew that it was a very tough decision that she was making but she knew she had to make it. It was a balance where she could not have both of these so different worlds.

She turned away from Brad and walked over to Grew saying, "Okay I'm going to come with you; let's get out of here."

Brad shouted at her, trying to move after her. "Marilyn don't go with him; you're just going back to what you left."

A policeman stepped in front of him, "Your not going any further, you stay right here. Let's just talk for awhile."

The police stopped him from following them. They stayed in a small hotel across from the park where Lisa and Grew had spent a lunch hour just before she had left the animal hospital to go back to school. The next day they both gave notice where they worked that they would be leaving in a week.

Years later Grew read over what he had written about that time, sometime after the two had got back together. It was all there in his notes. Feelings associated with the incident were still there-- bothering. He'd wondered so much about what had gone on, the coming back together with Marilyn so long before, wondered about the way life flows, how we never know what will happen the day after or the year after a decision is made, where we decide to go one way or the other.

As he looked back he could see maybe why it had all worked out the way it had. Would it have been better for her to stay with Brad? She wouldn't have had the freedom but how would the situation with his pregnant wife have worked out?. Would Grew have been better to let her go and maybe develop something with Doris? For sure the staff at the animal hospital, although quiet, had little respect for Marilyn. Do those that follow their heart or whatever live a fuller life? He wondered about his own life and where it went from there. There was no doubt that the story could have unfolded in a much different way than it did, perhaps in a gentler way but the story of each life unfolds not as we would wish but according to fate.

When looking at what he had written much later it was from a different perspective, the emotions were not as strong and how could he have known what was to ensue.

CHAPTER 10

On the Move

Grew felt so insecure when Marilyn had come back, scared of what to do then. How could he put it all right and was she back to stay? There was a lot of self-blame from his part. What had he done wrong? Should he hold her? Allow her space? Talk to her about why she had left and why she had come back? Years later, going over the chronology of events, he realized that she knew she had made a mistake in teaming up with Brad Hoare. The way she was she was susceptible to seduction. Brad had thought he'd be the only one. Grew eventually learned years later that his own ability to change people was very limited. People were as they were, guidance and talking could only affect them a bit and being judgmental was not the answer. People were unequipped to decide what others should do--support and understanding is all one can offer.

He had wondered about how Marilyn felt as they got back together. Did she think that she was now going to be persecuted for leaving? It was something hardly ever mentioned from then on, she knew what she had done, it was like the first baby thing, she was never blamed or criticized. It was something that had happened.

They had cautiously got into the same bed that night, like they were both in shock--strangers. Slowly he had put out his arms, a testing motion. She did not hesitate to snuggle into him, face him with tears in her eyes. Grew too, cried softly as he had kissed her. She was warm, her body was soft. She showed no sign of guilt.

When they had got in bed he was wearing underwear briefs and unusual for her, she had on a silk night thing that covered her body. It was not long before he was rubbing her skin beneath the nighty; the cloth was moving up her legs, her body, then she pulled her head away from him for a moment as she slipped it off.

Grew recalled the breathtaking feeling of being next to her as he had stripped everything from his own body, so close together for such a long time as he stroked her. She started caressing his body as they kissed, then she was holding his erect penis.

She had rolled on her back, bringing him with her, her legs spreading. His hand was in the soft, wet, warm center of her, gently stroking; he could feel her passion rising.

Slowly she told him. "That is all I wanted from you, to love me, didn't mean to get into this other stuff, with these other people. Remember the marriage doctor? I think he did teach me but then I applied it the wrong way. I couldn't live with Brad Hoare but have feelings for him. I don't want to talk about him though"

Grew never said a word, he just continued to hold her and listened, even though it hurt to hear her not so surprising revelation of affection for Brad Hoare. His hands moved softly around the smooth white skin of her body and legs, kissing her again, softly pressing as mouths opened. Slowly he worked his penis within her, for a long time they slowly moved together, gently loving each other. Later as the tempo increased, wildly kissing each other, mouths open, bodies thrashing at each other, it went on until a climax. Then there was a soft gentle holding again, caressing until they fell asleep.

They finished out their weeks work at their respective jobs, all the while looking over their shoulders. Looking for Brad Hoare to again reappear, Marilyn also had to be firm. She had made up her mind not to go with Brad but it was an unconvincing decision.

They all knew that Brad had another problem, finding support for a wife who couldn't speak, with four small children to look after. His affair was a fantasy that couldn't happen. He too would not have been able to satisfy Marilyn. Supposedly when Marilyn left, he faced fact, just as Grew had with his affair with Lisa, that it was over. A few years later they heard Brad died-- no reason given.

Marilyn and Grew packed as much of their belongings as possible into the Volkswagen. He couldn't remember what happened to whatever furniture they had but it must have been left in their Goodwood home. He did remember that there were four Corgis, two German Shepherds, a Miniature Poodle and a Siamese cat that were packed into the back of the bug. They had arranged to sell the place at Goodwood as soon as possible. There were just too many memories and ghosts.

They set off for Vancouver, determined to start life over again somewhere else. They did have a tent with them. They were so relaxed as they had driven around Lake Superior, stopping to camp when they had had enough driving, wherever a place looked suitable. There was a lot of laughter as neither criticized the other for whatever they had gone through. Could it be that Marilyn had actually missed being with him? It was like the honeymoon that never was.

As they drove through the empty country, absent houses but with the essence of nature everywhere, they had talked of what had happened to them, what they had lived through, where they were going and what was about to happen. There were long periods of time where no one said anything. One or the other would drive while the other watched the scenery, sometimes just discussing things in general. The little boy was a wonder as he too seemed to enjoy the scenery, and running with the dogs whenever they would stop.

Sometimes they would stop at small motels, buying simple things to cook or eat hamburgers picked up along the way or pitching their tent at campsites in the parks. There were long spells of quiet as they moved across the prairies, through miles and miles of nothing but grass and sky. In the mountains they stopped along the way, he and Charles chasing after each other while running the dogs. Time was enjoyable, at least for the boys. Marilyn would drive when it came to following the steep hills down the mountainside but she would be the first to admit that camping was not her choice of things to do.

When they reached Vancouver they spent some time with cousin Jack, then up the coast to visit Grew's father and sister living there. They never talked to the relatives of what they had been through. Back in Vancouver they went out to see his aunt in White Rock. She had been retired, living alone, an animal lover and happy to have them stay as long as they wanted. Grew found a job at a local veterinarian where the people were happy to receive the benefit of his trimming experience.

Six weeks after arriving in the Vancouver area they both were feeling sad. There was something missing in their lives. Was it a feeling that they had run away? They knew they couldn't continue to live with his aunt indefinitely although she was happy to have them. Their property back east was about to sell and they still felt in a state of limbo.

One day they had looked at each other, speaking almost together, "We do not belong here, we ran away from a terrible situation, we have left all our connections back there, lets go." Grew wondered if she missed Brad.

They had packed up everything they had started with and since they were so close to the American border--White Rock is as about as close to the American border as one can get--they decided to make their way through the United States. Grew remembered the climb being more gradual as they made their way up into the Rockies, than it had been in Canada. There was a pass that they came to, far away from anything but because it had been getting dark, they stopped beside the road and pitched their tent.

The next morning was one of the few times that he could remember of Marilyn sounding annoyed. She said, "Do not like camping. The ground is hard, we kept hearing trucks through the night, nowhere to go to the bathroom or cleanup, let's just get going."

He had driven quietly while Marilyn, Charles and the animals slept. Sometime in the day they came to a State park in Montana, still in the mountains. They then stopped at a picnic table, tied the Siamese cat to the table and proceeded to put some food together.

After walking the dogs they had thrown everything back into the Volks and started off again. It was Grew's turn to sleep.

Two hours later he woke up and asked, "Where is the cat?"

Marilyn pulled the car over to the side of the road. They looked at each other. She said in almost a fearful voice as if he was going to hit her, "Still tied to the picnic table?"

Grew was unhappy but only said, "Oh shit, do you want me to drive?" Then they had both laughed.

Swinging the car around, he headed back along the eighty miles or so. The cat was still tied to the picnic table. She meowed as all three of them and the dogs had gotten out of the car, coming towards her. She seemed happy to see them all as she had rubbed herself back and forth against everyone, dogs included.

They made their way across the Northern part of the United States, stopped for a while in various small cities like Fargo, skirted around Minneapolis and found their way around the South side of Superior, through the Upper Peninsula of Michigan to Sarnia and "home". Much of the time while traveling, he would study the map as Marilyn drove. They had stopped fairly often for the dogs to run but had kept on moving, both with the thoughts of getting to Toronto to find jobs and straighten their lives out.

When they did get to Toronto, Grew thought that they had stayed at Jill's rooming house for a little while but there was a lot to do as they looked for a more permanent place to live and try to get the jobs back they had before. They found an apartment above "The Dog House" which was close to the animal hospital that Grew had applied for and gotten his job back. Sandra was still working there or there again. Marilyn was also rehired at The Elegant Dog, a mile further up the road. He did not remember what they had used for furniture, whether they had brought the bed from Goodwood or there was furniture in the apartment.

The apartment was up stairs at the back of the building with its own entrance. At the bottom of the stairs was a small yard where Charles could play and behind that there was an alley where they could park. Soon after moving in they arranged for a lady to look after Charles in the daytime. Grew could not remember her name but they had agreed that Charles would call her Deedie.

This couple that could not have their own children, became so attached to Charles that they wanted him whenever they could, even on weekends. One day Marilyn talked to Grew about a conversation she had had with Deedie. Deedie had suggested that perhaps Marilyn, who always displayed an openness that encouraged people to propose the strangest things, might be interested in being a surrogate mother for a child for them. Deedie's husband would be the father and Marilyn would be the mother. It was before implants and artificial semination was rare.

As they drove back from picking up Charles, Marilyn and Grew, who were always able to talk about "way out things" discussed this proposition. He wanted to know how this fertilization was to take place to which she replied that it was an area that had not been discussed. After all they had been through, even though they could use the money that would go with the deal, it was never followed through with. Grew could see though that she was still open to controversial ideas; she had considered the proposition. Grew didn't think that Marilyn would be able to let another baby go. It was the main reason that they rejected the idea.

A short while after they had settled--both back to work--he was telling Sandra from the animal hospital, about their apartment, he asked her if she wanted to see it after work. She responded that she would like to. Marilyn had the car so they walked. When he got in the apartment he called Marilyn to find out just when she would be coming home, he was still a conniver but did not want her to walk in with Sandra there either. She told him that they were quite busy so would be late.

Walking with Sandra he showed her around the apartment letting all the dogs out to meet her and then outside for a few minutes. *(Again)* She was still in the kitchen when he returned, then followed her into the living room, the cat was brought out which she stroked for awhile, then put it back in the cage. They had found that since they were back the cat had taken to eating holes in woolen sweaters, perhaps revenge for leaving her in the park.

Something seemed to be holding Sandra back from leaving. She went to the bathroom, came back, and then stood there, sort of looking at him, she picked up a book. "So" he had said, "Oh yeh, lastly I've not showed you the bedroom, it is in here." he held the bedroom door open, she walked in with him behind her.

She stood beside the bed looking around as he came up behind her--put his arms around her, she didn't move so he brought his arms up to her breasts, fondling them. Since there was still no objection he turned her around, brought his mouth down on hers and it was a short step until they were on the bed, rolling around together like they were attached. He had kept kissing her while he moved his hands within her clothing--stripped off her bra and for a while sucked and squeezed her still magnificent breasts. It was not long before he had her dress moving up her legs as his hand had stroked the warm flesh. A quick rollover and he was divesting himself of his pants. She was naked before him, inviting him in with wide spread legs and the invitation was accepted, as he had sunk his hard penis into the slippery entrance designated for penises.

They copulated until he felt himself ejaculating inside her--not knowing whether she had a climax or not. It brought out guilt feelings, knowing as he did that Marilyn was still not happy. He did not think that this maneuver was going to make things better. It appeared that the roll on the bed was something that Sandra expected.

Sandra made her way out as he had held the door and thought about her, another unconscionable lover of sex, that made no demands and loved her dogs, was always pleasant but still had not been able to find happiness with her husbands. A few years later she had come to Grew's new place. She was married again. That next time when he had made a pass at her she politely declined, saying, "I have found someone who loves me for me, I'm not going to jeopardize things this time."

He gave her a ride to wherever she was going;--admiring her for the direction she had grown. Years later he saw her again, on her own but about to take on a new older husband for security. Later emails told him that too was not working out, but she had been successful showing her dogs. Further in the future when they had again connected, she told him that she had had twin girls. The girls had been adopted out but reconnected with her when they had grown up. Although she denied that they could possibly be Grew's, calculations from how old she said they were made him wonder. She never gave him the exact date of their birth and she never sent him pictures of them and for awhile he threw the numbers around in his head without satisfaction but it eventually passed from his mind.

Marilyn and Grew still had problems but were getting along pretty well. He never told her about Sandra. They were relatively happy in the now chosen environment. They had started taking in evening clipping by placing a perpetual ad in the Duncan Mills and Scarborough Mirror. For quite a while there were only a few dogs coming in but the ones they were getting were not only coming back but also recommending the service to their friends. There was the odd occasion where they got a wild screaming animal. At those times they would quickly tie a lead around the dog's muzzle to keep it quiet while they got the job done. It was time to find a better work place.

The number of night dogs had also been increasing to the point that they couldn't handle the business. Grew had the idea that a small place in an industrial area where they could live and would not bother neighbours, would be ideal. It was this type of place that he kept looking for and found an old house with a garage that was for sale on one acre of land on Duncan Mills Rd. two miles North of Steeles. He talked to the doctor about it for a kennel, wanting him to go in with them as a partner.

He also spoke to Dr. Gleason who said, "It is too far out in the country."

Dr. Relaishe did arrange a loan to be shared by him and a customer, for five thousand dollars. Marilyn and Grew had five thousand from the sale of the Goodwood property so in their usual adventurous spirit, went for the deal.

They bought the property for nineteen thousand dollars with five thousand dollars down. It was just in time because the landlord of the property over the pet shop had found out they were trimming dogs there and was doubling their rent,

Things were beginning to look up for the two of them. They got a kennel license from the town of Buttonwood that the previous owner had arranged. That man had been raising Chinchillas on the property, so a kennel license was not a problem. Besides there was no one around to complain. On one side was a company that moved industrial equipment, next to them was a wrecking yard, across the road were a gas station, a demolition company and a lumberyard. On the other side it was next to a ninety-acre farm.

It was the ideal place for a dog kennel and considered livable, for them that meant it would do--whatever it was. Without ever going in the house, Grew looked in the basement window, saw that there was no water covering the basement floor, looked in the kitchen and living room windows and did not find anything obviously wrong so the property was bought. The property was only sixty-six feet wide but six hundred and sixty feet deep. They knew there would be a lot of changes that they would have to make in the buildings.

A brother in law of Marilyn was a carpenter; another was an electrical engineer. They helped in the paneling of the living room. The kitchen was painted and the two bedrooms were wallpapered. The garage was converted to a kennel by building dog runs outside the back door. Grew's friend, Al Mitten, mixed most of the cement for these runs by hand.

Al Mitten was an unusual person that Grew had befriended at the dog shows. He was only about five foot nine, regarded then as somewhat of a joke by other dog people because of his unusual way of handling dogs. When Grew had spoken to him he recognized him as a diamond in the rough. Al had developed a complete understanding of the mental aspects of dogs. He had persisted in his efforts and had become a first class trainer, trained them for specific purposes, for the blind and specific guard work. Al by trade was a bricklayer, an expert in cement.

Another big run with a cement pad was placed at the back door of the house. This one was also done under the direction of Al Mitten. A relationship developed between them that saw a sharing of ideas and dogs for years--a lifetime friend. At Al suggestion a cement truck was brought in and he smoothed off the cement while Grew watched and learned. It was hard work but Grew was later able to apply the procedures in other cement work.

The place was brought into line within their finances. When the hydro people came, Marilyn talked them into putting an underground line into the kennel in their off time, done for a most reasonable cost. They had also put electrical fixtures with fluorescent lights into the basement so that the grooming could be done there.

Grew had then built holding kennels in the basement and the framework for a raised bathtub. He had also built a whole network of kennels along one wall of the garage, which became a kennel. Steel doors were ordered for some of these kennels to hold dogs that might be difficult. That was a good thing, other gates were made for the smaller kennels.

There were days and days of painting to be done. It was decided between the two of them that it was time for Marilyn to quit work first. The owner of the Poodle salon allowed her to drop down to a part time employment basis. This time when she was left at home alone her time was more productive. She met people who were a benefit to the business, she had the sign at the road changed. She designed, had printed flyers, cards and promotional material. She met some of the local business people and suggested to Grew that they join the Button Country Club, which he did not do, but she did. She also was in touch with local dog breeders in Markham and when one of the Buttonwood politicians wanted to move all dog kennels out of the township, this group of breeders formed the Markham Kennel Club that worked against this man's re election. She went to all the initial meetings.

They became part of the founding members of this group who hired a lawyer to fight the cause. The Markham Kennel Club, as a group campaigned vigourously for the candidate running against the one who proposed the anti kennel by law. Their candidate won and was later to become Mayor. Again a relationship was built that lasted for years, each time working for this candidate, until years later, he died.

The Markham Kennel Club also participated in parades and events going on in the community. As they continued as a group, eventually putting on annual dog shows, they always remembered to contribute part of the proceeds to community causes.

On a personal level it appeared that Marilyn and Grew were getting along pretty well. He couldn't remember too much conflict or mistrust. Their sexual relationship--if not dramatically great-- seemed to be on a level where each appeared satisfied, accepting of each other without mistrust. He sometimes recalled the incident with Sandra--wishing it had not been--wondering about his own promiscuity. He was aware of his own blame for the troubles they had been in.

There were some occasions that caused the old jealousy factor to arise. Gillian, a vivacious dark haired girl with a nice German Shepherd who had phoned for advice, Grew met at the animal hospital then gave her a ride to her home to see her dog. It was a nice dog. He believed that it could finish its Championship and made some suggestions. If given the opportunity he would probably have jumped into bed with her in a minute. Fortunately, he wasn't given the opportunity.

His friend Sid, came on the scene, he and Gillian went through a wild romance. However when Marilyn saw this girl, the old defenses went souring. Grew still felt he should be trusted defending his innocence with vigour, had done nothing but it was like she could read his mind. It wasn't fair. It was Gillian's friend, Sarena, who he later had an involvement with.

To defend his friendship with these two would probably have been better not bothering with. Unknown to him Marilyn was getting to know John Cooper, a local gentleman farmer who was in the early stages of breaking up with his wife. She had met him at the Button Country Club. John also had a son who was in the same kindergarten class as Charles. In this situation Marilyn would be looking for something to blame on Grew, who did not even know that John and her were friendly until much later.

Marilyn had finally learned that it was better not to talk about her acquaintances, or affairs. However as she became involved she would suspect Grew of the same. Perhaps she was psychic but her own wanderings might just have made her more perceptive.

Activities started occurring around the kennel. The grooming business was increasing, as was a certain amount of boarding. They were selling more dogs because of the proximity to a main road. After two years they had paid off the loan and made a lot of improvements. The lumberyard across the road, owned by Sam Rubinstein was co operative. His son Ralph had helped build an addition onto the kennel which Sam cleared the way for at the township permit offices. They never got the needed building permit but built the addition anyway.

Sam had a white German Shepherd, (It could have been part wolf) that they used to lock up in the lumberyard every night. He had been picked up at the pound. They called him Fritz. Grew first got involved with Fritz when Sam and Ralph decided that his nails should be cut. It appeared like a simple task to Grew who had done hundreds of dog nails through his time with the vets and his own business. But with both Sam and Ralph hanging on, he could not extend the front leg enough to get away from some of the longest teeth Grew had ever seen. When they put a lead around his mouth as a muzzle, it was the same thing. Fritz decided he was not going to have his nails cut. They never were, that anyone knew of.

CHAPTER 11
Dog Talk

There was a German Shepherd male that Grew liked when he saw it at the dog shows. A young man who worked up north at the nuclear plant owned it. Grew had agreed to show the dog for him when they had been living at the apartment. Rory was consistent with his protective German breeding; he was tough. While at the apartment this dog had given a slight bite to Charles, who learned with the experience not to maul every German Shepherd. It was not the first or last dog nip he was to get.

Around the time they had moved to the kennel, David arranged to have him bred at the Duncan Mills kennel to a nice looking female whose owner had also discovered Rory at the dog shows. Both David and Grew liked the bitch but weren't aware that the owner was uneducated about breeding dogs. After the breeding took place, the owner took his bitch home and tied her out on his front porch, his normal thing to do. Later when David saw the puppies he immediately called Grew to come and look at them, They both agreed they were not all German Shepherds. Years later with the advent of DNA the kennel club had enacted rules that there could be more than one father in a litter of puppies.

There was no question, half of the eight puppies looked like hounds. It was then that they found out about the back porch practice of the owner. She had obviously also been caught by a hound. David refused to sign the papers so the puppies were either given away or sold as pets.

A year later a person called Grew about a nine months old German Shepherd male that he was unable to deal with. He was afraid of the dog, which surprised Grew until he saw the animal. The man brought it out to the kennel and Grew could not believe that this dog would be so hard to handle at nine months. When the dog arrived the few people that were there, including David went out to the car to have a look. Grew had doubts that the owner would be able to hold him back or the leash would break because of the vicious display of the dog in the car. The snarls were that of a wild animal--terrifying.

As the owner brought him from the car, the dog was completely wild as it strained to come at Grew with teeth bared. A security lead with a strong choke chain was thrown to the man who was told to put it on the dog then bring it in the house. Grew stood on the arm of a chesterfield chair, slowly reached out his arm as he asked the man to hand him the end of the lead. The dog was held taught standing on his hind legs, snarling wildly as he tried to reach the newcomer holding the lead.

Grew pulled up on the lead sharply, holding the dog at arms length as he partly dragged, partly suspended in a hang, this wild thing, as he moved him out to the kennel. The dog was flung into a kennel at leash end, with the lead left on. Grew then agreed that he would give the man another German Shepherd puppy as soon as one was available as a replacement even though he had not sold him the dog.

It was one of Sarena's dogs that he used as a replacement, he had some sort of a deal with her, had been trying for some time to guide Sarena on a path to breeding better German Shepherds. She kept getting other advice though from Sid and the Henry's who had sold her a couple of dogs. She later imported a dog from Germany, thinking that it would be the answer, which it wasn't.

Sarena was one of those people, not too much younger than Grew, who were always a mystery. Her husband was a little English accountant, very quiet, hard to figure out. No one seemed to know where he worked except he always had a briefcase. Sarena never seemed to be too happy. She worked in the wholesale clothing industry as a salesperson and displayed her fashionable clothes on a well-formed shape in a most provocative way that made it look like she could be available. Grew never found the true Sarena.

The dog he took over from the man was named Rolf so they left him with the name. Some might wonder why Grew would take this unregisterable dog that was also unmanageable. It was because he had a job for him. Some time before, a company that was a mile south on Duncan Mills had approached him. It was called Brown Auto Bodies, they took basic truck bodies and converted them to be used for specific tasks They had a large yard, completely fenced, seven foot chain link around a building that would probably contain 200,000 sq feet. They had huge tires that they kept in the yard. Someone had cut through the fence and by a process of some sort of cutting tool, ruined a number of these tires.

Another associate of Grew, who he had met years before at Dr. Gleeson's, had made his living training dogs for several years. People were not quite sure whether John was genuine or not, he certainly obtained many training contracts for protection. John had gained notoriety years before when he had a group of Doberman Pinschers doing an act at the Sportsman Show. He had aroused the ire of dog lovers because he guided the dogs by snapping a whip. He was not hitting the dogs. The snap was similar to what eventually became a practice in dog training of using a clicker in conjunction with commands. John had been looking for a home for two older German Shepherds that had worked as protection dogs at one of his rich clients premises. One was solid black and was solid white. Grew and Paul Adams who sometimes worked on these projects with Grew had looked them over, deciding they looked formidable enough to put in the yard.

He soon found out that basically they were two nice dogs but animals that did not require expert handling so he placed the dogs in the yard with a couple of dog kennels he had come across and gave instructions to the foreman who was going to be the feeder. Until that man had the idea of how he was to care for the dogs, Grew had agreed that he would look after the dogs in the yard on weekends when the business was closed.

That summer, Brown Auto Bodies put a night crew to work in the shop. They had been warned about the guard dogs in the yard and not to go out there. It worked until someone forgot. It got hot and the doors were opened. It did not take long until the two dogs came wandering into the shop. The men shut down their machines and were successfully "treed", standing on lathes or whatever else looked high enough. The dogs didn't bark at anyone and in time wandered back outside.

At first the foreman wanted to know about the safety of his men. When he was assured that unless they provoked the dogs they would be safe, (they hardly had any teeth) the foreman and the company wanted the real thing. They wanted a man-eater. This is what Grew had found when the man delivered Rolf; he had found what they wanted, it was going to be money for the kennel with an ongoing contract.

The day after Grew had put Rolf in the kennel with a lead on he had wondered how he was going to get him out again. He went out to the kennel, looked through the steel bars, talked to Rolf for awhile, who was not barking that much. Grew tried to fish the lead through the bars while Rolf curiously looked at him. Rolf would not let him get it; he kept wheeling around just as Grew was about to hook it with a modified clothes hanger. He was surprised that Rolf hadn't eaten the lead.

It was time to act. Grew opened the door to the kennel; as Rolf rushed out he grabbed the lead. Rolf wasn't snarling then so Grew took him for a walk around the yard. It was like he had always been Grew's dog. They went through some heeling exercises that Rolf responded well too then he put him back in the kennel, this time without the lead and he was fed food. The way he went at it he acted like he had been starved for a week. The next time he had let him out inside the kennel Rolf came right to him, allowing the lead to be put back on. He was placed out in a run next to some of the kennel German Shepherds and right away accepted them as a nice part of life. Grew could see that this was one heck of a dog.

The dog was not large but a medium sized German Shepherd. There was obviously no hound in this dog. Grew also was aware of the proper structure of him. If he had had papers he could have been made into a great show dog, if he had ever been able to calm him down. Rolf was a rich black and tan, alert to a fault, with pronounced jaws. It was his look though, dominating as though there was nothing in this world too tough for him. All this was in a dog that was only nine months old. Grew determined that he would train him for Brown Auto Body. They wanted a tough one so he would give them one.

The next step was to train the dog some, he had to be trained not to take food through the fence, not an easy task. Rolf gobbled everything handed to him like a Piranha. At first he was handed meat through the fence that was spiked with hot pepper. Bang!

It disappeared and he was looking for more. Okay, next time he was given food tied to a set mousetrap. He didn't flinch a bit as the trap bar hit his nose. He just gave it a shake, and then took the meat off it.

This was going to be a problem, the dog continued to eat well and Grew thought he might respond to the mouse trap after he became better fed but it didn't happen. Using a rattrap finally completed the food refusal training. That did stop; thereafter he was considered successfully trained not to take food through the fence.

The dog turned out to be a most trainable animal and training was directed in specific obedience; it was coming along better than expected. Now the problem was to adjust him to the foreman. The first time he was handed to this man as Grew passed over the lead, Rolf got a piece of his pants. It scared him enough that Grew agreed for a certain price to put the dog in every night when they were finished work and take him out in the morning. There was another problem. Grew had been talking to the lawyer for The

Markham Kennel Club, who suggested he get Brown to sign a letter of responsibility; they refused and that was the end of that job.

Grew had spent a lot of time working with Rolf. He knew he couldn't put him in the Brown yard if their workers were going to open the building doors or even worse leave a gate open. That was why he demanded that they accept responsibility. Since they wouldn't he continued to work with him. Al Mitten, who had started to develop a good business of his own in protection work used to drop in at the kennel. He had taken an immediate liking to Rolf. In his English way (Al was an English former teddy boy) he called him Ralph. Perhaps the Rolf name was too German for him. In the trading off of dogs' process that Grew always seemed to lose at, since he had nothing for Rolf to do, he agreed to let Al have him. He couldn't remember ever getting anything for him but Al had helped him with a lot of cement work. Al had a small mini type car. Grew tied Rolf in the back seat on a very short lead so he would not be able to reach Al in the front seat. Al got in and by the time they reached Al's kennel Rolf had decided they should be friends

There were more stories about Rolf. About a year after Al had taken him over there was quite a fraternity of people working with dogs in a protective mode. Amongst the group were Hans Friesen. Someone who had connections to the provincial police had been asked to gather a group of these dogs with handlers to work with the police at a motorcycle rally. Their job was to stop the motorcycle gang from rescuing their buddies after the police had arrested them. The police would keep the arrested people in an area surrounded by the dogs. Grew recalled the plan as he wrote, he felt fortunate that it rained and the rally never came off.

The group of dog handlers was left standing around in the rain with their yellow raincoats shining with dripping rain. Someone started talking about the wild indomitable Rolf. Hans did not believe that any dog could be that difficult to make friends with. He was warned to stand back when Al brought Rolf out of his van on a lead, but Hans was one that seldom listened to warnings. He had even disregarded the advice of his doctor after he had a heart attack. Al

Mitten, who understood the concept never to ask the dog to back down from someone trying to make friends let the dog stand on a lead in front of him.

Hans approached the dog with arm extended. Rolf backed up a step which slackened the lead, Hans continued to move forward. There was a flash of movement towards Hans's arm. Someone then said, almost in a laughing manner, "Hans, take a look at the sleeve of your raincoat."

There was a U shaped piece out of the bottom of the sleeve of his yellow raincoat. Hans looked down at his sleeve. He hadn't even felt it go. Al had pulled Rolf back. Hans's expression went with his comment, "Jesus Christ, no one should have a dog like that."

The rest of the party laughed, Hans deserved bringing down a bit. It had been done so quickly that they had only seen the missing piece. No one seemed to actually see it disappear. A funny thing happened when Al put the dog back in his car. Al too was in a yellow raincoat and when he got in the car himself, Rolf started to go after him. You could tell Al was proud of his dog; they became a good team.

There were a lot of people who had taken a real interest in Rolf. People like Paul Adams who was involved in dog training and protection work as well as being part of the club demonstration team, had watched with interest as the story evolved. Paul had bought his second dog off Grew. Paul's new dog was probably endowed with all the right structure but was difficult to break from growling at judges. He did turn out to be a real good producer of protection dogs and was resold to a guard dog company. Paul, through his association with Grew ordered a German dog with complete German training degrees. As the two of them met the dog at the airport they expected to run into trouble getting him out of the portable kennel but to their surprise he was friendly in the kennel, being only concerned about getting out; he walked out of the kennel wagging his tail.

Around the same time, Paul Adams showed up at the Barrie dog show in the company of a gorgeous dark haired young lady. She was slim and tall with big brown eyes. Was she native? Right away Grew was aware of her sensual lips not being able to take his eye from her. Her name was Donna. Grew couldn't remember her last name but would never forget the graceful walk, the rolling cheeks behind as she walked away. Paul, had been on the outs with his wife, Mona.

Donna, who had a dog of her own, was helping him show his dogs. She had been living with her mother--had been involved with another man who she had had a child with. Grew also could not remember what happened to that child but it was not with her. Both she and her mother worked at General Motors on the assembly line. When he saw her later he realized she was not one to dress up. She looked like one more concerned with dogs than fashion.

Al, and brother John from England, who had come to help were now using Rolf at a private fishing club. They had taken on the job some time earlier. Their assignment was to patrol the area with dogs to keep the poachers away. One day Al and Rolf came across a big man who when told to get moving said, "Fuck Off"

When Al threatened the man with the dog, the guy produced a big stick and said, "Yeh! Go ahead let him go, see how he likes this."

Al reached down and unsnapped the lead. The dog was gone. Before the man was able to get one swing in, Rolf had gone straight for the man's testicles and the next instant had him on the ground with the man screaming in pain. He spent time in the hospital and was charged with trespassing. Rolf's reputation grew from there.

Al and John Mitten had their kennel north of Orangeville. He had also opened a pet shop. This led to him having all sorts of animals. Marilyn would listen intently as he told of his snakes and rats. Al was always a welcome guest when he would drop by to tell his own kennel stories, telling how the rat would chew at the snake unless the snake was hungry. Then the snake would eat the rat. He also had birds, turtles and fish, producing more stories.

The Mittens were doing very well as they expanded their security business. They also provided obedience classes at Rochdale College in downtown Toronto that was supposed to have been built as a hostel for youths in college. It turned out as a drug center for hippies who bombarded police with bottles and garbage from upper floors as they arrived on drug raids. Al was teaching obedience classes in the underground garage for the many dog owners in the building. This progressed to him having association with a Peter Smart as they created an in house security force for Rochdale, with dogs. These security people were a rough bunch, some were members of motorcycle gangs and others that in some way were connected to the dope dealing industry. Apparently the dog training was run on a straight business arrangement and from everything heard about it, people figured it was beneficial to all concerned. There was a connection to this training group that affected Grew.

Al was married had several sons and a little girl in his family. Like most people who make their lives with dogs, the boys did not seem to follow in the interest but were conscripted to help while they grew up. Al was close to his boys though and ran a boxing club for them and other boys around Orangeville. Later, Grew moved other dogs to the Mitten brothers; Al was a master at figuring out the rebels. Al eventually separated from his brother and moved up North, where he started all over again. Years later when most people would be retired Al was still training dogs, studying animal behaviour and from time to time having long distance phone calls with Grew. Although they worked with dogs in different ways there was always that connection that caused them to support each other.

CHAPTER 12
Dealing with Cancer

One summer Marilyn complained of a pain in her chest. Grew had just quit at the animal hospital because they had too much work to do at the kennel. They had also just decided to pay the Ontario Health Plan premium to cover medical expenses. They knew that if they didn't join up, if anything happened to either one of them they would never be able to pay. It is ironic that they at the same time did not invest in a life insurance policy for them both.

Marilyn went to see Dr. Gram about a small lump in her breast who suggested an X Ray. It was all paid for by OHIP (Ontario Health Insurance Plan). When the X Ray came back the doctors said they should do a biopsy. This caught both of them off guard but they were thinking it would be a simple procedure. Almost as a formality the doctor put a piece of paper in front of Marilyn to sign. It was a paper authorizing them to do whatever necessary if they found that the tumor was malignant. Marilyn and Grew looked at each other; both shrugged and she signed.

Quite a while later, where Grew had been waiting outside the operating room, Dr. Gram came out to explain. The growth had been malignant so they had done a complete mastectomy, removing one breast. Grew was shocked at the news but not half as much as was Marilyn when they told her. She had nearly died during the operation so it was some time before they even told her what had happened.

When Grew saw her she was quiet, not wanting to even talk to him. He could see she had been crying. As he tried to console her she talked of the butchery they had done to her. She had been totally devastated, even in her state of tranquilization.

The doctor talked to Grew about fitting her with a plastic bag full of liquid that went within the bra that would make her look good. The doctors worried about how he was going to adapt to what she had become but Grew never ever regarded that as a problem. Recalling the mess of bunched up skin taking the place of a breast, he did adjust to the disfiguration as well as anyone could but did find the mess distracting. Marilyn had been so proud of her breasts, regarding them as her most attractive feature.

She was not doing well at first but then, like a miracle her strength started to come back. Within a month she was back working with Grew at the kennel, then returned to doing part time work for the poodle salon. At that time there was a determination to beat the thing. People were supportive, welcoming her back to the world of the living. The follow up chemotherapy was something extremely difficult for any of them to handle. Marilyn was the one that had to take what it did to her, leaving her limp and depressed. Charles and Grew did what they could to adjust to this new person, their mom and husband that they were living with.

To ad to the concern, Dr. Gram called Grew in to talk with him a few months after the operation. He spelled out for him just what was being dealt with and that the life expectancy in these cases was only two years. What a shock that was. Grew didn't know what to do. He just felt like running but where to?

To add to the concern, Dr.Gram did not want Marilyn told that she would soon die. Grew wondered why and continued to wonder why, even long after the whole matter was over? Why would they tell him then tell him not to tell her? Imagine him going home, facing Marilyn, who said, "What did Dr. Gram say?"

"He just told me about the seriousness of the operation that you just went through. He told me it was Cancer, how they are going to treat it and wanted me to know that it was going to be difficult; told me that you were going to need a lot of support from me"

Grew hugged her as he held her but did not tell her about the prognosis. It was a bit out of character at the time for Grew to be hugging her. She might have been a bit suspicious about that. In Grew's heart he felt that this woman might just be strong enough to make it through. It wasn't about strength though.

They took it from there, day by day. Other people knew what the expectancy was but it was seldom spoken of. Grew's reaction was such that he really did not know whether he could get through it but had to try. They were all going to have to be tough. He felt sorry for himself, would like to have told her what was ahead, wanted to prepare his son but respected the orders of the doctors. It was to come up again and again.

During a session when Marilyn was back in the hospital, he was at a training session with the German Shepherd group. When it was finished for some reason or other Sarena kissed him on the lips. Maybe she felt sorry for him. It was warm and with feeling, a shock catching him by surprise. He didn't want to let go. It was at a time of extreme vulnerability towards affection. For some reason or another she had this impression that he was innocent but perhaps she knew as did everyone else what was coming up. Grew wasn't innocent but the kiss certainly stirred his desire. It was probably an innocent jester of support but became more.

It was the beginning of a relationship that went on and on with her over the following two years. He became her advisor with the dogs, advice that she usually did not follow, would be lover that never quite made it and friend through her various worries. She was a person wanting to be something, always a lonely person, had money to invest in dogs, never could learn the difference between what a dog should be and what it was. She was so quiet about her personal life, never complaining about her life with her husband who was typically less involved with the dogs. A person who had his own agenda whatever that was, almost inviting whomever to share his wife in order that he didn't have to spend time with the dogs.

Physically she was a very attractive woman that smoked and the wrinkles from it showed in her face but the rest of her body was built like that of a movie star Her body and the way she carried it were exciting.

Grew found it difficult to comprehend her conception of dogs. She was too kind to them. They were her kids that she hadn't had. To her it was inconceivable that a dog should not be kept because it was not worthy to carry on breeding with. She had paid people like Sid to finish the Championships on dogs not deserving then do a mind shift, as it was realized the championship title was an empty prize if other breeders did not accept the value. It was something that Grew had come to realize at an early stage of his dog involvement that breeding for titles rather than using a deeper knowledge of the qualities and faults of animals was a formula for breeding disasters. Probably that concept was responsible, more than anything, for the huge turnover of dog breeders.

These theories were the topic of discussion on many occasions as Grew rode with her to many dog shows. There was one show where they had gone together where he had been talking to another woman acquaintance about dogs. Suddenly that woman's new boyfriend took exception to him, attacking him with blows as he tried to dodge out of the way. Before the confrontation could get worse, a few friends stepped between and the attacker was whisked away.

Soon after, Sarena and Grew drove off in his Volkswagen bus. They stopped along the road, first to let the dogs out then they got into a necking session, from a kiss to where they became quite intimate. She let him fondle her breasts but would not let him get his hands on or in her, down below. From previous experience he had learned with her it had to be done a different way, sort of no hands below the belt. She would let him lay on her, kiss her mouth and breasts almost to orgasm but it was near impossible to get hands into her.

She was different about his penis. He couldn't determine whether she was just playing with him or was actually willing to have sex. She didn't want him to get his hands near her vagina but would freely work on his penis, jerking it until he would lose control, squirting on her legs, just as he was trying to stuff it inside her. They would both feel bad but with the previous conflict back at the show, he was already upset, not exactly the best time to be wrapped up in a sexual event. His home situation only added to the mental anguish--feeling additional pressure and not without guilt for what he was doing.

Meeting Sarena became a game after she had quit her job, preferring to stay home with her dogs. Her husband was usually out doing whatever he did so it was not uncommon for Grew to stop by her house "for coffee" when he was doing dog pickups or deliveries in the neighborhood. He found that most of the stopovers were short lived, either because of her schedule or his and he also found out that the best chance for results with her were when both of them had been drinking liquor, then he had to be careful to only have a bit because he was driving. She always seemed to have it on hand. Was she trying to seduce him?

One time as he was on his way out the door. She had on a flaring skirt. Grew kissed her at the door with a "Gotta Go".

She seemed particularly passionate that day but had stopped him when he had wanted to go beyond kissing and rubbing her inner leg right up to "you know where." As expected he was stopped there.

She kissed him at the door. This kiss went on and on. Soon he was pulling her skirt up her leg as they stood, his hand stroking the smooth skin on her leg, His hand reached her panties, pulled down on the cloth as they continued to kiss. She pulled them back up as their tongues pushed and sucked. His other hand was in her blouse, passionately pulling and squeezing her nipples, he could feel them hardening. He pulled down again on her panties, tried to get his hand between her legs as he backed her to the couch. They were still standing together.

This time he got his hard erection out, felt her take hold of it. She was fondling it, pushing the skin back and forth. Had she forgotten? Her panties slipped off her ankles as they continued to kiss. She was working his penis as she fell to the couch with her legs spread and he came right along with her, on top.

This was going to be it, he had her on the couch, was between her legs, directing his penis towards the pubic area, felt the slippery walls of her start to surround the knob. It was going to be tight. As he started to push he felt the pumping start within him. What was it with this woman? What was it with him? He barely pushed it in her when he ejaculated. She had to feel it going in.

She looked at him, "What is the matter? Why are you stopping?"

He looked at her feeling embarrassed, "Sarena, I'm sorry, that's it, I've gone. I'm sorry I couldn't hold it back."

He was disappointed at the way it had gone with her and sure she was too but he was to learn of the effects on him when he was in emotional turmoil. His opportunities with her became less and less after that, his own life at home was becoming too hectic. The pressure was building as day after day he continued to run the business. As the sickness in Marilyn continued, getting worse he was realizing himself that it was only a question of time. How and when was he going to tell Charles? The whole kennel business was falling more and more on his hands. He had back pain he couldn't explain as he made regular visits to the chiropractor.

Marilyn had been in for a second operation. This time they took the other breast off and both glands from beneath her arms. It was quite a while before she got out of the hospital. So amongst everything else on his schedule, he put nightly hospital visits.

For some time after this operation it was touch and go whether she would make it or it would be the end. They didn't know what would happen as each time they took her back they would try something else; they seemed to be guessing.

Grew was in a state of constant tension. When Marilyn would get out of the hospital or each time she went into one of her spells, almost running around like a confused animal or could not get out of bed, He realized that the authorities didn't know what to do or how each new experiment would work out. They just didn't seem to know. Grew didn't know what to do either. No one was telling him. He had back pain and was going to the chiropractor for treatments, that did not help.

Grew had to get more help at home, so even before the second operation they hired or at least gave room and board to the first of the unmarried pregnant girls. They became a story in their own right but their contribution did help the Tuckett's through the battle. There was Aile who came when Marilyn had been at home a lot, it was probably in the first year of the Cancer fight. Aile was about seventeen, blond, cute and pregnant.

Paul Adams enjoyed flirting with her. Aile kept close to Marilyn though, was not too involved with the dogs but was a big help in keeping the housework done. She was even a pretty good cook. She had come from somewhere on the Niagara Peninsula. Guess she had her baby.

Then came Karen, who was dark haired with a nice shape in spite of her pregnancy. She always wore dark clothing, was at the kennel for quite a while when Marilyn was in the hospital, enjoyed playing with the German Shepherd puppies which was good for them. She also learned about feeding dogs and a bit of training. Paul Adams came around quite frequently when she was there, becoming her self appointed tutor. He had a great gift of the gab and she was very receptive.

Karen's tenure was cut short when one evening with Paul and Grew giving her some of the basic ideas behind training dogs, with her on the end of a lead, a German Shepherd on the other, she started having pains. They were not sure how far along she was in her pregnancy at that time but the boys were beginning to think they were going to get some practice in baby delivering. They made a few phone calls then whisked her off to the hospital. She did have the baby so did not return.

The next one to arrive was Arlene. She was not pregnant that they knew off. Marilyn was going though a period of being home while Arlene was there. Arlene was a flaming red head from Nova Scotia. Paul took quite an interest in her to the extent that on her days off she spent that time at the Adams place. Marilyn and Grew were beginning to think that she had decided to live there instead of with them. She was not reliable there either. She borrowed Paul's car and disappeared. Later he got a call that she had decided to return to Nova Scotia, still driving his car. Paul had to head east in order to retrieve his car. After Arlene they decided that they did not need a house girl,

Marilyn was home. They felt they'd be better suited with kennel help. Pat Snow, married, English, a flirt with Grew and outspoken was hired in a hurry when Marilyn returned to the hospital. During the days, she did do the kennel work well but also spent time with Grew, as they chased each other around the house.

Marilyn came home and said in no uncertain terms, "Don't like her, too much to say and I don't trust her, get rid of her."

Grew talked to Pat and she agreed that it would probably be better if she didn't stay around if it was only going to cause more trouble. Grew had to admit she was fun but it would not work. He started looking again for someone else.

Marilyn, Charles and Grew did have some good times. When she was on the up side they would all go together to dog shows or work with dogs together. She could no longer do the dog walks but there were pictures of her posing the dogs. At that time she would run around the lawn a couple of times with the dogs, pose them and then have to sit down. She would take the phone and deal with most of the business things that had to be done. He kept wondering how he would ever get along without her; he wanted to discuss the future but how could he, without telling her what the doctors had said? Her sisters often came around and although they were never quite sure how things were going they were a support to her.

She was also quite involved with the Markham Kennel Club, helping a lot in the first year of her illness. When the club put on a walk, she walked with a corgi for 10 kg as part of a community walk. Other members of the club also walked with dogs. Marilyn would stop with the ladies she was walking with every once in awhile and she would rest but she was determined to keep going; she did finish.

There were times when she went off on her own. Sometime later Grew felt that she was probably seeing John from the golf country club--so busy that he didn't even bother about it. She never got around to telling him about that one.

The fluorescent lights over the grooming tables that the hydro boys had done where working out swell, He had improved on the wiring on his own; The tub setup was also okay, bringing it to table height at the edge of the tub. The tub drained into a sump hole where a sump pump pumped the water out the basement window to a ditch, then on to another ditch on the side of the road, environmentally poor.

Environmental things were not stressed in those days 1960's and 70's. Frequently the sump pump would clog up with dog hair, the sump hole would fill up, flood the basement and the system would have to be unplugged. There were times when Grew had to dig out the ditch, the hundred feet to the road. It was the grooming business that pretty well carried the kennel. Grew spent a good part of most days working on dogs that he had picked up from customers all over the east end of the city. The big part of the concept of their business was pick up and deliver. The customer would never see the dogs being groomed, better for control and efficiency.

There was really no discomfort for the dogs other than being subjected to brushing out. They were not always in good shape or willing participants, especially when there was owner neglect.

During this time when all these dogs were waiting to be groomed and Marilyn would be helping him get the dogs ready, he could see the torture that it was to her. Neither one of them often spoke. They just worked away but his admiration for her was so immense as he would look over and see the pain of her.

Then she would get to a certain level of the work being done and she would quietly say, "I'm going up stairs for a while."

Grew would answer, "Okay, go and get some rest, I'm okay here, it's not too bad now. Thanks for coming down, I know you're tired, see you in a while." and then she'd be gone, slowly up the stairs.

She would be back trying to help him the next day and they would go through the same thing again. They got through the Christmas rush but she was still spending a lot of time in bed. Grew realized that as much as anything, it was her that helped him get through her dying.

One time when she was in the bathroom a long time, he had called up from the basement, asking if she was all right. Finally she came out with a pill bottle in her hand, had been trying to be sick and told him that she had taken the pills in the bottle and thought she had taken them a second time, too many so she was trying to be sick. The bottle was empty. She was sort of staggery so Grew called the doctor who asked him to bring her up. Half an hour later they were at Dr. Gram's office.

After awhile the doctor came out and told Grew that she was all right. Then he asked Grew if he thought that she had tried to kill herself with the pills. Grew had not even thought of the possibility but when he considered it he thought it could be and then maybe she got scared or decided she was not yet ready to die.

Grew asked the doctor again if he could tell his wife the score, but he said, "If she wants to know she will ask".

Then the doctor told him that they wanted to do another operation on her; wanted to remove the pituitary glands. She was willing so it was arranged. They did the operation but after the operation she became totally disoriented. Nobody seemed to know what they were doing. Marilyn had helped so much through Christmas but with difficulties, they knew that they had to get help again. Her illness had become worse and by the spring she was spending most of her time resting but still kept answering the phone and door.

The next girl Grew hired, was an American girl who lasted two days, she quit on the second. She had to deal with a mongrel Shepherd that had put front feet on her shoulders and growled, "Who do you think you are telling what to do?"

That was enough, she came into the house and said, "Mr. Tuckett, I am afraid of that dog, I'm sorry but I won't be able to work for you." She was nice but Grew didn't try to stop her. Without further ado she had left.

Grew shrugged and kept working. It was in the spring when Marilyn had called down that there was another girl there to apply for the job as his assistant. Amanda Cook came down the stairs. She had long blond hair, fair complexion, almost freckled, sort of a dopey look to her blue eyes that appeared half closed. She was in blue jeans and loose shirt. She looked trim enough but he thought that she was not attractive enough that Marilyn would worry about her. "*Great, no makeup.*"

As Grew had looked at Amanda, very astute at recognizing attractiveness that was on the surface hidden, he smiled to himself. They had gotten rid of one woman that he was having too much fun with while Marilyn was in the hospital. That one didn't have enough sense to cool it. Amanda was twenty-one years old. Grew was thirty-eight. He thought this one might pass Marilyn's inspection but he also was aware of the beauty beneath. For a while they talked and she told him about working with horses but she was not too familiar with dogs. She seemed quite friendly and in spite of the spaced out appearance of her he had the impression there was intelligence there too.

He asked her if she thought she would be capable of going out to the kennel, taking each dog out of its inside kennel and putting it in an outside run. Was it the horse thing that had made him believe that she could? She thought that she could do it so he told her to be sure and close the door to the kennel building before doing anything but "Go ahead and do it, it'll be a big help to me."

He continued to work at trimming the dog he was working on. Ten minutes later Amanda returned. He asked, "Are they all outside now?"

She looked at him in a little bit questioning way, answered slowly. "Yes, that's what you told me to do, wasn't it?"

"Yeh that's okay. Did any of them give you any trouble?"

"No, I just put each one on a lead and led them outside one at a time, put each one in a run, took off the lead and shut them in".

He looked down at his trimming job as he asked, "Was the Shepherd cross all right?"

She spoke confidently, "He acted okay, didn't seem to mind me putting the lead on him, came right away".

Secretly he was elated, *she could handle the tough one*. "Did you talk to Marilyn upstairs when you came in.?"

"Yes, she sent me down, she said she wasn't feeling too well, but that if I was okay with you then I was okay with her." Then Amanda gave a cute sort of lifted smile at the last part of her statement.

"I've told you what the pay is, do you want to work for us?"

"Shuure". She extended her response, smiled some more with glowing white teeth. Grew hopped upstairs, Amanda heard mumbling and then he was back

"Okay, I've checked with my wife, she doesn't have a problem with you. You're hired, I've told you my wife is sick and won't be able to help us much but she knows all about dogs. She thinks she will get along with you. I'm sure she will help you as much as possible too, especially if you need to know something, you know what I mean, prices, breeds of dogs, that stuff".

Amanda started the next day. She told Grew some time later that she had been smoking pot and necking with a guy who lived in her building just before she had come to apply for the job. She was a little surprised that she got it, perhaps if she had been less dopey she wouldn't have wanted the job. The dope probably settled her so much that she wouldn't have noticed the dog growling at her.

Before leaving she went up to the bedroom and visited with Marilyn for a while. Grew was so impressed that she did that. But it wasn't to impress anyone, it almost became a habit of hers to check with Marilyn. Grew felt it was a sincere matter of caring for her. It meant a lot to Marilyn; they had a lot in common.

For the following several months, Amanda came to work early in the morning, let the dogs out, cleaned the kennels, fed them, cleaned the runs, then came in and helped Grew wash and groom dogs that he had picked up while she had been looking after the kennel. When she had finished the work before Grew got back, she would make tea for her and Marilyn and they would sit and talk. It was not uncommon for Grew to get home and find the two of them laughing about something.

They did not usually groom dogs on Saturday and Sunday so she got those days off. Grew looked after the dogs himself on weekends. Sometimes he would groom a dog or so but on those days people would have to bring them in. It would have been nice for them just to stop working but they couldn't afford to.

Paul, when he knew what the situation was had said, "You should just pack up and go somewhere, just the three of you." The likes of Amanda made the situation more bearable. Paul and his wife Mona were also an incredible help. There was nothing that they wouldn't do. They had this little group of support people that, looking back, were so evident. Right up front was Dick Edwards.

While Amanda and Grew would be working on the dogs, with him roughing out while she washed, or her blowing the dogs dry while he worked at finishing, her and Grew would talk. As she learned he would be telling her about what it was they were trying to achieve as he shaped each dog to emphasize its good points, while minimizing its faults. They also talked about life and the world. She had this funny way of looking at a map upside down and would say "Up south and down north". In a way she was a strange and individual girl.

Even at that early stage he could see that in some form or other she had great potential to work with him in the dog business. He had accepted that Marilyn was not going to get better in the long run. Marilyn also accepted that in her state, she couldn't help so reluctantly knew he had to train someone. They agreed that Amanda was as good a prospect as they could hope to find or at that point did she really care. Tactfully he was preparing for life after Marilyn's death.

Amanda listened well, asking questions as she worked along. He recognized quickly that she was a good worker and had an excellent way of handling animals. The animals related to her, never did he ever have to worry about the cleaning either. The kennels were cleaned every day, as were the runs. Any dog that got dirty would be brought in and cleaned up right away. She also washed dogs with care, getting them real clean without getting soap in the eyes. It would appear that she had the same horse training as Marilyn.

She had told Grew in the beginning that she had a horse. Every evening she would drive her Volkswagen up to the barn where the horse was kept and there she would work with him for a few hours.

She talked to Grew about how she was trying to train the horse to go over the jumps, make the moves that he was supposed to and how he was doing. She talked about left and right leads, driving into the bit, controlled gaits and about the young lady who was the star of dressage. Amanda looked at this person as a snob, loving any excuse to laugh at anything, either personal or professional that could be construed as Christalot's "fau pas". But there was no doubt she respected the ability of this girl.

Grew listened with interest as she spoke, often asking questions. It took his mind off the state that his wife was in. He knew she was going to die. It was a change to go from dog talk to talk of Amanda's escapades and her horse talk.

Marilyn went back in the hospital. When Grew had time to worry--which he did often in silence--he wondered how he was going to look after this little six-year-old boy after Marilyn was gone, wondered how he himself was going to take it when the boy's mother died and he wondered how much he should tell Charles before hand to prepare him for the loss.

One thing he did do was when an animal died, whether it was a puppy, a cat or whatever he would dig a hole and have a funeral. While he placed the dead animal in the hole Charles and he would stand beside the little grave with Grew leading him in a prayer for the dead animal. Charles was getting a perspective on death. Questions were asked and answered.

Grew spent so much of his time alone thinking, feeling sorry for himself and asking why this should happen to them. It was a selfish attitude but these were his thoughts when he would get off on his own. Should he have taken the chance to go on his own when they had been separated, was that his chance to get away? Was their life together worth it after they had got back together? Years later he was ashamed of even questioning, it was his panic. It had been more than worth it. The life experience with her was a joy. Another aspect was the raising of this little boy, the trials, the challenges, and the wonders at what to do, the pleasures, the rewards as Charles went on to the next generation.

Sometimes Amanda would ask if she could take the boy to the barn with her. Grew talked to Marilyn who was delighted to have him go, sorry that she could not go with them. Grew didn't think that she ever did get to go. Charles was allowed to go with Amanda though; he really enjoyed the diversion who he had become pretty close friends with. But Charles never really took to horse riding. Was it because of his mother putting him back on the pony when he was two years old? Not likely, he learned to take the knocks as he grew up, later through hockey.

Amanda had a boyfriend that used to pick her up quite often after work, a local farm boy who walked along with bouncing strides. Grew had not been too impressed with this guy, he seemed dull and talked little. Since his name was Bob, Grew referred to him as Bob along. This was a bit embarrassing one day while Bob was waiting for Amanda in the front room; Charles approached him and said, "My dad calls you Bob along". Grew did not have to see him too often, so it was not a big problem.

Spring turned to summer, Marilyn had good days and bad, in the hospital and out. Amanda and Grew continued to work at grooming the dogs and looking after the kennels. She was learning fast about grooming, an enjoyable person to work with. They laughed often as she told of her past adventures with men. These stories later got into more detail. For then, they enjoyed the simpler stories. Marilyn accepted Amanda without any signs of jealousy. Marilyn and Grew had still been having sex; she seemed satisfied. For him it was like having it with different people.

When she was overweight it was one thing. Then she went on her diet and as she lost the weight she became an active, aggressive sex partner as long as she could, but then she became so she had to stop for breath.

A litter of German Shepherds was born and Amanda decided she wanted one of the puppies. Grew was not in favour of it but really had no choice since she wanted to buy it. He didn't feel it was the best litter that he would be having. Arno was the father and a bitch that was tough German breeding was the mother. Dick and Barb Edwards also took a puppy from this litter. Theirs was considered the pick but Amanda's turned out to be better for breeding.

It got so he could not even deliver the dogs while leaving Marilyn alone. They had been going through a series of girls that were hired to help with the housework. At that time Amanda was the only one working and she went home at five o'clock.

In late August Marilyn was back in the hospital and could not get out of bed; they were afraid that her bones would break. Grew was relieved, his utmost fear had been to wake up and find her dead beside him, selfish but born of a fear. Even with deliveries he was still able to get to the hospital, Often Amanda would stay with Charles. In September, he spent the evenings with Marilyn in hospital whenever possible. Marilyn was very weak then. When Charles had spoken to her on his visit in hospital, he had asked her if she was going to die. Grew had been trying to prepare him for what he, by now knew would happen but he was not prepared for the question.

It upset him more than Marilyn. She hardly responded as Grew stopped him saying, "Charles, don't talk like that. I'm sorry he shouldn't ask that" Charles said he was sorry and gave her a hug. She hardly responded.

The next evening Grew quietly sat by her bed, alone with her. She too was quiet but did speak with some difficulty. The morphine was looking after the pain if there was any. When he left late in the evening he gave her his customary hug and kiss; he wondered if she even recognized what he was doing. He didn't want to see her die. Life for her had become a fuzzy existence from one day to the next.

In the morning he got the call from the hospital. It was early; he suspected the worst. They told him she had died.

Grew took Charles to the hospital with him. There they ran into a confrontation with the hospital staff. This little boy was insisting that he be allowed to see his dead mother; he had been told she was dead so wanted to see for himself. The staff and a hospital doctor spent half an hour trying to convince Grew that he should wait until they had fixed her up but Charles was insistent.

He continued to insist on his son's behalf until Doctor Gram said, "If you insist, they can't stop you." They had had enough of covering up. The torment of not telling her had caused so much stress for all of them.

Grew said firmly, "Thank you Dr. Gram, I do insist."

Six-year-old Charles stood beside the table where his dead mother lay. She was pale and lifeless. Charles had seen dead animals before so was not surprised at what he saw. Grew stood back, watching as this little kid took in what he was seeing, quietly inspecting every detail of her, almost expecting her to wake up but knowing she would not. Grew always believed that it was the right thing to do. He was relieved that it was finally over but wondered about tomorrow, the next day without this pillar beside him; they had been through so much together.

On the way home the two of them solemnly cried. There were no questions, no blaming God, luck or whatever. It was just a sorrowful accepting by the two of them of what had happened--their loss. When Charles and he got back from the hospital they were both in tears. Amanda looked like she was in shock too.

Some inner strength came from Grew and he said to Amanda, "Let's get the dogs done, I'll make some phone calls, cancel all the grooming for today, then we'll see about arranging a funeral."

Amanda looked even more shocked as she looked at him. Her big blue eyes seemed bigger. Things had soon been underway, getting onto the next phase in life.

His friend Dick Edwards, a pillar of support, arrived. He and Grew, who was in a daze, went about arranging the funeral. Dick had been preparing when this was to come--for his role. Within a couple of days the funeral was held in Markham. Grew would always remember standing at graveside with Charles in a way like the funerals they had held for the animals. This was different, the little boy cried and did not want to let her go. His crying was real, knowing she was going. The sorrow was there as they both cried goodbye.

Then it was over, Grew was picking up the pieces of life, and his new commitment was to raise this little boy to adulthood, until he too was ready to be turned out in the world. As time went by he always reminded himself of this pledge.

Grew was back grooming almost immediately, albeit in a daze for a while. Charles and he cried a lot as they delivered dogs together, in those early days, with Grew singing the Lord's Prayer. When Charles showed an interest in his songs he started singing folk songs as they drove along like "Bury me Out on The Prairie", and cowboy songs learned from his youth on guest and cattle ranches, Charles often between his legs, steering the van.

Grew had been sorry for the way things had worked out, sorry for himself, sorry for his son Down deep he knew it was better that she had finally died. Thinking about his life with Marilyn he recognized it as in a sense different from what might have been expected. It had been living to a strange plan. The rest of their lives this father and son were waiting to happen. They became very close as they rode together delivering dogs and then beyond. For him the steps of the plan continued in a bizarre fashion and no doubt it was the way it was meant to be.

Writing about the last days of Marilyn, very much later in the future the tears rolled down his face. He wondered why it had been programmed that way as he thought about his idea that every step we make is programmed, each person we meet being all a part of some plan. Why was it that he had been chosen to carry on and raise her little boy? Did he do a satisfactory job? People can only do the best that they can as they accept the responsibility and make the commitment, watching and being part of his growing up. Life seemed to go from one challenge to another.

CHAPTER 13

A New Beginning, New Loves

Charles had frequently asked Grew to sing for his friends, his many versed songs. Sometimes even Amanda would come with them on the deliveries, singing along with them. While they were working, Grew would go up to the kitchen, mix a conglomeration of hamburger, rice and vegetables, nutritionally sound, ready to eat before they left. After eating, they would all go along together, acting happy as they went. The laid back atmosphere took away from the grief and long hours worked. Almost at once Grew's bad back had disappeared.

One time while Grew and Charles were alone they had stopped at a donut shop, Grew got out of the truck first and went in. Charles came in a minute later. Then someone came in looking for the owner of the van in the middle of Sheppard Ave. Charles had released the park gear, throwing it into neutral. He was told that it was not the thing to do but was not necessary to get into an extended chewing out. It became their way.

By that time they had hired another housekeeper. They found a young divorcee with a son. Let's call her Cindy, willing to do anything at first. It meant that when they were late getting the dogs ready she would be there to look after Charles if he didn't go with him. But they became too friendly too fast, partly because of Amanda who pushed it and the girl ended up leaving.

Perhaps it was still early for Cindy to become involved with anyone, she had just gone through a traumatic time with her ex husband. Grew took her out a couple of times though while Amanda looked after the kids. Amanda also got a couple of wrestling matches going on the kitchen floor between all three of them, getting it started then getting herself out. Sometimes Amanda would get as involved as Cindy and Grew as they sprayed and threw whipped cream with other gooey food at each other. Grew noted the excitement in Amanda's face, she loved being on the edge, to be a part of the fun. Maybe it was part of her plan to get him over the death of Marilyn. If so he never caught on to it but did enjoy the activity.

A misunderstanding developed between Cindy and Grew as to where their relationship stood. It ended with a kicking open of her door in the middle of the night and near seduction. Cindy had given the impression early that there could be something happen between them. Probably Grew went too fast and too far for her. As it was, other friends were beginning to resent her taking over his life, cutting them out of their friendship with Grew. She tried to lock him out of her room when she had a change of heart. When the smoke cleared, she quit.

Amanda didn't even seem surprised or disappointed at the way it happened. He wondered if she too had been beginning to resent Cindy. Work went on like nothing had happened except for a while they then missed their roll on the floor, clothes tearing, food fights and then Donna started coming around when there was no Cindy there.

She had stayed away because of Cindy but said she only wanted to be friends. Between Donna and her mother their dog ownership was down to one dog. This was the same Donna he had met through Paul Adams. Grew did not know how involved those two had been but had always considered her as Paul's ex girlfriend that disappeared when he got back with his wife. Grew still found her very attractive even though she had put on some weight. Amanda was not too impressed with her even though Grew compared her to Sophia Loren, real earthy, like "Bitter Rice".

Grew and Amanda continued to work together almost as if nothing had happened. They continued to talk about life and her boyfriends, Grew's ex girlfriends, grooming dogs, breeding dogs, horses, training horses and dogs, philosophy of life and lifestyles.

Amanda talked of her pot smoking and some of the rough characters she had been involved with. It was then that she told of her youth and incomplete sexual activity with her biker gang friends. Supposedly Bob was not aware of any of this past history. They talked of expectations and virginity. She claimed that with all her sort of love affairs she was still a virgin. Even with this revelation she had become more and more explicit about her exploits. Grew had wondered if it was true, how in the world she had not given up this virginity thing. It became the topic of discussion itself. Grew himself had never been with a virgin so did not know.

There had been a friend of Amanda's called Judy who she had often gone out with before. Judy got into full sexual exploits but Amanda didn't. Grew had no doubt that she delighted in hearing Judy tell her in detail, of each adventure. It was part of Grew's discovery key to unlock her treasure. At his questioning, he could see the excitement in her face as she amusingly, laughingly got into descriptions of unsavory characters that were part of motorcycle gangs.

Necking with one individual who nearly seduced her she told of how he had rubbed at the crotch of her jeans, her not aware that the stitching was going. Before she was aware what was happening, he had worked through the jeans, at the cloth of her panties and had started a hole in them. Her own stories were weakening the threads in her treasured virginity. According to her portrayals it was her perpetual guardian in the gang that had rescued her from that scene. These stories, she got away with telling unchallenged for a while, bringing her virginity frequently into the conversation. Her gang guardian had also had his chances.

While she was talking one day, Grew felt it was time to tell her what her weakness was and how it could be done. He really believing it was quite possible, even though at that time he had no intentions of putting it into effect.

That day he said to her, "You know I have been thinking of these stories of yours. I think you are seducible. I believe that done right, exploiting your weaknesses, it could happen ".

He didn't tell her how it could be done; he should have just done it. She was really offended and went home and told her mother what was said. No doubt she had not told her mother about their conversation before this comment nor would her mother have known of the stories she had told him leading up to it. Her mother wanted her to quit work at once. Amanda was twenty-one years old,

Grew had never so much as made a pass at her, so she sure was not afraid of him. She said she really liked the job so didn't quit. He considered her too young for him, younger than his artificial cutoff age. Things were very quiet for a while, she just wasn't confiding in him anymore but he refused to take back what he had said.

Amanda was always trying to set him up with someone else. She had a friend, Lenore, who rode horses with her. Lenore was Amanda's friend but they were total opposites. Lenore was completely devoted to her horses, never did anything with men and probably she had a negative opinion of her sexuality. They, or Amanda decided to take Grew roller-skating. There was great anticipation looking forward to watching him fall all over the rink. They had arranged for Amanda, Bob, Grew and Lenore to go roller-skating at the Mutual Arena. What he hadn't told them was that as a young person he used to tear around the rink in the small town where he had come from. He had always been getting kicked out for zigzagging between the other skaters, whirling in circles, backward and forward, generally wild.

His sister had been more refined and had bought her own skates but he was probably a better skater. As it turned out he had not forgotten and was soon skating circles around the other three; he felt like a kid. When they came out of the rink he showed off by walking the guardrails beside the sidewalk on the way to the car.

It was suddenly like the yoke had been lifted, he could let loose again. Amanda's friend was too ingrained in conservatism and beside Amanda she would always be dull. Grew never even got started with her but got along with Cindy too well. She was blond, in good shape, medium height, flirtatious. Amanda promoted the relationship.

Amanda would look sideways at him and laugh. "She's got a big ass, GT".

Donna showed a real caring attitude towards Charles, started taking him places that Grew thought was a good diversion for him. He was to find out in time that his son could wrap women around his finger from a very early age, something he never lost. He knew just how to play on their sympathies. This trait of getting what he wanted was not confined to getting it from women.

There was a strange side of Donna. Grew found it and discussed her with Amanda that became a day-to-day conference topic. Even after going out with him several times she would not let him kiss her but allowed him to fondle her all over. He wondered what she wanted or why she even bothered with him. Donna and Grew did have many conversations about life and things. Donna was another he felt that had turned to dogs because of a feeling of being rejected by society.

She had lived with a man for a while. The impression left was that he had been abusive, however the way Donna was, wanting to fight with men, might have had something to do with that revelation.

The mother's cynical attitude about men, Grew had heard about from Paul, how Donna used to complain about this woman taking all her money, doling it out to her by the dollar. Donna was fairly tall. When Grew had first met her he was taken by her dark beauty but at that time she was fairly thin. Her big brown soft eyes and sensuous lips drew him to her even though she smoked. He detected she had intelligence within her that she didn't even realize.

Always bragging, how she could wrestle, holding her own with a man was a challenge. Grew got into these wrestling matches with her by trying to kiss her. There was no way she was going to let him do it though, it was a game for her to keep the men off that he never understood. She did not object to spending what seemed like hours rolling around on the floor with him. All the time this was happening, he was getting more than his share of "feels" while she kept moving her face away from his lips. Her body felt hot as they had played.

After many recurrences, he got the idea that kissing her was not the way to go. One night he spent a lot of time working his hands into her bra, pulling and twisting nipples, massaging the breasts, all without complaint, he worked a hand up her skirt, stroking her inner thigh, could feel the intense heat of her; she didn't close her legs. He put his hand in her panties, fingered her as she moaned, got her going, her mouth open. *Now he would kiss her.*

Approaching her mouth she suddenly spat in his face and said, "You bastard". But her mouth opened wide as she accepted his lips, his tongue, and her own tongue met his and played. Her lips were full, soft and receptive, wild, hot and turned on completely she responded fervently; he had found the key.

After continued feeling and passionate interplay, he had brought her to orgasm then he let her up, she moved across the room, she sat on a chair, reached under her skirt and pulled out a pair of black panties.

He knew they were soaked. "You wont hurt me will you? Please don't hurt me". She had sat on the chair facing him with her legs spread wide.

The way she had reacted was totally unexpected; it had shocked him, he felt he had just seduced something ordained by God as untouchable. She was on the brink of tears. He felt guilty and sorry for her, did not complete the seduction, he couldn't. When he talked to Amanda about it she was appalled at Donna spitting in his face but he hadn't even thought much about that. As he recalled it he could see in Amanda's excited expression that there was no love between the two.

To him it was Donna's concession that he had won, she had been seduced. Maybe it was him that had been seduced. He had the attitude at that time that if they were good enough to fuck they were good enough to marry, clearly an idea to be rethought. Later he did agree to marry her, promised that he would not have sex with her until after they were married, and he didn't.

They were married five months after Marilyn had died. The wedding was in the church up the road. Dick Edwards had put "Help" on the bottom of his shoes that amused everyone but the mother in law. The reception was brief and at the kennel. He remembered them going into the bedroom. Suddenly she was nude standing there before him. He remembered her looking too heavy, there was no excitement in the room for him.

"What have I done?" She was so hot and sloppy, so wild that he instantly ejaculated almost as soon as he was in her.

This became a problem in their sex life but over time sex became quite pleasurable with them. There developed a feeling of need, a kind of animalistic passion when they came together that if they had given their marriage a chance without interference from so many angles, it just might have worked. There were so many differences and much not talked about between them that the wheels fell off.

Grew remembered some good times; he remembered their honeymoon where they drove up the St. Lawrence, stopping at little heritage type motels along the way. It was like a different country. For a while the things that were to turn them against each other were far away. They did not argue nor even talk of things that they would not agree on. They enjoyed nice things like old things, nature and the animals. They took turns driving her car, enjoyed eating out and watching the big river flow by. The seaway was new, they explored its magnificence. Then they went home to the petty things that they did not work out; they had not discussed them.

Charles decided one day he was going to be the benefactor to the community. He took the money that had come in from dog trimming kept in a drawer and was noted by the bus driver, handing out ten dollar bills. Donna went with him as he went to the friends who had received the cash and asked for it back. The bus driver collected the rest.

On her own Donna took Charles out shopping. She was his mother and wanted to be proud of him. She decked him out in a suit and all the things that went with it. It was a gesture to be commended but he didn't want it. Grew was not too diplomatic in taking his side but Donna was not prepared to compromise.

There were other problems, mostly developing because she wasn't happy and couldn't find the answers. After work time was mostly spent at her mother's. Amanda and Grew were running the dog business, not an eight hour a day job. often laughing. Donna felt left out and was whenever there was a discussion about the dogs or kennel. Did she feel like she was an the intruder? Was that why she was always at her mother's? Grew too inwardly felt that his new wife was never around, never doing things that wives do around a house.

The only time they related was in bed, but even when he tried to stop so he wouldn't come so fast she kept going in her thrashing passion, wild, hot with her organ sucking it out of him. She had him going off too fast almost every time. Her body was electric. There was an earthy sense to her and he often referred to her, inappropriately discussing with Amanda, as Moonbeam McSwine from the Lil Abner comic strip. Her hair was invariably ruffled, looking dirty, with clothes unkempt. An invitation emanated from her rolling ass an invite for sex.

There was a time when he had felt close to her, really did care for her but the relationship just ran into circumstances. He was re roofing the new part of the kennel building, thought he would be doing it alone. It was on a weekend. Almost to his surprise he found her out there helping him, working right along with him. They were tired when finished and went out to dinner, he felt real close to her. When he thought of it later, he was sorry that their life together did not work out.

The usual daily pattern became a distance between them thing. Each day he would cook the meals, started while he was finishing off the dogs, as before, usually a stew or a combination started with hamburger that he called "Grew's Goo". Donna would wander in just in time to eat or she wouldn't bother coming until much later. She wouldn't call

Demonstrating no sense of responsibility to the relationship she wanted to keep her money to herself and let him look after everything else. They hadn't discussed these things before they were married, he hadn't even thought of it. With Marilyn, the money made went into a bank account and each took what they needed. There wasn't a lot left over but they had been doing all right.

It was obvious that the problems were developing very fast between Donna and Grew. All the time he continued to work with Amanda. Some of his friends had suggested that he had married the wrong one. He didn't want to but was beginning to believe it himself, too much fun with Amanda.

Sometimes she would come with him as he walked the dogs because she had her own pup now that she wanted to exercise. As they went they would sometimes run through the fields themselves as she wanted her puppy to run with her. One day during their lunch break, her and Grew had gone back to a creek bed that ran through the back of the field behind the property. It was grassy besides the creek, with large trees shading the flood plain.

She was wearing her usual men's blue jeans and a hang on T-shirt, loose and not tucked in. Donna had always referred to Amanda as being built like a man, without curves. He had taken her hand to help her down the bank and as she ran the last few steps he steered her into his arms. She did throw her face from side to side to avoid his lips for a few minutes but he caught the pattern, and their mouths met. His arms were already around her, then they moved under her T shirt where it hung loose, on her bare back he moved his hands up the smooth skin, soon realizing that she did not have a bra on--still kissing her--a soft kiss but leaving nothing to the imagination; it was real. He pushed her down to the ground. As he did he moved hands around to her front, pushed up the T-shirt-- uncovering magnificent breasts.

Confronting him were the most stunning set of tits that he had ever come across. The nipples were pale as per her complexion, but the breasts were so full, so firm, that he wondered how she managed to conceal them under the loose fitting things she wore. If she could have only seen, Donna would have been surprised; this was no boy.

Realizing the tits before him were so firm, pliable, and not even a hint of sag; he worked them with his hands as if he had just found paradise in the creek bed. Amanda just looked at him with the softest eyes. He knew that if he would go further with her, she would not resist. But there was so much love and trust in those eyes that he knew he had to stop. Right there he could have had her virginity but maybe he now understood why she still was a virgin. He pulled her to her feet, kissed her lightly and they walked back. Walking for a while hand in hand. There was a new relationship between them, neither one knew quite how to handle it. They finished the walk by racing together for the house.

When they got in the house he chased her around a bit until she jumped into the house bathtub on the main floor. He stepped in there with her and kissed her while they both stood, pressed together. If Donna had been more of a house cleaner she might have wondered about the footprints facing each other that they had not noticed or washed away. After that interlude they got back to work.

His new attachment with Amanda did not help his relationship with Donna. Now he really was in the middle and it was getting tighter day-by-day. Where was he to go from there? To make matters worse, Amanda had a fight with Bob, he never knew what that was about, (he could guess). They stopped seeing each other. She was quite sad about it but never dwelled on it; now he saw a quite different Amanda. She started taking her lunch breaks while she watched "Another World". Soon Grew started watching with her. It certainly was another world that they were living. Grew did not realize what this new world was becoming.

One evening when Amanda was going to stay for supper, she did that quite often since Donna wasn't coming home until later, Donna unexpectedly did come home. Grew told Amanda to take Charles for a walk with the dogs, confrontation time was at hand. While they were out he had a war of words with Donna that increased in intensity as it continued. He called her, on her absence all the time, the fact that he was making all the meals, doing whatever cleaning was being done in the house, the fact that she just wanted to ride along, contributing nothing financially, no effort or anything else, to their marriage.

She responded loudly about Amanda being there all the time. He said she could make a few meals from now on as he dumped the stew on the floor. She picked a mop out of a bucket that they always had kept there for clean up, (dog kennel), she charged at him, mop pointed like a spear. He saw her coming and let fly with the Corning Ware pot that the stew had been in. The handle on the side of the pot caught the side of her head as it was going by and opened up a gash. Donna was almost paranoid about cuts and blood. She tackled him and, they fell to the floor, him holding her down but then he saw the blood.

Together they got up. Right away she called the police, charging him with assault. Amanda and Charles came back in the house looking shocked when they saw what was happening. Charles thought his dad was going to jail. Police took him to the station and Amanda came along with Charles. They charged him but allowed him to go home. Donna went to her mother's where she stayed or went to their northern cottage for a week.

The two of them appeared in court in Newmarket the following week. The judge told them not to see each other until they came back to court again. That was another three weeks. By that time Donna had got pregnant by someone else and had effectively been replaced in the home of Grew and Charles.

Chances for reconciliation were at that point none existent. But that was not the total reason. In the time that Donna was gone on his own, Grew went to a drive in movie. He was very upset, it had not been a solution that he had wanted. He had asked Amanda to sit with Charles for him while he was gone. The movie was 'The Odd Couple". He couldn't get into the story so came home before it was over-- talked briefly to Amanda, telling her that he should have put Charles in the car and taken him and her with him.

For a while they sat talking, had a coffee but there was electricity in the air between them. He sat down beside her. Silence--soon she was in his arms. It was so peaceful, so natural for a while, they just held each other, they appeared so compatible together. He couldn't help it, his hands moved on her, to those ravishing breasts, massaged them, bared them, and sucked gently. He undid the fly of her jeans and was forcing his hand down the front as she held his wrist, trying vainly but gently to hold him back. But she was not closing her legs either.

His fingers had prodded and stroked in the wet entrance to her vagina, she was turned on, meeting his open mouth with her own, in a sweat, moving her hips as he fingered her, she was going with the fingering that was moving into her.

He moved back, easing her tight jeans down while she looked at him, not telling him to stop. They were off. He was working up between her open legs with his hard penis now in his hand, directing it towards the goal. He felt for the hole and found it closed, felt again with his hand, and opened her again. She closed again when his penis arrived. He looked in her face, at the tear; she was crying.

He stopped, kissed her watery eyes, softly touched her mouth, her lips, took her hand and pulled her to her feet. She got dressed and he patted her now covered bum as he saw her out the door. While Donna and Grew were separated Amanda would travel with him while delivering the dogs. He would often kid with her about stopping at a motel and having a "party" between them.

One rainy night he looked at her as she said, "Okay let's do it, there is one around the corner." They did stop. Charles must have been away or he would have been with them.

They went in the room, he ran a bath for her, and then watched intently as she removed her clothes while facing him. There was not a sign of embarrassment, she looked right back at him as first the wonderful breasts were bared then she slipped down her jeans and panties with one motion, off her ankles in a step. He could feel his erection as the bit of red fluff came into view at the pinnacle of her shapely pale legs.

While she sat in the tub he soaped her all over, he kissed her as he ran the soap over her delicate skin. She moved with the hands, yielding to their guiding touch, shared the touching, allowed him to work his hands between her legs, massage her golden hair around her vagina, slipping his fingers between the folds, rubbing gently and probing. She had stood up as he rubbed her dry, and then led her to the bed coming down with her--clothes were off as they faced each other, naked bodies warmly holding together. He rubbed her back, her warm pliant bum, his hands worked around to her front, between her legs to the golden prize. His gentle massage continued.

After awhile as his hand moved back and forth in the slit he could feel that it was not lubricating. He lay on her and teased with the knob of his penis. It only closed tighter. It became a hole that not even his finger could get in, there was something stopping him. Was it a fear of hers? Was it why she was still a virgin? It was closed so tight it was like there was no hole there. He went back with his hand but could not get any loosening at all even though she would passionately kiss him.

Though they kissed, they fondled, he was unable to take her. Then his erection went down. This time he could not get it up again. After a while they dressed and went home. She stayed the night at his place but she slept on her own.

Peggy had bought a dog from Paul Adams that was from a repeat of the breeding that created Arno who was a good one and Margo, one Grew had kept for his own breeding. Peggy's dog didn't quite turn out as well as the other two but Peggy became a friend of Amanda and Grew. She had also been a close friend of Marilyn in her last year of life, being there when needed. She kept going out of her way to be helpful. However Peggy did not consider herself close to Donna, another that believed he had married the wrong woman.

Years earlier Peggy had been a friend of another couple, the Davies. When the wife had died, Peggy had married the husband and they moved to Ireland. A few years later he had died and Peggy had returned. She had always been a supporter of the German Shepherd Club. When Grew had taken over as President she became treasurer.

She had remained a friend, relating well with Amanda until a few years later when she too had died.

Grew was still upset with his situation with Donna but his affair with Amanda was getting more intense. By the end of June and beginning of July there was a German Shepherd Dog Show in Ottawa. Amanda had decided to go with him but was supposed to stay with Peggy at the motel but her and Grew had a few drinks at the dance reception.

The two of them had been dancing very closely, it was a mixing of generations. Amanda had been used to dancing in the way of that time, standing apart, facing each other, usually not touching and shaking. But Grew had taken her in a way he was used to with slow music, holding her in his arms, the two of them hardly moving. That way they could keep in time together. They were to learn his way and her way to dance as their association was to continue.

He whispered to her, "Come with me, I want to show you my room. Peggy has already gone to bed, you can catch up to her later".

She obediently followed saying little if anything. In the room she lay on the bed and smiled, holding her arms out to him. Her eyes looked a little droopy, she had had too much to drink. He lay down beside her and took her in his arms. They kissed, at first softly, barely touching lips. The passion grew as his hands moved up her mini skirt, finding the waistband of her panties. Soon his hand was gently rolling the bud near her wet trough. Her body was becoming increasingly active, warm. She moaned as his fingers played her. Her legs spread, now devoid of those panties as he moved between her legs. His erect penis was heading for home.

This time he found the right place before it could close up. There was a substantial obstruction in the way but with her encouragement, her guiding hand, they steered the erection the way it was supposed to go, he just kept pushing, feeling the membrane tear, and then he was in the tunnel. It was tight, snug, as he pushed slowly deeper, not loose as he had lately been used to, out a bit, in a bit further, they went slowly back and forth until the fluid was coming from her.

Grew had continued to kiss her open mouth as together they made love. It was quite a while before he felt himself coming, by that time she had loosened considerably, was pushing her pelvis right back at this storming penis that was driving through her. Her muscles were holding this thing filling her warm initiated cunt, but the slippery walls couldn't keep still, it was becoming dreamy, she loved lifting her bum back at him while his hands lifted her. Then everything was loose, she was filled with his liquid too. Soon his hardness was declining and then her muscles pushed it out of her. She had had it, that was it. She was no longer a virgin. There was only a spot of blood. When she looked at him, he had fallen asleep, she cuddled up to him, wondered about what she had done, in awhile she was asleep.

The next day at the dog show Amanda appeared depressed. She was quiet, had not saved it until marriage. She really loved Grew but he had gone on to show his dog. She thought, *"he's almost forgetting me, like nothing happened."*

Margo won Best Female and he had seemed more interested in his victory than sharing the honeymoon with his new bride, as might be expected he missed the signals. Sometime later she talked to him of how she had felt. He tried to understand, recognized that it was such a traumatic turning point in life for a female, particularly one that had intended to wait for marriage. She did not make a big issue of it, but he later realized the significance of such a step for her, she had every indication that this man would become her husband forever.

As for Grew Tuckett, the dog man, in the space of a year he had seen his wife die, he had become involved with someone else and had married her. Then he had been charged with assault by that same wife but had deflowered a virgin and had moved her into his house and business. Life had become much different with new challenges.

CHAPTER 14
Life with Amanda

After that they openly lived together. She helped him with the dogs, the house, he still did most of the cooking but their relationship changed some. His ego was in its glory as he paraded this elegant young blond to the dog shows with him. With his associates she was quiet but friendly and was obviously very much in love with this man. Other dog breeders wondered just how he was able to bring out. one woman after another

There followed a time when he acted like he was 15 to 20 years younger; he was doing well in keeping up to this young life style as they spent time getting to know each other. She now had a lot to say in the business--not all wise.

They went to a rock concert out in a field with thousands of teenagers and young adults. The slept in the van overnight. Police on the concession roads that bordered the field surrounded the whole hundred acres. When he had got up to go to the toilet, walked out towards the road, suddenly headlights came on. The police questioned him as to where he was going. He thought that they had been pretty uptight in expecting some kind of riot but he did talk to them, then did his thing and went back to the van.

Amanda was awake so came with him down to the arena type bowl where a group was playing. They had laid in the field like hundreds of others, listening to the music. She started calling him GT. Then they had gone back to the van and made love. Whenever the youngsters at the concert would look at him they would ask if he was a "Narc". He had said no but later asked Amanda what that was, she said it was a narcotics officer.

If things were slow at the kennel, with all the dogs trimmed and ready to go home, sometime the two of them would take a drive out to the country with a few of the dogs, would often walk along a hydro right away, sometimes holding hands, sometimes running with the dogs or hiding on the dogs, forcing them to use their noses as they looked for them. This usually ended with a roll in the wild grass together or a chase where one ran after the other. On those occasions the chaser always managed to catch the prey.

Life was a love in, they went to dog shows together, stopped work in the afternoon instead of at lunch in order to watch the soap, "Another World" which they followed consistently, even if it meant they would not be delivering dogs until late in the evening. Often he would go with her while she looked after her horse or horses. She taught him how to groom them but was not too good at making a good rider out of him.

Too many of his old riding habits were still with him from his days on the cattle ranch and the Yukon. In spite of the paradise time he was having there was the nagging feelings about Donna. From time to time his worries about the court case emerged, he knew he really had not given her a proper chance to adjust, knew down deep that he had cut her off unfairly. Had it been because he had become involved with Amanda? A later look at the happenings brought out guilt feelings.

Another problem soon faced him where he was going to have to sell his property to the government for an eventual highway right away or hang on in a freeze where they would not let him make any improvements. He knew he had to have a new septic system. When he discussed the matter with Amanda he got the first indication of her immaturity. The government would lease back the property until they needed it if he sold it to them and would put a septic tank in at no cost.

She said something like, "Gee GT, I don't know, it's up to you," nothing more to say about it.

He wished he could have talked it out with Marilyn or even Donna. Years later he knew he would have been rich if he had held on but there were things he needed then, like the septic system; so he sold the property. He did make use of the money that he got for it and he had made an overall profit from what he paid for it.

They hired another girl to do the kennel work, Carol from Ottawa. She lived in and had her German Shepherd with her. Somewhere around town was a husband that she was separated from but they didn't even see him for a long time. Carol was a heavy girl but with a warm laughing personality, she had various affairs with different men in the dog fancy and had pretty well accepted life the way it was dealt to her--not the best deal.

At night Amanda, Carol, and Grew used to climb over the fence where the portable pools were sold from, across the road from the kennel, then swim in the largest of the pools, it was about four feet deep. Since no one else was around they used to take their suits off, swim in the nude. Grew used to wonder if the pool would overflow as he stole glances at Carol splashing, knew there was no danger of him straying in that direction.

The manager of the pools also became involved with the people at the kennel. They suspected that he was gay but he still took a special interest in Amanda, discussing his philosophies with her. He was also a pot smoker which Amanda had stopped doing. Grew was afraid Paul might get her back into it and wasn't all that sure that he was gay. He tried setting the two of them up (Paul and Amanda) together to find out, but only found out that Paul was very slow if not gay. Paul also got them all playing chess which Amanda introduced to Grew. He was not happy about her always beating him. He did not consider her to be much of an intellectual but she had sure made him look dumb when he played chess.

Amanda still had her games to play. One of the girls that had been hired was young, white blond and an out and out flirt, cute, medium build with everything in the right places. Dick Edwards was having problems getting along with his wife; she pretty well was left looking after their kennel on her own.

Dick started spending more time with Grew. They were both directors for the dog club. And Amanda was more into fun. One evening she got a clothes-tearing contest going after a few drinks with herself, the new girl, Dick and Grew. The two girls literally tore the pants off Dick, which resulted in counter tear with the two girls, and no one was left out, not even Grew. Surprisingly it did not end in an orgy as the young girl's spectacular silver haired vagina came into view. She instantly worked herself loose and headed for her bedroom where she locked herself in. Amanda, Dick and Grew were already naked by that time. A bit of time was spent stitching up enough of Dick's clothes so he could look respectable going home. It was a time when they shared laughter and fun without any hard feelings.

They decided to move Amanda's horse down to the kennel. There was a shed in the back yard that they had converted into a stable, then they fenced off the back part of the property. It wasn't long before she realized her horse was lonely for other horses so talked Grew into buying a horse for himself. They picked out a tough little horse that they figured he could handle.

One ride down the back yard with Grew hanging on for dear life, trying to make the horse stop convinced him that this little pony was not for him. The horse didn't go through the fence but stopped in front of it. It was Grew who kept going right over the top. It was soon after this that the horses got out onto the highway and were both killed. Someone had left a gate open. They suspected Donna?

Amanda was overwhelmed but then went looking for another horse, decided on a cross Arab\thoroughbred colt Her mother paid for it. She did not make the same mistake again and boarded this one out at a barn. She was not riding so much but still spent a lot of time working with the baby, teaching the little fellow to lead and generally adapt. Grew also had loved the style of this horse. It was a new time of irresponsibility.

The sale of the property went through to the highways department and then he rented it back. He then had money that he felt had to be spent on buying other property. He also bought a new van for deliveries and decided that Charles, Amanda and he should take a trip out west to see his family. They went by train, which was peaceful, had a room with upper and lower bunks. In the daytime they would watch the miles and miles of Canada go by.

Jack was taken with Amanda instantly and she found him to be very entertaining. He drove them around the city giving them the royal tour. They went out to White Rock to see his aunt, After a few weeks they were on their way back to Toronto. Charles had enjoyed the whole trip, was the only one not tired out. Day after day they sat watching it all go by, sometime playing cards, sometime Amanda flirted with the porter. She said she wanted to try out a black man, was almost in a mode where she felt she had to catch up for the sex she had missed earlier.

Many weekends before they had gone west he spent looking for suitable properties in the country. He would mark down numbers of good-looking places as Amanda and he drove over miles of farmland. When they got back Grew once again started looking for property without calling the agents. That caused Amanda to start refusing to go with him. Instead she went on her own up to the barn to look after her horse. One day while Grew was looking at the paper--Amanda was out at the barn--he saw what he did not believe as a price for a property. He phoned the agent who told him it was still available so he got in his car and drove, didn't realize just how far it was. It took him two hours to get there.

The property was fifty acres, had an old brick farm house, a barn, a steel cattle barn, a trout stream on the back, all on fifty acres. It was in high country next to ski areas. Grew could not believe it, he put the offer in that afternoon paying full price, even more down than they asked for. It was accepted but it was late when he got home.

Amanda had started supper something she seldom did. "Where you been GT, I missed you?"

"Bought a farm." Once more she was shocked.

It was bought as much for her as himself. He felt he could make the steel building into a boarding/breeding kennel and she could use the barn for her horse. It started out that way but didn't quite turn out the way he had planned. It was registered in his name but he never thought anything about that and Amanda never bothered about it.

From time to time there were other workers, more litters, more dog shows and Donna did not go away. She admitted to the court that she had responded to the fight by going out and getting pregnant and in due course she withdrew the assault charges. She would think nothing of calling, Grew would talk to her, and she always wanted to meet.

Amanda never objected to him meeting her, quite different than what he had been used to but he was no better than what he had been. On those occasions the session would start of with them talking rationally, then he would see it, something about her, she could have a lot of clothes on or little, maybe she would flash a length of thigh or cleavage. He would watch her for a while until she started to move past him and he'd snag her wrist as she went by pulling her to him, lips would smack together, his penis would jump hard, his hands would be tearing at her clothes, undoing buttons and zippers. His hand would be in her hot wet vagina before he had her clothes off. His own pants would be gone in a second, perhaps she would feign resistance but he would be on her, in her, pumping his groin at her equally responding body, smacking at her belly. Shortly he would be gushing his juice into her as she responded with her gyrations then the two of them would subside, soaking wet--guilty.

One time they had met at the farm, he was to deliver a dog to go up near her cottage. The dog was the one he had got back in a trade and better than what he realized. They went walking by the river, he was showing her the property. In the bush and while the flies bit at their bare bodies they made passionate love in the mud by the riverbank. He just couldn't resist her, in his van, in her small apartment in the city, always they ended their meeting with sex.

There was something about her that always said to him, "I wonder if I can still seduce her?" There was almost an animal attractiveness to her, something that said, "Sex". And as always it bothered him afterward, when he went back to Amanda.

At the time he delivered the dog to her, for a watch dog at her boyfriend's lumber yard, the one that had got her pregnant, the dog who liked to play with sticks later jumped over the fence and took a cane away from a crippled man. The next time a woman was shaking a stick at him and he went over the fence again. This time the victim had most of her clothes torn off before she gave up the stick. She was not hurt but the dog had to go. Suppose he thought it was part of the game. Years later Grew realized that dog would have been invaluable for breeding.

Now that they had bought the farm he had to figure out how to convert it into what they wanted. Through the summer they spent a couple of days a week driving there as they changed things. One of the first things was to make a suitable stable in the barn for the colt, which was now close to a year old. They spent a bit of time exploring the country around there and on one occasion came across a field with a number of horses in it. They saw a man who was called over.

Amanda took a fancy to a big rangy horse that the man told her was a handful to ride. She said that she liked him. "How much". She knew these were horses designated for the meat factory in France.

The man told her it was $200.00 so she asked him if she could try him out. He had a halter and bit but no saddle, she shrugged her shoulders as he handed her the gear and in a moment she had it on the horse and had jumped on his back. The horse took off, straight for the barn. Grew watched in terror as she ducked her head just as they went through the doorway. A few minutes later she was back out leading the horse. She talked the owner into throwing in the headgear that she had on the horse. She looked at Grew who didn't hesitate, just forked over the money. She rode the horse back to the farm.

Amanda wanted a baby by Grew. After it wasn't happening they had his sperm tested. It was a low count, therefore unlikely that he could reproduce; it just was not going to happen. They discussed it often, very lightly at first, talking over just who might make a good stud father for the child. Eventually he realized she was serious, she wanted to seduce one of his friends.

Dick Edwards was first choice but the problem was that he was too good a friend, so it wasn't going to be easy. They decided to ask him to help take some things up to the farm with them. At the last minute something came up that Grew could not go. They never told Dick's wife that Amanda and he were going up on their own. Amongst the stuff they took up was the bed and mattress. They had to take it apart to get it in the truck. When they got there the two of them unloaded the things, then put the pieces of the bed in the bedroom.

Dick asked," Do we put this thing together or just leave it the way it is?"

Amanda looked at him for a minute, wondering if she had enough nerve to seduce him, "It would help if it was up so that next time we come we could at least go to bed".

Dick was a very good handyman, he had the tools to do the job. "Okay, you hold this end while I fit these bars into the slots".

She came back, "I bet you can fit your bar into the slot?"

He looked at her and laughed, "You'll get yours someday".

"Promises" she threw back at him with a tempting look.

They had put the bed together and then brought the rest of the things into the house packing a lot of them in the bedroom, joking at each other as they did. When they were about finished she brought two bottles of beer outside. "Want a cold beer?" she asked him.

"Okay, sounds good to me", he said as he reached out his hand she handed him a bottle.

As they stood there drinking she said, "You look kind of hot like you've been working too hard, really you look like you need something on the outside to cool off. You should see the water down by the river."

"Oh yeh, and have you push me in, I know what you are capable of."

She said, "Why don't you trust me? You're always thinking I'm going to do something devious."

"That's right, let's just get these few boxes in the house before we do anything." He picked up a box and started into the house.

She had hardly drank any of her beer, as he went by her she spilled the rest of the bottle down the back of his pants. He yelped, dropped the box and took after her. She made a little circle then into the house, up the stairs to the bedroom-- looking like she was trying to close the door just as he got there. He was pushing on one side with her pushing the other. He won out and they both tumbled on the bed.

She said, "I guess you better get those wet pants off?" and went for the belt buckle.

He said, "Oh no you don't, you're going to get your bare ass beaten" and he was at the buttons of her jeans.

Soon they both were in their underwear but as he tried to roll her over on her stomach when his head was down close to hers she reached up and grabbed him around the neck, pulling him down to her. She kissed him and he responded, they joked a bit about where they were but she could feel his hardness on her.

As he was taking down her panties, she acted like she was trying to get them back up again as he kept pulling. But he was winning, her laughing as she relaxed, she wasn't struggling so much, just slowly moving as he got her panties off, a token struggle, she was hot, her legs willingly spread open as he descended on top of her.

She said, "Hey I thought you were going to beat my ass?"

"I got a better idea".

He pulled her legs up around his body, there was a quick adjustment in their positioning. She wasn't fighting him anymore.

Then it was in her, her legs slowly moving in the air above them as she felt his penis sliding back and forth, inside her slippery nest. As it moved within her she held him tightly with her legs as she pushed her hips up to meet his every thrust.

It went on, then their pace quickened, she could feel him coming, his hardness filling her, then as they lay still he kissed her tenderly, stroking the her. It looked like he couldn't understand why she wasn't upset, he felt guilty.

Grew wanted to know every detail of how she had done it. He was getting excited as she told him and got her going again too. As he carresed her warm body himself with every word she smiled, teasing him as she drew out the story. They then really got into their own sexual marathon.

They had to build another stall for the other horse that she called Crunch, and arrange for someone to be there all the time, or arrange with a neighbour to feed this guy. They moved Amanda and Charles, most of the breeding dogs and the other horse up to the farm. There was an assistant back at the kennel. Between the two of them they looked after the grooming business, three days a week. Grew was now working like to get things finished at the kennel in four days, then he was coming up to the farm to get things done there in three days. There was just not enough time. Peggy was staying at the house near Toronto. They had made arrangements with her that if they moved permanently she would take over the city place.

Of course there was the unforeseen. They bought a cheap car in order that Amanda could move around while at the farm. The farm was four miles from the nearest town. This car was to be driven there by Grew's assistant, a portly male student from Montreal who had the ability to make everything come out wrong. The first car he started out with, the motor burnt out on the first drive to the farm. They then made a deal with the second hand dealer to get another one.

The rush was on to keep both places going. In his time at the farm Grew gutted the cattle barn making pens suitable for dogs. It was his intention to have kennels within the barn, large open doors but runs built so that the dogs would only go outside when taken out.

It was an idea of an almost self-sustained operation. He had taken into consideration that the area was in the middle of the Snow Belt so there would be times when they could not get outside. Too much time was spent however rebuilding the stalls in the barn for the horses. It created arguments between Amanda and him as to priorities. It was something that would go on plaguing them.

The car they had dealt for was so bad that they had to put it in reverse to get up the steep hills near the farm. Low gear wouldn't take it. Amanda did get by with this car. Charles was enrolled in the local school four miles from the farm. They lasted till Christmas.

Amanda did not adapt to being in the country on her own either. She took the gun to bed with her each night and jumped out of bed at every sound. She was nervous when she went out riding. Whenever the neighbours stopped by she was uneasy, she was not another Marilyn that perhaps Grew thought she was replacing. Charles was okay, adapted to the country school, made friends with the kids that lived around there. When they went back near Toronto he was not unhappy though getting back to his old school friends. Years later, it was him that told Grew of the fears of Amanda. Amanda was not pregnant either so they decided to seduce another friend.

This one they knew would screw anything. It was Alex, so it was just a case of getting them together. It had to be done in a subtle way because he was a straight forward, ask a girl for sex type, the kind that would normally turn Amanda off. Usually she shied away from even talking to this man, considered him gross, he did have some nice daughters though so was rated as a good producer.

Grew arranged that she would meet him downtown, being "too busy" himself to get away, with information regarding the pedigrees of certain dogs. Amanda and Grew knew that if he met her he would first offer to buy her lunch, then a drink, then if she looked a little under the influence of the drink, suggest that he join her in a hotel room. After that it would just be a matter of not stopping him It went according to plan.

Again she relayed the whole thing to Grew just about as they had thought, she told him that when her and Alex got to the room he was like an animal as he stripped off her clothes, she didn't fight him, laughing to herself as to who was being seduced. Her respect for this man was not much as she realized he thought he was getting away with something. She felt he was okay sexually, did ejaculate and that was what she wanted. She saw him as a man without feeling, just wanted to screw. Years later Grew heard he had died. Amanda did not get pregnant from him either. Grew had another wild time with her as she told the tale of seduction.

Once again they were working out of the near Toronto location. They'd arranged for a friend of Pat Snow's to rent the farm with the idea that they would eventually work some kind of partnership deal. Grew's people would take in boarders then bring them to the farm. The renters kept bothering him about buying the place for themselves. He kept turning them down so after awhile when nothing could be worked out, they bought a place of their own near there.

Grew then arranged with the real estate people in Maxwell to rent it out. These people rented it to hippy's that were letting the place go to ruin. Grew never received any kind of rent, the real estate people only took the first month for themselves. In the meantime Grew was dealing with another project.

His pal, Al Mitten's pet shop in Orangeville was doing well so he became the expert advisor. A man came around responding to an ad in the paper for help. Amanda was impressed as he talked of setting up a pet shop. He too was a pot smoker, the fraternity that Amanda related to. He left them with the impression that he was going to invest in this thing. By the time they had it set it up they didn't even give him a job. They found a store, signed the lease and then started putting the pet shop together.

Lenore's father who was a handyman did the work required in the store. When an electrical inspector came around he would tell him he was the plumber or carpenter. When the other inspectors came around he was something else. One inspector told him to get rid of a bunch of wires that were prominent in the basement. When he did he threw the whole building out of phone service. When asked why, he gave the inspectors card and no one bothered him after that.

Al convinced Grew that he could not just get along with dogs and grooming. A pet shop had to have the works, so he helped set up the whole thing. Before Grew knew it he was selling descented skunks, fish, turtles, cats, rats, mice and snakes. He drew the line at selling tarantulas.

Wendy was working at the kennel at that time, The farm was rented out to the hippies who weren't paying, some dogs were being brought into the pet shop to be groomed but most of their business was still pickup and deliver.

When the first Humane Society inspector walked in the door he noted a snake curled around a stuffed cat at the door his comment was, "Boy that sure looks real". It was, or at least the snake was. Somehow the whole thing got through inspection, they were in business.

One of the other creatures they had inherited was a Komondor dog. Grew had originally got to know "Chaos" as his groomer. He had belonged to the wife of an ex football player. Komondors are groomed properly by splitting their mats which results in long cord like strings hanging all over their bodies. They stand about thirty inches tall on all fours (table height) and when they stand on their hind legs it is easy for them to stand with their front feet on a man's shoulders.

Chaos was offered to Grew because the lady was breaking up with her husband. He soon got a pretty good idea why they broke up. Chaos and perhaps most Komondors have strange personalities. Their purpose was to protect the sheep, they are big, agile, can knock a full grown German Shepherd off it's feet by a swing of its rear end. Their hair will fill the mouth of a dog trying to bite them before it can get into the flesh, they have the courage to take on most anything. Perhaps they will stick around a flock of sheep but they are terrible about sticking around home and do not respond to commands. Any attempt to discipline Chaos by use of force would result in him going after the would be trainer.

Containing Chaos didn't work too well either as he could get over fences. He used to hop the farm fences like a hurdler going over hurdles. What was finally decided for him was a special chain and heavy collar to tie him up, breaking other chains until they learned about him. When learning about Chaos there were days when the whole staff of the kennel were running down the center line of Duncan Mills Road in pursuit of this villain or following with binoculars, this dog that was flying over fences.

For Amanda, he was an ideal dog, fitting her personality to a T. Grew felt he understood why they got him when he tried to make the dog comply to some kind of authority. Chaos jumped right up on him as he stood, placing his front feet on Grew's shoulders, snarling in his face, with all teeth smiling. Grew felt the football player would have tried to beat the dog down when he did that which would only make him worse which in turn would make the man angrier and the wife more upset. Not the way to do it. Grew loved his response, loved dogs with the guts to "Stand Up" to a man. The first time the dog did this to him he grabbed both sides of Chaos's face by the hair. There followed a five minute growling session, dog and man standing toe to toe, man growling at dog, dog growling at man. After a while the growls of Chaos became less until finally he dropped to his front feet, they settled for a standoff.

This practice was part of what they do not train dog handlers about rebel dogs. In another instance Grew was called to a home where their terrier took possession of the living room couch. When they tried to chase him off with a newspaper he defended the territory, absorbing the newspaper blows with courage. When Grew saw this he took the newspaper and sat down beside the dog slipped a noose over his head and then led him off the couch.

The game with the Komondors became standard policy, Grew used to even do it for fun. Chaos learned it was just part of a game. It was the same with the terrier he loved the game of defending the territory. Chaos had another game. When he was tied in front of the house, as someone would approach he wagged his tail, barking, a steady repetitive bark. People didn't seem to understand, they would walk right up to him, after all he was wagging his tail. Then he would bite them on the ankle. A German Shepherd could never get away with what he did but they were only bruising bites at best, or worst.

Amanda once dyed him pink, parking him out in front of the pet shop. He stopped traffic. Charles took him to school for show and tell despite Grew's misgivings. Chaos acted like he spent his life babysitting, hamming it up for the kids.

The first time Grew tried to sell a baby skunk it latched onto his thumb and wouldn't let go. He shook it loose and never sold skunks again. The mice got loose, wandering through the drains to the store three doors down, one was killed by a male hairdresser with a broom. After that they setup a series of plastic tubing called "a habitat" they kept the mice in there. The folks left the house cat, Stoney, in the pet shop to discourage any breakouts. Through the night the cat knocked over the habitat and had all the mice trapped in a corner of the system.

Each day the fish man came in and replaced the fish thinking they were being sold. No, the girl who cleaned them in the morning just threw out the dead ones. They didn't sell too many fish. They did get a Piranha that fed on gold fish. It took a year to sell that one which had to be delivered. It was just about loose on the floor of the truck on the way to its new home.

Snakes were what attracted Amanda the most. They weren't in the business six months before she had several different kinds of snakes, some of which fed on other snakes. It was not that unusual to find a young boa constrictor half way ingested into a four foot king snake. In these instances, the Boa would be dead.

In order to feed the snakes Amanda got into the breeding of rats. That is what snakes eat. But even all the snakes they had could not eat rats at the rate the rats were being reproduced. Fortunately other snake owners found it to be a good place to buy rats.

There were other characters gravitate to the pet shop. Dave Harwin had bought a dog from Grew. It was a male that Dave had made a game with, of chasing traps that they sent up to shoot at with shotguns. It was called trap shooting. Dave was another pot smoker, a rough character who left this dog in his apartment while he was out doing whatever he did at that time. The dog used to spend time destroying mostly books but some furniture too. Eventually Dave married a Japanese Canadian girl but somehow their lives were too different.

When Grew took his Ontario Provincial Police friend to look at this dog for a potential recruit for the police force, the officer, who he had found dogs for before, fired his .45 pistol in the air as a test for gun shyness. Right away the dog was searching the air, throwing his head this way and that as he looked. The officer couldn't understand it so tried again with the same results. The policeman thought the dog was as crazy so rejected him. That dog Arno was the same dog that eventually went north with Donna as a guard dog. The police missed a good one.

Grew had got the sister to this Arno back too. She was smaller, well built, but the first time he had her out she was sitting at his side at a dog show. A friend approached handing him in a slapping motion a catalogue. Before the catalogue reached him, the dog had the man's hand. Fortunately, this person had also had an aggressive dog, was not hurt and had been drinking. He was impressed with the dog.

Grew had traded this one to Dave for Arno who he had a job for. He needed a male, his mistake. It was one mistake among others, the bitch would have been a great producer but Grew did not know it at the time. Dave Harwin was off on strange ideas of producing man-eaters. He bred her to an aggressive Doberman and kept puppies for his watch dog business that he had decided to go into.

Dave Harwin decided he was going to run obedience classes in the basement of the pet shop. Grew vetoed that idea, firstly because Dave's experience at dog training was derived from a few books he'd read. He was resourceful though and as an afterthought it too might have worked. Grew did not want the responsibility of the venture or to be tied to it. It caused a certain amount of animosity between them that was not resolved until Grew supported him in his watchdog venture. Grew gave him Arno back to work with and a two-year-old Saint Bernard, Barney that had been abandoned since he was five months old.

As Barney grew past a year old he became more and more difficult to find a home for. He would watch through the fence as they trained the German Shepherds in protection work getting quite vocal as he tried to get in on the action. Then when he was let into the kennel he would growl at anyone trying to get him in a cage. Grew used an aluminum snow shovel to push him into where he belonged. Barney was allowed to stay out in the runs for long periods of time where he would bark at everything going by.

There was a time when he was let in the kennel building when Grew was there with Jordan Sniderman. Jordan jumped up on the freezer while Grew forced the dog into the with the snow shovel pushing in Barney's face looking like some wild animal but he was not able to jump over the shovel

After Dave took him, finding an assignment for him in a wrecking yard, Dave worked with just the two dogs Arno and Barney for a while. Then he ran into trouble with the law. He lived in a second story apartment and someone had pinpointed Dave as a dope dealer. When the plainclothes officer's kicked in his door, Dave knocked out the first officer coming in with a pool cue. That caused the rest to do a job on Dave that put him in the hospital. Dave called Grew and he came to visit him where he was conscripted as the only one able to put the dogs in the compounds. There was no one else to handle them. There was never a question as to whether he would do it.

Grew used Amanda's car, a Nissan fastback, Barney was in the back seat. Grew came to a road that he had to turn onto and looked back over his shoulder, turning around only to be looking into the face of this huge St. Bernard. Grew reached his hand back to push him out of the way. "Get out of the way, Barney."

"Growww" was the response with snarling teeth shown to back up his answer.

Fortunately there were no cars coming, they got around the semi turn and Barney got to the job. Our hero was overjoyed when Dave was finally able to get back to his job. There were other adventures with the guard dogs.

Barney came back to the kennel for some reason lost in history and Grew tried to sell him again, this time for fifty dollars. A man and wife loved him but when the man kneeled in front of Barney, there was a "wuff" and a button was gone from the front of the man's shirt-- too much for that couple and they were gone.

Grew first spotted Susan in the front of the shop examining her finger. She had a splinter in her finger, which Grew removed for her. Susan was small with a beaming smile, sort of bubbly personality. She was built like a goddess in miniature with dark hair, blue loving eyes and a brilliant smile. She talked to Grew about her situation, (Grew the perpetual sympathizer). Her mother had left her father and returned to England then her father had died, leaving her and her brother, who might have been a year older or younger, The Children's Aid had taken her over but she had run away. With a boyfriend she had survived in Northern Ontario by breaking into cottages until she was caught. She was placed by the CA in a school, and also in a home across from the pet shop where she was not happy. She planned to run away from there as soon as she got the chance.

Susan kept coming back to the pet shop where they found her often stroking or cuddling an animal. She had another boyfriend who she wasn't able to see as much as she would have liked, the reason he was seldom in the pet shop with her. Grew would frequently talk to her when she started coming in more often, telling him more of what she was going through and why she wasn't going to stick around.

Grew tried to talk her into staying where she was but when it became apparent that she really was going to run away, he talked to Amanda, asking if they could put her up at the kennel for a while. She could help Wendy and even be company for Charles. Amanda, in her usual agreeable way went along with the idea without any concerns at all. So when she was ready to run they took her with them to the kennel. Grew could not remember where everyone slept but could remember scenes of Susan in Charles's room.

Susan adapted to the kennel, being a help to Wendy but he became concerned when he found her getting drunk with her boyfriend. They were boozing it up one evening. It was time to talk to Susan. He told her that if she were going to stay, she would have to abide by rules. She was crying as Grew spelled out the acceptable and unacceptable to her. Wendy stepped in, trying to tell him that what she did was not his business but he explained to Wendy that it was In a way he had accepted responsibility for her. It was his house and that was the way it was going to be.

After that Susan did comply, she was a good kid needing a bit of discipline. She lived there with them for awhile after that. Then she found an apartment with her boyfriend where she had a baby, supposedly by the boyfriend. When they broke up, some time later, (they really were too young the boyfriend's life became, getting drunk,) His family took the baby and Susan came back to the kennel and asked if she could stay for a while. They allowed her to sleep on the couch.

CHAPTER 15

People, Pets, Snakes

Lynn started coming around the pet shop. She had originally bought a dog from Grew to replace her German Shepherd who had got run over. She had arrived with a friend who somehow knew about Grew's dogs. Over the next couple of years Grew sold Lynn two dogs and she kept another for him.

The first two were called Spice and Toby. These were the dogs that she kept bringing in to get washed. A few years later something happened to Spice and Toby also they had ran afoul of a car, both at once. Grew was called in once again to find another German Shepherd for her. She lived in one of the better Toronto areas, had been married for some time and had a grown son and a teen-aged daughter. Lynn was nicely proportioned, looking a bit on the heavier side but maybe Grew would have just called it maturity. Was it because of her full breasts? In any case she was pleasant to talk with, a fun type of person who obviously could afford to have her dogs looked after. Her husband went out to work every day leaving her to her own devices. It appeared that they had quietly agreed to do their own thing without ever spelling it out. She brought the dogs in more than they needed to get bathed but they were housedogs. As a more than regular customer she received "wander around special privileges". At least no one ever tried to stop her.

Sam sold his interest in the lumberyard to his partner. The partner did not want Fritz so Sam approached Grew about taking the dog over. Grew had no use for him, did not want to take him but Sam kept after him, built an eight foot fence around a portion of the back yard, gave him a dog house to keep the dog in and provided him with food. The plan was to retrain the dog and find him another place to be a guard dog. Sam knew the alternative. The dog would be put to sleep by the new owner of the lumberyard.

Reluctantly Grew agreed to do this but he knew that he would have to spend some time training Fritz if he took the job on. Fritz was delivered to the pen, a pen with a step on the outside so one could get up on it and lasso the dog, thread the rope through the fence, open the gate and bring him out.

The first time Grew tried this he was amazed how well the dog responded; he was heeling around the yard like he had been doing this all his life. Not only that, but the dog did not seem to resent being corrected. Fritz would sit on command and lay down on command. Grew would tell him to stay, back out to the end of the rope and then call him. Fritz would respond like a competitive obedience dog. Grew could not understand why he was so obedient. Day after day Grew put the dog through his paces. Each day he was at least as good as he had been the day before and the two of them, Grew and the dog, were working like a team. Deciding it was time to trust the dog he opened the gate to the dog's pen and while Fritz stood there he threw the rope to lasso him. Fritz was only a few feet away, how could he miss?

Except Fritz didn't see it that way. As the rope came toward him he backed up, he dodged the rope, snuck past Grew and was loose in the main kennel yard. Grew called him. Fritz paid no attention, called him more firmly. Fritz paid no attention, Fritz walked over to a clothesline pole in the middle of the yard and lifted his leg. When he had finished urinating he took a look at Grew who wondered at the way Fritz was charging towards him, looking serious.

Fritz was serious, came right up to this man like he didn't even know him, gave a turn of his head as he went up on his hind legs, seeming to be saying, "Now it's my turn" and in an instant he had hold of Grew's thigh with those huge teeth, was shaking his head, digging deeper; he was serious.

Grew was in agony but had been through the being bitten route on many other occasions and had developed a certain amount of pain tolerance, reaching down and in a reverse motion he grabbed the dogs left ear with his own left hand and the dogs right ear with his right hand. With a lot of effort Grew managed to drag the dog off his leg, threw him up against the fence - teeth snarling back at him and trying to get loose, twisting his head back towards Grew.

What then? Grew started yelling for help. A young man called Bill who the day before Grew had threatened to fire if he didn't take more interest in the job came out from the kennel and saw the situation.

Grew yelled at him, "Throw the rope over his head or if you can, thread it through".

"Well I guess I'm not so useless now, am I", Bill said.

"Bill, I can't hang on much longer. If I let him go we could both get hurt, throw it over quick".

Bill put the rope over the dog's head, the only problem was that Grew's arms were also under the rope.

He said, "Okay, we gotta go with it this way Bill I can't hang on much longer. When I pull my arms out you tighten the rope then hand it to me. Okay?"

That's the way it worked, Bill handed him the rope and then took off and ran clear. Grew threw the dog off balance a few times, heeling fast around the yard, making him sit. Fritz did it perfectly knowing the game was over. Then Grew threw him back in the pen, slipping the rope off as he did. The next day it was back to the beginning but it was time to get rid of this dog.

Grew just had a couple of deep puncture wounds in both side of his thigh. His usual treatment for bite wounds was to put iodine in the wound and keep it open so it would heal from the inside. The same procedure was followed here. Bill actually kept working for the kennel for some time after that.

Grew never trusted the dog after that but kept working with him. When he got the chance he made a deal with Al Mitten who took Fritz, did a bit more training and put him to work. Al Mitten was an adventurous type of dog trainer who took the dogs that other people wanted no part of. He came around one day as Grew was working with Fritz. Al asked if he could take him home. Another rebel that Grew didn't have a place for was gone. As before Al turned him into a watchdog. Rolf, who he had taken earlier was doing fine in that environment.

Fritz also fit in well. Al would sell the dog to construction companies. The construction site would be boarded up with hording, at the night the dog would be left in the closed in area. During the day they would keep Fritz in a holding pen or crate that Al designed so that it could be opened into a yard without the person having to be in the yard. It was worked into the price for the dog. Al sold them the dog so that he would not be responsible for any damage the dog might do.

When the contract would be finished and the construction company moved out they would give the dog back to Al who would sell him again to another company. In between jobs Al used to use the dog as part of his demonstration team as he taught obedience classes at Rochdale College.

There was a soft nature to Al that related to dogs and women. He studied them to find the best way to handle each individual case. He had no stereotyped conceptions, flexible in his thinking, flexible in his training. Fitting into Rochdale was not a problem with him. He was close to their security people, a nondescript bunch of "outlaws" and got them using dogs.

Amongst them was Jordan Sniderman, son of a successful real estate agent, also a pot smoker, motorcycle repair man who had owned his own garage, member of motorcycle gangs, conception of women--"something to fuck", wore dark sunglasses, the motorcycle vest, pants and boots, weighed in at 265 lbs. Jordan looked scary and wanted to buy Fritz. After completing Al's training course, he did buy him which cost him plenty.

This man and this dog really hit it off; love that Jordan could not relate to with woman he threw at the dog. Fritz ate it up and responded by accepting that this was to be his life, - protecting him. At first one might wonder why he would need it, but in time Fritz's services were required.

Somehow $5000.00 disappeared from the Rochdale safe. Probably it was a good chunk of the rent money that came in at the beginning of the month. Maybe it was because Jordan was one of two or three people that had access to the safe that they determined that he must have been the one that scooped the money. Their system of interrogation was to hang Jordan from the eleventh floor window while they hung onto his ankles. How long can two men hang onto 265 lbs in this manner? It didn't take Jordan long to admit that he took the money even though evidence suggests that he did not. They never got it back from him anyway.

The police also questioned him and wanted him to be a witness on charges against the security people who had hung him from the window. It wasn't there first encounter.

His answer, "That for sure will get me killed, what kind of stupid assholes are you anyway?" That was perhaps the beginning animosity between Jordan and the police.

This was in a time before there was a Charter of Rights and police in Toronto were running roughshod over human rights. Jordan was a known pot smoker that they had tried to tie in with drug dealing. Jordan moved out of Rochdale and kept on moving from one place to another.

The first time Grew saw him he was walking up the driveway to the kennel. Grew's first thought was to lock all the doors and make like no one was home. However he didn't. He opened the door and talked to Jordan. The first thing Jordan wanted was to board Fritz for a while. Grew invited him in and they talked. Something about him impressed Grew; they got to know each other, Jordan told him the story of how he acquired Fritz and Grew agreed to board the dog.

Many times in the next months Jordan visited his dog, walked with Grew with the other dogs, many times he slept the night on the chesterfield in the front room. They often talked, Grew could see the bitterness and mistrust in this man, often argued with him, defending the good people in the police force, in society and the world. Their outlooks were probably totally opposite but Jordan had found a friend. Was the dog walking a therapy?

Jordan felt that eventually the police would break into wherever he might be, plant a quantity of dope in his premises and charge him with trafficking. The relations between him and the police had deteriorated. They had "raided" him before but the first one through the door would run into the dog that would have that person by the ankle. That would invariably cause a backing up of the police, there would be a standoff until Jordan could get his father on the scene as a witness, by then it would be too late to plant any dope.

It had happened on a couple of occasions and was the main reason for Jordan wanting to get the dog boarded out, he didn't want him killed. He had then come into possession of a semi automatic weapon and was resolved that on the next break-in, he was going out fighting but determined to take as many police with him as he could. He talked at length about this with Grew, who quietly listened as they walked in the fields. Grew calmly talked to him about not doing this thing, telling Jordan that he was worth more than that.

But the police had him in for interrogation more than a few times. He had upset the police by telling them of their home addresses, describing their wives and how many children they had. It is not surprising that he would make many of them anxious. It was not the best way to deal with police. Many police, at least of that day, were bullies at heart, they understood well the process of intimidation and this man was scary. They were not comfortable to have it all turned on them. They were out to get Jordan.

Jordan was changing. He and Grew often talked of the farm that he had bought in the country. He wanted to put Jordan up there and let him train dogs for him. Grew knew he was honest because his own working money for the business was kept in a drawer in the kitchen. Jordan knew where it was, had free access to it but had never touched it.

Amanda and Grew both lived at the kennel, she being an ex pot smoker too. Of course the three of them had many discussions. Jordan never bothered her by trying to get her smoking dope or by coming on to her. Grew was trusting him, felt he had been set up all along by the police. They were becoming very close friends.

There was one evening though when Jordan brought some chewy stuff. Grew tried a bit but didn't like it and it didn't make an impression, pretending to be high on the stuff himself, the two of them tried to get Amanda into her clothes ripping games, leading into a sexual thing but she locked herself in the bathroom and the idea was put aside. She wanted no games with this guy.

Grew also had the pet shop running by this time, where most of the grooming was done for the business, where Amanda and Grew spent most of their time when they were not at the kennel or delivering dogs. The other girls, Wendy and Susan, were at the kennel looking after the dogs These girls became really attached to Fritz. Many times Amanda would go home and Jordan would ride with Grew as he delivered dogs. They would get into discussions on life, right and wrong, women, and dogs. Grew felt this guy was mellowing and wished that he had had the opportunity to influence him earlier. Jordan was calming but still with disturbing sides to his attitude.

One day Lynn had followed Grew down to the basement to get dog food. It was a time when Amanda was not there. Since Lynn was going up the stairs before him, one step ahead, it was the first time he was aware of her nice curves, particularly the backside. Could she feel him looking or did she read his mind? When she turned around to say something one step above him, they were nose to nose, the same height. So, just on a whim he kissed her. He didn't expect anything, he just kissed her. He really did not expect her to keep kissing back but she did, superlatively, - mouth opened wide, nice soft tongue touching his, making the best of it. It was most pleasing.

When she backed off she expressed the opinion that he was too young for her. Maybe it was because of Amanda that she got that idea. They compared ages and found that they were within six months of each other. Lynn kept coming around more often after that. They became close, she was a dependable friend.

Barney had come back from Dave's and was again at the kennel. A German woman, who would be about forty-five years old, wanted a watchdog. She insisted that this was the dog for her so he was sold to her for fifty dollars. After that she was on the phone almost every day.

Barney would not let any of her friends in the kitchen, he kept growling at them. Grew told her to lock him in the basement when her friends came. She would then call back and say that Barney didn't want to go in the basement. Grew told her she would have to get him to understand he had to do what she wanted.

Finally it was decided that he was too much for her so Jordan and Grew went down to get him. When they reached the house someone there told them that she had taken him out for a walk. They pointed the direction and. Jordan and Grew went to look for him.

They found him, the dog saw them and came charging down the street dragging the lady behind him shouting, "Mr. Tuckett, I can't hold him."

Two large grown men looked around, saw a baseball diamond and headed for the fence. She was finally able to thread the lead through the fence to them. With an extra lead they were able to get him in a crate in the back of the truck and he was off again. Grew sold him to someone else who knew him from when Dave was putting him in compounds. They thought it was going to be easy, bought him with "a no return" agreement. Dave then got him back from them.

One of Jordan's friends was on the surface very much a respectable looking businessman. But underneath Jordan knew that this man was a very skillful second story man who got his kicks from breaking into high class residents, stealing them blind. He used to tell Grew about this man, Jordan related to it because of his own rebellion against society. Grew used to tell him that he was not doing himself any good by associating with this man, some time along the way this man would be taking him the wrong way and getting him in trouble.

Too late--one day Jordan and his second story friend were driving in Jordan's car and were stopped by the police and the vehicle was searched--still legal at that time; they found heroin. Jordan never knew whether it was planted by the police or that his friend, seeing the possibility of being searched, ditched it in Jordan's car. In any case Jordan was charged. It was what the police had wanted. It too was before the Charter of Rights, police were permitted to search or seize anything without warrant.

Jordan was soon out on bail. The police kept trying to make a deal with him about dropping charges if he would be a witness for them with the security gang. Jordan always refused, he did say though that he was not going to go to jail. When the trial came up it was in the same courthouse and on the same day as he had been subpoenaed to go to court as a crown witness in the other case.

He was convicted on the heroin charge but was let loose to attend the other trial. Instead of appearing he walked out of the courthouse, got a bus and later a taxi to the pet shop, appearing in a very wound up state, ready to kill himself or whoever got in his way. Grew did not know whether he even had a gun. He stayed in the basement of the pet shop until eleven at night. Grew brought him food and drink while he waited. They talked for a long time as they discussed what was going to happen then, Grew trying to calm his fears as they talked. He was surprisingly calm himself but not wanting a police encounter there.

This man trusted him. Grew was not going to bring the police in at that point but worried, knowing that really he was harbouring a fugitive. The alternative of calling the police might have got someone killed. Grew reasoned that it was better just to let him go, thought the police would be happy that he left the country. At eleven a car came for him.

Later Grew was told that he was driven to a small airport where he was flown to the United States and from there flown to Israel. Grew only heard from him once but he talked to his father a couple of times.

Fritz was again back at the kennel to stay. Wendy and Susan paid special attention to him and in time he became quite docile. A man came along who wanted a dog to use as a model for his ceramics.

Fritz was sold for a small sum to this man with hopes never to see him again.

Years later, the man was finished with him. Fritz would have been 12 years old. The man wanted to return him. Grew said "No".

People were bringing in their litters of kittens and the pet shop was taking them. Although some were sold the outflow could not keep up with the inflow. One day, Grew had had enough, a bunch of kittens and rats were loaded up, driven up to the barn on the farm. They were all turned loose to fend for themselves. They never took kittens after that and held back on the production of rats.

Amanda, Wendy and Grew where doing some shopping after work in a shopping center, Grew was sitting resting while they looked around. They came rushing back, they had found the ultimate public relations gimmick. Without too much resistance they talked him into buying "Sheba". Sheba was a seven-foot boa constrictor. The first thing was to have a special glass terrarium built for her. It was four feet high and cost $90.00. She stayed in it one night, even less. That first night she pushed up the glass lid, curled up on the other side of it and the whole thing collapsed. It was in their front room at the time. They had jumped out of bed at the sound. Amanda and Grew stood side by side as they looked at the snake curled up in the bottom of the terrarium with the broken glass from the lid all around her. They just sort of looked at each other and laughed, and then they went back to bed.

After that Sheba was allowed to run loose in the house. Her favourite nesting place was with the rats that slept in another terrarium without a lid. In the daytime the rats used to sit around the edge of the glass looking down at the cat that used to scratch his head, wondering what was going on. At night they would get down in the tank. If the snake was there they didn't bother her, they cuddled around her, giving her warmth. She didn't bother, unless it was eating time. Then she helped herself to the nearest. They were all in good shape.

Grew had come home one day and was sitting reading the paper on the chesterfield. It suddenly dawned on him that he hadn't seen the snake. He happened to look over his shoulder, there was Sheba, fast asleep, sunning herself as she stretched along the length of the backrest behind him.

They took the snake to a dog show only once. They had leased a booth to promote the pet shop. The snake was wrapped around Wendy's body as they walked in. It almost cleared out the whole dog show. The complaints started at once. People were clasping their small dogs to their own bodies as they tried to hide them from the monster. For some reason, Wendy who was a rather large girl and the snake who was full-grown, presented an ominous picture of terror.

Memories of the show superintendent screaming down at him, from the control room of the arena, kicking them all out, prevented them from trying that promotional idea again.

But Sheba still fitted into the picture. The snake went to show and tell at the school. Invariably Charles was asking Grew to bring one of the animals in. As he brought the snake through the door a woman teacher saw him coming down the hall; she did an about face and real quick disappeared through a door. The children loved the snake though, and Sheba acted like a pro.

As the pet shop survived, even if not prospering, Amanda's mother bought another shop that was about to go out of business, for Amanda. Jill who had had enough owned it. Essentially it was a grooming salon and not a pet shop. Grew wondered if it was a way for her mother to separate her daughter from him. It meant he had to have more help. Magdalena who had worked for the Edwards years before came to work for him. She was also a German Shepherd breeder who never learned what quality was. Grew only beat around the fringes of her life, an attractive dark haired girl with her own story

They got the extra clipping customers from the other place but it meant Amanda had to go there to work. She took most of the snakes with her which Grew was happy about; she kept them all in a large cage at the front of her store while she worked at clipping dogs in the back.

One day the fellow who was originally to be involved in the first pet shop with them, came to the new store and wanted to see the snakes. Amanda told him to go ahead and open the cages. There were two cages side by side, some snakes could not be with others. After he left she found one cage open and snakes missing from the other, one snake ingested into another. A king snake had almost completely swallowed a young python. Of course the python was dead.

A month later a woman using the washroom that was in the basement back of the pet shop connected to the apartment building was confronted by a four foot snake poking it's head out of the toilet bowl. The apartment and store management gave her a letter after that insisting that she get rid of the snakes. The snakes were brought back to the main pet shop.

Amanda's handyman father replaced a tap handle in their washroom with a round doorknob. It did the job so they left it. There did not seem to be any reason to change it but one night Grew woke up to the sounds of rushing water, he thought a pipe must have broken. He jumped out of bed into two inches of water that covered the floor of the whole house. The noise sounded like it was coming from the bathroom so he splashed his way in there and turned on the light.

There was Sheba with her head caught behind the "door handle faucet" and the wall, - stuck. He called Amanda; it took the two of them to pull the reptile from her trap. The house dried up, but the basement was like a watery cave.

Sheba was supposed to be an attraction for the pet shop. She came back and forth from the kennel usually with Amanda. When Amanda was trimming she would have the snake beside her in the back room. In order that people could look into the backroom to watch the dogs being trimmed they had cut a diamond shaped window in the wall in front of the grooming table. Sheba would do her snake dance, looking out the diamond window as Amanda trimmed the dogs. It did not really help business; people were afraid to come in the shop, much less leave their dogs for grooming, with the snake watching.

Amanda was having identity problems and one night spent the whole night at the university with an encounter group that was trying to understand what they and life were all about. Grew didn't attend but felt it also had sexual connotations. When she stayed out all night it bothered him an he was beginning to feel there were problems with this girl in determining just what she was and where she was going but she still wanted to have a baby. Also he realized that whenever they started on a plan of business she would distort it in a way that would make it impossible to work.

The pet shop could have worked as a dog shop, just selling dog supplies and grooming dogs. One day she told him that she had been talking to her friend Laura who was seeing an engineer who was separated telling Amanda all about him and the place he lived. Amanda had told her about her attempts to get pregnant. Both were very free thinking people who would discuss such a subject without embarrassment. Amanda had asked Grew what he thought about her trying to get pregnant with this guy. By that time Grew really didn't care because he knew she would do what she wanted anyway. He still had not given up on Amanda.

Thinking they had gone through as much as they were going to in that direction, he shrugged but also felt she should have the pleasure of raising a child. He didn't think he could stop her anyway. One thing he so liked about Amanda was the complete honesty. She never ever tried to hide anything from him but still she had to be given her head. It was how it was to be achieved that bothered him.

CHAPTER 16

The Return of Lissette

He said, "Well if you want to check the guy out it might be all right then we can talk about it. Okay?"

Amanda replied, "I'm going to meet Laura tomorrow night, we thought we would go to a show together. I am having my period now so it could be a good time to have a look at him without getting involved ".

"Alright, we can talk about him and the whole idea when you get home".

They went to the show together, her and Laura and afterwards she asked Amanda if she wanted to come back to meet Larry. She wasn't living with him but knew he would be home doing some draughting for his work. (Grew wondered if Laura had set that up. wouldn't put it past her) Amanda agreed to go. They used Laura's car to drive to the house a short distance away.

As Laura took them through Amanda noticed the fine furniture, leather covered chesterfield and chairs, classical decor. Laura showed her a kitchen laid out to utilize every inch of space in the best possible manner. They found Larry working on his material. Amanda was instantly taken by his outgoing friendly personality.

Laura introduced them, could see that what she had told Larry about Amanda was not something that he would disagree with. Laura was envious at the way she saw him take in the long blond hair, the full swell of her chest, the trim figure and long legs, she knew they had his full attention for the next little while. His draughting was done for the evening.

Larry was quick to offer to get them all drinks. Amanda was a little reluctant but was obviously impressed with this man herself; she liked his masculine physique, his good looks and warm smile. He handed her a drink looked her straight in the eye, his expression showed warmth but also obvious desire. "You are a sweet thing, Blue Eyes- long flowing blond hair, let me run my fingers through it". He reached out, boldly fingered the hair, let it flow through his fingers as he trailed it's length.

As this scenario unfolded, she had blushed, her white teeth showing in a smile as she did. Even as his fingers trailed through her hair, she took the drink and did not back away. He leaned forward, kissing her on the cheek. Laura just stood back, looking supportive, smiling at Amanda, with no signs of jealousy whatsoever.

They went into the living room, sat nursing their drinks for a while as they talked briefly of who Amanda was, what she was doing, her experiences with the animals that brought a lot of laughter. He talked of his business, the house and the connection of the house, the business, hopefully what it would lead to. They talked of his family, of Laura who was up getting them more drinks.

Amanda said, "Laura, you know me, you know I can't drink".

Laura responded, "Just take the drink, you're right, I do know you, so I made it weak." Amanda reluctantly took the drink, soon realizing that it really wasn't weak, She took it anyway.

As they were finishing their second drinks Larry said, "Let us show you the rest of the house." He walked over, took Amanda's hand and pulled her to her feet. She felt a little woozy already but allowed herself to be pulled up.

Larry put his arm around her to steady her as if he realized she was a bit unsteady but it was a flirtatious testing. "Are you alright, Laura hasn't been loading you're drinks has she?'

She shook her head, "No, I'm okay, probably just too fast to my feet, I'd love to see the rest but I have already seen the kitchen and your office?" She giggled a bit from the drink.

"Okay", he said, "All hands to the bedroom, the master's bedroom". Laura was up with them with her arm around Amanda from the other side as they moved into a dimly lit large room with a huge king size bed in the middle. Amanda was taken with the pastel, mauve of the walls, the black dressers, dressing tables and bedspread. A white thick rug covered the floor.

"Oh wee", she said as she took in the whole magnificence before her, "You must believe in comfortable sleeping or sleeping in numbers." She looked a little sheepish as she said that, thinking that she probably shouldn't have said it.

Laura pulled back the bedspread to reveal mauve sheets, "Go ahead Amanda lie on this thing. just see how comfortable it is." Laura was bouncing on the bed by then.

"No, I'll take your word for it". She didn't think it was such a good idea, she could pass right out with those drinks. But Larry had not removed his arm from her shoulder, now he turned her towards him, was kissing her on the mouth." *What was going on?*" It felt nice. She allowed her lips to part as his kiss became more passionate. She found herself being backed at the bed, then she was going over backwards.

All of a sudden all three of them were on the bed, and this guy was kissing her still. She felt she should be stopping him as his passionate lips worked on hers; his tongue traced little paths around and in her opening mouth. On the other side of her now was Laura whose hands were now also on her, stroking her soft hands so nicely on her legs under her skirt, between her thighs. *"What the heck was going on, now she wasn't sure whether they were Laura's hands or his, there were other hands under her blouse massaging her ample breasts"?*

Then the lips left her. As she looked over he was now kissing Laura who had divested herself of every stitch of clothing, her own clothing was loose with buttons undone from her blouse, untucked from the skirt. She could see now that it was his hand up her own skirt, giving her little thrills as he traced patterns on her inner thighs, moving his hands as her legs involuntarily gyrated slowly from side to side.

Laura had managed to get his pants off, his shirt was hanging loose. Amanda thrilled to the great mat of hair displayed on his chest as it peeked out from the shirt. She could feel Laura's hands on her again, under the blouse, felt the snap on her bra undone then suddenly her blouse, and bra were coming away from her body completely. She was naked to the waste. All this time Larry was caressing with such a smooth touch, her long legs that tingled to every finger touch. She was losing it; Thrills went through her whole being as the gentle stroking continued.

She looked over to see Laura's hand steer a rigid penis into her own waiting sex receptacle, as he lay between her legs. But he still did not stop fondling Amanda's legs, even as his body snapped into Laura who humped back to meet him. Even as they increased their tempo his face was now over on Amanda's body sucking her own stand up breasts, igniting her whole body into a heated frenzy. *"But I am having my period, she can't do this now, and even if I do I couldn't get pregnant, this would just be an exercise in lust."*

Her skirt had been pushed up, bunched right past her panties, displaying the rest of her figure. These panties now covered his hand that was underneath the cloth, stroking her vagina, fingering the slippery walls of the entrance, playing with that little bump, in spite of the tampon filling the hole. He was pulling down on those panties, then trying to get them off her legs as he furiously pumped on Laura.

Amanda reached down and pulled the panties up again. Then he was pulling them down again, he got them half way down her thighs the next time, which prevented her from spreading her legs as much as he wanted them spread. As he ejaculated into Laura, Amanda pulled the panties up again but then he was kissing her again.

"Wait just a minute, let me go to the bathroom", she said. He totally let go of her this time, letting her role off the bed. She was into the bathroom, pulled the string, removing her tampon, took off her panties. *"I can't help it, period or not, Grew or not, I am going to get it by this guy right now"*. She looked in the mirror at herself, "Slut" she said and went back to the bed.

Laura was working on him, bringing his erection back up as he lay on his back. In an instant Amanda was down beside them, kissing him with all her own passion. In a moment he had her on her back and was between her legs. She loved the feel as he pushed his penis slowly into her, moved it out, and slowly back.

Her vaginal muscles felt every muscle in the thing, her body was hot as she wrapped her legs around his body, conscious of the curly matt rubbing her sensitive nipples. For a long time they moved slowly, almost as if Laura was not there, but she was there, also stroking Amanda's legs as Larry screwed her. As their passion increased eventually to a wild thrashing crescendo she felt her own orgasm arriving with his. Then there was peace.

She felt Laura kissing her nipples running her tongue over her breasts, down her body, to the V between her legs. She was shocked as she felt the tongue on her, in her, but her legs spread and again she enjoyed the thrill of a new sexual experience. Laura also brought her to orgasm.

She told Grew of her experience with Laura and Larry. He didn't quite know what to make of it but felt that this one just wasn't an attempt to get pregnant, felt that perhaps she required more sex than he was able to provide. He could also acknowledge that she was actually seduced as he probably would have been himself in the same circumstances. He wondered how long this young lady was going to be satisfied with just him. So much of their relationship had been satisfying his ego.

Through the course of their time together this had come up from time to time. Times she had decided to go home to her mother's (her father had died) but she always got down the road and came back. He had become used to the possibility that she might eventually leave him but thought so much of her that he thought that he should give her a chance to find someone who she would be more suited to--age wise, someone who could give her perhaps a more conventional life style.

Grew did not realize that whatever she was she was not a person who would ever accept a conventional life style, she was different as was he. Years later he had his regrets but then second thoughts; she was different but maybe too different. He didn't believe that age would have made a difference. She never married but kept in touch--even years later.

It seems that she did try to get pregnant from the engineer, tried at another time but it too was unsuccessful. They also had a session with Grew and Laura in bed together with Amanda standing by watching. It just sort of happened, probably at Amanda's invitation. For some reason or other they were all in the bedroom, Laura kissed him and it didn't stop, soon he had his hands in her clothing with a cover over them; under the covers he removed their clothing.

Amanda who had gone out to answer the phone came back, looked at the two of them without anger. She said," What are you two doing in that bed?"

They just looked at her as she left the room. Laura came back to visit him again sometime later when he was alone. She was in the water testing business and he needed the well water tested and again they had a tumble in bed. It was nice. Grew had the feeling that Amanda had told Laura about the tussle with the engineer and they had agreed that to keep him happy they should have a session with him. Probably he'd have been happier if Amanda had come in the bed too but could understand why she wouldn't.

Grew brought home the book from the "Key Club". All these people wanted to switch partners. Amanda decided she wanted to have sex with a hairy man so they found one. Remember she was still trying to get pregnant and they did not believe that Grew could get the job done. He wanted to come in on her and someone else while they were doing it. She thought he had gone out the night it was arranged. He listened at the window, heard the noises of passion, tried to come in the front door but was so excited he didn't realize it was locked. Chaos barked as he tried to open the door.

Amanda told him later that the man had come in, they had talked for a while then she had escorted him to the bedroom. She had stripped in front of him, he in front of her. She did like his hairy chest. They kissed then he stuck it in her and they had sex. Even to her it seemed cold, a fantasy tried but gone wrong.

Another time when they agreed to meet a couple. The girl was gorgeous. She had won the nude model prize at a nudist camp. He also was a good-looking guy. They talked then left, supposedly to think it over and meet again if either couple wanted to. Neither couple phoned the other. Grew knew that what would have had to happen was that either he or the other guy would have had to have taken the opposite wife into another room to discuss it and then it could have happened. Amanda and Grew never tried it again, feeling there were just too many risks involved. It was never brought up again.

It was getting near the time when the divorce should come through. He wanted a couple of days away on his own so rented a room at a motel in Pickering. Then drove around the country not sure what he was looking for or what to do.

He arrived at a party that Carol, who was now on her own was putting on; a seventeen year old girl there that was still a virgin, was nice looking, Carol and her friend tried to interest Grew in devirginating this girl. He could not remember why he could not get interested. Why hadn't he taken on the task with the younger girl, she looked all right but was very quiet? Perhaps he was thinking that she too was being set up and the other two were just doing it for kicks. Anyway it didn't happen; probably he'd have felt very guilty if he had done it.

Five years after the breakup of Donna and Grew, the divorce finally came through. Amanda said as he read the official paper and showed it to her, "You're divorced, Now we can get married".

Grew knew she was serious, he was scared, "You must be kidding, but I know you are not. Can we not have a bit of breathing space before we do that again, I'm scared of it at the moment?"

"Okay" she said, "then I am going back to just working for you. I will not be sleeping with you anymore". When he tried to make love to her she resisted with such fervor that he stopped. She was working her angle for what she wanted but it was not the way to go. He was beginning to realize that she was not right for him.

There were a few uncertainties about their relationship, the way she steered his business attempts onto unconventional paths concerned him. He was ready five years before but not then. And onto this scene one day came Lisa. Grew was in bed, sick with a cold, it was a weekend because both Amanda and he were there.

Lisa had come to the door and Amanda had answered it, then she came in to see him. She said, "There is someone here to see you".

There was a strange look to her, it surprised him. He asked, "Who is it?".

"A very pretty lady" she smiled in her knowing way, like he had been caught in the chicken coup.

On his direction she showed Lisa into the bedroom. Lisa didn't understand who Amanda was and he didn't explain it at that time but she had a great conversation with him as they filled in the years that they had not seen each other. She had become financially secure but for Grew, too dependant on money. She left after awhile with a promise to come back some time. She didn't return until some time later.

He explained to Amanda just who she was, telling her the story, he had probably told her before, it was just a matter of filling the person into the reality.

Soon after that Amanda did go back to her mother's to live, taking Chaos with her. At the time Susan was still living with them, sleeping on the couch.

She could see that he was upset when he announced to her that Amanda had left. It was as much as he could do not to go after her, really did not want her to go but he knew that she was a detractor from everything he tried to do, every plan he tried to put into operation, ironically so much of what the pet shop had become was because of the things she had brought into it. He only wanted it to be a dog shop where he could sell dog food, trim dogs and even find better dogs for people. Everything else only increased stock and labour required to run the business.

He told Susan that if she didn't mind being alone with him there, she was still welcome to sleep on the couch where she had been sleeping. Susan was a real pro, she didn't bat one of her eyes as she looked at him, had been through so many upheavals in her life that she was almost oblivious to situations changing.

Amanda found her cause in and for life. She became, "Saved" devoted her life to Jesus. She joined the Baptist Seminary. She even got Grew interested but after going with her to many different churches he found one that he sort of related to finding more in the words of Jesus, than the process of being saved, but for awhile he thought he was "Saved".

Amanda did not believe him and he wondered himself whether it was only to get her back. He saw many in the church who he knew were only going through the motions but what right did he have to judge? None. The church itself was too aggressive for him in promoting their local church and collecting money and he faded from their influence. In time that particular church was no longer there.

Amanda, had kept calling, even when he asked her not to. 20 years later she was still calling, still not married, with all sorts of ailments. He was the healthy one; she had allergies and conditions that they didn't even know what they were. She blamed dog-washing chemicals, he wondered about the pot. She was always trying to bring him to the Lord, but his philosophy became somewhat anti religion, believing all religions to be mans rationalization for dying, still referring back to the words of Jesus, the Sermon on the Mount and the Sermon on the Plains. This became his simple religion. Amanda was still "saved", working for the Lord. Susan and Grew lived together for a while, him in the bed, and her on the couch. She really was a sweet kid but he had to wonder what their connection was. She would go down town often; before she went she would sometimes help him with the dogs.

One day she had wanted to look at a puppy but when she was finished she did not put it back, she forgot. Then she wanted a ride to the bus. He didn't see the puppy lying under the tire and ran over it. He was so upset he drove her to the bus but told her not to come back. It was probably fifteen years later that she did look him up again with the story of where she had been. He was so happy to hear from her. She was like his own child, would have loved to have had sex with her but she had to leave town, besides he was with someone else who was very upset at his elated response. Susan was doing okay and Grew hoped he would meet her again one day.

He was working on his own again, had sold the farm property, had sold the pet shop to the store next door for a small sum and was back working at trimming dogs out of the basement at the kennel. He was going to a church on Sundays and the people there were treating him well. There were a couple of incidents where some of the young girls of the church wanted to come out and see the animals, it was something that he could see no problem with. They were a bit old for Charles as he was at that time about 12 years old, they were around seventeen. They did come out but then wanted to keep coming out, a redhead and a blonde. The blonde lived with her separated mother, the redhead lived with her separated father.

It was summer when they arrived one day as Grew was on his way to the community swimming pool. They had their bathing suits with them, which were bikinis so he allowed them to come with he and Charles. In the pool he kept getting rubbed and teased by this pretty redhead, would be the first to admit that he was enjoying it and getting aroused. As he thought, back he thought she was probably maturing emotionally, ready to try out what she had. She came around a few more times and Grew was beginning to wonder about her approach, giving the impression that she frankly wanted loving--one of those danger signals he often missed.

He had a conversation with her father shortly after that who made it quite clear that he wasn't happy with Grew spending time with his daughter. Grew answered in a way that essentially said that it was okay with him if she stayed away. After that she did stay away. It was probably the best course to take because he was certainly aware of her willingness. Grew had been there before.

And then Lisa showed up again on his doorstep. He was pretty wrapped up in this Christianity belief at that time, even trying to talk her into the wisdom of it. It did keep them at arms length at first, which wasn't without regrets. She was even more attractive at this stage than she had been as a teen-ager.

She came by often as she was supposed to be picking up the coins at a coin laundry that her and her husband owned. She would walk with Grew through the fields as he walked the dogs and they would talk. She told him of the years that they had been apart. He thought she had told him of losing a baby but had decided not to try again or perhaps there was a reason why she couldn't have one.

As they walked, she went on about the overemphasis on the pleasure of sex. To her it had not been a good thing. It was done as a chore that she obediently complied with. Harry and her had had a couple of affairs each with other people but they too, at least on her part where disappointments.

They walked together through the fields with the German Shepherds. They went back to the creek where Amanda and he used to go--telling her of the relationship he'd had with Amanda, how he was now on his own. He imagined it was how the religion discussion came about.

Lisa was one that had had religion shoved down her throat from a little girl. Her parents sending her to school at a convent only soured her more on the whole idea. Grew thought that perhaps it had something to do with what seemed to him as a total lack of conscience. She had that quality of never looking back with regret, was able to accept each new experience on its own merit, their feelings for each other were still there though. As they started running through the field one day he lined her up and made a tackle on her bringing her down to the soft ground and as he continued to hold her for a few minutes, he moved up her body. She expressed her thoughts that they were going to have to contain their emotions, not get back to where they had once been. He kept lying there with her, she made no effort to rise.

He said, "Okay, if that is what you want to do. With my religious belief I shouldn't be doing anything that will cause you marital problems anyway".

They continued to lie there in the dirt talking about this thing, She said, "My marriage is not that good, the sex is yuh. Harry tries to watch everything I do, control every moment of my time, bugs him that he can't reach me while I am picking up the coins from the Laundromat. As for your religion, I'm like Amanda, I don't believe it, don't believe you are really changed that much."

He was still lying there with her as they were talking. He moved up closer so his face was next to hers and he kissed her. It was soft, gentle; the kiss went on for a while. She didn't pull back either and he made no move to touch any of her body parts. He really did believe in Christianity, thinking maybe he was being tested. If so, at that moment he wasn't doing too well but he was under some control.

The kiss broke and he pulled her up by the hand. As they continued to walk in the fields he still held her soft warm hand. Then she talked more about her husband, told him that even her doctor had asked why she still stayed with him. She said she needed the financial security.

When she said that and she often repeated it, Grew would remind her that she also had a well paying job, no responsibility of kids, just one cat and that it was dumb to stay somewhere if she wasn't happy. This guy had done a control job on her. It made Grew less inclined to respect the ownership of this wonderful person. Then Grew reflected back to times he stayed when he was not happy.

She went on about Harry's theories on sex which caused Grew to start his argument again as they walked back to the house, telling her that he thought that she had got it all wrong. He was not sure how many times this sort of scene unfolded. Obviously they were still very close, the feeling was dormant but still there. Now he was going to have to talk her out of all this crazy stuff that this ex cop had spoon-fed her. It became normal to hold her hand as they walked. It also became normal to kiss her as she left for the day but when Grew looked back at his own life it was not something to brag about either.

One day she came in the house and he made them some coffee. They were standing in the living room talking again where she was elaborating on Harry's concept of sex and her idea that it wasn't all it was talked up to be. There was an air of electricity between them; she talked rapidly. She almost seemed to be trying to talk around it. Grew caught her in an embrace; he picked her up, and carried her as she struggled, legs kicking, to the bedroom, putting her down on the bed.

Grew said, "Now stop talking and love me a bit."

She looked up at him saying, "I'm not sure this is a good idea, what are you going to do?"

"You and I are going to hold each other for a bit, you know how I still feel about you--wouldn't keep coming back if there wasn't something mutual. We don't have to do anything but just lie here together. I want to hold you in my arms. You know how often I have thought of you through the years? Even Marilyn said that I should have left her and made whatever arrangements you and I could have made. Did you know she was envious of our relationship, the thing you and I had going?"

He told Lisa of the experiences Marilyn had had with the marriage councilor, said he thought it had helped them. She lay there as he snuggled up next to her, talking with her; she was not trying to get up or even move. He moved closer beside her and took her in his arms again. They kissed tentatively and softly, going on for a long time before their mouths opened and they became more passionate. He was lying right up against her warm soft body, was sure she could feel the hardness in his pants. He started massaging her breasts that were not large but at least for him delightful, he worked his way under her clothing, her bra, massaged the bare flesh, then he stripped her to the waist as she sat up to accommodate the removal, letting him take things off for her.

He twisted gently on the nipples, sucked on her tits when she lay down again, brought a lot of the breast meat into his mouth then slipped his lips back to play with the nipples again for awhile. She was getting warmer as they necked. He released the button on the top of his pants, undid his own zipper, bringing out his now hard penis.

Then she rolled onto her back without direction or command and undid her own jeans. Grew watched as she slid panties and jeans down those enticing legs in one motion. He noticed the medium complexion of her skin, the great condition of the muscles, flat stomach leading down to the brown tuft. When the jeans were coming off he watched her bending those delightful legs to reach down to push them off her feet. He moved his mouth to the center of that dark patch of hair between her legs, gently separating legs as he did. Her hands took hold of his erection, she stroked it as he sucked on her; his hands were then moving all over her. They continued to stroke and play with each other. Then he was moving his body between her legs.

As she looked down at what he was doing, she said softly, "I don't know if you are going to get that thing in me. I didn't remember it as being that big."

As he came down with his body, looking into her brown eyes, he said, "It doesn't matter if I don't, It is so exquisite loving you like this. If I can't get it in I will just work it in the entrance, it is enough just to be so close and part of you."

With that he gently moved it between her legs to the center of that dark patch. She was right, the entrance was tight, and it wasn't going to fall in.

He put the knob there anyway, gently moving it around between the folds of flesh. It wasn't long before the lubrication of her surrounded the knob and he pushed. She looked into his face as he did.

She was feeling it. She was smiling. Gently and easily, snuggly it moved into her, a bit at a time, then out a bit, then back. She moved with him as they pushed at each other. It was truly joyful, a mutual effort towards the pleasure.

Then it was right in her, he moved back a bit, and in again. He asked her, "How does that feel? are you alright?"

"Just fine, full but spectacular, keep moving it back and forth just like that, just the way you are doing." and her hips moved towards him, slowly again. She was still smiling.

They were moving more and more together as they pushed together, then back. There was no fear of premature ejaculation here, this was a love match. They went on and on. Somehow he knew that it was right as she started to pick up the pace. Then they were furiously kissing again, their bodies quickened the pace till he was aware of their bodies slapping at each other, two physically right bodies pushing together as their organs played their music. Then he was coming and sure that she was too.

As they lay there with his penis embedded, but subsiding, he could feel the muscles of her pushing him out. He kissed her again as they lay there sweating.

She then said, "I am so stupid, I never believed that it could be that fantastic, all this time I have been living with the idea it was overrated. Anyone who knew must have known I was the problem. I'm sorry."

He kissed her again then said," Don't be sorry, a lot of it has to do with how we feel about each other. It was just as great to me because you are so incredible I have always loved you even though we were from a different time, a society that wouldn't allow our love. Now you have been programmed into materialism, it will be up to you whether you can go back now. Still it was all so enjoyable, even if it never happens ever again".

It did happen several more times, perhaps destroying his commitment at that time to Christianity. The old lack of conscience on her part was still there. Many times she would come by, he would lead her in the pleasurable sex play that Marilyn had picked up from the sex doctor. It was indeed a great time. Grew continued to council her on not being controlled as they continued to walk in the fields. Her visits were becoming more frequent, Grew got the idea that she was taking more chances. There was something about Lisa that was attracted to the adventure of taking chances. She was almost content to live under control as long as she could play her game, the game that said, "You don't really control me; you just think you do".

Lisa would drop by at any time but it was hard to tell when. He tried to stick around when he thought she would be there but then she wouldn't be able to show up and he would be disappointed. Other times he would have to go out, when he returned, there in the kitchen would be a love note from her. Sometimes when he wasn't there she would meet with Charles and they would take the dogs out for a walk. He too developed a caring feeling for her. Sometimes he would ask Grew about her, and he would talk softly about how they had worked together when she had been a student. Charles knew there was more than that and Grew made no secret of his attraction to her.

The two of them, Lisa and Grew would lie around in the nude enjoying each other. They would fondle and stroke until they brought each other to a sexual peak. Often they would change directions as they mouthed each other from each other's feet, sucking, and licking until they reached the special sexual places where each would dwell. Then they would jump into a wild sexual thrashing of limbs and bodies. Sometimes they would shower together, soaping each other's bodies before she left.

She would take her love lessons home though. Her idea was to try out what she had learned on her husband. Perhaps she was beginning to believe that she had not given Harry a fair chance. It was bringing them closer together. He was starting to enjoy sex with her.

He would ask, "What has got into you, are you my wife?"

After too quick a time with her and Grew together she announced one day that her husband was quitting the police force; they were going to the States to open a business. He had learned the Laundromat business as the best for taxes.

They went south to Georgia. Before they went her and Grew had more love sessions, she even took him to show the house that they were leaving. He was very nervous to be there so they didn't stay long. It was depressing to lose her again but he had expected it

CHAPTER 17
More Adjustments

Grew was feeling depressed after she left. He had never asked her to give up her marriage, to come live with him but he did realize that she was as close to Chloe as he could ever expect. There was no question though, he had offered nothing while she was still attached to her husband. It would have had to be her decision to leave before Grew could even consider getting back with her.

Years later he would realize the value of how close they had been. If there was ever, true love, they had experienced it. She called him from Georgia a few times. She too could scam a few quarters for phone calls. At first her and her husband enjoyed the new found love, but it faded, without the mutual total commitment. Grew wasn't surprised. She told him she had also had another affair with someone else, still searching, but it was empty. Her husband too had done the same with similar results. As Grew wrote his story it was a long time since he had heard from her but then she probably did not know where to find him.

After she left Grew felt empty. He talked to Charles about going to the west coast mountains to explore the wilds--his sanctuary. He agreed to take Charles friend, but they decided to advertise in the paper for someone to help with the driving. Charles and his friend were thirteen at the time. Charles laughed when he saw their name painted on the roof of the van.

It was a time in Grew's life when everything was about to change; he'd lost three women that he had been so close to. Did he ever love any of them? There was always the feeling of being on the outside looking at life as it went by. He wondered what he was going to do with the rest of his life, was there still a plan for him?

He developed a sort of Asthma that doctors contributed to years of breathing dog hair, so he had decided to stop the dog clipping business. He thought it was more the emotional distress of losing all his loves around that time; long before he'd committed himself to raising Charles as his first priority so the next step was to determine what else he would do for a living. First he was going to return to one of his first loves, the mountains; wanted to explore some of the back trails, places where few people had ever traveled. Charles looked forward to it too because on the back roads with no other cars he would be allowed to drive the truck.

The responses from the ad started coming in. There was one woman whose husband had left. She was really in a bad way, not the person to go on the trip but he did promise he would call her when he got back. Why should Grew remember her? He didn't know but her name was Margaret.

Then there was another called Eleanor. She was a person that worked at plucking hair out of women's legs and eyebrows. Is that called Electrolysis? She had a table set up in her apartment. When she phoned, Grew was about to go out to deliver the dogs. When she asked Charles what his father was like he said," Just great". She agreed to come to the house and was met by Charles. He confirmed his dad was great.

So when Grew arrived home she was waiting. If he was great, she was greater. She was of medium build and about five foot nine inches tall, had a very pretty face and nice smile. They hit it off right away so decided to go up the street to hit some golf balls; Charles went with them.

When they came back to the house Charles went out somewhere, he was a smart and good kid that left the two of them in the house alone. It wasn't long before the two of them were necking on his bed.

She had on these full legged slacks of light material that were so full they were like a skirt with a piece in the middle. The necking got quite heavy but he told her they could stop whenever she wanted to. She was kissing him wildly, he was kissing her around the neck, her ears, then he opened the front of her blouse.

Contained in a full sized bra were shapely breasts that flowed out without changing shape as he divested her of the undergarment. They were full, bouncy and she responded with obvious pleasure as he sucked, molding these things by hand.

He was moving his other hand up the leg of these pant things when she took his hand, just after it passed the knee, and stopped it saying. "I think that is far enough for now. I think we better stop while I am still able to stop."

"Okay" he said, "do you want to go out to the living room now? I have some wine".

"Yeh, let's take a breather The wine sounds fine."

They did stop, sat in the front room with their two glasses of wine. They kissed again in the front room then she said, "I've got to get going, I'll call you when I get home."

"Just give me another kiss before you go."

Then they were kissing again, then passionately, until he was pushing her backwards again, into the bedroom. She was backing easily, then they were on the bed again. In a while he was moving his hand up her bare leg under her spacious slacks again.

As her hand stopped the movement again, he took out his prick, putting it in her other hand. It did something to her. She loved it, played with it like a baby as she nursed it, with both hands, rolling the foreskin around, on and off the knob. Its as if she had forgotten to hold his wandering hand.

That hand was now moving up her inner thigh and before she could object, if she ever had intended to, it was massaging her clit, wandering into the wet cave and back. Legs spread without asking, she continued to love the hard penis.

There were no underpants on her, Grew found he could push the leg of these things right up, dangling around her hips with only one strand of cloth between her legs. He wiggled his body between her legs, pulled up to where he was face to face with her. Almost before they realized it, this hard thing she was holding onto, pushing the skin back and forth, was inside her. Grew was not sure whether it was her or him that put it in but it went in so smooth. Then her legs, those long shapely legs came up and fit around his waist, the cloth from her slacks hung loosely around her mid body and they fucked. There was an excitement to that cloth hanging, it was a symbol of a spontaneous decision, almost like sex at the moment of desire, on a table or floor.

It was enjoyable as he drove it into her with her body coming back up to meet him. Then they rolled over and she got on top. Grew didn't come so fast that way so they went on for the longest time, both of them, doing the marathon. They lay there for a long time before moving.

Grew went to her apartment the next time where they did it on the table where she treated her patients. She had put some greasy stuff inside her so it was a bit too slippery but nice and worthwhile. She wasn't available for the trip out West.

Grew ended up getting a guy who helped drive as far as Kamloops. It was a mile after mile trip across the prairies. They arrived in the mountains, near where he had decided to start. Near the base of 10,000 foot plus, Mount Tatlow where there was a trailer set up as a store. They bought some supplies and were told that if they left their vehicle anywhere in the woods, when they came back the tires would be gone. It was a scarier thought than that of meeting Grizzlies.

They also had with them a shotgun with bear slugs. He didn't want to shoot a bear but the gun was brought along as a last defense. The boys and Grew spent a Sunday morning shooting at a stump until a nasty ranger arrived to question them as to what they were doing. There was a sobering moment when one of the boys shot a hole in the tent, thinking the gun was empty.

As Charles drove the vehicle up the back road towards a lake called Taseko, the road suddenly veered around a corner up hill. As

Grew looked to his side he was aware of a creek about 200 ft below. He was scared, but then he was always afraid of heights. He just said," Keep going, don't stop till it gets flat."

It didn't bother Charles but it was a shocker for Grew, beginning to realize the danger they could get into just by getting stuck in those mountains. They parked the truck and together they climbed up the side of Mount Tatlow, but even that they gave up on as they climbed over burned logs, through swamps and snow. The trips up the mountains are not just a straight walk up, there are areas where snow has stayed longer in hollows, until when it has gone, there are swamps and there were no trails. They were concerned about the van so did not stay on the mountain overnight. He could see that to reach the top would have taken more than a day.

They got back to Toronto. Again it was time to decide what to do with the rest of life. Charles got all wrapped up in hockey, summer and winter so Grew got involved too. It was not a way of making a living but it was looking after his priority. For a while he continued to groom some dogs on his own but it is not something that you can do a bit of. When people want their dogs done they want them done soon. Often there was just too much to do.

Lynn came around to the house a few times, would usually have the dogs with her so her and Grew would go for a walk with them. Then she would put them back in the car and come in for a coffee. She was very upset one day as they had their coffee, she sat saying nothing, then after a silence she told him that she had found out that her husband had been fooling around with what had been her best friend. They had quite a conversation about it in which they talked about what her options were. Really there weren't too many. She could decide to break up with him or try to work it out. It seemed that at that time, she and her husband had been talking about it but were not getting anywhere.

As Grew and her talked they were in the kitchen. Grew said something like, she could always get even if she wanted to.

Then she said, "Yeh, with whom?"

It was dangerous territory, Was it something he wanted to get into? He said jokingly, "I'm available for a change."

He thought it wouldn't hurt to give her a bit of loving or make her feel that someone cared. At that time they were both standing in the kitchen. He reached out, took her hand that she gave to him willingly, pulled her into his arms and kissed her.

She responded with that wide-open full kiss of abandonment that she was so good at. They just stood there kissing.

Then he was backing her over the back of the chair as he pressed up against her. This threw her legs wide apart for balance, the whole front of her body up against his body with legs spread, him leaning over her. She was really bent far back, she couldn't move. He could feel her body against his erection, right where it would be felt, in the clothed valley. Through her sweater his hands worked at unclasping her bra, as he moved to the side. She knew what he was doing but was caught but he had dragged it out long enough, she had not known how far he would go. It was very exciting for them both but he didn't want to take that extra step. He did get the bra undone, which set her into a panicky state of getting herself together again. As he had her backed over the chair she had kept repeating, "My back, my back."

He let her go and she straightened herself out. It had made her feel more wanted, she was obviously excited, seemed to forget her other problems for the moment. Grew felt that she had really got turned on, he could have gone further if he had wanted to but he didn't think it was what she wanted or needed, not yet.

It was a beginning though, it certainly didn't stop her from coming back. She would walk into the house often without even knocking, obviously without fear of him. From time to time he would try to steer her into the bedroom saying, "Come on, neck with me on the bed".

At first she wouldn't have any part of it, saying, "I've got to go." and so she would but the attention was making her feel good. He would go back to work doing whatever he was doing--wondering a bit about her--she had really turned him on with the bra unfastening scene.

One day she said, "Okay" because she was menstruating. She came and laid on the bed with him. After necking for a while she let him get between her legs as their kissing became more passionate. She had tight blue jeans on, which Grew knew he would never be able to get off without her help. They went through a mock sex thing with her legs wrapped around his body, a dance that got very active, body slapping against body. It was the first, but such sessions continued.

Awhile later when this scene was repeated, he started getting under her sweater with his hands on to her bra covered tits, which she never made any objection to. After that it wasn't long before he got the bra right off, sucking those lovely things, they were that, there was something about them that was really special, blue veins tracing throughout.

It seemed to turn her on even more, She would suddenly jump off the bed, rush out of the house again saying, "Gotta go, see you again". She would be doing herself up, as she was going out the door.

One day she came while Grew had been in bed sick or just tired. Guess it was cool out or he was having chills because he was in there in his long underwear. When she came that time she knocked on the door. He threw a pair of jeans on, and came to the door to let her in--told her he had been in bed because of the way he was feeling so was getting back into bed but she was welcome to come in there to talk to him.

A bit to Grew's surprise she came in the bedroom. He got back under the covers keeping his jeans on. She lay down beside him outside the blankets and they kissed. She was a superior kisser. He reached out from the blankets, fondled her tits through her sweater and asked her to get in the bed with him. She said that she was having her period so couldn't do anything anyway. Then she was getting in beside him.

She pulled back the blankets, sliding in, pulling the blankets over them both with their jeans on. She moved into his arms which was nice, before long he had her bare to the waste, working on those pale blue veined tits with the nice nipples just begging to be sucked.

While he kissed her and his hands played titty, then he would suck. It went on and on as they played together.

He had a great hard on that his jeans were restricting. He said," Hold on a minute, it is too hot with my pants on with this long underwear underneath, have to get rid of something". Getting out of bed, he was sure that his penis pushed the cloth out.

While she lay there watching he undid his pants, slipped them off. He also took his top off leaving him with just his long underwear; then he got back in the bed beside her, and went back to kissing that inviting open mouth. His bare top rubbed up against her tits, skin to skin.

He slid over her, got on top of her with his legs between hers and they went back to doing their mock fuck again. After awhile he slipped to the side as he tried to get her jeans down. He got two buttons undone at the top, was trying to get his hand under them but they were too tight, still he did get them down a bit. Then she was pulling them up again, buttoning them even as he kissed her. He took it as a "NO".

He needed something though and slipped his hard prick out of the long johns, found her hand--placing it on the hard thing. She didn't let go, his act didn't seem to bother her. In fact she stroked it gently back and forth as Grew continued loving her, massaging the breasts, kissing her, sucking around her neck. She was getting into the prick manipulation thing, pulling the foreskin back. She was Jewish so probably had never seen an uncircumcised prick.

Then he was at her pant buttons again. This time he was surprised when she didn't stop him, let him get all the buttons and zipper undone--was sliding the jeans off her legs. She was letting him do it. She didn't have panties on either. As he looked for the hair he could see she was shaved. She lifted a leg so he could get the jean leg off her ankle she said to him, "You wont fuck me will you?"

He looked in her face, kissed her again as he pushed her nicely shaped legs apart, looking under the blanket. He rolled between her legs directing his prick that she was still holding towards the smooth cunt, long johns were off straight away. He took over holding and directing his prick, pushed in the area for a bit with his knob then put his hand around the area feeling for the clit and felt the string; she really was menstruating.

As he pulled the tampon came out so easily and then he pulled her legs up around him with no resistance from her and his prick almost found its own way into the smooth wet channel, an ideal fit, so warm smooth and slippery. She moved with him.

Then she stopped moving when he was in her full length, said to him, "I've never done it before with other than my husband. Please can I ask you to take it out? Take it out...please."

As he lay there with his erect prick warmly buried in her, feeling the glove like fit so nice, so tight on his penis, he answered "Even if I take it out now you wont be able to say you have never slept with anyone else. I am in here now so we are going to do it." With that he started taking it in and out.

She was going with him, throwing her body right into it, her middle smashing back against him, her mouth opened wide as they almost violently sucked each other's mouths together. But it was her body rhythm, she was good, excellent. That hole kept driving back and forth on his prick, she even rolled them both over, and then she was on top, smashing her hole on and off the impaler. They both came in great orgasms. She rolled to the side and he slid out.

He thought she looked so proud as she got out of the bed naked, strutted to the bathroom. His impression was that she looked better naked than clothed a real picture woman. She told him that she had not had an orgasm for a long time, even though she had second thoughts about getting into this thing she had no regrets. She said, "What kept you anyway, I thought we were never going to do it?"

It happened again in the house a few days later. He found it equally as great but by that time she was starting to have guilt feelings. Afterwards they had coffee as they talked. She let him know that it was causing her real guilt feelings.

One other time much later, he had been somewhere with Lynn to check out a dog for her, they were back at her house. He had her in the study on the floor with her top off, those blue veins leading him on. She would have had sex with him right on the floor but he asked, "When are the kids coming home from school?"

She looked up into his face, she would have taken the risk. She said, "In about five minutes"

He said, "Okay, I better go then, but I don't want to."

Grew associated with her as a friend for quite awhile but sort of felt that she had told her husband about them. He became involved with someone else too that knew there was something between Lynn and him so she became forbidden territory. When he did phone her leaving a message on her machine, she didn't call back. He often wondered about that real classy lady.

Now it was time to start finding his life again. There was a feeling of not knowing what he was meant to do, for that moment having lost track of any plan. It was not in him to pray for guidance but in some way as he had walked he had waited and wondered just what he should be doing. He had enjoyed the experience with the farm, a little sorry that it had gone. Property ownership had largely been the only reason he had any money at all. He enrolled in a real estate course. Six weeks after it started he was licensed to sell, starting out by doing the very basic thing of knocking on doors, day after day going out talking to people. There were breaks where they had meetings in the office; to him a distraction because as all they ever did was do the praises of those who had sold something. It was very basic motivation, a pat on the back initiative.

He did get a listing after a couple of months and in time did make a few sales but he needed direction, which he wasn't getting; the whole industry seemed embroiled in cutthroat procedures that the school had taught against. As Grew looked back, there was no room for someone who cared about the people they were working for, the people selling property.

Margaret invited him to a party that she was having at her house--a nice lady but depressed because of the husband that had left. Everyone had left the party but Grew. It wasn't long before they were into embraces, then into her bed. Sex was nice with her but when she was on top he was massaging what he though was a breast but it felt strange. He looked up and realized it was her hanging down middle; it bothered him at the time, realizing there was a certain amount of turnoff possible from physical differences. He'd overlooked the distortions of Marilyn's breasts, why couldn't he overlook this? As he looked back, Margaret would have been more acceptable if she had not been so depressed; yet later he had polarized to other depressed people, only to eventually move on. Positively he was not ready to accept someone solely on her wealth--not ready to be kept. The house she lived in was a mansion.

CHAPTER 18

Real Estate and The One Parent

While doing his washing at a Laundromat he saw a flyer on the notice board about a one-parent group. Soon after going to a few of their outings he joined the group; sold a few properties through his association with them and would have been well to stay uninvolved with anyone in the group just work towards selling their properties. Marriage breakups were a great source of finding properties for sale.

It wasn't how he looked at it though; he was starting to enjoy the people, their dances and the days they spent out at picnics. It didn't take him long to find that most of these people were in someway attached to someone else. There were not too many of the women available and since he wasn't much of a drinker, one beer if that; Grew became the designated rescuer.

There was a time when they had stayed overnight at someone's cottage. There were people sleeping everywhere. One man who had just gone through a messy separation was staggering through the yard dangerously close to the canal. Grew spent most of the night, with Mary, one of the other none drinkers, consoling, keeping this man from harm to himself.

There was also a woman there who he had taken home from one of the dances, which had ended in her bed. The entrance of her teen-aged daughter had interrupted sex with her. Grew didn't know whether there was a feeling of rejection left over from that or not but at the overnight event she took the occasion to chew him out about something he had said, perhaps it was an attack on his perceived Puritanism; his position would seem odd. There was definitely a difference in his philosophy that put the children as a priority. Philosophy to have fun, damn the children was common in the group; to many children were left on their own. Grew was later given the opportunity to vent his opinions when first he was asked to host their weekly local TV show, then took over as their local president, promoted by Mary. The old feeling of being on the outside, looking in was there again, okay as long as he didn't talk about the things that he considered wrong-- but he did.

Yet he was no Puritan. There was a youngish engaging woman who had been left by her husband. She had gone out with some one they considered was out to take advantage of her. She was expected to be at a meeting where the group was worried about her; it was decided that Grew would go over to "check up on her". As he arrived Nan was just issuing her guy out the door. Grew hardly knew this woman but she invited him in; she was having a coffee so he had one with her. He could see that she was feeling down and for some reason what started out as a simple hug and kiss, progressed to necking; the previous guy must have warmed her up because before long Grew was playing with her ample breasts, as she was stroking his penis in a most exciting way.

Grew remembered the scene, couldn't remember whether her panties were off or on, maybe he'd just shoved them aside--but there was enough room for him to work. Her body was lovely as were the legs flailing on either side of his body as he worked his finger around in what felt like a wide open, warm responsive hole in the middle of it all.

They were on the couch, her knees were up, legs kicking the air, and his body was between them, nearing that warm hole when the phone rang. Their mouths separated as they looked at each other. His inclination was to let the phone ring but it was disturbing. She said, "Can you answer it?"

Finally he said he would get it, "Don't go away."

It was Mary at the meeting, saying that everyone was waiting for them to get there before starting the meeting. He looked over at the couch at the "prey" or "prize" to see Nan putting herself back together. He said, "Okay, we'll be there".

They got their things together, and then drove in one car to the meeting. Some time later he had supper with this lady--with some expectations but accepted that she was too young for him, but as he thought about it, maybe she wasn't. She was someone that could let it all go sexually. That supper evening he also had another concern.

Yet Nan and he did have a rapport. They became very good friends, even after she married again and moved out to the country. Grew regarded her as one of his favourites. She too had been married young and had grown in a different direction from her first husband. When set free, the qualities in this lady emerged, making her a better person.

It was on that evening at her place having supper when her and Grew had determined that they were not going to complete their previous sex tryst when he asked to use her phone; he wanted to check up on someone else. Denise who he had met through the real estate, she had been in a bad way, had just learned that her husband was cheating. Grew had been giving her moral support.

He had met her by knocking on her back door one day, asking if they were interested in selling their property. She invited him in but expressed the thought that at that moment they weren't. They shared coffee as her children played. Then they went outside where her and Grew continued to talk. When he was about to leave, they stood almost together looking at each other. He knew then that there was more going on that she would have liked to have talked about like a silent invitation to return--so he had.

Later she had invited him to a night yard party they were having; told him about her friend who she thought would be a good match for him. It turned out that he spent more time with Denise at that party. Her husband spent time with the one that she had brought for Grew. It was all right with him because the two of them related well, as apparently did her friend with her husband.

Denise was an artist. She showed him many of the things she had painted which he was impressed with. They were her creations but she also did art commercially, which gave him thoughts about things she could do for real estate. She showed him a project that she had done for a development, which he went to look at. She had done a professional job but he was unable to get the listing for the houses.

Another time that he came by she told him that they were going to move to Alberta because of her husbands company that had transferred him there. She was sorry to leave but they planned not to sell the house but to rent it out--told him then that she really did not want to go but was going anyway.

Then she dropped the bomb, she found out the friend she had tried to line him up with was having an affair with her husband. There was closeness between her and Grew and as he was leaving he had offered to take her out to supper before she left. They made a date to do that, he kissed her as he was leaving. It was a warm friendly kiss--held too long--leaving the promise that there could be more.

It was two days before he was to take her to supper that he had called her from his friend Nan's house. She sounded very distraught, hardly able to talk as he tried to question her but she didn't want to answer. There was a concern as he asked her if she was there alone, she just said that the kids were there but that her husband wouldn't be home that night. When asked if he could come over she said that she would be all right.

He didn't think she was all right, so told her that he would be there in five minutes. She said, "No, don't come"

He briefed Nan a bit about the story, said that he was going to go to see if he could comfort her a bit. Nan gave him a funny look, she had seen this man's comforting, but understood. They kissed as they parted.

As he came in to Denise's he could see that she had been crying. He asked her, "Denise, what is the matter?"

She said, "My husband has gone out of town for a few days, but before he went we had a discussion in which he told me about the affair that he had been having with Patricia. It was certainly more involved than what I had thought but really things have been less than they should have been for some time."

While they stood there he took her in his arms, just holding her for a while. She broke free turning to the side saying, "Come on in for awhile. I really am happy to see you. You don't need to get bothered by my problems though."

She stepped aside as he walked through the doorway. She made them coffee then brought it into the front room.

Denise was one of those quiet people that one would think nothing would ever bother about five foot eight, probably one hundred and thirty pounds. Her body seemed to have strong limbs. He had noticed a long rump, not particularly obvious breasts. She was not adorned with makeup, her blond hair flowed straight, not precise, around her shoulders, surrounding a face, somewhat weathered, that this hair often obscured when she bent forward. It was a face without distinction because everything was normal but there was a look of character. This came out when she talked, intelligent conversation--a pleasure to listen to.

After handing him his coffee as he sat in a single chair she sat down herself in another chair about three feet away. He had sat there purposely so she would not feel he was on the make. If he had sat on the chesterfield it might have given another impression. She then would have been in the position to sit beside him not to offend him or sitting elsewhere to let him know there was no chance. So he sat in the chair. This man was learning his craft.

She talked, him quietly listening as she told him of her grief. As he finished his coffee he put the cup on the floor beside him, reached out his hand for hers and she willingly placed her warm hand in his.

For what seemed like time standing still the two of them sat there holding hands in their respective chairs. He could feel the warmth of her hand. She had calmed noticeably, conversation had become more humourous, light discussion on things that had happened but he didn't let go of her hand. It was almost without words when he looked over to her and their eyes met. He knew and knew that she did too.

Standing up, still holding her hand, he moved over to her chair. She said simply, quietly stretching the words, "Noo, Noo."

But he reached down, putting one arm under her legs, the other around her back and lifted her, carried her into the bedroom without her trying to block his progress at the doors, placed her gently on the bed and as he did laid down besides her. As they lay there he put his arms around her and they kissed. Almost casually, as time stood still he had his hands under her clothes, massaging her bare skin. Her bra was easy to get off as was her sweater. Her breasts were not big but that had never bothered him before. When she was down to just her panties she excused herself saying, "I'll be right back" and she was off to the bathroom.

While she was gone he pulled the covers back to expose the sheets, removed all his own clothing, and lay there with his prick reaching for the ceiling.

She said something on her return but he didn't remember what it was, thought it was something about there being no commitment to go with this. Whatever, it didn't bother him and he saw no reason to answer.

They continued their lovemaking; that is what it was, lovemaking, it was very unhurried, he enjoyed every muscle on her legs, every feel of every piece of skin as they licked and stroked each other from head to toe, culminating in a complete capture of his penis, tightly clasped within her, until they had satisfied each other. He knew she had enjoyed it as he had. There was something about the way they were doing it, strictly for the pleasure of the moment. It was a prize for both of them.

Two days later her and Grew went to supper, had an enjoyable time. Afterward she had come back to his place with him. They went to bed again; the sex was more than enjoyable. After he had come in her, she took his penis, again sucking it so masterfully that after awhile she brought it back to full erection. Then she was on it again, sinking it into herself. As she sat on top of him, she rode his penis for the longest time. It was infinite pleasure until finally they came again.

Denise left soon after that. He received one letter from her from Alberta. She wanted him to contact her through her friend, which he tried to do. She left him Pat's phone number but did not give him her last name. He phoned the number, which said that the number had been disconnected. So had Denise and Grew. It was time for him to start rebuilding his life. Even though it was stated that there was to be no commitment, Grew felt that this one who had gotten away could have been more than a superior sexual experience. She had the intelligence and a compatible outlook on life. When he had known her she was in a state of confusion, faced with trying to put her own marriage back together or moving on. Grew never heard from her again.

Years later he had had a similar tryst with a woman that he had met a week before New Years Eve. They had both returned to a dinner he was invited to on New Year's Eve everyone else had plans to go somewhere. So he and Rebecca had walked a snowy cold wooded road together until she had come back to his apartment. She couldn't stop shivering and as he held her she still shivered. He had rubbed her body, then under her clothes had taken off her top and massaged warming bountiful tits. He had just kept stripping her and then took off his own clothes. He was neither erect nor embarrassed, but took her into his single bed and got under the covers with her. For an hour he caressed her until she was warm. She noted as she looked fondly into his face, "Where in the world did you come from?

They had gone to church together at midnight and he had returned to her place. For the next month they had read to each other from religious teachings, they had danced together in her apartment in the nude to the strains of "Unchained Melody". They had slept together and had walked together and danced together and sung together at the local legion hall. They had read to each other and he had read to her while she bathed.

The wonder of her screaming orgasms eventually gave his penis rebirth and eventually one evening, his penis again rose to full magnificent past expectations and as they clung together with this thing embedded within her, their orgasms came together in a fantastic explosion of love. The peak had been reached as Grew had learned the wonder of love as being a giving thing.

However outside forces conspired, that could not endure the wonder of what they had discovered and achieved. It was the unmistakable peak with nowhere to go but down. It was as if their pleasure had superseded the need for God. She had been in states of depression and elation, the pills prescribed he couldn't afford nor were they covered. Outside pressures eventually negated their love. Three months later they too had gone their own way. As he had recalled the brief association with Denise he could not avoid the comparison.

Mary was the center of the one parent group. She was a none smoker or drinker, as was Grew, and the brain behind whoever was president at any time. Her and Grew also had the same priorities about children first. She not only was the cornerstone of the branch they were in but also was the inspiration, the motivation of the whole organization. She was the rock that kept things going.

She was a widow with a son that was a few years younger than Charles so naturally there was some association that developed between the two boys. Mary was not a glamour girl but a person of extreme common sense. In some ways the mother mode that she displayed with her son, she extended to both Charles and Grew. She took over watching his finances and doing his income tax. While she worked at her day job she would come home to the supper he had prepared. He became quite close to her. There was never a question of trust and for most of their association, for a long time he respected the commitment of the relationship. While she did her evening meetings, if he did not go with her he often would stay at work, at first trying to sell real estate. She also started coming with him to his German Shepherd meetings, which he had started attending again.

They had become closer when she had designated him to host a weekly sitcom on the local television station that dealt with matters of the one parent group. At first it worked out well but as might be expected; Grew's questions to the children on air became more and more controversial. A few of the members started to object and some of the skeletons started sneaking out of closets.

Mary had convinced him to run for the president of the group. He had served as president of dog clubs at various times. With her backing he won. When he would put his president's messages in the monthly newsletters, some of the members found them pretty hard to take. Years later he found copies of them that Mary had put together for him. He didn't think he was so hard but these people hurt too much to hear the truth. They were used to being felt sorry for. So Grew finished out the year and then was defeated at the next election.

In the one parent group, although they were supposed to be all separate single entities, there were couples that it was understood belonged to each other. That is what they had become, although he could dance with anyone he chose, at the dances, the other women accepted that he was taken, going home with Mary.

Mary maintained her own apartment but the relationship got closer with Grew when she started eating at the kennel property that he was still renting from the highways department. Then she wanted to buy a reasonable piece of country property so Grew spent hours, first looking for something that she had described to him, then he drove her to look at these places. They spent a lot of time on the road, learning every side road from Toronto to Lake Simco.

While president, not yet with Mary he got a call from a woman one day, he decided to interview. She was the wife of a doctor, who had moved out. Grew went alone to her place. Somewhere he had written about the experience but had lost those notes but remembered sitting in her front room looking and studying pictures from Life magazine, side by side with Cathy.

As they sat, the two of them discussed the various pictures, life itself, what was going on in the world. As Grew thought back, he remembered the atmosphere becoming thick with the two of them, tell tale stares at each other, touching of hands, sitting down side by side, the moments of silence, the cautious turning towards each other, until the turn was made, they faced each other. The air was electric between them, why?

They looked at each other, the same look both ways, and then she was in his arms. It was passionate, wild, a scurrying and flinging aside of clothes, hands in her bra, it coming off, his own pants down, her legs spreading as her skirt came up over her waist, hands in panties, the wild clashing of teeth, mouths and tongues. It was spontaneous, almost a wild sign of the times.

Then she stopped. "It is too late."

Her children were due home. They could see the bus coming around the corner. He met her children as they came in; Cathy and Grew were dressed by then. His write-up was called, "The Interview". There was never a place to get it published, certainly not in the monthly newsletter. At the first dance Cathy attended she was obvious, apparently drunk, she hung on man after man. Her reputation was becoming established.

Some time after that time when Cathy, who was striking but with the pains of life showing in her face was then a member of the club; she was at one of the club dances. It was while Mary was still living in her own apartment. Somehow as Grew was dancing so close to this woman that she was, "eating out of his back pocket", as it was described, followed through with him taking her back to his place. At an opportune moment, the two of them had snuck out of the dance when it looked like no one would notice. They had sex in his bed, his room facing the driveway onto the property. In the middle of their fun they could see the lights come up the driveway. It was Mary. There was no commitment to her at that time. The lights of the house were off. He never answered the door; Cathy and Grew continued to make up for lost time, completing the loving that had been started so long before. It was a mutual sharing of feelings, physical, without apology, very good. But this lady was into things that were far beyond Grew. He knew it so never pursued her further.

When he saw her sometime later, she had been in therapy for her problems, was apparently cured of her dysfunctional behavior and was married to a dentist.

There were other incidents that happened before Mary and Grew became deeper involved. Eleanor, The lady who had come to see him before he had gone west with the boys, called one day. He had invited her out. Grew realized she wasn't just coming for a friendly visit but as was Mary's custom she showed up either at the same time or before Eleanor arrived. Grew kept a friendly gathering going for a bit, quite expecting Mary to leave again when she saw he had company but she too felt that she had ownership rights on Grew, at the time he was oblivious to it.

Suddenly Eleanor stormed out. Grew caught her as she was getting in her car, he talked to her for a minute, trying to find what the matter was. It was too late; she made it clear that she was not going to share her time with him. In all fairness he should have told Mary that he had arranged something with this lady. Even if the two of them had left together. It is a shame because he did find a lot in common with Eleanor, he did not feel he wanted to be owned by Mary but she was taking over.

Mary and Grew had also become better and better at "dancing" together. It got so she understood every crazy move he was likely to make on the dance floor. To keep the interest he kept trying new things, watching what the experts were doing;. He would watch them, figuring how to do those things, as he was becoming quite a skilled dancer, but never an expert.

Mary spent more and more time sleeping at his place. She helped with the buying of food until it got to the point that the only thing he was paying for was the rent and his car expenses. Even so he was running out of money as he kept trying to keep going in real estate. In desperation, he took a job working for a security company that employed man and dog teams. They supplied the dog, an animal very good at what he did. The dog and Grew would spend fifteen hours a day looking after a compound that was connected to a construction expansion project.

The young inexperienced but know it all supervisor kept trying to get Grew to tone down the dog but Grew refused. Grew started looking for something else. Lincoln View hired him almost as soon as he put in an application, as night security in one of their smaller malls. Mary used to bring him lunch in the middle of the night. They would talk. They were the only people in the mall, so she would walk with him for a short time as he did his rounds. Her intelligence was beyond question, always a pleasure to talk with.

When he was alone he would write descriptions of what people were wearing as he described the dress of the manikins in the windows. It kept him awake. He also brought books to read. One was "How to Live to One Hundred" another was, "How to Get Your Boss's Job" then there was "Dress for Success". All these books were beneficial in the direction he was then moving. One of the store managers had referred to him as the security with white sox.

Enjoying the work his real estate work went from part time to no time but he didn't care to be a boss anymore either, so did as he was told. Water was pouring out of the parking lot; a water main had broken. He organized the repair but could not find the mall manager or security supervisor. After continuing to call various people within the organization, most of who were at a managers meeting, he was able to contact a manager from another mall in the chain who authorized the several thousand dollars worth of work. The mall was back in running order by the next morning.

Later they moved him to the afternoon shift. While on that shift he enjoyed moving from the pool hall at one end to the bowling alley at the other end. Both would have the hockey games on so he would follow a bit at one place then a bit at the next. The tough guys at the pool hall, for some reason did not find him a threat, complying with the regulations he was required to enforce; there was a rapport.

He was transferred to another mall. It was bigger, it had a young security supervisor who was a bit of a wild one himself. Grew and he got along well, as he did with the assistant supervisor. The assistant Leroy was a large black man who had at one time, run in world competition racing for Jamaica. It was a subject they both enjoyed discussing. Grew too had run longer distances, but only in school.

One evening they got a call from the drug store that there was a man in the store with a snake. Grew arrived first, was met at the cash check out, by a man in his twenties, with a four foot snake wrapped around his arm. The girl had backed away from the counter, When Grew approached the scene the smiling man pushed the head of the snake towards him.

Grew told him that he should know better, "Right now, just leave everything on the counter, and then come back without the snake."

The man pushed the snake towards him in a threatening way saying, "I'll put the snake on you".

Grew knew the snake was harmless, had been on the other end of that scene. His hand darted forward, grabbing the snake behind the head as he told the person, "I am not afraid of your snake and will squeeze its head off if I have to."

The man looked amazed, now having to argue about trying to get Grew to let go of his snake and not to harm it, just as Leroy arrived.

Leroy's comment was, "I'll take care of the man, you take care of the snake."

Grew carried the snake out the door. As Leroy talked sensibly to the man, they escorted him out the door. Outside Grew handed the man the snake and told him about his pet shop with all the snakes.

The man laughed as Grew told him about the adventures with Sheba and the rest of the snakes. Leroy and Grew walked back with mutual respect for each other. They felt they were a good team.

On night shifts he continued to try and put together his book on German Shepherds. He was finding that he was missing too much information needed. He did not have enough German books.

He came home one day and said to Mary, "If I am going to continue with this thing I will have to go to Germany."

To his surprise she was all for it, almost before he realized it, tickets were bought, with the whole trip arranged. Grew had a terrible fear of flying. He spent hours at the airport, watching airplanes land. There were many times while he watched that another plane would come in every minute or two, all safely. After awhile he began to realize that he was probably safer in the air than on the road. They rented a little car in Frankfurt and for the next three weeks traveled back and forth across Germany. Many of the old breeders were at first reluctant to speak to him but after they realized some kind of sincerity in his questions, they opened up. Often it was late at night that they got away. They stayed in small hotels as Grew learned the basic German words to ask for room and food. There was a lot of sign language.

They watched the dogs herd their sheep, understanding the special nature of the German style. The dogs kept the sheep in the designated already cut areas, moved them down roads to the next location, over to the side when cars came along, through gates. Then they constantly circled the five hundred sheep they were looking after. Grew and Mary went to sheep herding trials, working trials, all the time Mary supported his efforts with class, never complaining about not fulfilling any of her desires.

They did visit a large castle, hiked through a bush, trying to find their way. The bush in Germany can be as difficult to get through as that in Canada. This also was not Mary's thing but she dutifully went along. This was part of Grew's life long quest to get to the top of things to see what's on the other side.

The last few days in Germany found them in a small city near the airport. As they looked for a room he asked a man on the street about "Zimmer". He was an older gentleman with a cane, he waved it in the air and pointed to what looked like a garage. Obediently they went to an ordinary door and opened it. There were large vats that looked like they were used to distill liquor. A man in there, pointed to another door that Grew opened. There they found a large restaurant, full of people. He went to what looked like a checkout, asked the man for a "Zimmer". The answer went on for a long time.

Another man sitting nearby smiled, then said that they had a room but had to prepare it. He also had stated the price and suggested that they sit down and have a meal in the meantime. They sat with the man and his wife had a most enjoyable evening of discussion with these total strangers. Grew came away totally impressed with the hospitality of the German people. The room was something that you would expect in the finest hotel in Canada. It had luxurious settings. He particularly remembered the lush full-length towels. The bed was the same quality.

After three weeks, Grew thought they had had enough of each other. He could remember an incident as they approached the airport, in a traffic circle with all the signs in German. He was driving, kept asking Mary which turn off to take as they went round and round in circles. She didn't know, she couldn't read German any better than he could as he was trying to avoid all the cars that kept coming on the circle. He saw something that looked like air something and took the road. It was the right one.

Back working at the shopping center, there was an evening where Grew was confronted with a lady that was quite drunk. She had left one of the bars. They had told her to leave, but she was distraught about something. Perhaps she had a drinking problem associated with depression. There was something about her that indicated that she didn't think much of herself. Grew the perpetual sympathizer, sat on a bench talking with her.

She was a musician with the symphony orchestra, a violinist. She talked to him of her music, telling him that she would like to play for him. This woman was lonely, he didn't know too much more of what the problem was but knew the alcohol had not made it better.

She was a nice enough looking lady, not a glamour sort but good body shape, only slightly carrying more weight than what would have been perfect. Their conversation went on, she didn't want to leave. There was another guard on duty that he radioed, letting him know that he was tied up for awhile. She told him she lived across the street. If he would walk her home she'd play the violin for him.

This was not something that he should have been doing but it was just part of him, living on the edge, trusting people. He walked across the parking lot and street with this lady, whom he didn't even get the name of. She staggered as he supported her but the alcoholic effects had lessened. They went up the elevator, she searched for the right key to her apartment, and then opened the door.

Inside. She took off her coat, Grew could see the nice shape of her body, full breasts and hips, hidden within her simple dress. The knee length dress also exposed her shapely legs as it climbed her thighs; as she sat she almost fell on her couch.

Soon she was removing a violin from a case and as Grew sat facing her she started playing the most spectacular music. It was relaxing, he sat enjoying the sound for a while. Then she was putting it away.

He told her that he had to get back to the mall. She thanked him for getting her home, and then as she faced him she was suddenly kissing him. She was in his arms and he was kissing back. It was nice, her body was firm, smooth as he stroked his hands over the skin of her legs. She was letting him stroke or feel wherever he wanted, even though he should have been breaking free, could feel the skin getting warm as they continued to kiss. It was taking on that invitational warmth. This was Grew standing there, not too quick to turn down opportunities like this. He remembered her bra coming off, not sure whether he had removed it or she had. The rest she took off herself until she was nude, then lying there before him.

He was stroking her all over but there were all sorts of warning bells going off in his head. She was such a beauty as she lay there, she was moving with his hands, spreading her legs, taking his hand in hers and putting it within her.

Still kissing her--hanging on the tightrope--to proceed or not he knew if he was going to stop it had to be soon. With all his will power he did it; he stopped. He suddenly backed off telling her, "I can't keep going with this, you have been drinking, I am supposed to be working, you'll hate yourself, I have to stop."

She got angry with him then. Unfortunately he thought she believed that he did not find her desirable, but he did. It was not the time to make love. If she had come back to the mall while sober it is possible that they might have had an affair. However even though he resented Mary's possessiveness, there was a feeling of commitment that made him believe that if he was to be involved with someone else he had to break it off with her. Was he maturing in his conceptions of attachment?

There was another near miss while at that mall. A woman who worked in the chocolate store, Carol, used to talk to him about her abusive husband. It was her second one. He thought they were getting along fine until she confided in him one evening while things were slow in the mall. Then she was separated from her husband. She moved into an apartment close to the mall with her two kids. He got Carol to come out to a one-parent dance and introduced her to Mary, danced with her a few times, finding her to be one of those super dancers that just fit everywhere while dancing. She was long, lean but with enough flesh to make it comfortable. She also had shoulder length brunette hair, a pretty face and adorable smile. No wonder she found someone to go home with from the dance.

A short time later Carol invited him to supper. Mary was in Florida with her son. He had not allowed Charles to go, he was trying to break away from her. Carol was home with her teen-aged daughter who they joked about as being the chaperone. After supper her daughter fell asleep in the bedroom.

Carol and he danced for a long time, she had on some kind of longish black dress that folded over in front. Grew put his hand between the cloth folds and held a warm breast that was unhindered by a bra a bit surprised at the fullness, the lack of support needed.

It was so soft as he massaged the flesh, pulled gently on the nipple. They looked at each other, kissed gently, tongues stroking together, enjoying the feel, their bodies close together. His erection pushed against her flat belly. It was like Judy all over again. They didn't even realize her daughter was asleep. There was only the one bedroom and they both agreed not to risk her walking out into the living room, catching them in the middle of sex. He was to meet Carol again a few years later and regret that he did not pursue a relationship with her. She was class.

Eventually the kennel property deteriorated to an extent that the house became difficult to live in. The basement kept filling with water. They kept burning out sump pumps. Mary bought a property near Lake Simco with a house in a small community. All the time they had lived together, the dogs were kept outside. They bought fencing to reconstruct the garage so that they could keep the two dogs, much the way they did in Germany.

Now he was living in her place, feeling subject to her rules. He didn't mind keeping the dogs out of the house but there was always that feeling of being a kept man. He had no control over his own finances. His RRSP's were nothing but Mary kept enhancing hers.

Even with their differences, Mary was still willing to come with him out to the mountains. He wanted another try at getting to Taseko Lakes, in the wilds of B.C. If they could get that far the map showed a trail that went over another ridge of mountains to an area reached from Pemberton B.C. It was behind the area he had hiked as a boy, always wondering what was on the other side. There had always been this strange attraction to the mountains.

She and her son Bill drove with him across the country, sharing the driving until they reached Kelowna. There they exchanged vehicles with her sister, using their four-wheel drive Bronco. Mary was always worrying about it getting scratched. It had a short wheel base, did not drive well on the highways but it did get them up to the lower Taseko Lake, a forlorn uninhabited area.

To get there they had to go up a road that followed the side of a hill so narrow that Grew had to walk in front, signaling right or left. If it was too close to the bank; it threw the back perilously close to the edge. If closer to the edge they could go over. All this was on an angle that increased the drop over the side more and more as they climbed. It was not any easier on the way down. Some of the roads were barely trails with branches on either side. And she worried about scratches.

Driving back through the Rockies, across the prairies was an ordeal that rivaled anything they had been through. They had had enough of each other. Her son Bill kept whining and complaining to the extent that Grew got him alone; he told him that if he didn't shut up, he was going to get off at the next town and catch a bus back on his own. It had some affect but only enforced his resolve that this relationship was over. Things just weren't working out between Mary and Grew but they kept going. There was always this feeling of being kept by her.

He had received a promotion to supervisor of security in a larger mall. It too was something that Mary was opposed to him taking. His feeling was that she didn't want him to become too independent.

He arranged for Charles to go west to visit with his sister. He was now eighteen, was no longer in school, and was trying to find his own niche. For many of his teen years they had concentrated on his hockey skills, there was a feeling he could have made it if he could develop the right attitude.

Mary attended meetings with the one parent group often at night so Grew would stay in his office at Don view Mall, either working on security procedures or doing work on his book, the perpetual book on dogs. She would pick him up when she was finished and they would drive home together.

There was a lady working in a doctor's office that was down the hall from the management office in the mall on the third floor. Grew had seen her walking in the mall. She always seemed in a hurry. One day he found her walking ahead of him up the stairs. As always Grew was aware of the nicely turned ankles that followed up to nice calves disappearing into a white cotton dress that covered her knees.

As she went up the stairs, on impulse he reached out, taking hold of her ankle; she stumbled. Then he hopped up the stairs catching her elbows before she could fall. She looked around at him in the strangest way, a questioning. He was not sure whether she was even aware that it was him that caused the stumble. He met her later in the mall and asked if he could buy her a coffee. She accepted and for the length of time that he could squeeze for lunch they sat on a bench in the mall and talked. There was so much to talk about as they shared opinions that were so synonymous. Then she had to go.

Shortly after, when Grew was alone in his office in the evening, he stopped to go to the mall for something to eat. In the mall he met the office secretary of the doctor sharing office space with the doctor

Silvia worked for. As they ate together, they talked. She told him to forget any ideas about an affair with Silvia. She was married to a policeman and had two teenage children. According to Elizabeth, Sylvia was not about to upset her life.

Grew was disappointed, wondering why Sylvia would spend so much time with him if she was really happily married. He also had his own thoughts about the wives of policemen who regarded their wives as chattels, thoughts went back to Lissette, her expressed feelings of being a possession. He was not about to give up on Silvia, she was really nice. Perhaps Elizabeth, who was divorced herself, had her own agenda yet he considered her too young for him to get involved with. (that is a laugh). By the nature of his conversation with Elizabeth he also felt that her and Sylvia did not have a lot in common. It was Sylvia he wanted.

A short time later there was a rose left for him in the management office. He assumed that it was from Elizabeth and went into the doctor's office to thank her. Unfortunately he made a mistake. The policeman's wife had left him a rose. He had been told that she was happily married. It was characteristic of her behavior. He could see that she too had the capacity to reach out, get herself involved with what she wanted. Grew was certainly impressed by the rose, taking it as a message.

Again they had lunch together when Sylvia met him the next day in the mall. He ate his peanut butter sandwich, she had a small lunch that she also had brought from home. They started to compare notes on life as they sat in the mall and then walked together as Grew patrolled. The doctor that she worked for left the office from twelve o'clock to two, then he started seeing patients again for the rest of the afternoon, sometimes into the evening, so she had about a two hour break in the middle of the day. This doctor worked on different days than the other doctor so although both assistants were there together in the office in the morning, in the afternoon they were there on alternate days.

Soon after that, Sylvia asked him if he wanted to go for a drink at lunchtime. He didn't have his car there but she had hers. They drove down to a hotel that was close called The Prince. They had just one drink then returned to her car. Their talking was getting more personal, more into detail about past experiences, mates and the inadequacies of their present relationships. They also talked about their children that were the main reason that she had stayed with her husband.

She talked of the way she felt she was being controlled. Again the control was so rigid that this woman too, got into the game of doing things on the edge, testing the control, almost tempting her husband to catch her. Still, according to her tales, she had not become involved with another man sexually until a short time before Grew met her.

When they returned to the car they were sitting in an almost empty parking lot. He kissed her and she responded with open mouth, flickering tongue as the mouth to mouth continued, a hand went to her breast massaging the nipple under the layers of cloth

CHAPTER 19

A New Love

She didn't object as he undid a few buttons on the uniform, then it wasn't long before his hand was working with wiggling fingers under her bra. The flesh felt nice, was warming up as they continued to play their game of discovery. Her breasts were full, the nipples hardened in his fingers.

They were running out of time. He thought they both knew that nothing was going to happen in the parking lot. After awhile they stopped the necking and went back to work. Grew did have a certain amount of flexibility but was required to be around the mall. He carried a radio to communicate with the other security on duty.

Sylvia started briefly mentioning a professor that she at first referred to as "This Chap". Grew thought it was a strange way to refer to him but was more interested in the stories that she told about him. As he looked back he thought he was entranced with her stories as much as anything. However everything about Silvia gave the impression of class. He felt that to become involved with her was taking a step forward.

Even so, there were things in her background that took her to the edge of a nervous breakdown. Her fingers had broken out, sometimes she would nervously rub them. Grew thought when they met it was under control, but some of the signs were still there. Her boss, who invariably got involved with his attractive women patients would have liked to get involved with Sylvia also but she did have some hard, fast rules, like not getting involved with the boss. Besides she thought it would put her in a position of being just one of the lovers. Her position of non-involvement minimized any feeling of possessiveness about him from her part.

The professor was a frequent visitor to the office. The routine became Sylvia's job to administer the needle, sometimes without the doctor even seeing the patient. As she got to know Grew she gradually let him know the rest of the story. Perhaps it was his enthusiastic listening that was a polarizing factor that brought them together. So Sylvia went on about her thing with the professor.

One day he had come into the office, she was alone at the time. His eyes met hers and she blushed as he reached over the reception desk, all of a sudden he was kissing her. She just melted right there, knew she would do anything for him. They met shortly after when he was at a conference at the Inn On The Park. She had trouble meeting him because she had to take her son to a hockey game. She left her son, Clark at the game then came to the hotel and her and the professor had lunch in his room.

It was an interesting meeting that wasted little time. She was aware of the difference from what it had ever been with Mark, her husband. It was gentle, timed so that they both would get the release, thrilled with passion. It was related to Grew how she felt when she had to leave. They had laid around in the nude, both in love, feeding each other the food from the fruit basket. It gave Grew an idea about what she wanted in love. This was a passionate woman, in limbo.

The clandestine meetings continued between the professor and Sylvia. He was catholic, married, with grown children. He embellished her with gifts, often she stayed with him on overnight trips while he attended business meetings or conventions. He talked of setting up an apartment for her but never talked of leaving his wife. Before Grew came along the thing he had been trying to arrange for Silvia was to go with him to Sweden, a trip he was doing for the school board. But she had wanted more, now she wanted the man, not just to be his mistress. When he had left she had decided their affair was over, then she met Grew.

looking back Grew saw some of the same adventurous spirit that was in him, walking on the edge. She was even more daring than he was though. It was a motivator for her, the excitement that she had missed in her dull existence with the policeman was not enough. On the other hand she needed someone to slow her down a bit from time to time. Many times, as they loved and she was asking Grew to stop, she was disappointed that he had not taken control.

Sylvia and he managed to sneak a lot of time together. Where was Mary during those times? There were times when they would meet after his work when he was waiting for Mary to pick him up. He had stopped writing his book. There was at least one evening in the week when the doctor had late hours. On those times Sylvia would work late. If it coincided with a time when Mark was working late and Mary was at a meeting; Sylvia and Grew would then go for a walk.

One evening when she had changed to her track pants, they walked over the highway bridge to a small park not far from the mall. They were there alone but could see people out in front of their houses. They lay down together behind a grassy knoll where they could still see the people. It was her game of pushing temptation to the edge.

Their necking had got heavy as they lay there, his penis out, enjoying playing with it as it hardened in anticipation of where it was going to go. He had gotten his hand into the hair, down into the wet gap between her legs. It was obvious that this time she was going to let him fuck her. He had her track pants down to her knees, was laying in such a way that he could slip it into her from the rear, didn't know though whether she would have gone along. He had kept telling her that he wouldn't do it to her unless she was willing; could see though as he recalled the incident, that she did not want the responsibility. She wanted to be taken.

He could see the people, could hear them talk; he thought they were coming their way. As he peeked over the knoll, there they were, almost in front of them. They pulled up their clothing in a hurry, stood up as they started to walk, hand in hand, laughing as they went. It was very close. She said, "You weren't going to stop, were you?"

He answered, "Sylvia, I want you but I just don't want you sexually, I want to share life with you, almost got you this time, I wasn't about to stop"

A life together was something he could offer that the "Chap" was not able or willing to do. It impressed her. They snuggled together as they walked back to the mall. The two of them were in love. He was going to start separating from Mary.

Another time, it was a Saturday, it was raining and still they walked in the park by the Don River. They climbed a knoll and went down together on the top. They were sliding in the mud as he was working her track pants down. He was about to get it in her right there on a Saturday afternoon; they got caught in the mud beneath the grass and suddenly they were sliding downhill, both half dressed.

There were other stories that she entertained Grew with about the professor. She had met the professor at the hotel where he had a room, was giving a presentation on education, all dressed up in white trousers and sports coat, ready to go for his presentation when she arrived. He wanted her to wait for him in the room but there was an hour to wait until he had to attend the function so they went for a walk through the forest trails that surrounded the hotel, through the flood plains down to the river. In a wooded enclave off the trail they got into a loving session off the trail, discovering the side trail, leading him in there, it was Sylvia's excitement craving factor.

The passion had become wilder until his pants were down, her dress was up, and he was fingering her, hand in panties. It didn't stop, she was on her back, lying on the bare ground, her panties pushed aside. He was on his knees pushing her delightful bum up to his penis. As she lay there watching him rise above her she was suddenly taken with fits of laughter. His white trousers were smeared with mud at the knees. No doubt it was the same mud on her bum. She seemed to think that he had to give his presentation that way. It was another of Sylvia's stories but was consistent with her way of taking things to the edge, the quest for often-humourous events and even jokes on people. It was part of her "Love of Life".

In the time when she was supposed to be on lunch between twelve and two, when Grew could get away from the security they would spend time in the doctor's office in the back room. There were times when he got her on the examination table, kissing her wildly. She was in it with him, sucking tongues, passionately kissing. One time he had undone the upper buttons of her nurses uniform, one hand squeezed pliant tits, bouncing the flesh of her breasts. Alternatively, he was pulling nipples; she seemed to love it. Then one hand was stroking up between her white clad legs. His hand continued to stroke further and further up the valley until it was rubbing in the center of her sexuality, feeling the opening spreading under the sheer material. It felt damp and hot.

His hand moved up the covered slightly rounded belly, feeling the hair beneath, over the top, pushing it all down with his hand, the panty hose was going south, no panties just hose, it moved easily over her rump as she wiggled side to side, half way down her thighs, wide open in front of him. He moved over between the raised legs pushing them before him into the air, delightful stems there in front of him, as they waived freely in the air. Then he had hold of her bare hips in both hands, moving his fingers on, into the soft buttocks, squeezing.

As she tried to back away he held her, stainless steel of the table made it slippery for her, she couldn't get away. His hard prick was out leading the advance. The knob was feeling the wet of her open cunt when she called out to stop. But he didn't, she pushed backward but he was holding her on the slippery table, she couldn't get away. He moved forward and all of a sudden it was going in.

She was nailed and as he kept coming she lay back on the table, lifted her legs and started raising her bum to meet the thrusting penis. They continued to move back and forth at each other, gradually they increased the pace. It was a nice fit, she was warm and slippery. It was almost like they had been doing it for some time as their passion and speed increased, then the ejaculation. He fell on her and gradually he subsided. It was like a marriage, something they wanted together.

Grew had to find places for his dogs. So talked to Al's brother, about taking them for watchdogs. It was a mistake, he was preparing to get away from living with Mary. John took them but unlike Al, he did not appreciate the value of these two dogs so eventually found homes for them.

Grew had to make it clear that he was going to a dog show without Mary. He was going there to judge. He made a point of telling her that he was leaving, had taken an apartment near where he worked. There was a lot of discussion but Grew was persistent.

It was not so easy for Sylvia to get away. She announced to Mark that she was leaving, that she was going away to Nova Scotia for a few days. Knowing it was going to happen, he even accepted her going away but did not know that she was going with Grew until after they came back.

CHAPTER 20

Changing Partners

In Sylvia's fun way they got into it in the motel. She sent him out to get ice with only his underwear on. When he came back the door was locked. For a while he banged on the door as quietly as he could. She wasn't opening it and he could hear her snickering on the other side. He went and hid in the stairwell for a while then came back. She opened the door and for awhile they chased each other around, trying to put ice on and in the underwear of each other. It was such a fun time.

She came with him to the dog show and later to the dinner put on by the club. No one asked who she was but she also enjoyed the company of some of the club members while he was judging and at the dinner.

Then they had to face the reality of what they were about to do. She did move in with him, as did his own son, into the other room. There were some adjustments to be made between the two of them. She felt that Charles should have had some counseling when his mother had died but he and Grew couldn't see it. Grew did go to a councilors for one session who couldn't see the need for it either so that idea was dropped.

Mary accepted the breakup but soon after married another member of the one parent organization. Years later she admitted that it was her mistake to do that. After that marriage they found out that her husband had Leukemia and died a few years later. A few years after that Mary died.

Sylvia on the other hand, was having real problems of adjustment. She felt she had abandoned her son, in fact he did get through the summer but had been conditioned to having his mother do everything for him, so was about to drop out of school in the fall.

Mark would phone and when he would upset Sylvia, Grew would take the phone from her, tell him that she was with him because that is what she had chosen to do and did not have to have him doing power trips on her. When he came back at Grew, telling him to put her back on the phone Grew said "no", and hung up.

This put Sylvia into a panic as she said in a loud voice, "Oh my God, You hung up on Mark. What will I do now?" There were still elements of control.

"Nothing, You do not have to be intimidated by him or anyone. You had a right to leave if you wanted."

They waited for him to take the next step but he didn't. He had too much sense for that. His job was too important, he couldn't jeopardize it by getting into domestic violence.

They stayed together for a while that summer taking a camping trip where they could hike through the rocks, north of Lake Superior. They had picked up a tent, were camping in a campground north of Barrie somewhere. It was their first experience sleeping out in a tent together. They snuggled together in the cold. The ground felt harder than it had before. They made it through the night and as he bathed in cold water, shaving with a disposable razor, as it scratched across his face he wondered if this camping thing was something for him.

The next day they reached the north side of Superior, camped on Batchewana Bay. Sylvia and he ran along the beach, miles and miles of sandy beach with no one there but them. They took off their suits as they bathed in the nude. It was their first experience in doing that which they both loved. She tried to get pictures of him but he kept avoiding her efforts. He didn't know why he didn't get pictures of her. This was a woman to behold.

That evening as they studied a cabin looking over the water, empty at that time they nostalgically wondered whether it was something that they might have one day. But she was lonely for her kids; she had to find a phone. They drove miles, nearly to Sault St Marie, until they finally found one. The next day, lonely for her children, she had decided to go home. She missed them too much. They had become her reason for living. She had given up on her husband years before. Grew eventually moved to Sault Ste Marie and years later visited Batchewana Bay again, still taken with its beauty, even though by then it had become more inhabited.

For a while they lived together with Grew's son in the other bedroom. They never knew when Charles was coming or going and although he was nineteen he was still very unsettled, had managed to wear out his welcome on the west coast; he had a great opportunity to play hockey with the local team that could have led to better things but his preoccupation with girls got him off course and into financial trouble. He was acting a bit like his father. He used his hockey equipment to get money and never got it back. It was part of his seedy side.

Sylvia was still not content; the restlessness showed. Her husband was willing to take her back even knowing that she had cheated. She talked to Grew about her son and how he was so upset about her leaving that he was going to quit school.

It was Grew's way, he didn't interfere, it had to be her decision. She did go back but they kept seeing each other. It went on for that whole winter, through the next summer and fall, but by the end of the year Grew had told her that if she wasn't going to leave by February first, he was going to stop seeing her.

It was a very difficult time. Grew spent a lot of time on his own, in the parks, following trails through the bush; he would meet her when he could, quietly they walked and talked, her telling him of her son's frustration about the things between his parents. Her son did quit school anyway, found a job in a nursing home, enjoyed working with the disabled, always going to go back to school which he never did. From time to time he took psychology courses. Grew thought

Clark was trying to understand his own depression that perhaps he inherited. Sylvia recognized it; which only made her more caring.

There was no question that he was her favourite, years later she bought a country property by the sea with her son, something they could both work on, something keeping them connected.

Sylvia was a very "up" person. Her and Grew would meet after the courses she was taking--learning business and computers--while Grew took Human Resource Courses, paid for by the company. They would discuss where they were each going, to a certain extent helping each other with the written part they had to put together. It was a pleasant time. There was a lot of time that Grew spent alone though, aimlessly walking in the parks or following rivers to the roots, climbing through rocks or up cliffs. Again, it was some kind of exploration, taking him back to what he did as a youth.

Grew could see that it couldn't go on forever so he had issued his ultimatum. He phoned her at home one morning. Mark had hearing problems so it would be her that answered the phone. Grew asked her to meet him. She came right away.

She agreed that it couldn't go on. It was January when she took the apartment near where Grew had moved to. This apartment was across from the mall. In fact it had the same underground garage as his apartment. So although officially Sylvia was living in one apartment building, she was seldom there. Mark never did seem to figure it out. He often got in the lower door to her apartment that is never difficult to do and would knock on her door. Even though it was classically decorated and with her classical furniture making it a showpiece apartment, they seldom spent any time there. Her daughter and her husband lived in the apartment owned by them, inherited from his family.

There were times that life hurt, times when she would go to family gatherings where he knew Mark would be there. She arranged a birthday gathering at one of the restaurants at the mall. Both her children were there, Clark's girlfriend and Sylvia's daughter's husband. They were just starting to eat when Mark walked in. Grew was working at the time and could not afford a confrontation so he left. Her children knew they lived together, had learned to accept it, the daughter reluctantly.

Sylvia and Grew had many good times together, both of them loved hiking in the woods. She would say that she didn't want to go there so he would back off. Then she would feel bad that they weren't going where he wanted to go and she would agree to go too. He would then insist that it didn't matter. Sometime they would do the thing, sometime they wouldn't. Often the situation was reversed. She had been used to being controlled so was having trouble adjusting to be part of the deciding force. Grew only realized it was that way, as he recalled their life together.

She had lived for twenty-five years with her husband deciding everything. Grew wondered if after many years on her own, there had been a lot of change in her life. They did have so many similar interests but she was always more daring than he was. She was the one that would keep exploring through the woods when he would be wondering if they could find their way back.

One time she was walking on the slippery rocks on a landfill in Lake Ontario, in February. She slipped and fell in. If Grew had not been there to pull her out, he didn't think she would have made it. He rushed her to the car and got her clothes off, then wrapped her in a blanket. It was just part of the way she was. A man had drowned by slipping off similar rocks in the lake.

Grew did not always handle well the way she had become through the years, of being controlled He could have been more supportive and understanding. Even the lifestyle of her boss, who had been playing games with the women he was involved with had caused Sylvia to doubt everyone. She had told Grew about a time when he was coming in at the airport, she informed two of his girlfriends that he was coming in and they both met him. This was the sort of joke Sylvia would play, maybe not funny. Yet she glorified in playing such jokes on people.

They also went to dances but every time that they did, when there were friends of either one of them there it would cause trouble if he danced with the women. Sylvia wanted to be fawned on which

Grew had trouble doing but he did try. He was independent and in that sense fitted in better with the way things were between Mary and him. He was the man she went home with. However Sylvia and Grew became more synchronized and it became a pleasure to dance with her.

A phone call came one day from Susan. She had found his address through the dog club. He arranged to meet her at the Orangeville dog show where Sylvia and he were going. Susan was still her effervescing self. She told him of how she had gone with the circus, eventually ended up in Winnipeg. She had two children and a boyfriend but no husband. She had done some writing, had done a children's show on TV in that city. Grew was amazed had how well she had done. She was a survivor.

Her and Sylvia got into a discussion on drugs. Sylvia had gone through her own problems with her children and drugs as had Susan herself. They had very opposing views but Grew felt there was the other factor with Sylvia--jealousy. She did not like the way he looked at this young lady who was now 38 and Grew didn't blame her for that but the debate could go nowhere and it did not.

Sylvia agreed to take a trip with Grew to his mountains; he loved the coast mountains. Rather than drive they flew to Vancouver and rented a car from there. As they drove up the Fraser Canyon he showed her the immense beauty of this area that she had never been in. They did drive up to Williams Lake and for a while he talked of taking her to see his friends in the Chilcoten and on to Tatlayoko Lake. They got into a real disagreement over the matter. It was one of those times when he couldn't win. At first she didn't want to go there because he had been there with Mary, then she was annoyed because he agreed not to go there and then she wasn't good enough for his friends. So he said that they would go. Eventually in silence, since he was driving the car, he set off south through miles of cattle country, open range, part of the Chilcoten but on the eastern edge. It was as if they would never get through it.

When they came to steep drop offs, Sylvia would take over the wheel. There was something about driving on the edge of cliffs that seemed to affect Grew's equilibrium so at such times she would take over. He would study the map, trying to determine what roads would be passable, and then off they would go. They came to a rock formation that was full of greenish rock, breaking off pieces to take back with them. Then there was a deep gorge that they would have to drive down into in order to cross the river below. They decided on a different route.

As they left that area they followed a steep grade on the east side of the Fraser. He wondered why she was going so fast. There were no guardrails, the drop off was extreme to the river below. When he asked she said, "Look behind us."

He turned around and saw a huge logging truck loaded with logs about one hundred feet behind them, he wasn't slowing down. Grew didn't think he would have been able to. He laughed as he said, "Hurry up; and go."

They reached Lilloet then from there he thought that they could take a road that would lead through valleys to reach the other side of the Taseko Lakes. From there they could take trails or logging roads and approach these lakes from the other side, up in the alpine country where the trees where scarce with grassy meadows. As they followed a gravel road on the west side of the Fraser, with Sylvia driving, he looked out, down to the river far below, wondering about the wisdom of this decision. He had learned before that in this country, a dot on the map with a name did not mean there would be a town there but usually at least a gas pump.

They proceeded along miles of lakeshore he believed it was Downton Lakes that were a creation produced by damming up rivers to produce hydro, forlorn country, mile after mile of desolation with no one to be seen. They came to a little village called Gold Bridge. It not only had a store it had a motel and a restaurant. It was time for them to splurge so they did. The first night they slept in the car but then spent another night in the motel. They had this thing about camping. They were going to do it until they had had all they could take--roughing it.

It was a Sunday so the logging trucks were not working, they were allowed to go up the logging roads. They followed a rough road up into the mountains that headed north. It was the direction to the ridge protecting the Taseko Lakes. Then the map showed trails.

They drove as far as they could go then left the car, proceeding on foot. It was like a road but there were some huge washouts that prevented the car from getting through, so they walked on. A few miles from there they heard this screeching sound. Grew told Silvia that it was the sound of vultures, but really did not know. They kept going, following the trail. Then they heard the sound coming their way out of the heavy underbrush along the side of the road. Suddenly one hundred feet in front of them, was a baby bear that looked like it had lost its mother. They knew what that meant. The baby saw them, decided they looked nice, so came running towards them at a gallop.

It was on the side away from where they had come. They knew what they had to do. This was grizzly country, so they started back at a run. At one point Grew turned around to snap a picture of this little thing, smaller than a dog, wanting to adopt them. Then they kept going as fast as they could until they reached the car. They laughed as they started back. On the way something attracted their attention, just off the road lying in the afternoon shade. It was a deer. It must have been resting time for most of the animals.

When they got back to the town they took the motel room for the night and had supper at the restaurant. They went exploring finding an old gold mine in a closed up town called Bralorne. There was no one there but a caretaker who said that nothing, including the mine was open. They were beginning to realize that they were in gold country. People were standing in the middle of creeks, panning for gold. Another had brought a backhoe from Vancouver and was digging up the river bottom for the same reason. They decided to get involved. They knew the same road they had come on continued on until it dropped twenty five hundred feet to the Pemberton Valley. From there they could get to Vancouver and did.

On the way down the road they looked at a mountain that on the map was shown as Green Mountain. From the contours shown, it looked like they could climb it since it was shown at seven thousand feet in elevation. They left the car on the side of the road, and then started to climb. By the time they reached the snow line, this was in the middle of July, they had climbed for several hours. They frolicked in the snow for a while and then Sylvia wanted to continue on upward to the top. Grew could see the evening shadows closing in, did not want to be stuck up there after dark. It was a time that he had to be persistent. She was determined to go on but where they had come from would be too dangerous to get through at night.

She gave in and they returned to the car. It was pretty dark by the time they found it. They drove for a while until they came to a crossroads. There was a picnic table there so they pitched their tent and stayed the night. It was a decent place to camp. The next morning they took the summer road down the mountain. The scenery was absolutely astounding looking up the Pemberton Valley as they wound down, one switchback after another.

Grew had convinced Sylvia that second gear was put in these cars for a reason, so by that time she had consented to use it which took away from the perpetual smell of burning brakes.

They went to Vancouver, bought gold pans then returned. They spent another two days panning for gold. Standing in icy water with their legs numbing, they scooped up pans of dirt from the bottom and shook it down. It was fun doing but they never found any gold.

They returned to Vancouver and stayed with Grew's cousin for a few days. He introduced them to Wreck Beach where he, Grew and Sylvia climbed down a steep slope. They bathed in the nude and then came back for more, for a few days. Grew was cautious in the water only going out neck deep but then stepped in a hole and went under, thought he would drown, could see them recovering his nude body. He did manage to swim to shore. Jack, a lifelong bachelor, and Sylvia took to each other right away. Eventually she realized that he was enjoying her nude form and they didn't go bathing again. It was time to return to Toronto anyway.

He loved the time at the beach with Sylvia, enjoying all the splendid bodies, being amazed at the numbers and the unconcern, he still had those feelings of wonderment. There was the person selling marijuana, wearing nothing but a belt with a purse. How could you put undercover agents there? Climbing the hill from Wreck Beach was steep, although difficult there was something special about it.

He wondered at the time why Sylvia would be surprised at cousin Jack looking at her sexually, she was an exquisitely built woman. He thought the issue had come to the surface when Jack seemed to think nudity also was okay at home. They never went to the beach again.

Then they drove to Cape Breton from Toronto to judge another dog show, got into an argument about the Cabot Trail which Grew had never heard of but Silvia was determined to travel around it. After back and forth giving up on the idea they took off with her driving. She was right it was splendid. Most of the way his eye stuck in the viewfinder of the camcorder. There was one hill they were coming down which was so steep that Silvia was crying out that the brakes wouldn't hold. Grew was under the front panel of the front seat by the time they hit bottom. What they got on film was a scramble of pictures but the voices and sound were something that fit well with the overall video.

Sylvia and Grew would often talk of all the women that he had been involved with. It was ironic that they figured out that she was the 19th. S is also the 19th letter of the alphabet. So it was at a relatively new part of their relationship that he had started referring to her as number 19. Often when he couldn't find her in the mall he would page over the PA system '19'. It worked well until a new manager of the mall was hired and one day asked what the page 19 was for, he was informed that it was PA testing.

Silvia's daughter had decided to move back to Toronto so not only did they have her son living with them but her daughter, her husband and their two children. The daughter who always used to give him dirty looks anyway used to do things like setting the toaster so he would burn his toast in the morning and preparing the coffee so that his morning coffee was like dishwater.

His first step was to get a mailbox in the mall, which Silvia was not happy about. It played on her insecurities, wondering whom he was getting mail from. It was neither but he knew that at sometime someone was going to have to move.

One day Sylvia's granddaughter who was about 4 years old kept banging on the keys of his computer while he was trying to write-- the book again. He told her to stop and she wouldn't so he squeezed her wrist. It left a red mark and Silvia told him about it. Silvia also told him that her son and law had stated that she did not have good luck with men. Grew objected to the fact that Silvia allowed him to say that without comment from her.

Clark's dog bit or snapped at the little girl. (no wonder). They decided they could not take further chances on him so decided he would have to be put to sleep. Grew had to hold the dog with Sylvia there. Her son would have no part of it. The girl working for the vet was so upset that Grew consoled her. Sylvia got all in a tether herself. Grew was beginning to see there was no winning.

He decided to get an apartment of his own so talked to the landlords of the apartment across from the mall. They asked whom it was for and when he said himself they said they had a basement apartment vacant that he could move in right away, they would find something later. He took the apartment and informed Silvia. She wasn't happy but went along with it--even helping him move.

She went from buying a condo with her children that she wanted Grew to go in with, to getting her deposit back when the kids wanted to move back west. She went with them and found a man who turned out to be not only a drinker but also a gambler. When she got him out of her house he also turned out to be a stocker. So she sold her house and quit her job, one she had gotten because of the computer courses they had taken and when Grew caught up to her again she was living a secret life hiding from this person who was also a hunter.

For three years Grew pined over Silvia but knew in his heart that she was something that he was not likely ever to get back. He did go out with a number of women but none could fill the void, she was truly unique but then so many of the women he had been involved with had their own uniqueness.

Years later when traveling to Vancouver he had looked her up again. They met and together made a steak dinner, watched a movie and although it was not intended they did have sex and slept in the same bed for the night and had sex again in the morning. But a new life together was not to be. The next day they had met with his cousin Jack, the three of them sat in a restaurant for a few hours before he had to once again head east. Through the whole time Jack had mocked his relationships, particularly one where he had married a woman, where the whole affair had turned bad, she had charged him with assault, where he had eventually fired his lawyers and defended himself, - and won.

That was one that had cost him dearly, through the whole affair he had lost the kennel he had bought with her to her lawyers expenses. He had paid the whole cost of buying it. Of course at that time the case was before the courts, but when he had been in touch with his cousin again, he had been told that Sylvia did not want to see him again and would prefer that he did not call or write. He wondered if there was something going on with her and Jack. It was a few years later that he heard that Jack, who was a heavy drinker, but with money, had died on a cruise around South America. Grew never heard from Sylvia again.

CHAPTER 21

Joanne and On

Grew needed one assignment with the Toy Group, Group five to get his certification to be an all breed judge. It was for a club where he was a member, the Markham Kennel Club. He was only judging at the Friday show, which made him available to work at the Saturday and Sunday shows as a volunteer, helping with driving judges back and forth to their hotels and the airport, always a few things to do and fewer people to do what was required.

His wide brimmed hat that he had started wearing because of an eye operation seemed to attract women, times when he was riding the bus, women made a point of talking to him. He was on his own again, so some of these casual meetings progressed to somewhat further involvement, but nothing permanent. He had gone through so much with women in his life that he was becoming reluctant to get into anything that wasn't going to go anywhere. He was writing his memoirs.

After finishing his judging assignment around noon, wandering around the dog show looking for a place to sit down, relax and think over how he had placed the dogs and the unusual things he had discovered in the ring, he looked at a dog food display with a strange name and asked the young lady with the display what the name meant.

Joanne was all smiles on a weather beaten face. He thought that she had probably spent a lot of time outside working with dogs, had on short denim skirt, which brought his attention to long well, shaped most enticing legs. She was not noticeably developed in the chest, which made him think that she could be thought of as underdeveloped, but he had been surprised before by such looks.

What did draw his attention more than anything was the look of superlative condition with flat stomach and an overall look of muscle rather than fat, her face was surrounded by somewhat scraggly hair that looked like it needed cutting, combing or both. None of these things took away from an overall look of youth.

There was a distinctive soft look to her expression that he was sure many might be inclined to miss. Did he see a general lack of self-esteem or was it truly a look that she had decided that how she looked personally didn't matter? Was it her own self-confidence as to what she was, that kept her going? Maybe it was a combination.

He tried to guess her age as she chatted quietly and pleasantly with him. She explained the great qualities of this dog food, detailing the technological breakthroughs encompassed in the food. What she was saying took him back to some of the dogs that he had raised that lived their whole lives with problems that might have been diet related.

Every few minutes she would chuckle or laugh, smiling while she talked to him. He couldn't help thinking about the positive impression she was giving out. In spite of her pleasant projection, her face gave out another message; he could see the signs of past trauma, an indication of sadness beneath the surface, buried in the lines not hidden on that face. Still as Grew recalled, she was flirting.

They discussed the dogs he had judged after learning she bred Doberman Pinschers. It had always surprised him that occasionally he would come across a dog that had won multiple Best in Shows, Like the Maltese he had just judged that when judging it, he had run fingers down the front legs through the coat, only to find the legs were crooked-- so wrong. Or others that got away with slipped stifles.

After awhile he came back to the same booth and there was a man sitting with her. When he started talking to her again he referred to him as her husband.

She laughed out loud saying, "He is not my husband."

Grew said," I'm sorry, I thought maybe he was. Boyfriend?"

Again she laughed, "Come On. He already has a wife and I don't have boyfriends that have wives."

She expressed a delight in the Miniature Pinscher that he had placed first in the Group. His reaction was to realize that this girl had a good knowledge of animal structure. The little dog was a prize that was not always rewarded enough for the quality that he was. They had gone on to discuss dogs in general and that is when he found out that she was a Doberman breeder that had sort of given up on the dog shows and later other reasons for not showing, there was someone, perhaps a past love, who had been trying to catch up to her and as dog people know, that is where they can be found.

In what seemed like several hours of conversation with this delightful person, where she continued to chuckle and Grew continued to enjoy pleasing legs that periodically crossed and re crossed, showing a bit more thigh, they found a lot of agreement about dogs. He kept hoping for a look at more of those legs as she shuffled around, was she teasing him, reeling him in?

As they were getting along so well he asked her if she would go to the club dinner with him the following evening, having established that both were unattached and lived alone. He had no idea how old she was but was guessing somewhere between thirty and forty. It didn't matter as it was only to be a one time thing. He had thought with some sorrow that she was too young to think of anything more.

To his delight she accepted and he picked her up in the car that the club had rented for him, she'd combed her hair and cleaned up nice, a new image which made him feel good, straight nose and clean jaw line were now more obvious, classic beauty but still not completely hidden was the story in her face of past trauma.

The conversation had been light, somewhat teasing by her and suggestive by another judge, all taken in fun. She became the central attraction of two of the older judges and one of the young ones. After the dinner he dropped the judges off first then drove her to where she had parked her car.

As they had stood by her car he kissed her on a warm mouth, ran his lips over the skin of her neck, warm and responsive. He wondered if he should have taken her back to his apartment, not far from the show site. Not yet he had decided. Before leaving he pushed her up against the hood of her car feeling the firm body pressed against him, legs spread and the skirt up as he pushed forward--wondering later if perhaps he had moved too slow. This girl was exciting.

He was not sure whether he could even sexually perform, not having been active since Silvia had left for the west, still in a state of celibacy, not particularly by his own choice. Later he found that she would have kept her dogs waiting, would have come home with him. There was some kind of mutual attraction. When he had still been with her they made a date to go out to supper the following week, even agreed that she would pick him up.

They had got to the Keg restaurant late, only had one drink, had the food of the day but stayed until closing. It had been like there was no end to what they could talk about. The look on her face was so relaxed as they had discussed dogs and people they knew in the dog game. It was most pleasurable. Why can't it always be so simple, where the better times of two people is enjoyed by each other?

When she drove him home he asked if she wanted to come up and see his pictures, elated that she accepted. There was no question of worrying about her safety or lack of trust. She just willingly accepted the invitation and came up.

Pictures he had taken over the years, which encompassed a wide variety of dog pictures also pictures taken at the mall in fashion shows and various pictures of scenery in mountains were in his albums. He brought out the videos with slow motion studies of how animals move and why some structures in their build are more efficient than others. The time was again passing and he had not touched her to that point. She must have wondered if he ever would.

It was getting late and as he put the stuff aside all of a sudden he was kissing her. She was responsive and so much a part of their making out, not a matter of him trying to seduce her while she feigned resistance, but a coming together of two willing bodies wanting each other.

Grew got a real thrill out of lifting in both hands her full length skirt as he came between her legs, boosted her up to the table as he stood and wrapped those gorgeous treasures of legs around his body. He pushed himself against her and was aware of the thin look of her but not lacking in firm muscle, so enjoyable to be wrapped up with.

Her ample breasts that emerged from somewhere, he massaged, dove his tongue into her mouth and she responded by pushing her firm tongue back at his. He sucked on it, nibbled on it gently, chewed her lips, nibbled her ear sucked along her neck; all the while he was pinching gently her nipples and could feel his hard erection pushing up into the panty covered valley. He wanted her badly, she wasn't stopping him but he felt it was late and she wouldn't be able to stay all night. He wanted to save it for a less hurried time. It must be a sign of maturity that he was able to cut it off at that stage.

The next Saturday he met her after work, helped her stack what seemed like mountains of clothes as she did her laundry in the Laundromat, must have taken a fortune in coins but she seemed to have the money. She kept sending him to a convenience store for more coins as they washed and stacked. As they were finishing up she asked him if he would like to go to her friend's house to play cards. He told her that he had not played cards since working on the tugboats but would give it a try just to be with her. It was not too far from where she lived.

He enjoyed the evening as they played some kind of doubles game, looked at these friend's two German Shepherds, very impressed with the older one and expressed the idea that he would like to see them in daylight and videotape them. Too soon it was one o'clock in the morning and Joanne said that she should go home and look after her dogs. Grew offered to sleep on her couch to avoid her driving all the way back to his place. She must have thought him to be some slow character, not wanting to be involved with her.

When he had made some suggestive remark at her friend's house the lady said, "You wish".

Did it mean that she knew Joanne and that she would not get involved with him or was it the older man thing? When he got to her house he met the dogs. The house was a wooden two-story structure, not large. The dogs were in portable kennels upstairs and as she let them out two at a time they jumped all over him before going outside. She had excellent voice command of them all. They were her family. The dogs gave a few sniffs around him, mouthed his hand and played. There was an instant acceptance--the test.

As he sat on the couch, Joanne came and sat beside him, he put an arm around her and right away one of the dogs put its muzzle over his arm and looked up into his face.

He got the message, "What ever you intend to do with my mistress, I want you to know that I am here as her protector, so be careful."

Mockingly, without fear, he patted him on the head and said, "Nice doggy".

The couch covers were still wet so he added, "These covers are wet I can't sleep on them."

She calmly said "Okay" nothing more.

Together they went to the roll out from a couch bed in her room and together spread the sheets on it. They were wet too but neither of them said anything. When the bed was made she started getting undressed so he did the same, a mutual feeling of embarrassment but they were both soon in their underwear, her in her bra and panties and him in his jockey shorts. Was it to be a platonic sleep? What would happen next? They got into bed and without even a whisper she came into his arms. That was so nice. They kissed long, unhurried, and deep and forever, it was getting even nicer. He could taste the smoke from her cigarette and reminded himself that he wasn't going to get involved with a smoker. It was a bit late for that though. It felt good to be unclasping a bra again and thought that he must have appeared to be doing it with practiced fingers. His hand reached down and traveled fingers along the smooth skin of her inner thighs around her curves to the classically formed behind. It was something that stood out even when clothed. His hand moved casually back between and up into the hair between the puffy folds of her vagina lips and massaged in the wet. It had felt so precious.

His penis, still not as hard as it should have been, perhaps with a bit of apprehension, found its way almost on its own into that slippery warm thing as he moved between her legs that then moved around his own legs and nestled gently around his waist. They moved to a side position so naturally and without hurry as he had sunk into her. His legs came up behind her, the cushion of that so nice bum pushing against his thighs. He dug his hands into that superlative butt as he pushed his now hard prick into her.

She had responded as they worked into such an enjoyable rhythm, he could feel the stiffness of his thing, not lacking anything now becoming the proud stallion as he quickened and she followed like an experienced dancer, together driving at each other in a furious crescendo. He could feel it coming, the slippery glove was warm but holding as they slipped back and forth and he ejaculated.

They had continued to hold and cuddle, to nestle, to love and to fondle. For a long time she had sat on him, smiling down, her hair falling to the sides as it framed her now relaxed looking face, so ecstatic. She got it up again inside her but for then he did not come again. Then they both fell asleep, he had been vaguely aware of her sliding to his side. They had snuggled together, in a love sleep.

At one point he was aware of her teeth grinding and wondered if it was because of the tension she was under. Through the night he got out of bed, made his way up the stairs to the bathroom. The Dobermans started barking but quit when he sad, "Shssssh".

In the morning he awoke with a semi erection; proudly he lay there on his back, thinking of the night before as he gently stroked himself, *it had been some accomplishment*. He started to feel the reality of the body beside him, he took her hand and put it on his erection. Gently she stroked it back and forth until he could feel a real stiffness developing. He couldn't believe it. THIS WAS SOMETHING BIG. He thought, *"I am not going to live through what I am about to do but I am going for it anyway"*.

He spread Joanne on her back, wiggled between her legs as he spread them apart and gently slid the big thing into her warm, wet, slippery softness where the legs came together, could feel the sensations as it slid all the way in. This time he started driving at her hard, as she equaled the rhythm coming at her. He wondered how this smaller built girl could take it all, but she did. The exercise reminded him of riding an Arabian horse, so smooth, so coordinated and as they increased the ride to a gallop it was both of them going full speed, sweating and driving into a wild passion. He could feel it coming, could feel her inner muscles contracting around him and then they were there and collapsed together, just laying there until he could feel the diminishing erection being pushed out.

He exclaimed as they lay there, "I can't believe we did it again."

They had gone back to sleep still cuddled together as they did. Then the dogs were complaining about it being time for them to go out. She sounded a bit annoyed as she got out of bed, put on a golden colored top and started for the stairs. She bent over at the head of the bed, suppose it was to put on slippers. He peeked down and was treated to a view of that pretty bum, the lovely legs and the puffed lips, pinkish, showing between her round buttocks.

Through the week they had met again at his apartment. It was not long until they were in bed again. Her car broke down outside of his apartment and all attempts to get it started proved fruitless. She called someone about looking after her dogs and they settled down to share another night together.

When they got to bed there was a lot of fondling and loving of each other but he was unable to get enough of an erection to stay in her. She tried about everything including sucking and licking this prick that was now sore from all the new activity and temporarily out of retirement. He worked his hands and mouth all over her, working within her until his hands were sore and she was closing up. She too was tired but it was like they both had something to prove, which they didn't have.

Their last effort was to have a bath together which was fun but they had trouble adjusting limbs around each other in the bathtub, both trying to squeeze their bodies into the tub and he was trying to squeeze into her, all to no avail. They had an enjoyable time drying each other off then collapsed in bed where they were soon asleep, snuggled together.

In the early morning he had an erection and rolled between her legs again. She was wet and receptive and soon they were at it again until he ejaculated within her. He had a tough time getting through the day at work.

He was at her store on Saturday as she finished work, brought steaks to take to her place, she did the cooking, a lovely job of preparing the supper. He too had worked on that day and was tired. When they went to bed she patiently worked with him and his reluctant erection. He got it in her and it went on and on for the longest time in a splendid rhythm of sex but he did not ejaculate. With the stroking and loving he had done and the endless "just fucking", obviously they were both worn out.

They had drifted off to sleep in each other's arms, he woke up to an erection but thought the full bowel might have had a bit to do with it but he was also thinking of the pleasures of this woman's body. This penis thing was beginning to crave the ravishing thing beside him again. He started caressing the body beside him; her hand moved over and took over on the penis and they moved together again.

He simply said to her," Sit on me".

Then she was rolling over his body, sitting on top of him and guiding this thing into her, riding him, posting as she rode, up and down while the impaler stood rigid as she slid on an off of it getting warmer and warmer, throwing off covers, sweating together, going faster in the action. He was starting to have trouble keeping up to her as she drove herself onto his spear. He lay there as she drove on; the excitement of her was wild. He reached up and sucked at her mouth, gently nibbled her lip, they laughed as they went on, furiously thrashing their bodies together. They were both soaking wet as he rubbed hands on this wild wet body, loving the feel of the sweat as he rubbed her all over, the lovely slippery rump, the slick long legs, spurring him on. He could feel every muscle she had, a perpetual motion machine running on sweat. He could feel himself coming inside her, what a fantastic thing.

He had rolled her off to the side as he was coming, stiffened all over and it was there. She stopped and soon was closing the hole pushing the thing out. They fell asleep again and it was another several hours before they awoke.

That day they relaxed together and he could hardly keep her awake. (No wonder) He watched television as she slept beside him. Grew realized what a breathtaking woman she was; wondered what it was that seemed to make them feel they had something to prove, it was like they were trying to fuck each other to death. It was such a divine experience.

At one time one of the Dobermans came and dropped a pair of Joanne's panties at his feet. What was that supposed to mean? After awhile she got up saying she had to go to the store. This was the tired side of Joanne, quietly surfacing as they went off together. They walked through the supermarket first, picking up a bit of this and a bit of that. She seemed to be waking up. Later they took the dogs through the fields, again talking about the different aspects of the dog game. He got her talking a bit about her past but it was hard to get it out of her. He was aware he was with the teeth grinding quiet worrier and not quite sure how to deal with her, much better when wrapped in each others arms setting a record for sex.

As they walked further and started to relax she told him of living with a man for eight years, when they had split up he had taken the property and she had taken the dogs. This was one of those girls who would not risk losing one dog to a man so that was the way their assets were split. This man had harassed her for some time after the split so she moved from the area where she had been, stopped showing dogs, as he would have been aware of it being the place to find her.

Grew thought that if her sexual prowess with him was as he had experienced and she had been with him for eight years, he too would have found it difficult to give up. He wondered what it was that had made her so determined to get away from this person. With more discussion it came out that this man was not only cruel to her but the dogs. If she had only been with the right person, they could have turned it all into a great thing. Thoughts like these eventually got Grew into another relationship that almost dragged him under.

When they got back to the house Henry was there. She still claimed that there was nothing going on between her and Henry yet he never saw Henry with Joanne while he was with his wife. That day she was giving Henry the cold shoulder, perhaps it was a message to Grew that this man did not own her.

The next day there was a call from someone who she said was her father. It upset her terribly. Almost at once she went outside and started fooling around with her car, one that was in the house garage, the first time Grew had seen it. She changed one wheel and then agitatedly said, "I just don't have the patience for this today." If he had known what he later learned he should have grabbed her and just held her but he didn't. He just followed along trying to be in some way supportive.

They went back to the friend's place where they had played cards. Together they took their two German Shepherds out in a park and while they moved them he videotaped them in motion. He often used the tape of the older one as an example of ideal German Shepherd movement often wondered if she ever got to show it for them. Probably her self-imposed exile from the shows prevented that. He also had lost track of the tape.

That night the two of them went back to his apartment where she cooked them a superlative Thanksgiving dinner. Grew was totally moved with appreciation. Even as he thought of what she had done, he realized that in some way he had let get away a special woman. His son had not called to even suggest dinner together, he was getting married.

The following week he called to ask him if he could bring Joanne to the wedding. He said it was probably okay but that he would have to get back to him. A few days later he called and said that it couldn't be done. They didn't have any extra room. At first he told him then in that case he wouldn't be going either.

Grew did go; it was a mistake. This girl needed every bit of support that he could give her. She had been angelic to him. Whether her and Grew would ever have made a life together she deserved a chance.

The wedding party was nice and he did make a talk that brought tears to his eyes as he talked of the two of them growing up together more as pals than father and son after his sons mother had died. There was a lot of applause. He then sung one of the songs he used to sing to him, tried to get into the dance but at these things there is always the fear in the women that someone is going to pick them up, he missed Joanne, left early and in his rented car headed for her place.

Joanne was cool, answering his questions with one-word answers. He was not getting through to her at all, it brought out the incapable side of him.

He said. "Do you want me to stay the night or not?"

The wrong question and he got the wrong answer. She said. "I don't care"

Of course she did, she was hurt bad. She needed him and in his stupidity he didn't know how to get past it, so he left. He told her," In that case, if you don't really want me to stay I am going to go home."

He had walked over to where she sat on the couch and said," Good Night" as he kissed her.

She had expected him to stay the night; she was just doing her disappointment act. He should have allowed her silent protest, supporting her in any way that he could. Instead he presented to her an unfeeling person, another in a line of unfeeling people that she had been involved with. Sure she was feeling sorry for herself for being left out. She was having second thoughts about him.

They never did get back together. It was a super brief interlude. Grew had been this route before with women who had so much hurt from their past. Things never did quite recover with the family of his sons wife and often as he thought back could not even remember his sons wife's name. He seldom heard from his son but he was always responsive when called. Not going to the wedding would have perhaps saved something with Joanne but there was always a question, whether her problems were beyond what he could help with.

For the rest of his life there would always be an appreciation for the brief interlude he had shared with her. Even if he could not re establish her confidence he still had such a life lasting feeling about what had been between them.

The old man finished reading the draft, that he had written years before; it seemed to end without a conclusion. Before ending things with Joanne he remembered one young lady he had talked to while standing on the bus on the way home and in some way had convinced her to come home with him where he eventually divested her of her clothing to take her picture and she had cleaned up the cigarette butts left in the apartment by Joanne. It was funny because when Joanne was later in the apartment she asked who cleaned up the butts and him not wanting to confess his story of the other girl, said it was the cleaning lady. He had forgotten much of the wonder of the brief time with Joanne, but when he had looked at his notes it all came back.

In the time since her he had seen other women briefly Then he remembered meeting someone through a newspaper dating ad, another dog person. It turned out to be a disaster. He had dated her but she had a married boyfriend. Amidst back and forth turmoil. The old man did marry her anyway after he had retired from his security supervisor position, bought a kennel for the two of them. That turned out to be impossible as he was forced to endure her boyfriend's input at the kennel. The boyfriend finally died but she found another. Probably her and the boyfriend had conspired from the beginning to use some poor sucker and it looked like he was the victim. They had not counted on the boyfriend dying.

The relationship with her had gone back and forth until it ended with as he was on his way out the door for good she threw a cup at him that shattered over his head. A physical wrestling match ensued;

then after he let her up she went outside, put bruises on her face and called the police. He should have followed her.

That night and one other time he had spent the night in jail where he had enjoyed discussing life on the other side with those also brought in for various misdemeanors. His lawyers were costing too much so he had represented himself, learned the particulars of *The Canadian Charter of Rights* from the library and finally the case was dismissed and they divorced--which he also paid for. The assault case had gone on for two years--then the kennel was sold. He had fought his way through a court case, on her false accusations but in defending himself had learned invaluable lessons on the law. However her lawyer took the money from the sale of the kennel for her fees. Later he had moved north to a retirement community, Elliot Lake and took courses, useful later when he went to university.

His two years in Elliot Lake had more benefits as he hiked the surrounding hills with hiking groups and alone, attended their Karaoke nights, flowing over the dance floor with abandon and joy.

He did find a poem in his writings It was there from his Elliot Lake English classes where he first started to learn how to express free verse poetry--perhaps not quite proper but he enjoyed his own poems.

Old Man Thinking

Old man thinks back to the life he led, to the wilds of Chilcoten or Yukon days, moving camp as rain came down, too cold in the saddle, walking, holding horses tail with bold mud spilling over boot tops. He being the cook built the fire in the rain, clothes drying by fire till the men were fed.

Untold life was of horses, dogs, women and sea, of times as cook in a camp floating in a bay, of climbing waves in the night in kitchen of tug with fright that next wave would swamp the boat or if tug should stall to be crushed by scow that followed behind--with death to all.

His women were lovers of horse or dog or snake. These women he loved until one by one, had to leave. Was it all behind? Were there no pleasures to follow? Would life from now be just to write of those times? Tales to remember to provide joy and to read, rhymes he could follow when memory also decided to leave?

He had met Ramona at a party held by a mutual friend and connected immediately. While it lasted it was a pleasurable relationship. He walked her home through the snow, harmonizing "Summertime", only hugging her at her front door but the next week she had called him and they went on another torrid affair, walking everywhere through the snow, him cooking for her, bathing her while she read to him from the bathtub, helping her wash the bedding that she did every day but it was the dancing together at the Friday night dances that caught the attention. They flowed like they had always been together. He was in great shape and felt free as they walked in the snow.

Lovers Winter Walk

They walk hand in hand through woods and path. By day or night, more by night when stars and moon alight the stage where lovers pause together. What hath been placed before with backdrop of blackened blue? The snow crystal diamonds flashing to a silent tune in snow, that in time too will disappear, soon be gone for another year. Even though they knew it would be so, as time changes and love warm hands in cold squeeze, pause and contemplate their own place in time, and they watch for that moment when heaven appears to come down and touch the earth and they walk the heavenly path that no one else sees.

He made friends with a retired history professor that had a suspended drivers license, DUI and as he drove him to the isolated lakes in order to fish they had conversations as to the state of the world and on occasion came close to getting stuck in the bush miles from home. His upgrading courses led him to realize that as a senior he could go to university and only pay student fees. At first he ignored the information but after hiking the hills for two years his professor friend was going to teach English as a second language in the orient so was leaving. It was time to go.

The old man remembered when he had been in Elliot Lake and could recall some of the reason for going there but before that his memory was vague. There were even parts of his brief affair with Joanne that he had remembered. How could he forget? It was such a fantastic few days, something to remember for a lifetime.

Before leaving Elliot Lake he had reluctantly joined an entertainment group in which they voice synced, (not actually singing but mouthing the words) but his relationship with Ramona had turned sour, she had been searching for a man who could afford her medical bills and that was not Grew. After the kennel and marriage fiasco he was left with little money--didn't have it to pay so eventually their affair crashed. Although she professed love for him she did marry another with a better pension who died two years later and then she married his best friend.

She had been an exquisite dancer that almost turned his head as is seen in the poem above but it was her that realized that he was not what she wanted. He too soon realized he was better off without her-- could not afford another fiasco.

While taking courses in Elliot Lake the teacher who taught English would drive him home at night, he was getting a crush on her while her husband was out of town on a course; he would walk her back to her house or run with her, but he was determined not to get involved again, afraid of the consequences. One day after driving him home she asked, "What would it take to get you to stay in Elliot Lake?"

He knew what it would take and for a moment considered asking her into his apartment. He was shaking in the dark as he thought how nice it would be just to hold her in an embrace, he came down to earth and said, "Don't go there." It was treading on dangerous territory.

As he sat on the mall parking deck, that years later collapsed killing two women, the bare trees of fall faced him. He wrote this poem. He was leaving and felt remorseful. It was clear he was not over the loves he had known in Elliot Lake.

The Poet I Am

Now that I am old with still tales untold was it God that told me to be a poet? This one who sees dormant sticks of fall, tries to understand, as it all unfolds, if sticks still feed the roots hidden, as trees stand tall or are roots the only reason they stand like myself, wet boots clinging to earth?

This person that learned from Kipling to trust himself and that all men count. Yet to be a poet? God please, not a poet. To tell my tale of my touch on earth, here and there, while out on the trail, not enough moss gathered of any worth. Who refuses to age with friends that touch through life, never close too much; yet share pleasure with each friend but only to lend.

Just to see the same go their way as dogs and pets in other game; they too die too soon, what a shame. This man who touched lips to some without commitment, same lips that pressed on virgin breast, and more, who has lain with wives of own and others; and swam amongst the sparkle of eyes. Each one remembered as a special prize.

These woman he loved that didn't realize the score. Oh such memories of love and all without shame. No, no shame, no resentment or rancor or blame, part of memories written but never spoken. Why this mouth, these lips, to be so outspoken? Lips that refused to leave the youthful fountain, where I touched on sea and sky and shared adventure and climbed each mountain trail from north and west and east and south, until come tomorrow, move on, all destined to end.

All only for today, is what is shared, not to follow unto age, or death-- all fought against like hell until earth time becomes buried ashes, beneath a plaque. A stranger will read about a man, who touched on earth with words from Kipling about what it was worth; as in peace I finally rest.

All his connections had been severed and he was walking up the trail to the school when he met another lady who wanted directions to get down town. He told her how to get to the mall and they talked for awhile, he told her that he was moving to Sault Ste Marie, detailing why it would be a better place to retire. She was a military widow. He suggested that if she called him there he would show her around the city and surrounding country; he gave his phone number and simple directions to get there.

Two weeks later the lady from the trail did phone and came to Sault Ste Marie and kept coming back. She kept coming back for a few years before they rented an apartment together. Years later they had passed their tenth anniversary living together and their lives kept going as a couple but they never married.

CHAPTER 22

Chloe

The old man took many university courses, usually three subjects each semester and he just kept taking more. In the summer he and his new partner journeyed all over Canada from one coast to the other, studying the geology and geography he had learned about in the classes. There were other courses where he enhanced his knowledge of computers that enabled him to save so much of what he had written, yet he continued to lose material in the labyrinth of computerization, all the poetry written disappeared as did his notes about his early life.

On their ventures they climbed the not so high mountains that were in the back country around where they lived, almost got stuck on a local ski hill in the summer and they searched for fossils in Nova Scotia. Nuclear facilities were studied and visited. He gave a talk to geographers at a convention on the possibilities of nuclear energy as the way of the future. They also visited hydro dams and coal conversion plants that piped CO_2 into expired oil wells in the earth. They followed river sources in the United States. He walked across the headwaters of the Mississippi. He got a B.A along the way but after ten years he had quit university and wrote a book about history, politics, people and religion. The B.A. was never considered very beneficial other than to put on his letterhead, but it did enable him to hone his researching technique useful for his writing.

This was the material that had been placed on the computer of a now old man, an old man that realized there were many things from his past that he was no longer clear about. He read the forgoing story of Grew Tuckett and wondered, since he did not recognize most of the names, if it was all about him or was it an accumulation of stories that he had gathered through the years. He assumed they had been changed but if so he had trouble sorting out which name attached to which person.

He was flabbergasted at the affairs of the dog man. Could that have been him? He remembered spending a lot of his life working with dogs and realized that perhaps many incidents could have been about him but maybe there were tales of other people too. Since sex was essentially a thing of the past in his life he had almost forgotten how breathtaking it had been, how splendid the women in his life had been, with some conniving exceptions--women that had used him but some of them he did not remember at all from what had been written.

He found it great to read though, he could feel some of the excitement. There was some recollection of him having an affair with a women that worked in the mall that had been married to a policeman that she had left and who he lived with for some time. His memory was foggy as to why they broke up but thought she had decided to go west with her grown children. There was another policeman's wife.

He loved reading about his time with Lissette, a little shamed at the first affair but he reveled in thinking about when she found her way back to him, even though for a short time. it was so long ago, he could not remember all the thrills he had enjoyed with the women in his life.

Amanda had called him one day so he remembered a lot about her, she had changed so much from the years before when she was twenty or so but she tried to preach to him and their conversation had eventually degraded to the point that he did not want to talk to here anymore. She was on Facebook and he unfriended her.

The old man realized most of this story was more than 30 years old so he again went to the computer looking for a follow-up but there was nothing there; there were no compact discs, only some floppy disks in his cupboard but he had nowhere to read them as that was no longer a feature of his present computer. He did find some hard copies of two stories he had copied and stowed away. He looked at them for awhile but in the end became disgusted at his own stupidity for getting involved and then marrying the one. He had called that story Quicksand and if it were true he was fortunate in getting out. However he read about the very fact this had happened caused him to read up on the law, defend himself and get the case dismissed, even though he had lost the cost of what he had invested in the kennel involved. Yes, he was lucky to get away from that one but felt a sense of pride in what he had accomplished in getting away and then going to university.

When he read the other story about Elliot Lake it was almost as bad, him becoming involved with a widow there, seduced by her dancing and singing ability. There were some things she did like sleeping all night with her first husband after he died and charging an ex lover with rape that was bogus that all bothered the old man. He had gone to the police and asked why the man had not been charged, They said he would have to ask his girlfriend. When he did she became angry. A meeting with her ex revealed in a photo album the extent of their involvement before she had attempted to have him charged and as the other suitor had confessed to him, "I am no longer able". Again the old man was fortunate to get away.

With his new friend in Sault Ste Marie things developed quickly they had a number of common interests and both were willing to share pastimes. There was a time when they went to the horse race track and stayed a few days--in Fort Erie where he had the kennel. They had driven across Canada and the northern United States stopping at small motels. There was a motel owner that had driven them down into a gorge in Montana when he was told of the interest in Geology where they looked up at the ragged cliffs created from millions of years of river erosion. They had picked berries for a few

days in a place off the Hope Princeton highway in British Columbia--
had stayed with friends she had known through being in the military,
stayed with her relatives and his as they passed through the country.
On other years they had stayed with others on the east coast and
dug for fossils in the cliffs of Nova Scotia-- driven to the end of Cape
Breton to visit other military friends. They made full use of their
retirement as they explored the country. stopping from time to time
to talk to people he knew in the dog business or dog shows.

He thought of the time they had camped at Ivanhoe Lake and
while there, had journeyed over to the Groundhog River--had driven
down a back road then hiked to a waterfall. He had stood on rocks
and dug into the gravelly bottom filling a pan with bottom sand,
shaking it, trying to find gold. In turning around he had gone into
a spiral and as he fell the gold pan went before him. He landed ass
first in the pan--no injury. When trying to hike out of the area, he
had fallen, unable to continue; he was so tired he couldn't get up.
With the help of his angelic partner he had crawled out of the woods.
She had helped him up and he had walked the few steps to the car.

It was a similar situation when in summer they had climbed the
ski hill to the top, they had made their way down a shallow ditch as
they had made their way to the bottom. She had got out of the ditch
but he had kept going until the sides were too high to get out. It
took the efforts of both of them as she pulled on his arms to get him
out although he probably could have made his way to the bottom
through the deepening water.

Together they had faced life, her driving him to dog shows or just
discovering the world they lived in; together they solved the jumble
puzzles in the daily paper or watched the quiz programs on TV. She
had her favorite crime programs that he often would not watch but
she would watch his favorite soap operas with him. She did her Tai
Chi without him and often he would walk alone when she felt he was
going too fast or did not want to go where he was going.

They joined the local dog club and contributed as much as they
could. One spring at the dog show she expressed a tiredness. At first
she thought she would just go home and rest but people at the dog

show convinced her to go to the hospital. After a number of days and many tests they put her on a pacemaker and from there she got back to her energetic self. While she was down he started making the meals and kept doing most of them when she was well again, From early on in their relationship he had been making the bread, trying different combinations.

Kidney stones were found after some pain in his back. An X-ray showed the stones but he refused the operation, preferring to go along with natural medical ideas he had read about on the internet or heard about from a doctor friend. Three years later an ultra sound revealed that the stone had shrunk in half.

He also had some issues with waking up with a start--thinking he was dead. After sending him to a sleep clinic he again refused to follow advice. When watching a post on Facebook his attention was drawn to a devise that stopped snoring. He felt from reading the information that it was connected to his sleep problem, they called it sleep apnea. With some experimentation it was felt he could put together something for his own use. After many tries sewing pieces of stretchy cloth together with Velcro he was able to perfect something that allowed him to sleep through the night and eliminate his snoring. When he combined it with a 3 mg Melatonin pill it gave him a deep sleep, making it no longer necessary to have his daytime naps. He also stopped having the wake up dead dreams--at least they lessened.

Through the winters he would walk the halls of the apartment building always trying to get in his half hour of walking, seldom venturing outside for his walks. In spite of various small ailments he did without medication and stayed in shape. There was a bout of Pneumonia where they sent him home right away with seven pills for seven days. He thought the pills would kill him but after seven days he was starting to recover and soon after almost like new.

He did became a watcher of the obituaries, noting that so many people of his age and younger were dying. It encouraged him to work harder at staying in condition but knew in time it would all end. His hearing had been diminishing but was able to understand most conversation on the TV by adjusting the sound. Of course his eyesight had diminished quite a bit earlier. His one eye was kept operational with the adjustment of glasses but sometimes he wondered just how long he would be able to see to write. He developed carpel tunnel syndrome in his right wrist and he got a sleeve to stop the numbness. With whatever difficulties passed his way he was always able to adjust without complaint, no cane, no artificial devises, he just kept going, surviving the best he could.

The years passed, so many friends died along the way but with the odd trip to the emergency he was kept alive. One day in winter he went outside to walk, he missed the snow and cold weather. It was so fresh, he found it exhilarating. As he walked through the park and along the side of the river, he murmured a song from long ago, his steps matching the beat of the song. He thought it was "Shine" it had been sung by Frankie Laine, *"Just because my hair is curly, just because my teeth are pearly---- Just because I always wear a smile...always dress the best in the latest style, that is why they call me Shine."* He couldn't remember all the words as he became tired, like he had been when he was in the bush and could not get up. He sat on a cold bench; he would rest for awhile. The cold sunk into his body. He thought back as if dreaming. He remembered his first wife Evelyn, yes that was her name--not Marilyn. She was troubled, had affairs, was sick for two years with Cancer then died at age 33. He and his son had carried on and he thought back and wondered how they had survived--but they did. His son played hockey, a lot of their time was spent at games. He remembered the dogs, thought of some they had and how he had worked with them and other peoples dogs, sometimes getting bitten.

He smiled as he remembered visiting his niece in Edmonton, them staying in her brothers house while he was in hospital, him grooming out the cat--so many of the places they had stopped at, like lake Saskatchewan; it was an artificial lake, a testament to what man can really accomplish with a bit of effort.

Suddenly he remembered some of the other women that he had affairs with and he wondered what it was that made him attractive to them, looking inward at himself, he seemed so simple. How was he able to attract his present partner and have such an enjoyable life with her for so many years.

Then the cold was really getting to him but he still couldn't get up. He felt like he was in a dream, a dream where he was climbing a rock slide with Chloe as he had done before. On another day she had gone up the slide before him and he had refused to follow the first time, afraid that the rock slide would start moving and take them down with it--but he had stayed at the bottom, waiting, the worst place to be. There was a cross they could see on the top of the mound; it could be seen from the bottom. He remembered they had tried again on another day, it was Mount Zion, not far and inland from the little village of Thesselon that sits on the shore of the St Mary's River in Northern Ontario. The second time they tried to climb it he worked his way up the side of the slide and in the last twenty feet he had used the slide with her help to get to the top, just like they had done before. He was up there with the cross. In his dream he was up there again. It was a rugged cross, pieces of a tree tied together with twine; somehow it had been forced into a crack in the rock. He thought briefly of the song *"The Old Rugged Cross"*

He could see for miles in three directions, the whole world was before him-- all flat. Then he felt warm and remembered so much more about his past, his memory was returning, he was remembering all sorts of things that happened in his life. He remembered Lissette from when she had knocked on his door and her name was not Lissette. Was his memory returning? He remembered Sylvia and the many memorable years he had spent with her but that was not her name either. Life that he had lived passed through his dream, all the memorable and enjoyable events he had lived through were there. And then he was flying off Mount Zion--but he couldn`t fly? But he was, from the top of Mount Zion until the dream ended. They found his frozen body the next morning. He was smiling; he looked so happy.

Printed in the United States
By Bookmasters